SHADOWBOXING

ANNE BARWELL

ECHOES RISING, BOOK 1

A game of cat and mouse across war-torn Europe.

LACEDRAGON
PUBLISHING

ISBN: 978-0-473-54818-6 (mobi)
ISBN: 978-0-473-54816-2 (print)

First Edition published by Dreamspinner Press, 2012
Second Edition published by DSP Publications 2016

Although this story is a world of fiction, it is set against a backdrop of actual places and events. While many of the locations used are real, some liberties have been taken for the sake of a good story. Some of the buildings appearing in the story, although still intact in 1943, did not survive the war, while others still stand in present day.

ALSO BY ANNE BARWELL

Slow Dreaming

On Wings of Song

The Sleepless City

Shades of Sepia

Electric Candle by Elizabeth Noble

Family and Reflection

Shifting Chaos by Elizabeth Noble

CO-WRITTEN WITH LOU SYLVRE

New Zealand Romance

Sunset at Pencarrow

Magic in the Isles

The Harp and the Sea

*To everyone who has waited, encouraged, and stalked for this
story since its inception.
Thank you.*

ACKNOWLEDGMENTS

To Susanne for beta reading and hours of discussion, and all her help with the German; Angela for all her support since the very beginning of this story, beta reading, and brainstorming sessions; Reesha for her enthusiasm for this series, despite coming late into it; Sharon for always commenting for each new bit as I wrote; Lou for her friendship and support; Laura for encouraging me to finish this story; and Julia who sent me maps and postcards when I began writing it.

To my writing and reading communities for your support and friendship, in particular RWNZ, and my Facebook groups Anne's Books and Brews, and Kiwi Authors Rainbow Readers. A special thanks to the New Zealand Rainbow Romance Writers group—you guys rock.

Gillian and Emma for all their support, friendship, and awesome accountability.

T.L. Bland for her wonderful cover art.

Desi for editing.

To my family. Love you

And last, but in no way least my friends at Upper Hutt Science Fiction Club and Hutt City Libraries.

CHAPTER ONE

David Reuben hadn't changed. His unruly, too-long dark hair still met the top of metal-rimmed glasses, and his shirt was creased as if it never had the privilege of being introduced to an iron despite his trousers being neatly pressed. His appearance had always reflected the contradictions of his personality, but his eyes were now tinged with an out-of-character sense of sadness and worry. Kristopher sighed loudly. He reached across the table to offer comfort, acting on instinct rather than common sense, then quickly withdrew his hand when he realised what he'd done.

They'd known each other a long time, having become close friends at university although they'd studied in different fields. Kristopher's passion was physics, as he was intrigued by how the specifics of the universe worked and why, while David, acting on a genuine desire to help those less fortunate, had decided to become a doctor. After graduation they'd drifted apart, but Kristopher doubted David was aware of the real reason.

Kristopher regretted so much about their friendship, especially how he'd eroded the closeness they'd once shared to what was left now. Part of him didn't want to remember the painful memories and the guilt of what he'd done, but at the time he'd convinced himself it was necessary. David was a good-looking man, and while the physical desire Kristopher felt for him was not as strong as it had been, enough of it remained to remind him why their friendship could not be allowed to develop further. Seeing David again, however, Kristopher wasn't so sure he'd made the right choice. Perhaps he should have been honest with himself, and with David, instead of taking the coward's way out and choosing not to face the reality that he was falling for his closest friend. But now, seven years later, it was too late. The spark that had once brought them together was gone. Kristopher had deliberately killed it.

David sipped his coffee, not having said anything since their initial greeting. Kristopher wound his fingers tightly around his cup, trying to ignore his restlessness and curiosity, knowing David would speak when he was good and ready. David had requested this meeting, which in itself was unusual. They tended not to meet in person, although they still kept in contact through Kristopher's sister, Clara, and the occasional letter. Those letters had become rarer since most of the Jews had been rounded up in February—David having escaped because of his position at the Jewish hospital.

Even so, he'd taken a huge risk meeting Kristopher in a public place. Not only was he a Jew in a Kaffeehaus, but he wasn't wearing his yellow star. If someone asked to see his papers...

The door of the Kaffeehaus opened. Kristopher glanced over his shoulder to see a tall man in a dark suit enter and walk over to sit at a table on the other side of the room.

David lowered his cup onto the table with shaking hands, gazed at the man, then returned his focus to Kristopher.

Kristopher wanted to ask David whether he was all right but decided against it, as he very obviously wasn't. Once he would have had the right to ask anyway, but not now. Focusing his attention on the steam rising from his coffee didn't help him ignore the emotions he'd thought long resolved, so he settled on drinking it slowly in measured sips instead.

Eventually, David removed his glasses and reached over to place his hand on Kristopher's. "Have you any idea what kind of people you are working for?" David spoke quietly, as always, but with an underlying tone of fear Kristopher hadn't heard before. He'd always envied David's control over his emotions. "Have you any idea of their real agenda?"

Kristopher snatched his hand away, his heart thumping. Why had David come to him? Surely he couldn't have presumed to use the closeness they'd once shared to further his agenda?

"I'm a scientist, David, trying to make the world a better place, just as you are. We are advancing science and this is for the good of the Fatherland." The last sentence came out sounding like the mantra it was. Kristopher's doubts were always dealt with efficiently when he repeated those words. The device and his research had the potential to be dangerous, yet he still clung to the hope it would be used to benefit mankind, rather than someone utilising its potential for catastrophe.

"You always were naïve, Lehrer." David raked a hand through his hair and replaced his glasses, adjusting them when they slipped down his nose. "Wake up and take a look at what's going on around you before it's too late." An edge of desperation and fear sharpened his voice as he lowered it to almost a whisper, as though he was talking about the end of the world.

"Too late? Too late for what?" His earlier fears of being used vanished at David's tone. Kristopher's voice rose in pitch, all attempts of hiding his conflicting emotions lost as he tried to desperately work through his rapidly growing confusion.

David shook his head, unwilling to say more, his eyes darting nervously around the small Kaffeehaus before his gaze settled on the man who had entered several minutes earlier. "I have to go. I've said too much already."

"Wait!" David was already halfway out the door before the word was out of Kristopher's mouth. He pushed his chair back, ready to follow his friend, then hesitated, suddenly unsure what had just happened.

"I saw the God of Death today."

"What?" Kristopher scrutinised his sister, Clara, across the dinner table, noticing too late the slight smile turning up the corners of her mouth. He studied his soup bowl for a moment. "I wasn't listening, was I?"

"No," she said, shaking her head. His being distracted was a standing joke between them of late. He'd be thinking about the events of his day, and Clara would divulge something far-fetched to see if she could win his attention. Some evenings the stories she spun would be completely ridiculous; this one was a little closer to home, considering her profession. "Honestly, Kristopher, the world could end and you'd never notice. Were you thinking about your project again?"

Kristopher nodded. Often Clara knew him better than

he knew himself. He usually looked forward to these conversations and the lighthearted banter and teasing that accompanied them, but tonight it failed to capture his attention.

Dinner at the Lehrer residence would be an extremely silent affair if not for Clara. He shuddered at the thought of just him and his father sharing their evening meal, each ignoring the other because they were focused on their own thoughts. Formal dinners were one part of his life he'd discontinue in an instant, given the chance. He'd be just as happy sitting in a park somewhere with a packet of sandwiches, rather than playing the dutiful son. Paul Lehrer, however, certainly never worried about the opinions of his children in regard to the running of his household. Each night was a repeat of the same scenario, food served on fine white china on an impeccable white linen tablecloth, a servant hovering in the background ready to top up glasses if required. Kristopher hated it with a vengeance. The routine was stifling, a reminder that even though he'd gone his own way in life, as Clara had, his father still maintained parental control on some level.

"Kristopher?" Clara's voice softened when her brother still didn't reply verbally. "Kit?" Her use of the nickname their English mother would have used always got his attention.

"Sorry, Clara," he mumbled, forcing a half smile. "What were you saying?" He'd spent the last few days mulling over an equation. The answer was so close he could almost touch it. Although his obsession with the problem was not healthy, for the moment, it consumed him to the exclusion of all else.

"One day you'll find a pretty girl to distract you from your equations," Clara teased, taking a sip of wine. "If you can find one prepared to share you with whatever project you're engrossed in."

Instead of laughing as he usually did, Kristopher mentally winced. A part of him had always yearned to find someone who would listen to his ideas and want to be with him. He didn't want to only live for science, but until he met the right person, he didn't see any reason to change. He'd dated a few times while he was at university, knowing he should attempt some semblance of a social life, but hadn't connected with anyone he'd met.

Except for David.

"David Reuben missed our meeting today. I asked at the Jewish hospital, but all they'd tell me was that he didn't come in to work," Clara repeated when he didn't acknowledge what she'd said. She met his gaze. She seemed tired, more so than usual. Her voice lacked its familiar fire. His sister always managed to sound enthused about everything, the spark in her voice often ensnaring others into assisting her with her current charity case. One of the reasons Clara became a doctor was because she couldn't resist someone in need, but the long hours she was putting in at the hospital, in addition to the extra volunteering, were beginning to take their toll.

She brushed an errant lock of dark-blonde hair off her face in a gesture of annoyance. Clara wasn't just tired; she was also very much on edge. He wondered how long she'd felt like this. Judging from the pallor of her skin and the lines around her eyes, the stress had been building for some time. Why hadn't he noticed before now?

"Have you managed to find out why?" Kristopher glanced at their father, but he was slowly sipping his soup from his place at the head of the table. Often it seemed that the long hours he spent running the family business were a higher priority than time spent with his family. Many of Kristopher's earliest memories consisted of being in the care of his sister and various nannies while his father spent long hours at the bank.

"No, but I'm worried about him." Clara ignored the way her father's eyebrows knitted together, his spoon paused just above his bowl when he looked up from his meal to glare at her. Father never approved of their conversations of late and was still under the illusion that his show of disapproval should be enough to divert the subject material to something deemed more suitable.

"David wouldn't disappear without telling anyone. He was very involved in his work and wouldn't leave without good reason." A slow, cold feeling crept through Kristopher as memories trickled through his mind of their meeting the week before. David had been scared, his words, both spoken and not, more ominous than ever. Surely Clara must be mistaken. He was only allowed to practise medicine at the hospital, but that hadn't stopped him doing what he could to help those in need. After the law banning Jewish doctors from practising medicine on non-Jews had passed five years ago, Clara had used her influence to secure David a job at the Jewish hospital, and discreetly called on him for help with patients who sympathised and would not report either of them.

Kristopher shivered. He reached for his glass and took a gulp of wine.

"Do you really think he would have had a choice?" Clara rolled her eyes. "You're so involved in your project that you haven't noticed what's going on around you." She paused before continuing. "He's Jewish."

Frowning, Kristopher placed his wineglass on the starched linen cloth. "So?" Why would that be a reason for it? While the Jews had to follow a different set of laws in regard to some things, David had always been careful to stay out of trouble. He had done nothing wrong, and this could not be anything to do with his assisting Clara, or she would have mentioned it earlier.

The sudden silence in the room was broken by the sound of Paul Lehrer dropping his spoon onto his plate with a loud clunk. "So?" he reiterated, the outrage in his voice resounding across the room. "They are Jewish. What other reason is needed? Better that they are rounded up and sent somewhere more *suited* for their place in the scheme of things. We must not lose sight of the fact that the Jews are nothing more than parasites interested in taking control of the economy for themselves."

Gripping the side of the tablecloth, pulling the fabric into a hard ball in his hand, Kristopher fought to repress what he really wanted to say. How dare he? He'd suspected his father had disapproved of his friendship with David but had never heard these arguments voiced before.

He shoved back his chair and stood, still struggling to quell his anger. "Father," he said in a low voice, his tone devoid of the disgust he was feeling. His stomach twisted, threatening to expel its contents as he eyeballed his father. "Most of these people have spent their lives as useful contributing members of German society. You have no right to judge them just because their beliefs are different from ours."

"Someone has to protect the future of the Fatherland. The Nazis will lead us into a glorious new age."

His father had always believed in looking after his own interests alongside those of the German people. He'd never turned down an opportunity to spread his own "empire" and to meet potential customers, especially those connected with the upper echelon of society. His work was more important to him than being there for the milestones in his son's life. Not even Kristopher's graduation ceremony had been enough to drag his father away from it.

While Kristopher agreed in principle that something needed to be done to help the Jewish people, and had read about how some of them lived, that did not mean they should be considered a threat. After all, David was still a qualified doctor. He helped people, as did Clara.

"These people might need help, Father, but relocation without their consent is not the answer." Kristopher leaned towards his father, knocking the contents of his wineglass over the table in anger.

Although the relocation of the Jews had been ongoing for some time, it didn't mean he agreed with it. Usually he said nothing and allowed his father to state his opinions without arguing with him, but tonight he couldn't stay silent.

"I should turn you over to the authorities for this treason! How dare you question me, question the ideas of the Führer?" His father turned an interesting shade of white, his hand shaking as the temperature in the room seemed to drop several degrees.

Clara stood, leaning over to place a hand on each man's shoulder. "I think we should leave this discussion for another time. Father, I'm sure Kristopher is tired after a long day's work, as are you."

Muttering something under his breath, Paul Lehrer pulled away from Clara. "We will discuss this further in the morning," he said coldly, stalking out of the room.

This was far from over. Holding on to his standing as head of the household was of utmost importance to the elder Lehrer. Losing control in public was even less of an option than being disagreed with in any shape or form in front of the servants. Was it really so hard for him to listen to his son's opinion?

Kristopher sighed, wishing not for the first time that his mother was still alive. From what Clara had said, their father had been much more approachable before he lost his wife. When she died giving birth to their only son twenty-nine years ago, part of her husband died with her. All Kristopher had of his mother were the stories Clara told him and the old photos she'd shown him. While Clara's slightly darker colouring was closer to their father's, Kristopher inherited his blond hair, pale blue eyes, and slender build from his mother. It—and his name—was another reminder to his father of what he lost. For all intents and purposes, Kristopher was orphaned when Kristine Lehrer died. His father tolerated him because society dictated he should, although it often felt to Kristopher as though he was disliked and blamed for the death of the one person his father ever truly loved. In Kristopher's mind, his family consisted of himself and Clara. She was ten years older and was always there for him. Discussions such as these only served to confirm that feeling.

"Are you all right?" Clara wound a stray lock of hair around her finger as she studied him.

Sitting down, Kristopher leaned back against the hard wooden chair and took a deep draft of wine when the serving man refilled it. "No, I'm not!" he snapped, guilty after he saw the hurt on his sister's face. She was the last person on whom he should be taking out his anger.

Clara nodded to the servant, and he backed quickly out of the room, following her unspoken request to give them some privacy. Someone would return later to clear the table.

"I'm sorry." Kristopher buried his face in his hands for a

moment. He'd always felt things deeply, even if sometimes he didn't possess the strength to admit those emotions to himself or others. Clara told him he empathised with others because he cared. Kristopher found that difficult to believe now. He'd cared so much he hadn't noticed what was going on under his very nose. The work he was involved in was so important and absorbing that he didn't have time for anything else.

Had this absorption cost the life of a friend? He'd entered science to advance the quality of life of those around him, and yet become so engrossed by it he'd ignored reality. When had he stopped caring, stopped noticing?

"Maybe you should get an early night. You'll cope with Father better in the morning if you do."

She was right. Discussions with Father, especially when they couldn't be avoided, usually upset him even when he wasn't tired. Herr Lehrer was only interested in his own opinions. Kristopher had once hoped he and his father would grow closer as time progressed, but instead they were drifting further apart. Kristopher's refusal, as son and heir, to take over the family business, or show an interest in it, only rubbed salt into an already existing wound. According to his father, Kristopher had shirked his responsibilities to their family name by choosing to become a scientist.

After a brief hug to Clara, Kristopher said goodnight and climbed the old wooden staircase at a snail's pace. Trying to digest the information about David, Kristopher was barely aware of the rail under his hand as he trudged towards his bedroom. He'd ignored the fear he'd seen in David, permitting it to take a back seat to his work. What had happened to his friend?

He quickly changed into his nightclothes, leaving the curtains open slightly so he could observe the stars. After climbing into bed, he pulled the crisp white sheets over himself and lay his head on the pillow, hoping sleep would bring some respite to his confused state of mind. A dark cloud passed over the clear night sky, obscuring the small pinpricks of light. Where was David and what had happened to him?

David's disappearance must be connected with the Nazis. He'd read something months ago he'd dismissed as fiction. What if the stories on the leaflets circulated by the underground group, White Rose, had some element of truth to them? The rumours of concentration camps were no longer as easy to ignore as when he'd first heard them. What had really happened to David and the other Jews? Clara always chose her words carefully. If she said he disappeared, she meant just that.

Dr Kluge, the head scientist on the project, and the man Kristopher answered to directly, had always spoken highly of the Nazi party. Kristopher sighed, wriggling further down the bed. He would not help them or allow them to use his work to bring harm to others. But he was only a scientist. This couldn't be connected to what was befalling the Jews.

"Have you any idea of their real agenda?" David's words echoed through Kristopher's mind until he finally drifted off to sleep.

He walked slowly, taking comfort in the familiar regularity of his breathing and the echo of the leather soles of his shoes against the hard pavement. They were loud in the apparent absence of life. He was in his own neighbourhood. These were the streets he saw each morning from his bedroom window when he started his day.

What had happened to all the people? He turned at the rumble of an engine from behind him, just in time to observe a large covered truck pull up to the sidewalk. The brakes screeched when the driver came to a sudden halt. Kristopher moved back into the welcome safety of the shadows, shivering as a dark shape slithered through the street, leaving a sense of coldness in its wake. Death moved through the empty streets and buildings; he could smell it, sense it. He pitied its victims.

A plaintive cry for help echoed through the silence.

"Kristopher!"

Carefully, Kristopher edged out from his hiding place, from the safety of the shadows, just in time to see David being ushered into the back of the truck by a group of soldiers.

"This is your fault." David tried to pull away from the well built man who held him. "I tried to warn you, but you wouldn't listen, and now it's too late."

Kristopher stepped forward, placing himself between his friend and the vehicle, only to have one of the soldiers bring his rifle up to bear down on him. As he reached out to Kristopher, David had his arms pulled roughly behind him before he was thrown, none too gently, against the side of the truck, his head connecting with a dull thump.

"Do you want to join your friend?" asked the soldier. "It can be arranged very easily."

The sharp intake of breath he heard was his own. He opened his mouth to protest the rough treatment but couldn't get the words to form. One look at David, still trying to free himself despite the blood dripping from his forehead, brought Kristopher to a sudden halt, fear for his own safety quickly becoming paramount.

"I can't help you," he whispered. "This isn't my fault. I didn't know."

"Wake up and take a look at what's going on around you before it's too late." David's eyes lacked their usual spark; his spirit was already dying. Kristopher remembered the creature he'd thought of as Death. His friend would soon be one of those sating its hunger.

Kristopher stood frozen. He tried to force himself to move. He'd left it too late to help David, too late to help the others he could see cowering in the back of the truck.

The soldier shoved David into the rear of the truck. Then he turned to stare at Kristopher before joining his prisoners. The street spun momentarily when Kristopher registered the expression he'd just seen on the man's face. He both despised and pitied Kristopher for his cowardice and lack of action.

So did Kristopher.

After the truck drove away into the darkness of the night, Kristopher stood, knees bent, breath rasping, alone once more on the quiet street with only his thoughts and growing feeling of guilt. He hadn't known. How could he?

"I'm sorry. I'm so sorry," he whispered, although his apology would never be heard by the one person who needed to hear it. Looking up again at the once-clear sky, now completely covered in darkness, he dropped down onto his knees and screamed the words again, trying to purge himself of a sin he'd never forget or be forgiven.

"It's not my fault." He closed his eyes, seeking respite from the images embedded in his mind, lashing out when he felt strong arms around him. The soldier had come back for him.

"Wake up, Kristopher, wake up!" The voice wasn't a soldier's, but Clara's.

Relief flowed through him as he opened his eyes. He was on the floor next to his bed, Clara leaning over him. He let her assist him in getting back under the covers, taking comfort from her gentle touch as she stroked his brow, her fingers cool against his damp forehead.

"It's all right, Kit. It was a bad dream." Clara would look after him. She always made things right. He took a few ragged breaths, snuggling into her when she held him close. Once he grew calmer, she disentangled herself, tucking the covers around him before settling herself on the chair next to his bed.

"It was only a dream," he whispered, more to himself than to her, taking refuge in the security of the soft feather pillow and allowing sleep to claim him once more. "Only a dream."

CHAPTER TWO

Kristopher shifted uncomfortably on the hard wooden chair in the reception area outside Dr Kluge's office. He glanced at the clock on the wall once again. Had Kluge forgotten they were supposed to be meeting that morning? He felt a twinge in his back, the ache a physical reminder of his growing frustration. He stretched, sighing when it didn't offer the relief he'd hoped for.

His bad start to the day was getting progressively worse. Although he'd managed to go back to sleep after his nightmare, he'd spent the rest of the night tossing and turning and mulling over the events of the dream. He hadn't decided whether his restless night was the result of an overactive imagination after the news he'd received about David, the guilt which followed it, or a combination of the two.

The expected lecture from his father over their conversation the night before hadn't gone well either. Although their argument was due in part to his own lack of sleep and irritability, Kristopher still wondered why he bothered attempting to talk to his father in these situations. Neither he nor his father ever compromised their viewpoints to reach an agreement, and in this particular instance, it was sheer luck his father hadn't turned him over to the authorities after some of the comments he'd made. Kristopher was skating on thin ice, and they both knew it. One more argument, and the fact they were family wouldn't matter. His father's loyalty would be to the Fatherland and the "greater good."

Sighing again, Kristopher reached into his lab coat pocket for his pad and pencil. If he had to wait for Kluge to finish his urgent meeting, he could at least spend the time doing something useful. Jotting down the equations he was supposed to be working on would serve the dual purpose of occupying his mind and distracting him from his present train of thought.

A search of his pocket supplied him with his pad, but he couldn't find the pencil. After another look proved fruitless, he emptied the contents of both pockets onto his lap. The pencil he was sure he'd returned the last time he'd used it was gone. Sitting here doing nothing was not an option with his present state of mind, and he also couldn't afford to waste the time. If he went back to his own office to retrieve one, he ran the risk of missing Kluge, which wouldn't be a good idea. Kluge preferred his staff to be both prompt and efficient.

Neatly organising the small pile of odds and ends before returning them to his pockets took care of another minute. Kristopher settled back in his chair, his fingers tapping out the rhythm of the Bach cantata he'd listened to in his office earlier that morning. He glanced around the room, taking in details he usually didn't notice. The paintings in their gold frames lining the walls were in stark contrast to the sparseness of the rest of his surroundings. It surprised him that Kluge bothered with such things, but it wouldn't have been prudent to refuse such gifts from the Führer.

He edged his chair back, wincing when it scraped noisily against the polished floor. He stood and began to pace across the confined space. He yawned, automatically covered his mouth with his hand, and his elbow connected with the closed office door. To his surprise, it opened, the tired hinge squeaking in protest to reveal Kluge's desk in all its glory. An accumulation of months of paperwork covered it, piled one on top of the other in an intricate balancing act.

Surely Kluge wouldn't mind if Kristopher borrowed a pencil while he waited? If he wrote out the equation, he had more chance of making sense of the problem that had eluded them both for some time. Kluge didn't have anything in his office Kristopher hadn't seen before. He had security clearance to everything in the building.

A few moments later, he sat behind Kluge's desk. "Pencil, pencil," he mumbled under his breath. "I don't believe this. All these papers and no pencil." Spotting the object of his frenzied search, he leaned over, his sleeve catching the edge of one of the many documents littering the large desk. A stack of papers tilted towards the floor. Kristopher cursed and shot out a hand, but he narrowly missed the errant manuscripts. He shoved back the heavy leather-backed chair and fell to his knees as he began to gather the papers together quickly, hoping he could tidy up before Kluge returned. Muttering a few choice curses, he wondered if the day could get any worse.

His eye caught a sentence written on one of the documents, and his breath hitched, his immediate problems forgotten as he reread it, convinced he must be mistaken.

We look forward to putting these plans into reality. Such

a device will ensure the continued success of the Fatherland during this war against our enemies.

Kristopher dropped the remaining papers with a thud and kept reading, the coldness running through him reminiscent of how he'd felt in his dream the night before. Shifting from his knees into a half-squatting position, he almost lost his balance because of how much he was shaking. He reached out with one hand for the support of the desk, trying to recover his bearings. The words on the page he was holding stood out as he read and reread them.

This couldn't be right. They couldn't seriously be considering using his research to build this bomb and use it against the enemies of the Fatherland. The consequences would be unthinkable, bringing about death and destruction on a scale never seen before.

"Have you any idea what kind of people you are working for? Have you any idea of their real agenda?"

Kristopher had only seen what he'd wanted. He had focused on the honour of being chosen to be part of a team alongside Dr Kluge, a man he'd admired throughout his studies. He'd kept telling himself their research wouldn't be used as a weapon that would end the war in a way nothing else could.

Everything he'd helped develop could be used for destructive as well as peaceful purposes. Although bombs had been dropped on both sides, he still hadn't believed someone would consider building—let alone using—a weapon that would make all the destruction up to this point look like nothing. Kristopher remembered the Allied bombing of Berlin three years ago, and the stunned look on the faces of his fellow Berliners. This would be much worse, and many more lives would be lost.

Massaging his temples, Kristopher slumped in the chair,

a searing pain piercing his head. He took a deep breath. The room spun when grogginess and the need for fresh air combined to overwhelm him.

He couldn't allow the panic to win. Furrowing his brow, he attempted to ignore the thumping in his head. He needed to take one breath at a time, in and out, in and out. He could do this with focus and repeating the mantra until his breathing evened out.

Minutes later, the aura of calmness he'd convinced himself he'd achieved shattered with the sound of footsteps in the distance. They grew louder with each moment, boots clicking against the polished wooden floors, marking off the time until he was caught.

There would be consequences for going through Dr Kluge's papers without permission. The fact he was Kluge's assistant would be inconsequential, especially when it became clear which particular papers he'd read. He no longer wanted to be a part of this. Although what he'd just read had shown him how naïve he'd been, he was not stupid. The Nazi regime had no room for loose ends. Everything he'd seen and heard over the last week pointed to that very clearly. He'd disappear like David, never to be seen again.

A lone tear trickled down his cheek, falling to smudge the ink on the sheet of paper he held between his shaking fingers. He wasn't sure whether he was crying for David or for himself. He had to get out of here. Once he could think, he might be able to figure out what he should do, or whether there was anything he could do.

This was something he couldn't ignore. He couldn't avert his eyes and pretend he didn't know the true purpose of this device he'd worked so hard on. How could he live with himself if he did?

The footsteps paused then began once more, but this time they grew softer, eventually dying away completely. Kristopher let out the breath he'd held. He'd had one narrow escape. It would be foolish to expect another.

It only took a few moments to gather the papers together. Kristopher placed them back on the desk, hoping it looked much the same as it had before he'd disturbed it. He peered through the slight crack in the door; the corridor was empty. Better to leave than risk his fears of being caught becoming reality.

Kristopher sighed in relief as he closed the door behind him. He started walking to his own office, his mind in chaos, the pain in his head growing with each passing minute. He hadn't realised just how much so until his foot caught on the doorjamb between the two sections of corridor and he went flying.

"Herr Dr Lehrer. Are you in need of assistance, sir?"

Kristopher blinked, suddenly aware of a soldier stepping in front of him, bending to help him to his feet. The man was several centimetres taller than Kristopher's own one hundred and seventy-eight. His dark-blond hair was cut short in military fashion, and brown eyes with a very slight hint of green to them scrutinised Kristopher carefully. He pulled away from the man's touch, trying to regain his sense of composure. A small shiver ran through him, and he used the gesture of brushing imaginary dirt from his lab coat to try to calm himself, all the while hoping his hands weren't so clammy to be obvious.

With how nervous he was, he didn't trust himself not to blurt out something that might be construed as incriminating, especially if asked any awkward questions. "I'm fine. Thank you for your help."

He spoke the words with much more politeness than he

felt like giving. The soldier—Schmitz was his name, if Kristopher remembered correctly—was only doing his job as one of the select unit of soldiers "protecting" the small group of scientists who worked on the premises. Looking out for their safety, and therefore that of the project, would fall under the banner of that duty.

"I'm fine," he repeated at the glint of amusement in Schmitz's eyes. Kristopher took a deep breath, trying to control both his anger and growing panic. No need to arouse suspicion and draw more attention to himself. "Thank you for your concern, Herr Obergefreiter, but it's really not necessary."

Schmitz nodded, appearing not to notice the now-cold tone in Kristopher's voice. "If you insist, sir, but I can escort you, if required."

His voice was even, though with enough of an inflection to prevent it sounding like a monotone. It reflected the calmness his demeanour projected, which was in direct opposition to how Kristopher felt. Schmitz's tone felt soothing, and for a moment Kristopher wished he had someone to talk to. "That would be appreciated, thank you," he said without really knowing why. This wasn't someone he could trust. Under the circumstances, everyone on this base was a potential enemy. If anyone got an inkling of the thoughts running through his mind, his life would be in danger. Yet he needed desperately to talk to someone, anyone. He groaned aloud, and Schmitz paused, one eyebrow raised in what Kristopher could only translate as a look of concern.

Choosing to ignore it, and Schmitz, Kristopher continued walking quietly, increasing his speed to overtake his companion. He needed to be alone. Why wouldn't the headache leave him be? This problem wasn't going to just go away if he ignored it either, but like his headache, was becoming worse. But what could he do? He was only one man. He couldn't halt the project now. Voicing his objections would only get him thrown into prison, or worse.

"Are you sure you're all right, sir?" Schmitz's impassive soldier's mask gave nothing away, which made it impossible to guess his intentions, and his voice suggested only polite concern. Even so, Kristopher couldn't help but wonder the reason for that concern. He wasn't thinking logically, but that realisation didn't make the feeling vanish.

"Sir?"

With the repeated questions about his well-being, Kristopher suspected Schmitz would keep asking until he got a satisfactory answer. Schmitz hadn't been stationed there long, a few months at the most, so hopefully this was only a sign of him being overzealous in performing his duty. As the war progressed, the men drafted into the Army seemed much younger than when he first joined the project. Schmitz appeared to be in his late twenties, early thirties at most, so close to Kristopher in age.

"Just a little tired, thank you, Herr Obergefreiter," Kristopher answered politely, realising they were outside his office door. Maybe having an escort was a good thing. Who knew where he might have ended up otherwise, given his current state of mind?

Schmitz stood to attention, gave a small salute, and continued on his way. Kristopher lingered for a moment, watching him leave, then took refuge in the sanctuary of his office. Leaning against the closed door, he concentrated on the smooth wood against his back then moved over to his desk. He felt sick to his stomach, and his brow was covered in perspiration. That Schmitz hadn't noticed anything was amiss was a miracle. Kristopher needed to go home and claim illness before anyone else saw him. Or he could attempt to pull himself together, which he doubted would be successful. Nothing would calm him now. He placed his head in his hands, trying to ignore the feelings of despair threatening to overwhelm him. What was he going to do?

"You're working too hard."

Kristopher looked up with a start. He must have nodded off again. Ever since the revelation several days before had turned his organised world on its head, he'd suffered from severe insomnia, to say nothing of a total lack of any kind of peace of mind. The first nightmare could only be considered mild compared to what now plagued him each night. The news about David had only been the beginning; he could see that now. How could he not have noticed what the Nazis were doing in his own backyard? These were the same Nazis to whom Dr Kluge had promised to give the plans and his and Kristopher's continuing assistance in ensuring those plans became a reality. Kristopher couldn't stay with the project, not now. Although an easy decision to make, putting it into practice would be difficult.

"You're going to make yourself ill." Clara had given up waiting for an answer. Kristopher opened his mouth to protest, then closed it again. He couldn't tell his sister why he looked like this. The less she knew, either about this turn of events or the project itself, the safer it would be for her. He fought back an urge to giggle, slightly shocked at his reaction. No one would be safe if the Nazis got their hands on the work he'd done for the project. The world would go to hell, and he doubted anyone would put up a plaque to congratulate him for his contribution.

"Yes, Mama," he said, pleased at the slight smile the

term of endearment evoked from her. Clara was all that and more to him, and had been for as long as he could remember. He would not allow her to become involved in this. He was well and truly on his own. Kristopher shivered at the truth in that statement. He had no one to turn to for help. Even if he found someone, which was doubtful, all he'd achieve would be to place them in the same danger he was in. He'd helped to dig this hole. He needed to make things right, if only he knew how. Part of him wanted to give up right then and there, rather than enter into a battle he doubted he could win.

His hands shook. He strengthened his grip on the side of the easy chair so Clara wouldn't notice.

He needed to pull himself together. The longer he put off a decision about what action he should take next, the more difficult it became to think clearly. He was convinced the other scientists were already talking about him, having noticed the change in his demeanour. To make things worse, he was sure he'd seen Obergefreiter Schmitz out of the corner of his eye on several occasions. Allowing Schmitz to walk him back to his office that day had been a major miscalculation on his part. Schmitz was watching him. The more Kristopher thought about it, the more certain he became. On several occasions, he'd turned, positive someone else was in the room, but he'd never caught the man in the act.

Perhaps he was being paranoid. The combination of a guilty conscience and fear would do that, wouldn't it?

"Go to bed before I carry you up those stairs myself." Clara paused, giving him the once-over with her practiced medical eye. His colleagues might have bought the story he'd spun about being under the weather, but he doubted she would. Lying to his sister had never been an option, and that was not about to change now.

So instead of arguing as he usually would when she insisted he needed an early night, he nodded meekly. If conceding to this prevented her from asking too many questions, so be it. Once he was in his bedroom behind the privacy of a closed door, he wouldn't have to keep up this act. He hesitated, his foot on the bottom step. Although tempted to ask her for something to help him sleep, he decided against it. While he needed the rest, drug-induced slumber wouldn't be any more dream-free than what he'd already experienced.

"I've been so naïve," he muttered, shuffling up the stairs to his bedroom. "Naïve and stupid."

After undressing quickly, he slipped between the sheets and wrapped his arms around the big feather pillow just as he'd done as a child when he was scared to go to sleep. Clara had always reassured him that the specters haunting his dreams weren't real. When she'd sat with him, her presence had comforted him until he'd drifted off to sleep. Unfortunately, although he'd like to believe they could be, these new nightmares were not going to be banished by a few words.

He rolled over in bed, biting down on his lip in an effort not to scream. Instead of succumbing to the desire to leave his mark on the world through science, he should have followed his original dream to become a professional musician, but that idea was one he'd discarded long ago. If he survived this, he was turning his back on science forever. Right about now, a small house in the country and a violin would be all he needed to achieve happiness.

That, and someone to share his life with.

God, he was so lonely, and doubted that was ever going

to change. Who in their right mind would want anything to do with him, knowing he was a part of this?

Kristopher pulled the pillow around him tighter, slamming his fist into the mattress. How the hell had this happened? All he'd wanted to do was help people and make the world a better place.

Reaching for a handkerchief, he blew his nose noisily. He was ashamed of his inability to act and couldn't escape the fact he was a coward. While he couldn't continue to work on the project, he couldn't just walk away and ignore its existence. Where was the strength he needed to confront Kluge? He ran his sleeve across his still-dripping nose and shivered. What could he possibly achieve by doing so? He'd only bring further attention to his objections, and in all probability sign his death warrant in the process.

The silence that answered him was broken only by the occasional sound of vehicles on the road outside. Kristopher burrowed down further into the blankets, trying to warm himself against the chill of the room. Placing a hand on his chest, he could feel his heart finally slow to a steady beat as he tried to find some source of inner calm. He had to find a solution. He couldn't continue on like this.

"God, help me," he cried out silently, repeatedly, before his mind finally stopped struggling against the advances of sleep.

Evil prevails when good men do nothing.

Kristopher walked the same street just as he had that first night, but since finding the letter in Kluge's office, his surroundings had changed, subtly at first, but with each subsequent night the sense of death had grown. The buildings around him were now ruined shells, and the only sign of life was his own. Even the Gestapo truck was no longer present. Shivering, Kristopher pulled his thin coat around himself more firmly, but nothing would rid him of the chill.

He was surrounded by death, Clara's words at the dinner table coming back to haunt him.

"I saw the God of Death today."

This was his doing, a consequence of his inability to act. Although he couldn't stop this evil, he needed to find the courage to leave the project and to ensure it would never become more than the glimpse of a possible future.

Kristopher laughed, the small sharp sound echoing among the ruins that were the result of the device he helped create. He'd focused on how it could be an energy source to benefit mankind, rather than how easily it could be warped into something deadly. This was once a thriving town with people going about their business and children playing in the streets, honest and innocent people who were unaware of what people like Kristopher did behind closed doors in the name of science.

Now total destruction was all that was left.

He couldn't stand up and be counted as a good man after this. A good man would not have buried himself in his work to the extent of not noticing what was going on around him. A good man would have listened to David and acted in time to save him. A good man wouldn't be so worried about saving his own skin that it paralysed him from taking the action needed to attempt to put things right.

This world was grey, different shades of neutral rather than distinct black and white. It didn't have room for vibrant colours or the emotions of joy and love he'd always associated with them. Everything positive was dead, killed alongside the people. Kristopher recalled his dream from the previous night: of children screaming, burning alive, calling out to him to save them. In it, the city was an inferno, the only noticeable colour the bright red of flames falling from the sky, until that too was gone, swallowed by the ash of destructive grey. He'd walked through it unscathed, but something inside him had died with the people he was unable to save.

He'd bent down to cradle a whimpering child. She looked up at him and pointed a finger. "Your fault. This is your fault." He'd wept over her lifeless body as she drew her final breath, knowing full well she was right. This was a burden of guilt he would carry for the rest of his life, whether this became reality or not.

No wonder Clara thought he looked like hell. He'd woken screaming, unable to stop shaking and too terrified to attempt to sleep again. This latest nightmare only served to remind him why.

"What do you want?" He lifted his head to the dark sky and screamed his question to whoever might be listening. What was the point? Nobody was left to listen. Everyone was dead. The air around him was still, the smell of death permeating every part of him. Not even vultures circulated to prey on what was left of the population.

Unable to face the memories of his dreams, or the proof of them still around him, he buried his face in his hands. What could one man do? He didn't need this responsibility; he wasn't ready for it. Surely there was someone else? Someone without as much to lose, someone better equipped for the task at hand.

A quiet voice interrupted his reverie. "You need to act, to follow your conscience, to stand up for what you believe to be right. You know the project you are working on will lead to this if it is allowed to fall into the wrong hands. Something has to be done now. Soon it will be too late."

He spun to see a slender woman kneeling behind him, over the body of a small child. "I didn't think anyone had survived," he told her. Why hadn't he seen her before now?

The woman's lips pursed, showing her disgust, then she rolled her eyes towards the sky. "Survive? Why would you want to survive this? Even those who do will feel the effects for generations to come. You know the evil that is planned, and yet you say nothing, do nothing."

"I'm only one man," he protested. "What can I do?"

The woman's expression softened.

For a moment he thought he knew her, but how?

"My poor Kit," she whispered. "You have to do what you know is right." Eyes the same colour as his met his gaze, and realisation hit. He knew why she seemed so familiar. Her appearance was similar to what he saw in the mirror each morning and yet not.

Kristopher took a sharp breath. He put the obvious into words. "Mama?" he croaked, his voice catching. She was beautiful, blonde hair falling over her shoulders in waves, her smile projecting a radiance and aura of inner strength he didn't possess. The old sepia photographs didn't come close to doing her justice.

Kristine Lehrer gestured for her son to come closer. She laid the body of the child she cradled gently down onto the dusty sidewalk. Kristopher needed no further invitation. This was something he'd longed for his whole life, an opportunity to hold and be held by the mother he'd never known. Laying his head on her shoulder, he felt the softness of her skin and hair against his. Clara's hugs had never felt like this, however much she'd tried. A mother's touch was unique and something he'd never had the privilege of feeling, until now. He brushed his fingers gently across her cheek, craving the contact like a drowning man clutching on to a life raft.

"I'm so sorry," he whispered. His body shook, the tears coming hesitatingly at first, then flowing as though they would never stop.

She stroked his brow softly, waiting for him to stop sobbing before pulling away, a stern look on her face. "You can't go on like this, Kit, you know you can't. It's time to take responsibility for your actions." His mother's tone was gentle. She moved closer again, placing both hands on his shoulders, but the firm way she held him suggested she wasn't about to tolerate his behaviour. "You have the power to stop this. Stop hiding and take action."

Wetness splattered across his hands. He glanced down, not wanting to see what he suspected was the cause. The consistency was not that of rain but rather of something he'd seen too much of over the past few nights.

Blood.

The red liquid dripped onto his clothes from the sky, seeping into his skin as he frantically began wiping his hands on his coat in a misguided attempt to be rid of it. He was already stained in guilt, in death, in blood. He'd left it too late to save himself, David, and all those he should have helped.

Kristine Lehrer spoke again, but this time her voice showed no sign of humanity. Her tone was cold and harsh, born of a nightmare. "Their blood is on your hands, Kristopher Lehrer. You have to stop this nightmare from becoming a reality."

Backing away, Kristopher fell to his knees when he felt the first wave of pain from the torment of rejection, self-hatred, and everything he'd feared in life all rolled into one. He had failed himself, his mother, and humanity.

He reached out for his mother, seeking forgiveness but already knowing he wouldn't find any. "Mama!" he screamed. She started to fade before his eyes, a wraith disappearing into the fine damp mist that had appeared out of nowhere, bringing with it a sudden burst of cold. Kristopher forced himself to his feet too late. She was gone, and he was alone.

"It's all right, Kit. It's just another nightmare." Clara leaned over him, stroking his brow. For a moment he felt disoriented, his memory struggling to mesh her features with those of his mother's in the dream. Taking a few deep breaths, he took comfort in the familiar smell of her perfume before struggling to sit, wrapping one hand around the cotton sheet. His knuckles were white.

"It's not *just* a nightmare, Clara," he told her, trying to pull himself together. "It's the future. A future I'm helping to create." He swallowed hard, shivering, trying to control the urge to run to the bathroom and vomit. The handkerchief he'd used earlier was gone. He looked under the pillow but couldn't find it. Clara handed him a clean one and watched him wipe his lips. All he wanted to do was to pretend the nightmare hadn't happened, but it was far too late for that now.

Clara shook her head, dark-blonde curls falling over her face. She took the handkerchief from him and folded it neatly over and over. A minute passed before she spoke. "I can't believe you'd be involved in something evil." She touched his chest with her hand as she climbed onto the bed next to him and rested her back against the headboard. "You feel too much for others in here."

He snorted. "I feel so much for others I don't notice what's going on around me until it's too late." Kristopher pushed her hand away, feeling guilty when he saw the hurt reflected in her eyes. Clara was only trying to help, but how could she when she didn't know the specifics of this situation? He couldn't answer her unspoken questions, however much he wished differently.

"Is there something you need to talk about?" The tone in Clara's voice reminded Kristopher of his mother in the dream. He pulled away, shaking, and she wrapped her arms around him, rocking him like a baby. He felt foolish, needing her in this way. He was no longer a child, although the dream had left him missing his mother's touch more than ever.

They sat for a moment, until Kristopher spoke again. He was reluctant to move away from the safety of her embrace, but he couldn't hide in it forever. "I can't. It's not... safe." He sat upright, forcing himself to withdraw from the comfort she offered. "I want to tell you, but I'm scared, I'm so scared. Do you understand?"

Clara nodded slowly. Realisation flashed in her eyes before disappearing. "This is about work, isn't it? Should you be involved in this project if it's having this effect on you?"

"I can't... Don't ask me. I can't." Kristopher stifled a sob. He hated hiding the truth from her, but he couldn't take the risk of his shortcomings placing her in danger. He concentrated on steadying his breathing. If he seemed less agitated, perhaps he could ease her concern. His mother was right. Running away was no longer an option. He spoke again, this time with more control. "I have to do something, but I can't tell you about it." He reached over and gave her a quick kiss on the cheek. "Promise me you'll understand. Please?"

"I *do* understand, more than you realise." Clara slid off the bed; her eyes were covered in a fine mist. "Promise *me* you'll be careful."

Kristopher frowned. From her tone... somehow she did understand, but he didn't have the energy to work out why. "I promise, but I have to do what is right." He would confront Dr Kluge in the morning and to hell with the consequences. He couldn't continue to do nothing. If the Nazis didn't kill him, inaction would.

"I love you." Clara put her finger up to her lips, leaning forward to touch his forehead in a familiar gesture of trust and affection.

"I know you do." Kristopher let out the breath he was holding. "I love you too."

He watched her leave the room before settling back against the pillows, feeling calmer than he had in days. The worry about how or what he was going to tell Kluge was still there, but for some reason it didn't seem to matter as much as it had. The fight within was resolved.

CHAPTER THREE

Kristopher paced outside Dr Kluge's office, waiting for him to return. He glared at the ornate clock on the wall. It taunted him with its slow, loud ticking, a reminder that the life he'd grown accustomed to was about to end. He wasn't certain what exactly he was going to say to Kluge, just that whatever words he used would be the last of importance he'd have to worry about for some time.

His trek across the floor halting midstep, Kristopher jumped when the creak of door hinges alerted him to Kluge's return. Kluge stopped at the entrance to the reception area, his brow creasing into a frown when he noticed he had company. He peered at Kristopher through thick spectacles for what seemed like forever, one finger idly stroking the end of his beard.

Kristopher cleared his throat. His reaction was ridiculous. He was the one behaving out of character. Kluge's response was nothing new. "I need to speak to you about something of the utmost urgency," he said quickly. The words were formal, but if he managed to keep the emotion of out of his speech, he had a better chance of seeing this through.

Kluge continued to give him the once-over for another few moments before finally replying. "So, young Lehrer... what is this subject that requires the 'utmost urgency'?" He enunciated the last two words slowly.

Kristopher fought the urge to flee. Somehow Kluge knew what his protégé had taken days to find the nerve to tell him. Kristopher clenched his fists, forced himself to uncurl them, then took several deep breaths before following Dr Kluge into his office.

The briefcase he carried, carefully deposited next to his desk, Kluge settled into the chair Kristopher had occupied several days earlier. He then indicated for Kristopher to sit. Kristopher declined, deciding it would be better if he stood. If he were already on his feet, he had a better chance of making it to the door once he'd said his piece, although he wouldn't be able to escape. He'd just have to take whatever happened and hope it would be quick and painless.

"I wanted to talk to you about the project," he began hesitantly, shoving his hands into his lab coat pockets to prevent wringing them over and over. The calmness he'd felt last night when he'd made his decision was gone. Reality and fear kicked in, banishing any good sense he might have had left. He met Kluge's gaze directly, disliking the coldness in the man's eyes. Had it always been there, and was he just noticing it for the first time? He'd chosen to ignore so much. He deserved whatever came his way. Ignorance was no excuse, nor was deliberately choosing not to notice.

"When I joined the project, I knew our research could be used to create a weapon. However, I kept telling myself that, although it was part of the war effort, it still could be used to benefit mankind." Kristopher paused, then continued. "I have recently discovered proof that the Nazis intend to build this bomb."

As he spoke, the inner tranquility he had felt the previous night began to return. Although he was quaking inside, his voice didn't reflect his turmoil. Putting his opinions into words for the first time brought with it a sense of taking control of his life in a way he'd never felt before. Everything in his life had led to this point, to standing up for what was right. He'd fought the one thing he'd needed to do. He'd learned his lesson. Even if it killed him, he wouldn't fight destiny again.

"Well, of course we intend to build the weapon. We're at war. And what, might I ask, is this *proof* you've discovered?" Kluge's voice held an underlying tone very clearly warning Kristopher not to cross him.

"I found a letter." Kristopher's calmness didn't waver. In contrast, Kluge appeared pale, reminding Kristopher of his father's reaction during their conversation several nights before.

"You found a letter? Pray tell how you managed to *find* this letter? Am I correct in my understanding that you have rifled through papers that do not concern you, Herr Lehrer?" Kluge tugged out a large handkerchief from his pocket and wiped a layer of perspiration from his brow before leaning heavily on the desk.

"Do not concern me?" Kristopher's tone changed to one of ice. "I have been with the project for over a year now, Herr Kluge. My calculations were instrumental in the great leaps forward we have achieved. If there are any plans to use this device for whatever reason, peaceful or otherwise, I have every right to be informed." He leaned forward, placing both hands on Kluge's desk. "I found the letter by accident while I was hunting for a pencil. I didn't deliberately go through your papers as you are attempting to imply."

Kluge opened his mouth, then closed it again, his skin taking on a distinctly greyish hue. "You are working on the project merely because it pleases me to use your intellect. What I decide to do with the plans has nothing to do with you."

"Giving them to the Nazis is wrong," Kristopher protested. "Think of all the deaths that will result from this!"

Sinking back into his chair, Kluge poured himself a glass of water from the pitcher he kept on his desk. Kristopher continued talking but kept a close eye on his superior. Once Kluge called for a guard or reached for the telephone, Kristopher's life would be over. He couldn't escape the consequences of what he'd done, but he needed to get his point across so he could go to his death knowing he'd done what he'd set out to do. His outlook was pessimistic, but also realistic. Once he started on this journey, his life, or what remained of it, would change forever.

"I mistakenly thought you were like me, working for the advancement of *all* mankind. We are not God, Herr Kluge. We do not have the right to judge others, and that is exactly what we are doing by building and deploying this weapon." Kristopher took a deep breath. He was warming to his topic, his tone growing louder and more animated as he finally gave voice to the thoughts that needed to be shared. He hoped Clara would be proud of him for doing the right thing, although he couldn't help but wonder if he would ever see her again. "There is still time to destroy the plans and refuse to give them the information they need to take this any further."

Kluge took a sharp breath and mopped his brow again. He looked distinctly unwell. Kristopher's head began to spin, along with the room, and he sought refuge in the chair he'd refused earlier.

"How dare you presume to tell me what I should be doing?" Kluge sounded angrier than Kristopher had ever heard him, his voice rising in both volume and pitch. "I do not need to explain myself to anyone, let alone you. You might be used to getting what you want because of your privileged background, but don't think any of that matters to me." He glared at Kristopher. "You will not be leaving here. There are consequences for speaking such treason."

He gripped the edge of his desk with white knuckles when he stood, swaying slightly. A whistling sound came from his throat with each breath. "You little upstart! This is, and always has been, *my* project." He took another sip of water, rubbing briefly at his left arm with his free hand before putting down the glass. For a moment, Kristopher debated asking Kluge if he was feeling all right but dismissed it. Kluge had made it clear that compassion had no part in this conversation.

Instead, Kristopher allowed himself a glance at the water pitcher. The cool water was very tempting, especially with his mouth so dry. He winced when a sharp pain hit him between the temples but fought the urge to put his hand to his head and massage it. He was not going to show any sign of weakness nor give Kluge victory on any level.

"Our benefactors can be here within the hour. I'm sure they will be keen to hear you repeat what you have just told me." Kluge reached for the telephone. Kristopher stood, his eyes darting towards the door. "Worried, are you?" Kluge laughed, a short, sharp sound that suggested he was anything but amused by the situation. "You should be."

Kluge began dialing. Time slowed as the metal circle moved clockwise and then spun back again, ready for the next number. Kristopher leaned over the desk and wrestled the receiver out of Kluge's hand. He jabbed at one of the square silver buttons with his index finger, cutting the connection.

"Lehrer, what the hell are you doing? How dare you!" Kluge stretched out his hand to seize the telephone from Kristopher, who stopped him with a strong grip on his wrist. He yanked free from Kristopher's grasp. The veins standing out on his neck signposted the fact he was clearly not used to someone questioning his authority. "Once my superiors arrive, you will regret this. I will..."

His voice trailed off, a cry of pain escaping his lips. One hand clasped at his chest. "I. Will. Not. Tolerate..." Kluge's movements were jerky. He grabbed Kristopher's shirt, pulling him close in a sudden unexpected motion.

"Get your hands off me!" Kristopher hissed, trying to disengage Kluge's fingers. Once free of the viselike grip, he shoved Kluge backwards to put some distance between them. Kluge jerked again, his body thrashing violently. He pitched forward and his head connected with the sharp end of the desk with a sickening thud. He fell to the floor and was still. Stacks of papers flew in all directions as Kristopher scrambled past the desk to reach him.

"Dr Kluge?" Kristopher whispered, dropping to his knees, fingers searching quickly along Kluge's neck for any sign of a pulse, any sign of life.

He couldn't be dead. He couldn't be.

Kristopher placed his palm in front of Kluge's mouth, waiting, hoping to feel the reassuring warmth that would give some hope he was still breathing. Nothing. Kristopher opened Kluge's mouth to check for obstruction to his windpipe. He gagged, tasting bile. Kluge's tongue was half bitten through, the incisor still maintaining a death grip on its prize.

Kristopher wiped his brow. He still had one last task to perform to be certain Kluge was dead before he could allow himself the luxury of fighting his own body's reaction to the scene in front of him.

His breathing heavy, he edged forward. The flesh under Kluge's shirt felt clammy yet warm. He cringed, but brought his head down to listen for any sign of a heartbeat.

Nothing.

This couldn't be happening.

Kluge was dead. One lifeless eye stared up at Kristopher. The other bulged unnaturally out of its socket. The pool of blood from Kluge's head wound spread across the only rug in the room, the white Persian carpet staining red.

He stood, reached for the telephone, and began to dial, then returned the phone to the cradle before completing the number. He couldn't call for assistance, and it was too late to get Kluge medical help. He doubted the Nazis would believe Kluge's death was accidental, especially with the way Kristopher had behaved over the past few days. The grey hue of Kluge's skin, his laboured breathing, and the way he'd clutched at his chest before collapsing suggested he'd had a heart attack, but it would still be Kristopher's word against that of a dead body. He couldn't take the chance.

Kristopher laughed nervously. How much was his word worth? Kluge was dead. At first glance it would appear death was the direct consequence of a blow to the head delivered by the only other person at the scene of the crime. He'd just given them the perfect excuse to be rid of him if he refused to continue the work they required.

Even in death, the look on Kluge's face mirrored the disgust he'd felt when Kristopher had confronted him. The expression could be interpreted to suggest he hadn't died peacefully. Kristopher had once read that the recently departed resembled someone in a state of sleep and were "at peace." Whoever had come to that decision needed their sanity examined.

He swallowed. The longer he was in close proximity to the body, the more difficult it became think rationally.

Taking a deep breath, he tried to slow his heart and regulate his breathing. The last thing he needed was to have a heart attack of his own. But he couldn't stay here, that much was obvious.

He had to keep his composure. He poured himself a glass of water from the pitcher he'd noticed on the desk before. The glass wobbled in his trembling hands. The water did nothing to quell the dryness in his mouth. A few sips later, it slipped from his fingers and shattered when it hit the floor.

The sound ricocheted through him, stretching his nervous system to the breaking point. Unable to ignore his body's reaction any longer, Kristopher dropped to his knees, bent over the wastepaper basket, and vomited repeatedly. His stomach continued heaving for a few moments after expelling its contents. He wiped the back of one hand across his mouth, wrinkling his nose at the strong stench of what was once breakfast. Stumbling backwards, he knocked several piles of papers off the desk when he reached out blindly to steady himself. Pain went through his hand when he caught it on the sharp edge of one of the pieces of broken glass. He ignored it. At this rate, it wouldn't matter that Kluge hadn't managed to make that telephone call. The noise would suffice as an invitation to anyone to enter and investigate.

He closed his eyes, calming himself, trying to act as though nothing had happened. Perhaps if he left the room before the body was discovered, he might have a better chance of survival. A thin trail of blood ran across his hand from where he'd cut himself. Some of it had already dripped down the side of the desk to seep into the leather of Kluge's briefcase. More blood; that was all he needed. The room spun wildly, memories of the dream from the night before bombarding his mind. He had to focus. He reached into his pocket and bound his cut hand with his handkerchief, then used the clean end of it to wipe the briefcase. This was crazy. He couldn't undo what had happened. Still he had to try, even if only to hold on to some semblance of logical thought and reason.

In a sudden gesture of frustration, he threw the leather case against the wall, the sense of twisted satisfaction that washed over him afterwards, taking the remainder of his nausea with it.

He quickly realised what he'd done wasn't particularly bright. He sighed and crawled around to gather up the files that had flown loose in the collision after the lock on the case had parted. Reading the title of the file he was holding down with one knee, he gasped, not believing what he saw. The file he was leaning on was the one pertaining to *the* project. Why wasn't it in the safe where it belonged? He flipped through it quickly to make sure the information was all there, excitement washing over him in an adrenaline rush.

This was his chance to put things right, to make sure the project did not go further. He hurriedly shoved the file back into the case and then froze. What exactly was he going to do? Only one complete copy existed as far as he knew, but he wasn't certain if the Nazis were aware he was capable of replicating the information. He would have to destroy the file, then disappear.

That wasn't going to be easy. The Nazis had spies everywhere, and he did not know anyone who would help him. He wouldn't ask Clara, nor would he consider death as an option. He couldn't do that to her, not after she'd spent so much of her energy taking care of him. Someone had to get the information about this device out to the rest of the world. He had helped to create it. He would make sure the project was only ever used for the benefit of all mankind, but where the hell was he supposed to find the people he needed to ensure that happened? How could he trust anyone now, let alone convince them to trust him?

Click.

Kristopher turned. The office door was opening. In one fluid movement he gripped the briefcase firmly beneath one arm and bent to retrieve a piece of broken glass, holding the jagged edge in front of him in a feeble attempt to defend himself.

The newcomer took in the situation at a glance, one eyebrow raised in an unspoken question. His eyes flickered onto what had once been Kluge, then back to Kristopher, and finally came to rest on his precious cargo, the briefcase containing the culmination of a dream now better described as a never-ending nightmare.

Kristopher debated for all of a second the chances of his success if he tackled the man head-on, then decided against it. Apart from the extra height, Schmitz's uniform probably disguised a well-developed physique. He also had the advantage of military training and the gun he held. Kristopher's opponent possessed some degree of intelligence.

That much was obvious by the inquiring look on his face and the way his eyes seemed to penetrate Kristopher's, searching for an answer. For an instant, Kristopher was sure he glimpsed a depth to those eyes, and the man behind them. He edged back a step, taking comfort in the solidity of the desk digging into the small of his back, the sensation grounding him while he attempted to place the pieces of the puzzle together.

How much had Schmitz seen? His expression did not reveal anything.

If Kristopher surrendered now, everything would be over, and the Nazis would win. He wouldn't give up, no matter what the odds. He gripped the glass fragment tightly, ignoring the sharp pain as the rough edges scratched against his palm, the red liquid seeping into his shirt cuff already stained with the blood he'd earlier unsuccessfully attempted to stanch. He took a step closer, trying to look menacing, fully aware that on a scale of one to ten he wasn't achieving even a one.

They stood staring at each other, or rather Kristopher stood staring. Schmitz leaned back casually against the door without shifting his gaze. After a few moments with Kristopher's ragged breathing the only audible sound in the room, the Obergefreiter pulled himself to attention and took a step forward. He lowered his gun and placed it in its holster before holding out his hand for Kristopher's makeshift weapon.

"Herr Dr Lehrer," he said softly, the tone of his voice low, an expression of disbelief fleeting over his features. "You're one of the most brilliant minds in this institution, and yet *this* is the extent of your plan?"

CHAPTER FOUR

"My plan?" Kristopher tried to control his annoyance but didn't quite succeed. "I don't have a plan." He changed his tone to one of sarcasm. "Do you honestly think I would be standing here waving a piece of broken glass if I had a plan?"

"Good point," Schmitz admitted, his hand still outstretched, waiting for Kristopher to surrender his weapon. His brow creased, the earlier expression of disbelief changing to one of curiosity. He indicated the room. "What happened... exactly?"

"Herr Dr Kluge had a heart attack. He fell and hit his head." Kristopher attempted to back up further, but he had nowhere left to go. Standing his ground, he gave Schmitz what was hopefully an icy glare. "Have you come to hand me over to the Nazis?" Whatever happened he didn't intend to go easily.

The corner of Schmitz's mouth turned up into a half smile before he shook his head. "I'm here to help you, Herr Dr Lehrer."

"You expect me to believe you?" Kristopher wished the

desk behind him would disappear into thin air, although that still wouldn't be of much help as Schmitz was blocking the path to the only door. "I know you've followed me for the past week." He noticed the slight look of surprise on Schmitz's face with a degree of satisfaction.

"You need to trust me, Herr Dr Lehrer." The initial surprise disappeared quickly, his voice unfaltering. Kristopher felt a pang of envy. While he often projected an air of indifference, using it to cover any inner turmoil, the way Schmitz had his mask in place was almost an art form. Watching him, one could believe the calmness was an extension of the man himself.

"Give me one good reason."

"The Nazis will be here in—" Schmitz consulted his watch. "—approximately ten minutes. Either you trust me, or you tell them what you've just told me. I doubt they will believe your story." His voice softened. "I do."

Kristopher studied Schmitz, wanting to trust him, needing to be able to trust someone. The Obergefreiter had a point. The choices available were limited. When he'd lost his footing, Schmitz had helped. He'd seemed concerned. Kristopher had fought his instincts then. Maybe that had been a mistake. He'd always had strong feelings about whether a person could be trusted. Ignoring his misgivings often preceded disaster, Kluge being a case in point.

He placed the glass fragment on the desk and removed the bloodstained cloth from the cut on his hand. The blood resumed its flow for a moment in response to the lack of pressure on the wound, then trickled to a stop. Thankfully his injury was only a small flesh wound after all. "All right," he conceded, "I am going to take a risk and hope you are telling the truth. You are right. My options are limited, and I have nothing to lose and everything to gain."

Schmitz nodded. "Herr Dr Lehrer—" he began, but Kristopher interrupted him.

"Kristopher, please." He watched carefully for a reaction, hoping for confirmation his trust wasn't going to be misplaced. "If we are going to work together, I'd prefer it be on a first-name basis."

"My name is Michel." Michel took a sudden interest in Kristopher's appearance. Kristopher blushed under the unexpected scrutiny. "Take off your shirt."

"I beg your pardon?" Kristopher stammered, growing even warmer.

"Your shirt is covered in blood," Michel explained. "The guards will notice." Deliberately ignoring Michel's expression of amusement, Kristopher followed his gesture indicating the chest of drawers in the corner behind the door. He had the distinct impression Michel was enjoying this on some level, or maybe that assumption meant the earlier paranoia he'd felt about Michel wasn't entirely gone yet. "Herr Dr Kluge keeps a change of clothing in the bottom drawer. Find something suitable. I'll keep watch outside and make sure you aren't disturbed." He paused. "Does your hand need redressing?"

Kristopher shook his head. Again Michel had showed concern Kristopher hadn't expected. "It's fine. I'll wipe the rest of the blood from it, and it won't be noticeable." After doing so, he stripped off his shirt quickly and rummaged through the drawers for something that might fit. Buttoning up the clean shirt, he shoved his old one into the drawer and rearranged what was there to fill the gap. He grabbed Kluge's woollen coat from the stand and slipped it on, completing the outfit. It was cold outside, and it wouldn't be sensible to make a detour to his office. Luckily he and his former mentor were a similar height, and Kluge's coat was very close in colour and style to Kristopher's. It hung on his slender frame, although not too noticeably.

A brief nod of approval from Michel, who was standing by the door and keeping watch over the corridor outside, indicated they needed to leave. Kristopher retrieved the project files from the briefcase and secured them inside his overcoat, where hopefully they wouldn't be as obvious, before joining Michel in the corridor.

He took one last glance at the scene inside and the life he was leaving behind.

What would happen now? Michel seemed confident, much more than Kristopher was, but under the circumstances that wouldn't take much. At least he was no longer alone, though hopefully Michel had the contacts they needed to get out of this mess. Michel had placed himself in danger by offering his help, and if something happened to him because of it, Kristopher would never forgive himself.

He strained his eyes and joined Michel in surveying the corridor for possible adversaries, groaning inwardly at the glimpse of long blonde hair in the distance and sound of light footsteps heading their way.

Margarete Huber. It had to be.

Kristopher shivered. He disliked that woman but had never worked out why. Something about her unnerved him. While she seemed demure enough, he suspected she had less than pure intentions towards him. The few times they'd been alone in the same room, she'd reminded him of a predator, and he had the uneasy feeling she viewed him as her prey. In hindsight there wasn't anything too inappropriate about her behaviour, although her resting her hand firmly on his knee made him uncomfortable, especially when it had begun to slide upward before he'd told her to remove it.

Attempting to look as nonchalant as possible, Kristopher followed Michel in walking slowly to the exit. Did he think they were just going to walk out the front door? Kristopher snorted. And Michel had the nerve to complain about the lack of a so-called plan?

"Are you going home early, Herr Dr Lehrer?" Margarete arched one perfectly sculpted eyebrow at him and came to a standstill, catching his arm in hers. He pulled free, sending an icy glare in her direction. "I do hope you aren't feeling ill." Her false tone of concern evoked a shudder from him. "Poor dear. I'm sure I could help you if you'd just give me a chance."

He refrained from voicing his retort. *When hell freezes over.*

"Herr Bauer was looking for you, Fräulein Huber," Michel interrupted.

Margarete glanced over her shoulder, her expression reflecting what Kristopher decided could only be guilt. He was certain her grandfather's influence was the only reason her presence was tolerated at the institute. Being related to someone with both a scientific and financial interest in the project had its advantages.

"Be sure to contact me if you do decide you want my help." Margarete's tone made Kristopher all the more certain she would be the last person he'd call.

"Thank you for your concern, Fräulein, but I will be fine." Kristopher carefully removed all traces of emotion from his voice by answering her in a flat monotone. If she suspected the true cause behind his less-than-well appearance, both he and Michel would be in grave danger.

He waited until she was out of sight, then turned to Michel. "It won't be long before she puts two and two together. Margarete might be lacking in some social skills, but she is not stupid. The sooner we leave, the better."

Michel nodded and picked up his pace, Kristopher increasing the length of his step to keep up. When they approached the gate and the guard station, Michel glanced around the compound, weighing the situation ahead. The two guards on duty were both heavily armed, the MP40 submachine guns they carried far outweighing the firepower of Michel's 9mm Luger.

Kristopher's knowledge of hand weapons was limited. Clara had once dated a soldier who was only too happy to explain the attributes of the "beautiful but deadly" Luger to her younger brother. He remembered well his sister's reaction when she'd found out. Poor Hans had learned quickly how protective Clara could be. Her ex-boyfriend was probably lucky she hadn't arrived home earlier and caught him expressing his admiration for the speed with which Kristopher had learned to actually use the weapon. Those few lessons several years ago were his only exposure to something he could now use to defend himself if he had one in his possession, which he didn't.

The years he'd spent at the university fencing club didn't count. He doubted any Nazi would come after either him or Michel brandishing a sword, and besides, Kristopher hadn't mastered the art of using one. He'd only joined the club to find out what David had found so enthralling about the sport.

He shook his head to clear it. This was not the time to get distracted by a trip down memory lane. He needed to keep his wits about him. It would be two against one if they were challenged. Kristopher knew he would be no match in a serious fight, and with the odds already stacked up against them, they certainly couldn't afford to draw any more attention to themselves.

"Is there a problem, Obergefreiter?" asked one of the men.

Michel shook his head. "No problem, SS Unterscharführer Müller. Herr Dr Lehrer is feeling unwell and requested I help him to his car." He reached out towards Kristopher in a gesture of support, and Kristopher followed his lead by swaying and pretending to lose his balance. The guard eyed them suspiciously. Kristopher swallowed, offering up a silent prayer for help.

"Should you be driving in that state, Herr Lehrer?"

Kristopher fought the urge to run when he and Michel turned to see the head of security for the project, SS Standartenführer Holm, standing behind them. *Verdammt*. It was just their luck he had chosen this time to make a spot inspection of the guard station at the front gate. No doubt he would be hoping to make an impression on the important, expected visitors. "Schmitz, escort Herr Dr Lehrer to his home."

Unable to believe their sudden change in luck, Kristopher let out the breath he was holding. "Thank you, sir," he said, the suspicion this was too easy niggling at the back of his mind. Holm was good at his job. He wouldn't fall for a ruse like this.

Holm nodded and saluted. "Schmitz, when you return, I wish to see you in my office." What did he want to see Michel about? A dozen different scenarios went through Kristopher's mind at a frightening speed, followed by a reminder that Holm would hardly let Michel out of the compound if he were under suspicion. "Good day, Herr Dr Lehrer."

Glad of Michel's support, Kristopher continued to lean

on him while they walked slowly through the small side gate. Once through, Michel tensed and pulled Kristopher into the shadows, fingers over his lips asking for silence. Moments later the main gates swung open and a large black staff car, flying the swastika flag of the Nazis, drove through, then stopped briefly at the guard station before continuing towards the main complex. Only privileged visitors, such as those affiliated with the Nazi party, were permitted to bring their vehicles through the front gate. The members of staff who could actually afford and obtain petrol under the current shortages used the small car park directly in front.

Signalling his compliance, Kristopher shifted Michel's hand, noticing how gentle his gesture was, despite the urgency of the situation. Michel was not like the other soldiers stationed at the institute. He was someone who cared, however much he tried to hide it. Something more was definitely going on here than met the eye, but Kristopher couldn't work out what exactly. "I hope you know what you're doing," he whispered to Michel. "You *have* had experience in smuggling out people and information before, haven't you?"

His question was met by silence.

"Michel?" he prompted.

Michel replied with a minute shake of his head. "No," he stated. "Never."

With that, Kristopher's peace of mind, or rather the little of it remaining, wavered and almost disappeared. He stared at Michel, searching for a sign he wasn't serious, but didn't find one. Wonderful. How were they going to get out of this alive?

Michel seemed to be watching Kristopher just as carefully. He coughed before turning to lead him to somewhere hopefully a good deal safer than where they were at present.

"Kristopher?"

"What?"

Michel had better not be making another crack about the lack of planning behind today's events. Kristopher snorted. At least *he'd* admitted from the start he didn't know what he was doing. He blushed. Michel had only admitted to not having any experience with *this* kind of situation.

"You can let go of my arm now."

Michel knocked briefly and waited. They'd left Kristopher's car several blocks away and finished their journey on foot, hoping it would be far enough from their destination not to give away their location. Kristopher shivered. Michel had led them to the back entrance of the same Kaffeehaus where he'd had that final conversation with David only a week ago. If only he'd known at the time that meeting his old friend would be the catalyst for his current situation, the unravelling of what had passed for normality in his sheltered life. He shook his head. Poor David. If Kristopher had been more approachable, maybe it wouldn't have come to this.

If only...

No point crying over spilt milk. The past was gone, and although his mistakes were clearer in hindsight, he had to look forward, to try to fix this mess somehow. He doubted he'd be able to save David, but he had to think about his and Michel's safety. Kristopher fingered the inside pocket of his coat, checking, not for the first time, that the precious files were still there. He could not allow the Nazis to use his ideas. His hands were covered in enough blood, and he wasn't prepared to add more innocents to the list of those he'd already unintentionally hurt.

The door opened cautiously, and a dark-haired woman peered through, eyes widening when she took in the situation. She had brown eyes, a shade lighter than Michel's but without his hint of green. She was slightly built, and stood about twenty centimetres shorter than he did. "Michel?" She opened the door a little wider, disapproval reflected in her expression. Her gaze flickered between the two men, finally settling on Kristopher, although her next question was directed to Michel. "What are you doing here?"

Michel placed his foot in the door to ensure it remained open. "I didn't have a choice, Elise. This is Kristopher. He needs our help."

"I know who he is." Elise wasn't impressed. "Are you trying to get both of us killed?"

Kristopher bit back a comment of surprise, wondering how she knew who he was. He supposed being the only son of one of the richest men in Berlin would be enough to get him noticed. He'd never thought of it before now. Hopefully it wouldn't turn out to be too much of a liability in his present situation.

"I didn't have a choice," Michel reiterated. He stood his ground, refusing to move.

"Please, Elise." Kristopher held out his hand in what he hoped was a friendly greeting. "Michel's right. I need your help." He glanced at Michel quickly, then refocused his attention towards Elise. Her decision could make the difference as to their chances of survival. By now the body would be discovered and too many people had seen them together not to draw the obvious conclusion. If Holm hadn't already doubted Michel's loyalty to the Third Reich, he would now.

Kristopher amended his original statement. "*We* need your help."

Elise hesitated for a moment, eyeing Michel cautiously before fully opening the door, her body language reinforcing Kristopher's initial impression of her. This was not a woman who would tolerate any nonsense from either of them. Any sign they'd lied to her and they would find themselves back out on the street. "Get up the stairs quickly," she told them. "Everything's in the usual place. Keep quiet, and I'll be up in a few hours after we've closed." She disappeared through an inner door, and Kristopher heard the background noise of the busy Kaffeehaus before it closed, leaving him to follow Michel in silence.

"I don't think she trusts me," Kristopher noted, taking in his new surroundings. The double bed filled most of the floor space, leaving room for only a small table, a chair and the old wardrobe in the corner. Midafternoon sun streamed through the one tiny window, although it did little to add much warmth to the room. How long would they be safe here?

"Elise can't afford to trust anyone she doesn't know, and neither can you." Michel strode over to the window, checking the street below before indicating another door to his right. "There's a sink in there. Have a wash. You'll feel better."

"Thank you." Kristopher looked Michel straight in the eye. "I mean it, Michel. I know you've taken a risk to help me, and I want you to know I appreciate it."

"I'm not the only one taking a risk. Make sure you remember that." Michel bent down to undo the catches of the battered leather suitcase he'd retrieved from under the bed. Kristopher waited for him to elaborate on what he'd said but after a few moments of silence decided he was wasting his time. Michel had said what was needed and the conversation was over.

Silently Kristopher walked into the small bathroom and closed the door behind him. He rubbed at the mirror with the threadbare towel he'd found hanging over the back of the door and examined his reflection. He looked awful. His eyes were bloodshot due to lack of sleep, his skin paler than usual, and his hair hung limply over his forehead. He filled the basin with cool water and splashed his face, hoping it would help him to at least feel more human.

His mind raced, trying to make sense of everything so far. While he'd known his life would change once he'd confronted Kluge, the reality of it hadn't really sunk in. Discovered with Kluge's body, Kristopher had acted on instinct, not truly comprehending just how much trouble he was in. But now the adrenaline rush he'd had earlier, which had enabled him to make his escape with Michel, was beginning to wear off, leaving in its place a sense of... nothing.

He groaned aloud. To be honest, he wasn't sure exactly how he felt. Logically he knew he was scared, that he ought to be scared, but a part of him was still reacting as though this was all a dream and any minute he'd wake and find himself in his bed at home.

Home meant Clara. To him the two were interlinked and a refuge he could always return to at the end of each day. She was the only person he'd ever felt truly comfortable with. In her presence he could be himself, Kristopher... Kit. Not Kristopher Lehrer, wayward son of Paul, not Herr Dr Lehrer, prodigy of Dr Kluge, but Kit. Without that, what would become of him?

He finished wiping his face with the towel. At home it would be replaced with a new one without thought and would not be allowed to become this thin, but here the situation was very different. Glancing down at the expensive dress trousers he wore, he realised he'd always taken his social and monetary standing in life for granted. There would no longer be a meal provided at the end of each day without question. For all his issues with his father, Kristopher had to admit that Paul Lehrer had ensured his children had everything they needed to lead a comfortable life.

Kristopher laughed, then stopped, surprised at his reaction. After all, wasn't being provided for, as the price for at least attempting to live up to his father's expectations, the very thing about his life he'd resented? In a twisted way, fate had provided him with the opportunity to move on and maybe become the very person he'd always yearned to be.

"First things first," he muttered under his breath. On the run for murder, theft, and God knew what else, and he was planning his future. He was definitely losing his mind.

His hands twisted the towel over and over. He took a few deep breaths. No point in alarming Michel. He had enough to worry about. After returning the now-damp towel to its original hanging place, Kristopher strode back out into the main room.

Michel looked up from where he was sitting at the table. He seemed thoughtful. "Feeling better?"

"As much as I'm going to be," he answered, giving a small smile with his reply. Maybe Michel did really care? After all, everything Kristopher had seen so far seemed to suggest that scenario. Or perhaps it was just wishful thinking? "Is my being here going to be a problem?"

"You've taken a great deal of risks to get this far." A determined expression crossed Michel's face, and he shook his head. "I am certain the priorities of this mission will be changed to include your safe passage out of

Germany." He slid the case back under the bed and looked Kristopher up and down. "You need to change your clothing into something less conspicuous. The cut of your suit draws attention to you, and you want to blend in rather than stand out." He opened the wardrobe and pondered its contents for a moment. Finally he pulled out a pair of grey flannel trousers and a nondescript cotton shirt, then held them out in front of him as he obviously attempted to gauge the sizing. "These might fit you. Try them on, and let's take a look." Turning back to the wardrobe, Michel chose a dark-coloured, woollen zip-up sweater to complete the ensemble. "It's cold. You'll need to keep warm."

"Thank you." Kristopher took the clothing from Michel and headed back into the bathroom, wanting some privacy to change. "See you in a minute." He almost regretted that decision when it brought home just how small the bathroom was, but he managed to only hit his elbow on the side of the sink once. Reentering the room, feeling quite pleased by his accomplishment and how well the clothes fit he... stopped.

Michel stood by the bed, clad only in a pair of under-shorts. The earlier assumption about his uniform hiding a well-developed physique was quite an understatement on Kristopher's part. Michel was... extremely good-looking. In fact Kristopher would even go as far as to use the word *gorgeous* to describe him.

Oh God.

Blushing, Kristopher stammered his apologies and ran from the room, seeking refuge in the small bathroom he'd just vacated. He splashed himself with cold water. What the hell? One look at Michel... Glancing down, Kristopher willed the bulge in his trousers to disappear. What was wrong with him? This was not the reaction he should be having in response to seeing another man in a state of undress.

His heart was thumping, his skin flushed.

Kristopher groaned.

He wasn't going to react like this. He couldn't, not after putting all this behind him last time. He'd been taught that a man's attraction for another man wasn't natural. His belief those teachings had to be right had prompted him to back away from David in the hope that some distance between them would make it easier to ignore the desire he'd felt when he'd walked in on David in a similar state of undress. If he was going to burn in hell better he do it alone than drag someone he cared about down with him. Hurting David by cooling their friendship was supposed to be better in the long term for both of them.

Yet, he'd still felt an echo of physical attraction for David the last time they'd met, although the emotions that had once accompanied it were very much mellowed.

That attraction, in hindsight, had at least been easier to hide. He'd never had a physical reaction to David to this degree. David had been, and still was, a good-looking man. Michel... Kristopher licked his lips, his mouth dry.

Michel looked amazing. He was muscular, yet not overly so. A fine smattering of light brown, almost red hair dusted his chest.

These thoughts were not helping.

"Kristopher, are you all right in there?" Michel asked.

"Fine. I'm fine. I just needed to um... adjust something." Kristopher hated lying, but he wasn't about to admit the truth. He didn't want to see Michel's disgust reflected in his eyes. No one needed to know. It wouldn't happen again.

This had to be a side effect of the stress he was under. Getting out of Germany would be very dangerous. No wonder his body was reacting in ways it shouldn't. After all, it wasn't every day he discovered everything he'd believed in was a lie and the ideals he'd spent his life working towards weren't worth the paper they were written on.

Seeing David again had also brought back memories and the emotions of the time they'd spent together as friends.

Kristopher walked out of the bathroom, trying to appear more nonchalant than he felt. "Sorry about that," he mumbled, hoping he hadn't made a total idiot of himself.

"No problem." Much to Kristopher's relief, Michel was now fully dressed. The dark trousers he wore suited him, as did the plain button-through shirt. He looked very different from the German soldier who had accompanied Kristopher to the Kaffeehaus. After pulling on a brown polo-neck sweater over his shirt, Michel reached into the wardrobe for a short jacket and peaked cap in a slightly darker shade of the same colour.

"So, what happens next?" Kristopher decided to focus on something besides how good Michel looked in his new outfit. "Are your superiors, whoever they are, sending in backup, or are we on our own?" It made sense that Michel must be working for the Resistance and therefore the Allies. "Are you allowed to tell me if they are? You keep telling me I should be careful who I trust, yet you trust me, although I'm not sure why."

"Because I know you," Michel answered absently, lifting the corner of the curtain and peering out into the street below.

"You've only just met me." The answer came automatically, before Kristopher had time to think it through. He narrowed his eyes. "Exactly how long have you been watching me?" The question came out almost as an accusation, the feelings he'd tried unsuccessfully to suppress disappearing to be replaced by a growing coldness.

"Long enough." Michel's answer sounded deliberately vague, not to mention extremely annoying. He'd only been assigned to the project a few months ago. Did that mean he'd had Kristopher under surveillance the entire time?

Kristopher sat down on the bed, racing to digest this new information. "Why were you watching me? Who are you working for exactly?" Had he misread Michel's intentions completely? His voice rose in pitch as his earlier frustration channelled itself into anger. "How do I know you didn't have something to do with Kluge's death? There are poisons available that can mimic the symptoms of a heart attack. This whole scenario could be an intricately thought-out plan to get me to trust you."

"Kristopher, your paranoia is getting the better of you." Michel sighed. "You're under a lot of stress, and you're not thinking clearly." He sat down on the bed next to Kristopher. "You can trust me. I give you my word on that." Their eyes met for a moment before Kristopher turned away.

"I'm sorry," he said.

"It's all right." Michel's voice had a gentle quality to it, but was tinged with a degree of sadness. He got up and walked over to the door. "I have to go meet my contact, but I shouldn't be long. Get some rest. We'll talk later. And Kristopher..."

"Yes?" Kristopher didn't look up from his examination of the knots in the floorboard.

The door creaked open.

"Be careful." The door closed quietly behind Michel, and he was gone.

"You be careful too, Michel," Kristopher whispered to an empty room. He buried his head in his hands. He hoped they would get the opportunity to talk properly later, although he had no idea what he was going to say. He knew what he wanted to say, but they were words he dare not speak, let alone thoughts he could permit himself to acknowledge.

Already he was thinking of Michel as a friend. When had that happened? Despite his words, Kristopher wanted to trust Michel. He needed to trust *someone*. Yet, hadn't his naïveté in doing just that got him into this situation in the first place?

After crawling under the bedclothes, he lay staring at the ceiling, examining the cracks in the plasterboard until he was familiar with each and every one. How was he going to survive this? He doubted this would end with a happily ever after. Even if he and Michel escaped with their lives, what then?

Hopefully Michel's contacts had some answers or at least could provide safe passage out of Germany. After that... he'd worry about it if and when the time came. By then he might know the correct path he needed to take.

You be careful too, Michel. His final words to his friend repeated in his mind as he slowly drifted off to sleep, unable to fight the exhaustion of both mind and body any longer.

CHAPTER FIVE

Michel glanced around the Sankt-Michael-Kirche, the old kneeler creaking in protest against his weight when he slipped into the pew next to the confessional box and assumed the correct position for prayer. The church was fairly empty, not surprisingly, considering Mass had finished a few hours before. The two men standing outside under the archway had looked up from their conversation, given him the once-over, and then continued talking.

The heavy doors leading into the red brick building had probably kept out their fair share of armies in the past. Churches had long provided sanctuary for those in need.

He bowed his head, pretending to pray as he examined his surroundings in detail, taking note of any potential escape routes. Turning at the sound of voices behind him, he noticed a man a little younger than himself, with dark-brown hair, nodding in response to something his companion had said. The second man, black-haired and of a similar age, indicated one of the confessionals with a shake of his head and shrugged.

At first impression the two seemed nothing out of the

ordinary, but something about them piqued Michel's curiosity. Whatever they were doing in the church, it certainly wasn't to offer prayer to the God many Germans hoped would help them win the war. Most of the ordinary people of Berlin went about their business unaware of the true horrors their Führer was inflicting on others. Many of the people who came to pray here would never venture past their own safe little corner of reality.

Even if they did, Michel doubted it would make much difference, but at least it would be a start. Someone had to do something. After all, wasn't that one of the reasons he'd joined the Resistance? He couldn't stand on the sidelines and watch, waiting for someone else to act first.

At moments such as these, he missed his older brother, Corin, the most. Their parents had argued with him over his decision to follow in Corin's footsteps, not wanting to lose another son, but this was something Michel needed to do. He couldn't allow Corin's sacrifice to be for nothing.

The brunet raised his head and met Michel's gaze straight on, returning it with a stare of his own. Piercing black eyes sized up Michel before shifting back to the confessional. The assuredness and preciseness in his action suggested that whoever he was, he was certainly more than just the working-class man he appeared to be. Clothes might help disguise a person's true identity, but body language was the key to successfully blending in. To give the man credit, a casual observer probably wouldn't have noticed, but Michel was a practiced infiltrator whose very survival during the last six months had depended on deflecting attention from himself.

Michel shifted his scrutiny to the black-haired man. He seemed more nervous than his companion, the air of impatience he projected combining with constant glances towards the front door of the church. Both men were several centimetres shorter than Michel, but the second man was of slighter build than the first. Checking his watch confirmed several minutes had passed since the agreed time he was supposed to meet his contact. According to his instructions, he was to attend confession first, although it appeared someone had gone ahead of him as the light was still on. That would explain the impatience of the men he was observing. Including whomever they were watching in the confessional, and the two outside, added up to a team of five. He hoped these men were more experienced in espionage than present appearances suggested, or they were not going to be able to give him the help he required.

His thoughts wandered back to Herr Dr Lehrer—Kristopher. Michel felt sorry for Kristopher, who was bearing up under the strain extremely well, considering he'd had everything he'd ever known pulled out from under him. Michel couldn't help but admire him. Kristopher was much braver than he probably gave himself credit for. Far more experienced men had cracked under less pressure. Clara Lehrer had been right in her assumption it would pay to keep her brother under close surveillance. Michel sighed, doubting Kristopher suspected his sister's involvement with the local Resistance cell. Kristopher might be brilliant, but that was certainly balanced out by his naïveté. For someone partially responsible for the weapon that could make the difference in winning the war, he needed to learn a lot about the world around him.

Hopefully Kristopher had taken his advice and was resting in preparation for what was ahead. Safe passage out of Germany was not going to be easy. Holm would have put together a Gestapo unit and sent it after them shortly after Kluge's body was discovered. Even without recent events,

Michel's cover was in jeopardy. Although he had been careful, Holm's suspicions were growing, and a detailed background check had been ordered on Obergefreiter Schmitz. Sooner or later it would have become obvious he was not who he appeared to be. One look at a photograph of the original Schmitz would be enough, let alone that the man's first name was Leo, not Michel. He'd made the decision to keep his own first name so he'd react to it on instinct rather than hesitating when called by another name. It had saved his life on several occasions, but Holm had the resources to dig deeper than most, and once he had the information he required, Michel's fake identification papers would be worth nothing.

He'd prayed he'd be able to complete his mission before that happened but hadn't expected the situation to work out this way. Although Kristopher's defection wasn't part of the original mission parameters, it had always been only a matter of time before he realised the project wasn't exactly what he believed. Kluge's death was an unexpected complication, but it had also served as the catalyst to convince Kristopher he needed to leave. Unfortunately, though, it also gave Holm a reason he could give the public for an arrest warrant for Kristopher and saved the job of constructing a propaganda story to dispel any sympathy from those who might be tempted to harbour a fugitive. The Gestapo were efficient when it came to tracking their enemies and even more so when it came to dealing with them. Michel didn't want Kristopher to ever be on the receiving end of that particular brand of interrogation.

Keep safe, Kristopher, until I return. Michel offered up a silent prayer. During the six months he'd watched Kristopher, Michel's concern for his continued well-being had grown. After all, it made sense not to let anything untowards befall him. Lehrer was important to the mission, and if the Gestapo got their hands on him, it could jeopardise everything. Michel had seen enough of Kristopher's abilities to realise he was perfectly capable of reproducing the files he'd taken, if required. Unfortunately, his former superiors were most likely working under the same assumption. The Nazis were not in the habit of taking no for an answer, and Michel was under no illusions of what they were capable of doing to ensure cooperation. A shiver ran through him at the thought of Kristopher in the clutches of someone like Holm.

Michel could not allow that to happen. He would protect Kristopher and keep him safe, whatever it took.

The light on top of the confessional blinked off, and an old man walked out, a dazed expression on his face. He muttered something under his breath too low for Michel to hear, glanced behind him, rapidly made the sign of the cross, and then repeated it. He then, to Michel's surprise, prostrated himself in front of the altar and called out in a loud voice, "God, I beg your forgiveness for leading such a boring life."

Someone snorted. Michel turned in time to see the brunet he'd observed earlier roll his eyes. Whoever was in the confessional masquerading as the local parish priest had an interesting sense of humour. He wondered idly who was in charge of this mission. The brunet certainly didn't seem surprised by what had just happened.

Michel tentatively opened the now-empty confessional and entered, wondering what he was getting himself into. Whatever the priest had said to the old man was definitely atypical of the penance Michel remembered receiving in the past, courtesy of the clergy of the Catholic Church. Surely they couldn't be condoning this behaviour, although he was sure Father Johannes would have agreed for someone to temporarily use the confessional as a meeting place. He'd helped the Berlin Resistance on more than one occasion.

Playing the part of a priest would be the safest way of doing this for the person on the other end of the confessional, especially if he were caught. Father Johannes too, despite his protestations, knew to deny knowledge of anything or anyone if that happened. He would do his people more good here than in a Gestapo cell or a camp.

Michel knelt as the priest opened the small mesh window dividing the two compartments. Searching his memory for the correct phrasing, Michel spoke the precursory words for the sacrament. Confession might be good for the soul, but in his occupation, some things were better left unsaid, even to a priest.

"Bless me, Father, for I have sinned," he began. "It's been two years since my last confession and—"

A bored-sounding voice interrupted him. "Just get on with it, will you? I hope your sins are more interesting than the last person's. I damn well hit my head when I started to drift off…"

The priest paused to catch his breath, and Michel spoke quickly, before the man could continue his tale of woe. "I'm homesick, and I'm often tempted to click my heels together and say 'there's no place like home.'"

The moment's silence was followed by what sounded suspiciously like a very loud sigh of relief. "The answer to your problem is to follow the yellow brick road."

Michel arched an eyebrow in the half darkness. Was this his contact? "Toto?" he asked.

"In the flesh. What took you so long? You've no idea what I've been through in here." He paused. "How can I help you, my child?" Toto snickered. "Sorry, I've always wanted to say that."

A loud creak was followed by the sun streaming through the now open confessional door. Michel blinked rapidly at the sudden change in light. The "priest" standing in front of him proffered his hand in greeting, although he was careful to keep his voice low so they couldn't be overheard. "Matthew Bryant. Matt."

"Gabriel." Michel considered giving his name rather than his codename, but he didn't trust this man or his team that far as yet.

Matt indicated the almost-empty church. He might have been dressed as a priest, but his demeanour was nothing like any member of the clergy Michel had ever met. Bright blue eyes twinkled as he led Michel to the pew with the brunet and his companion. "Come on. I'll introduce you to the rest of the team." Matt's German was flawless, even down to the prominent Berlin accent. He appeared well-trained, at least in that regard, and Michel suspected the man's attitude covered a very keen mind. Matt had light brown, close-cropped hair, and at least six to eight centimetres on the two men in front of them, easily standing at one hundred and eighty.

"I'm surprised you didn't give that poor old man a heart attack," the black-haired man commented dryly. He indicated Michel. "This is Gabriel?"

"Gabriel, meet Zhou Liang." Matt nodded towards the brunet. "Ken Lowe, our wireless operator."

Michel hid his surprise at the Chinese name. The man was taking a risk being in Berlin, although Michel could only see the hint of that side of Liang's heritage, now he was closer. He would survive if he kept his head down and didn't attract any attention. Maybe. His role on this team, which Michel noticed Matt hadn't specified, must be an important one.

Returning the social niceties with a brief nod, Michel refocused on the business at hand. "There is a change in mission parameters."

The three men exchanged puzzled glances.

"This was supposed to be a simple mission," Matt pointed out. "Meet the contact, retrieve the schematics for this weapon from him or her, head for home, and give the Nazis a good kick where it hurts, if required."

Liang rolled his eyes. "It never ceases to amaze me how you manage to translate a complex mission into such simplified terms, Bryant."

"It's a gift." Matt grinned. "And that's Captain Bryant to you." The tone he used was far from serious, and Michel doubted the words were meant as a reprimand. However long this team had worked together, he suspected they were used to the differing idiosyncrasies of each member.

"What is this change and how will it affect the strategies we have already put into place?" Ken spoke for the first time, *his* tone brusque and to the point. His eyes narrowed as he waited impatiently for the information about to be imparted, obviously preparing to make any required adjustments.

"Herr Dr Lehrer, one of the scientists working—" Kristopher's survival was important to the mission, especially as he was capable of reproducing the plans. The original orders needed to be adjusted to take that into consideration. Michel amended his statement. "One of the scientists who *was* working on the project will be accompanying us out of Germany."

Matt whistled. "That's one hell of an addition to the

original orders." A frown crossed his brow. "How do we know we can trust him? Why suddenly change sides?"

"He can be trusted," Michel reassured Matt. "Kr—Dr Lehrer has undertaken a great deal of personal risk to get this far." He glanced at his watch. "We can't afford to waste any more time discussing this. It's imperative we reach him before the Gestapo discover his location."

"And that would be?"

Someone else needed to be aware of Kristopher's location. If they were stopped before reaching there, Michel was more at risk of being taken into custody. For the moment, Matt was an unknown, as least as far as Holm was concerned. That gave him an edge Michel no longer possessed.

"Elise's Kaffeehaus. It's on the other side of the Spree, just—"

Matt cut him off. "I know of it." He lifted his head sharply, his initial surprise quickly hidden. "You'd better fill me in on these changes on the way." He exited the church, giving the statue of the Archangel Michael standing guard on the roof a curt nod before beckoning to the two men Michel had seen talking outside beforehand. It only took a few words to explain the situation to them and to give clear instructions on how to reach the Kaffeehaus. "Walker, Palmer, go ahead and make sure the area is secure. We don't want any little Nazi surprises, do we?"

His next words were spoken in almost a whisper, the momentary look of sadness and regret gone so quickly Michel wondered if he had imagined it. "I wonder if it still looks the same as it did before the war."

∼

Elise knocked on the attic room door. "It's me, Elise," she called softly, not wanting to alarm Kristopher any more than was needed.

After a few minutes, he peered out cautiously, rubbing his eyes and yawning, his half-focused gaze suggesting he wasn't yet fully awake.

She felt a pang of sympathy for him and doubted he really had any idea of the trouble he was in. "I'm making some tea if you want a cup," she told him. "I'll be downstairs."

"Sorry," he mumbled politely. He glanced at his watch and frowned. "I hadn't realised I'd slept for so long. I... um... don't want to put you to any trouble."

Elise bit back the comment on the tip of her tongue. He was causing trouble just by being here. Surely he must realise that? She gave him a smile instead. "We've closed for the day. Besides, Michel would want me to look after you properly."

At the mention of Michel's name, Kristopher visibly brightened. The two had bonded, or at least Kristopher thought they had. That was interesting and unusual in itself. Michel usually didn't evoke this kind of response in someone, as he was usually emotionally distant from others. He couldn't afford connections, with the stakes involved while working undercover. If anyone ever suspected he wasn't the role he played, it would be very dangerous, not just for him but for those he was in contact with. But then, she and the others in the Berlin Resistance faced the same scenario every day. Elise had no doubt what would happen to her if the Gestapo ever discovered she'd harboured Jews and other so-called enemies of the Fatherland since the legislation against them had been enacted.

"I'll be there in a moment," Kristopher promised. "Thank you."

Elise made her way down the narrow stairs and busied herself making the refreshments. She retrieved two cups and saucers, then placed them, a pot of freshly made tea, and a milk jug on a tray. The light outside was fading, causing darkness to fall across the wooden dish racks lining the wall to the side of the sink. She ran her hand slowly down the peeling paint, remembering the fun she'd had working out the colour scheme when they'd found the old building and realised its potential.

Matt had been so sure this location would be ideal for setting up business as a Kaffeehaus. It was their dream, or so she'd thought at the time. Unfortunately, the years they'd spent here together before the war had shown them both their relationship would not last the distance, and he'd decided it would be for the best if he returned to America. Elise had clung to the memories haunting the Kaffeehaus for months before finally accepting he was right. Since war had broken out between their respective countries, her thoughts turned to him often, and she wondered what he was doing and whether he was safe. Matt Bryant was not the kind of man to sit back and let others do the fighting. He'd be involved in the war effort somehow.

She turned briefly at the sound of light footsteps on the stairs. Now was not the time to lose herself in memories of the past. Kristopher offered to help her carry the small tray over to the table in the middle of the room, and she accepted graciously, noticing with some amusement that despite his current predicament he'd managed to keep his manners intact.

"Thank you." She settled into one chair and indicated he should take the other available seat. Matt had insisted they paint the Kaffeehaus in bright colours, although she had been equally firm that the two dark-pink chairs in which she and Kristopher now sat remain out of the public eye. After all, it would not be good to scare off the customers.

"Aw, Elise," he'd replied with a twinkle in his eyes, telling her not to be such a spoilsport.

"What?" Elise was suddenly aware of a gentle hand on her arm. Her resolution to ignore old memories was working even less than usual today, for some reason. Kristopher frowned. Had she missed his last comment? "Sorry, I was distracted. Would you repeat what you just said?"

"I was saying that I really appreciate what you are doing for me... for us." Kristopher wrapped his fingers around the heavy crockery cup, as though taking some kind of solace in the weak tea he was sipping.

Elise nodded. He did seem genuinely grateful, which surprised her, considering the reputation his family had in Berlin. Or rather the reputation his father had built. Clara Lehrer was completely different from her father and worked tirelessly to help the small Resistance cell since its inception. Even when most of them had been wiped out or had gone into hiding earlier in the year, she hadn't faltered in her resolve to offer medical assistance to anyone in need, whether German or Jew. She was a doctor, and her job was to help people.

Perhaps Clara's younger brother was more like her than their father. Elise certainly hoped so. Michel's perception of a person was usually very accurate.

"Herr Dr Lehrer—" she began, but he interrupted, a half smile creasing his lips.

"Call me Kristopher, please."

"Kristopher," she continued, then paused. Sticking to

safe topics of conversation might be better. The less she knew about the specifics of what he was involved in, the safer it would be, both for her and her "guest."

"You're wondering what we should talk about because you don't want to give away information you shouldn't." Dr Lehrer—Kristopher—was more astute than she'd given him credit for. "It's all right," he assured her. "I understand. Neither of us can really trust the other, and that's probably the best approach, given the circumstances."

She reached out one hand for the milk jug and accidently brushed her fingers against the hot teapot. "Shit!" she exclaimed in English without thinking, sucking the sore finger in her mouth before running it under the cold tap.

"Are you all right?" Kristopher voiced his concern in English as well, which he spoke with a British accent, and Elise looked at him in surprise. "I speak English fluently," he explained. "One of my nannies was English, and Clara insisted I learn the language..." His voice hitched slightly. "My mother was English. She was from London."

He'd lapsed back into German with the last sentence, his eyes glazing over, as he appeared to lose himself in seemingly painful memories. Elise wasn't sure how or whether to respond, so she allowed the silence to hang between them for a good few minutes before she finally broke the ice.

"I grew up in America," she explained. "My father is... was... German. My mother, American."

"Was?" His voice was gentle, full of concern and sympathy, and she felt herself wondering, with some guilt, whether she'd been a bit harsh towards him when he'd first arrived.

"My parents are both dead," she explained. "We were living in America when Mother died and Father decided it would be for the best if we moved back to Germany. He died a year later." Matt had travelled to Germany with them and stayed with her after her father passed away. They'd bought the Kaffeehaus six months later.

Kristopher's tone grew wistful. "I've always wanted to travel," he told her. "I want to see the world, to experience some of its history for myself. But Father was always too busy, and then my studies began to take up most of my free time." He laughed bitterly. "Maybe I'll get to do that now, although I was hoping to travel first class and see all the tourist attractions, not run for my life with the Gestapo at my heels."

He rolled his eyes, burying his head in his hands for a moment. "Dear God, I am losing my mind. I know I'm in serious trouble, but for some reason, I keep having these strange thoughts about how things have happened for the best." His gaze met hers as he dropped his hands, and Elise noticed for the first time the depth reflected in his pale blue eyes, and the fear. Kristopher was more than aware of the seriousness of his situation.

"You're not losing your mind," she reassured him. "Your world has turned upside down." He wouldn't be here drinking tea with her if it hadn't. "Give yourself time."

Nodding slowly, he took another sip of tea, lapsing into silence as he stared out the window at the approaching darkness. Elise glanced at the clock over the door, surprised by how late it was. Michel should be returning soon. In the meantime, she'd attempt to lift Kristopher out of his melancholy.

"We lived in America for nearly twenty years," she told him, pleased to see his interest piqued. Stories were always a good way to distract people from their worries. "During that time, Father decided to foster children from the local orphanage and try to give them some stability in their lives."

Matt had been one of those children, ten years old and the only survivor of a house fire that had taken his younger sister and both his parents. He'd had no other family to take him in.

"Your father was a good man." Kristopher smiled. "I hope the orphans appreciated what he did for them."

"Most of them did, yes." Elise grinned. "I was an only child, and I enjoyed having others to play with, even if we did get into quite a bit of mischief. I remember the time Matt decided it would be fun to suck lemons in front of the local brass band. We sat in the front row, and as the trumpet player began his solo, we carefully and loudly made a show of eating them in time with the tune he was playing." She laughed at the memory. "The poor man had trouble reaching the high notes. I can't understand why, really."

Kristopher chuckled. "I can imagine. It would be quite embarrassing suddenly finding his spittle deserting him in his hour of need." He shook his head. "Matt sounds like quite a character. I almost wish I could meet him."

It appeared as though Kristopher possessed a decent sense of humour. Her opinion of him climbed another notch. "Maybe one day he'll—"

A knock on the front door interrupted her, the loudness of it echoing ominously through the empty Kaffeehaus.

She exchanged a worried look with Kristopher, the humour they'd shared forgotten in their concern. Kristopher stood, voicing the question she hadn't dared put into words. He was shaking. "Do you think it could be...?"

Willing herself to be positive, Elise shook her head. "Until we know for sure it's the Gestapo, we're not going to assume the worst." She glanced at the door, ignoring the knot forming in the pit of her stomach. "You need to hide. If they find you, all of this is for nothing."

He bit down on his lower lip, his knuckles white as he gripped the side of the table.

The banging became more insistent.

"If this is the Gestapo, and they get even an inkling you're here, you need to be prepared to take action." She spoke slowly, emphasizing each word carefully. "You. Need. To. Run. Do you understand me?"

He nervously brushed back a stray lock of hair from his face. He hesitated, his gaze lingering on the door. His already-pale complexion turned almost grey. He swallowed. "I can't. If they suspect you've helped me..." His voice shook. He paused before continuing, his tone firmer. "I won't let you suffer for what I've done. It isn't right. I've done enough of that in the past, and it stops now."

"This is SS Standartenführer Holm. I order you to open this door in the name of the Führer, now!"

Oh God.

Elise grabbed Kristopher's arm and pushed him towards the back door. "Matt told me once that there is a time to run and a time to fight. How long you survive in this world depends on having the common sense to know which one to choose at any particular time. It is time for you to run, Kristopher." She lowered her voice. "I'm going to try to convince them they have the wrong place, but if it doesn't work..."

Elise didn't allow herself to see his reaction, but instead ran to the door and opened it, plastering a look of annoyance on her face. "Can't a lady go to the bathroom in peace, even in war time?" The annoyed glare the comment provoked from the tall, slender blond man in the uniform of the SS gave her a degree of satisfaction.

Pushing her rudely out of the way, Holm didn't bother to answer her question. She'd taken too long to answer the door. "Search the place," he told his men. "I don't want anything left unturned."

Elise backed up against the counter and reached behind her to feel around for the handgun she kept there in the hope it would never have to be used. Silently she willed Kristopher to get out, to get out now.

"Lehrer's here," yelled one of Holm's men. "I've got him." Another shot was followed by a shout, the sound of the kitchen table overturning and several gunshots.

"I want him alive and fit enough to convince that cooperating would be in his best interest," Holm called out, his tone one of annoyance. "The same goes for that traitor, Schmitz." His next comment was said under his breath. Elise strained to hear him. "Of course, Lehrer is the priority. If Schmitz just happens to suffer an accident while he's being brought in, I can't be held responsible." He looked up at her, examining her with renewed intensity. "You don't approve of my methods, Fräulein Schuster?" Holm smiled, his lips thinning before he reached out to pin her hands behind her back, her fingers dropping the gun to the floor with a clatter.

"Tsk, tsk. You weren't actually planning to use that, I hope." Holm raised his voice. "Herr Dr Lehrer, I suggest you show yourself if you want the lady's good health to continue." He picked up the gun she'd dropped, raised it to her head, and began to count slowly. Elise closed her eyes. She wouldn't say anything; she wouldn't beg for her life. Holm could die in hell before she'd give him the satisfaction.

Her only regret was that she hadn't seen Matt one last time.

CHAPTER SIX

Michel froze when several gunshots pierced the quiet Berlin night. "Kristopher...," he whispered. *No. Please no.*

Beside him, Matt looked up with a jerk. He swore loudly. A few moments later, another lone shot followed the first couple.

Walker and Palmer skidded to a halt, doubling back from where they'd gone on ahead.

"Elise's Kaffeehaus." Walker panted, trying to speak and catch his breath simultaneously. He and Palmer appeared much younger than their companions. Michel wouldn't be surprised if this was their first assignment in the field. "Gestapo..."

"Matt..." Ken's previous harsh timbre was replaced by something much gentler, but Matt ignored him and shook his head.

"No." His voice shook, his words partly echoing Michel's thoughts. "Not Elise. Please, not her, not now." Matt leaned heavily against a nearby lamppost, his eyes glazed over.

"We don't know who fired the shots, sir." Palmer took

over the explanation. At least he could pass for German if he stayed quiet and kept his head down. Hopefully it wouldn't come to that, but there were no guarantees which way a particular mission might go. Michel had had that fact reinforced on more occasions than he cared to remember, but too many lives depended on them with this one. It had to succeed. "The Kaffeehaus is swarming with Gestapo, but there is no sign of anyone else."

"We need to ascertain precisely what has happened before we move in. In order to do that, we will have to get closer." Ken took charge—although Matt was the ranking officer, he appeared to be in no state to give orders. Whatever his relationship to Elise, this was not the time for him to be dwelling on what might be happening in the Kaffeehaus. Getting Kristopher and the plans to safety was still their priority.

"It's damn obvious someone's been shot." Matt visibly pulled himself together, although his voice hitched slightly before the word *shot*. "We need to get in there quickly to minimise damage. Gabriel, take Walker and Palmer and secure the back entrance. Lowe, Zhou, you're with me. We'll secure the front."

"What if there's another exit?" asked Liang, disengaging the safety on his handgun.

Matt shook his head, his matter-of-fact tone verifying prior knowledge of both the Kaffeehaus and its owner. "There isn't. Not unless Elise has done some major renovations, which I doubt."

"We're probably more than outnumbered by Holm and his men." Michel pointed out the inadequacies of the plan. "It would be more sensible to size up the situation first, as Lowe suggested, before we move in. The shot might be merely a warning. We don't know for certain that someone is injured. If Dr Lehrer and Elise have been captured, it would pay to wait until…" His voice trailed off, a grotesque image entering his mind—Kristopher lying on the floor of the Kaffeehaus, his fair hair stained red with the blood dripping from a single bullet hole to the temple. Michel quickly pushed it away. Holm needed Kristopher. He wouldn't risk killing him. Elise could be used to ensure Kristopher's cooperation. It made more sense that they were both still alive.

"I don't care." Matt's previous calm was replaced by an edge of desperation that made him both unpredictable and dangerous. "I'm not just sitting here and waiting. To hell with procedure." Ken sighed and attempted to lay a restraining hand on Matt but was pushed away. "I'm still in charge, Ken." Matt eyed Ken. "Do you think I should step down?"

Ken shook his head. "No. But procedures are there for good reason. You're emotionally involved, Matt. It's clouding your judgement."

"There is nothing wrong with my judgement," Matt snapped. Ken shrugged but didn't argue the point further. "We go in and we go in now."

Liang turned to face Matt directly, his expression unreadable, his brow creasing into a frown. "All right, Bryant, we'll do it your way, but don't attempt to play the hero because I am not going to come to your rescue." His tone softened momentarily. "I understand why you are doing this, but don't lose sight of the reason we are here." He moved forward, following Matt and Ken into the darkness.

The dynamics of this team were certainly interesting for a military task force. Liang, in particular, did not seem very concerned with following the chain of command. Ken, too, had voiced his opinion when he thought their commanding officer was not thinking logically. Walker and Palmer, in stark contrast, stood to one side silently. Walker fidgeted with a loose strand of cotton on his jacket, winding it around his fingers, then unwinding it. Palmer checked the safety on his gun over and over as though he didn't trust it would fire correctly when needed.

"Keep your weapons at the ready, but don't use them unless there is no choice," Michel told them before signalling they were heading out. His hand rested briefly on the small knife hidden in his belt, his mind going over the various scenarios they might encounter and the best way to deal with each eventuality before refocusing on the task ahead.

Getting as close to the Kaffeehaus as he dared, Michel dropped into a half crouch, motioning the two men behind him to be silent. Shadowy figures moved through the building, a blaze of light illuminating each room as it was thoroughly searched. He hoped Kristopher had either hidden the plans extremely well or had them with him when he'd escaped.

Michel edged closer, trying to make out some of the conversation taking place inside. He needed to evaluate the situation before considering breaking cover. If the Gestapo had the plans and Kristopher was already... dead, there was no point in going further and risking any more lives. Retreating and regrouping would be the best option. Michel shivered and fastened the top button of his jacket to keep out the cold he suspected was not wholly related to the current weather conditions.

"Herr SS Standartenführer Holm, I've found them." Müller's voice shattered the silence before the light was extinguished in the attic room.

Damn. Was he referring to the plans or to Kristopher

and Elise? Michel strained to hear more, trying to stifle his annoyance at the fidgeting going on behind him. He turned, placing one finger against his lips to remind Palmer and Walker their very survival depended on no one noticing them. Catching a slight movement out of the corner of one eye, he quickly refocused his attention towards the Kaffee-haus. Someone was attempting to enter through the back door.

He frowned. Why would someone want to sneak back inside? The moon slid from behind a cloud, illuminating the figure trying to blend in unsuccessfully against an organised pile of crates outside the back wall of the building. Blond hair shone like a beacon, giving the enemy a clear target they couldn't miss at close range.

Kristopher?

Michel hissed over his shoulder at the two men behind him, telling them to stay there. He didn't want their incompetence risking Kristopher's life further. Ignoring their muffled protests, he ran to Kristopher, hoping to reach him before it was too late. Already moving again, Kristopher glanced around, edging along with his back pressed up against the crates. Acting on instinct, Michel propelled himself the last few feet, his body connecting with Kristopher just as he took a couple of steps past the relative shelter of his hiding place into plain view. Knocking them both sideways, they landed together in a crumpled heap on the ground. Michel wrapped one arm around Kristopher's waist and placed a hand over his mouth before quickly dragging him back into the darkness.

Kristopher sank his teeth into Michel's hand, and brought his leg up in an attempt to kick his assailant in the crotch. He kept struggling, determined not to be restrained easily. Michel strengthened his hold, whispering into his captive's ear. "Kristopher, it's me."

Immediately Kristopher went limp, the fight leaving him. He twisted so he could see Michel's face and pulled his hand away.

"Michel."

Michel brought his now free hand up to press a single finger against his own lips as a warning. He loosened his grip on Kristopher.

"Thank God." Kristopher continued in a whisper, following Michel's advice. His eyes reflected his relief, although he was still breathing heavily.

The voices inside rose in pitch as they approached the outside door close to where Michel and Kristopher were hiding. Michel dropped into a lower crouch, and Kristopher, having shuffled around so they were now side by side, quickly followed suit. They couldn't be discovered now, not when they had got this far.

Holm didn't attempt to keep the annoyance out of his voice as he dressed down his men. "Herr Dr Lehrer is merely a scientist. He has no combat experience. How could you allow him to escape?"

His second-in-command, SS Obersturmführer Reiniger, replied in a respectful and apologetic tone, "We thought we had him, sir."

"Thought?" Holm asked, a note of sarcasm entering his voice. "I would have *thought* you knew better than to let your guard down." He paused. "So he overpowered you and escaped?"

"No, sir. Müller heard a noise, which he thought might be Lehrer, but it turned out to be a cat. Lehrer was already gone... sir."

"We won't be making that mistake again, will we,

Reiniger?"

Michel could imagine Reiniger bringing his heels together sharply and saluting. "No, sir, we will not." Reiniger was very concerned with appearances and would not appreciate being made a fool of in front of his superior officer. He also had a tendency to hold grudges, a trait Michel had discovered to his own detriment. This, unfortunately, made him all the more dangerous, and probably added to his determination to apprehend the man who had caused him to "fall from grace" in Holm's eyes.

They needed to leave. Michel placed a hand on Kristopher's shoulder, signalling they needed to move out. "Kristopher...," he whispered, trying to instill the gravity of the situation into that one word.

"I can't," Kristopher hissed. "Elise is in there, and I heard a gunshot. If she's in trouble, it's because of me. I won't be responsible for any more death or suffering." His voice shook. He pushed Michel's hand away.

"You can't blame yourself. Elise knew the risks. She wouldn't want you to place yourself in danger. We are leaving. Now."

"You may leave if you wish, but I'm not leaving Elise in there with Holm." Kristopher's voice was low but cold.

Michel admired Kristopher's courage yet wondered how he could be so naïve. Did he truly think giving himself up would help Elise in any way? "We don't know she is still alive. We are leaving. Now!"

Still Kristopher refused to move. Michel snaked his hand around him and began to drag him from the scene. Kristopher dug in his heels, his previous stubbornness turning to anger. "How dare you? Elise needs our help."

Michel drew Kristopher closer, turning him so they were facing each other. Kristopher's breathing sounded ragged, his forehead covered in a fine sheen of perspiration, and his face was white. Placing one hand on each side of Kristopher's face firmly but careful not to hurt him, Michel made sure he had no choice but to listen.

"I know you want to help her, but now is not the time." Michel knew how Kristopher felt, wanted to tell him this would work out, but couldn't bring himself to say something that might be comforting now but turn out to be a lie later.

"They have the plans."

"We need to get you to safety." He'd worry about the plans later. Kluge was dead. Michel couldn't allow the Nazis to take Kristopher into custody. "That's the priority."

Kristopher tried to shake his head again but couldn't with the way Michel held him. "Damn the priorities. I won't do this. I can't." His voice cracked into a sob, his tone bordering on hysteria.

"Yes, you can, and you will." Michel didn't wait to hear the rest of Kristopher's words and grasped him firmly around the waist, then lifted him off the ground before he had a chance to react.

"What the hell?" Kristopher struggled, his voice rising several notches when he was hefted over Michel's shoulder. "Put me down!"

Michel began to run towards where he'd left Walker and Palmer, grunting in exertion with the extra weight he carried. Kristopher might be of slender build, but he was a lot heavier than he looked.

A shout came from the Kaffeehaus. Someone had seen them. Carrying Kristopher like this would slow them down too much. "If I put you down," he whispered sharply to Kristopher, "we have a better chance of escaping. But if I do, you are not surrendering to the Gestapo, not while we have the choice not to. Do you understand?"

Silence.

"Kristopher?"

He felt Kristopher nod his head and paused long enough to let him down to the ground. "Keep going straight ahead. You'll find two men in their early twenties, one well built and tall, the other slightly shorter and thinner." Hopefully their descriptions would be enough for Kristopher to recognise them. "Stay with them until I get there. I'm going to buy us some time."

"But..." Kristopher didn't want to leave Michel; that much was clear.

"Go. Now." Michel gave Kristopher a push and dropped to a kneeling position, reaching for the Luger he'd hidden in his jacket. "Now, Kristopher." Not waiting to make sure his directions were followed, he fired the weapon once, then twice at the oncoming soldiers, then a third time, the last shot aimed at the sole light source in the alley. It hit its target with deadly accuracy, plunging the area into sudden darkness.

The men pursuing them cursed loudly, fumbling around in the dark. Michel permitted himself a small smile and headed in the direction he'd sent Kristopher.

Walker was waiting at the end of the alley. He had his weapon in his hand and aimed it at Michel when he approached. "Who's there?" he called, nervousness in his voice. "Gabriel, is that you?" Michel mentally rolled his eyes. That these men had survived as long as they had was a miracle, as they obviously hadn't much field experience. Matt needed to be credited for keeping them alive so far.

"Lower your weapon," he ordered, glancing around. "Where are Palmer and Herr Dr Lehrer?" Surely Kristopher had managed to at least reach one of them?

"Herr Dr Lehrer?" Walker appeared embarrassed. "Do

you mean the blond gentleman?" He holstered his gun after Michel nodded. "He wouldn't tell us who he was, sir. Just that you'd sent him and... We were expecting someone older. Sir."

Michel raised one eyebrow. *This should be interesting.* He hadn't heard any gunfire so he presumed Kristopher was safe, but wondered what happened during those few minutes it had taken to stall their pursuers.

"Palmer has him over here, sir." Michel followed Walker quickly to a nearby park on the next street over from the Kaffeehaus. The entrance was tucked between two small buildings a few hundred metres to the left of the main walkway so wasn't immediately noticeable in the dark, despite being lit by a single streetlight. A small clearing stood in the middle of a grove of trees several minutes walk into the park, the path illuminated by a series of old-fashioned lampposts. Luckily it was before ten, or the park would already be in darkness apart from the phosphorescent paint marking the outline of the path at intervals. Kristopher sat under one of the trees, his hands raised and a frustrated expression on his face as he attempted to convince Palmer the gun wasn't necessary.

"Michel, could you please tell your friend I'm on your side." Kristopher started to lower his hands when he saw them approach but quickly raised them again when Palmer made a show of waving his gun. "I know these men aren't part of the German Army but—"

"What makes you so sure we aren't?" Palmer asked suspiciously.

"For one thing, your weapons are Colt .45s, which are usually American military issue. We Germans prefer Lugers. Secondly"—he pointed at Walker—"when you were speaking English earlier... your London accent is fairly prominent." He said something in English, and both men stared at him.

Michel stifled a smirk. While he didn't speak English, Kristopher's last comment had obviously got the message across. "Palmer, lower your weapon. This is Herr Dr Lehrer. He can be trusted." He gave Kristopher a nod of approval.

Kristopher lowered his hands gratefully and stood up. Michel had mistakenly been led to assume the information he'd received about Kristopher was fairly comprehensive. It would be interesting to learn what else was missing from the dossier Clara had supplied. Even under these circumstances, Kristopher's mind was still sharp. His fear and earlier near hysteria hadn't dampened his powers of observation in the slightest.

"If you were so convinced we weren't German, why didn't you tell us who you were?" Walker asked. "It would have saved us all a lot of trouble." He glanced at Michel, suddenly aware he might have stepped out of line. "Sorry, sir," he mumbled.

"You were so busy assuming I wasn't Lehrer, I decided not to waste my breath convincing you otherwise." Kristopher shrugged. "Besides, your conversation was... interesting." He smiled. "I also knew Michel—Herr Obergefreiter Schmitz—would be along shortly. It was easier to wait." The smile faded, and his eyes shifted out of focus for a moment. "Did you manage to lose them?" he asked Michel.

Michel nodded. "For now, but probably not for long." He issued further orders to Walker and Palmer. "Go find Bryant and inform him that I am taking Herr Dr Lehrer to another safe house. I'll get a message to him when it's safe." Had he underestimated them? Perhaps they might survive this mission after all. That at least one of the two had used his initiative and suggested retreating to this park rather than staying where they risked being seen definitely raised the odds at least a little more. "Don't engage the enemy under any circumstances. If Bryant and the others are not where you expect them to be, make your way back to the church."

The men nodded. "Yes, sir." They saluted and headed back into the darkness. Michel watched them go and then returned his attention to Kristopher.

"Are you all right?" asked Kristopher, shivering. He wasn't wearing a sweater and the shirt he wore wasn't adequate protection against the cold.

"I've slowed them down, but that's all." Michel deliberately didn't answer the question. Physically he was fine, which was all that mattered. "We need to go. It's more difficult to track a target if it's moving." He slipped off his jacket and offered it to Kristopher. "You're cold."

"But..."

"We can take turns wearing it and both keep warm." Michel was still wearing a sweater; he'd make sure Kristopher stayed warm.

Kristopher opened his mouth to protest further, but before he had the chance to speak, tyres squealed from the nearby road. Doors slammed, feet pounded, and dogs barked.

"Dogs." Kristopher paled. "They're using dogs. We can't outrun them. I've read about their tracking ability. You should go. It's me they're looking for, not you."

"We're not splitting up. The priority is to get you to safety, and to do that we need to stay together."

"You should have listened to Herr Dr Lehrer and left while you still could, Schmitz."

Michel spun to come face-to-face with SS Obersturm-führer Reiniger.

Michel drew his weapon and aimed for Reiniger's gun hand, but the man laughed.

"Michel." Kristopher's voice sounded choked. Michel turned to see Müller standing next to Kristopher, the barrel of his gun pointed against Kristopher's temple.

"Lower your weapon, Schmitz, and place it on the ground at your feet," Reiniger ordered with a smirk, "unless you'd like Müller to prove how difficult it is to miss a target when it's at close range like this."

Michel glanced between the two men. He had one gun to their two, and Müller wouldn't hesitate to follow any orders. Even if their orders were to bring Kristopher in alive, it did not mean he could not be hurt, and that was a risk Michel was not prepared to take. He lowered his gun, allowing it to fall to the grass at his feet, and then slowly raised his hands in surrender.

CHAPTER SEVEN

"What the hell is going on in there?" Matt slipped his Colt through the concealed opening of his cassock and secured it into the waistband of his trousers. The disguise, although a little cumbersome, did provide him with good camouflage in the darkness. He'd already gotten rid of the rabat and collar and would do so with this, too, when he had the opportunity and time.

He edged further forward.

"They appear to be searching the building room by room," Ken said when Matt crouched beside him. Matt nodded, trying to make out details but without much luck. Shadowy figures turned on the light in one room, then the next.

Matt shivered, praying Elise wasn't badly hurt or worse. As much as he wanted to storm the Kaffeehaus, Liang was right. They needed to wait for a sign to show them what their next move should be. So far logic had prevailed, but Matt wasn't sure how much longer he could ignore his need to know what was happening. His imagination providing him with possible scenarios was killing the tiny sliver of hope he had left.

Ironically, the first time he'd prayed in years, and he was masquerading as a priest. He wasn't sure what Father Joseph would have thought of that. Matt hoped the old man would be pleased his young friend was doing his bit for the war effort but knew it would be accompanied by a slight frown of disapproval for the way he was dressed. He didn't think of Father Joseph often, although they'd stayed in contact until he'd died just before Elise's family had moved back to Germany. Father Joseph had approved of Elise and her parents. They'd been good to all the children at the orphanage, not only those they'd fostered. Matt had lost his parents and sister in the house fire a long time ago, but he'd never forgotten them or the priest who had taken him in afterwards.

"Herr SS Standartenführer Holm, I've found them." The light coming from the attic died shortly after the man's voice called out to his superior. Them? What or who was he referring to? Matt groaned inwardly, fighting the urge to draw his weapon as he tried to stay calm and not think the worst.

Holm was the Gestapo officer in charge of this operation. According to Gabriel, Holm was very capable and should be treated with caution. Getting old Dr Lehrer out of the country was going to be a fun addition to the task already ahead of his team. Perhaps it would be a good idea to convince Elise to come with them to America. She wouldn't be safe in Germany after this. The life expectancy of a known collaborator wasn't very long, and they already had an extra person coming with them, so what was one more?

If only she'd come with him the first time he'd asked.

Matt sighed. By the time he'd left Berlin for America, their relationship was over, although he suspected she'd not accepted it until much later. He wasn't sure what went wrong between them and didn't regret the years they spent together. They'd remained good friends afterwards and only lost contact because of the war. She'd wanted them to get married, but the idea of it had scared him. He loved Elise, but he wasn't in love with her. He also wasn't convinced she was the person he wanted to spend the rest of his life with, and although they'd never kept secrets between them, he'd never shared a part of himself with her or anyone else.

"There are at least half a dozen men under Holm's command." Liang slid in beside Ken, giving his report, his British accent more pronounced when he switched languages from German to English. Spying on the Gestapo was not the safest of occupations, and they weren't being subtle about it. It seemed pointless to keep speaking German under the circumstances, at least until they moved position again. "And no, Bryant, I didn't see anyone else, although I did overhear him dressing down one of his men. Apparently this Dr Lehrer has escaped."

Matt nodded, relieved at least something seemed to be working in their favour. Maybe if the Doc had escaped, Elise had too? After all if an old guy could get away—

"What the hell?" The words carried clearly through the quiet night air, and the three men exchanged glances as the Kaffeehaus suddenly came to life.

Shifting his weight onto both elbows, Ken trained his binoculars back towards the building. "Something's happening. The Gestapo are in pursuit of someone…" He shook his head, running a hand through his mop of dark hair in a gesture of frustration. Ken hated not knowing what was going on in any given situation. Matt had discovered that very quickly when they'd first met nearly two years ago. Both had joined up shortly after Pearl Harbour, met during basic training, and become good friends. "Whatever is happening seems to be taking place at the rear of the building. It's difficult to tell—"

"Gabriel is supposed to be covering the rear," Liang interrupted, rising to his feet. "Maybe the Germans have become aware of his presence?" He looked at Matt, as though waiting for an order to move in. For someone without a military background, he seemed keen to be fully involved in this mission, and more than just in his official capacity as the only person of their team capable of confirming the authenticity of the plans they were here to retrieve.

Matt frowned. "I doubt it. He struck me as being very careful and efficient. Maybe if this Lehrer is on the loose, it's him the Germans have seen?" Or Elise. No, Elise would have more sense. She'd be long gone if she'd escaped. Maybe that was what the shot was—a warning fired at her and Doc Lehrer as they'd escaped. That made sense.

Whatever was happening, they needed to move in. The Gestapo had done enough damage for one night, and the thought of them in Elise's Kaffeehaus—their Kaffeehaus— annoyed him. He couldn't sit here while the bastards went after her. At the very least he could slow them down, even if he couldn't stop them.

Two loud gunshots sounded in succession, quickly followed by a third. "Damn," muttered Ken. "The only light's just been hit. There's no possibility of seeing anything clearly from this distance now."

"Sneaky bastard," Matt muttered under his breath, grinning, guessing who was responsible. He would have done the same thing under the circumstances. The pursuing Germans wouldn't have deliberately shot out the only light source when it would be helpful in tracking their enemies. It must have been Gabriel. If he was still free and had the situation under control, it also meant there was a good chance Elise was still alive.

He pulled out his Colt and motioned for Ken and Liang to follow. "It's time we showed the Gestapo that it doesn't pay to mess with the good guys."

Liang and Ken exchanged amused looks before they drew their own weapons. "I'm almost afraid to ask which one of us is Tonto," Ken said dryly.

Matt grinned. "Hi-Yo, Silver. Come on. Let's go catch some bad guys." Ken glared at him and Matt laughed. "Aw, Ken, don't be such a spoilsport."

"Typical," muttered Ken. "He gets to be the Lone Ranger while I get stuck as the horse." He and Matt moved out quickly, turning to gesture Liang to follow.

Liang stood there staring after them for a moment, shaking his head slowly. "Americans." He sped up to narrow the distance between them.

"There is an alley very close to the back entrance to the Kaffeehaus," Matt told them once Liang had caught up. "We can survey the situation from there before moving in." Approaching the alley, they were careful to keep to the shadows. The moon couldn't decide whether to stay behind the clouds to provide them with cover or show itself and give away their position. Still, they were safer than if they'd tried to remain undetected on a night with no moon and therefore no shadows to hide in.

"Captain Bryant!" Walker skidded to a halt in front of them, Palmer almost colliding into him as he followed closely behind.

"Where's Gabriel?" asked Matt.

Both men stood, hands resting on their knees in a half-bent position while they caught their breath. Finally, Palmer spoke. "He's taken Herr Dr Lehrer to a safe house, sir. Told us to let you know he'd contact you when it's safe." He hesitated before continuing. "Lehrer called him Michel... Obergefreiter Schmitz, sir."

Matt nodded. It made sense that Gabriel—Michel—had worked undercover at the project in order to get the information they'd needed. At least he and Lehrer were safe. "Was anyone else with them? A woman?" When the questions were answered with puzzled expressions, Matt added a description, hoping it would help.

It didn't.

"She must still be in the Kaffeehaus. Shit." Matt voiced the only conclusion left open.

"Ssh," hissed Liang, who was on lookout. "I hear something."

Motioning his men back, Matt pressed up against the wall to avoid being seen. They quickly followed his lead. Moments later the squeal of rubber against the road signalled the arrival of a large truck pulling into a sidewalk further up the street. An SS officer opened the rear door and stood back to allow several men accompanied by dogs to exit the vehicle.

"They shouldn't have got far," someone said, the authority in his voice giving a fair indication he was in charge. This must be Holm. "Reiniger, take Müller with you and head towards the park. Tell the rest of the men to spread out so we can cover more ground."

"Yes, sir." Reiniger snapped to attention. He was a tall, slim man, light-blond hair barely noticeable under the cap he wore.

"Bauer wants them both taken into custody with a minimum of damage." Holm's tone hardened. "While we need to follow those orders, often incidents in the field can complicate such matters." He paused. "Do you understand me?"

"Yes, sir," Reiniger replied. "Is there any particular potential incident you wish me to be aware of, sir?"

"I'll leave that up to your discretion, Reiniger. Of course if they resist arrest, use whatever means necessary to ensure they don't escape. We have the plans, so at this point our main concern is ensuring they are not duplicated." Holm laughed, and Matt shivered. Whatever the story was with him, this Lehrer, and Michel or whatever his name was, must have annoyed the hell out of him. "And of course, at least to my understanding, now Herr Dr Kluge is dead, the only person connected to the project capable of doing that is Lehrer."

"But Herr Bauer..." Reiniger dared to question Holm's orders. Matt guessed Bauer must be someone higher up than Holm on this chain of command.

"Herr Bauer isn't running this recovery operation. I am. After all, we did our best to bring them in unharmed. Traitors to the Third Reich need to be dealt with appropriately." Holm sighed. "Do I make myself clear? Oh, and Reiniger? I am returning to headquarters shortly. Do not disappoint me."

"No, sir. You can count on me to *execute* your orders, Herr SS Standartenführer."

This Holm was definitely a nasty piece of work. Hopefully Gabriel had gotten Lehrer well clear, or their chances of survival were not looking very good. Matt shuddered. That last line of Reiniger's and the emphasis on the word *execute* had left Matt with no doubt both SS officers would prefer their prey dead rather than alive.

A few minutes later, the area was quiet again, the sound of dogs and men growing fainter as the search for the fugitives drifted away from the Kaffeehaus and the alley behind it. A car door slammed shut and an engine roaring to life confirmed Holm's departure. The Kaffeehaus finally appeared empty.

"Right," Matt told the others, "I'm going in. Lowe, Zhou, cover me. Walker, Palmer, head back to the church where it's safe and await further orders. We need someone there in case Gabriel and Lehrer show."

"Matt." Ken's voice was gentle, but firm. "You don't need to do this. Liang or I can—"

Matt interrupted him, his tone harsher than he intended. "I gave you an order, soldier. Cover me. I'm going in." He hated having to play the command card with Ken, but had no choice. Elise would be scared, so better she knew the person going in. His knuckles white, Matt gripped his Colt tightly, surveyed his surroundings one last time, and ran quickly to the pile of crates by the back door.

She was still as organised as ever, he noticed with a grin. The crates were stacked neatly, reminding him of how much she'd hated a mess. Everything always had to be just so, a place for everything and everything in its place. She'd complained about his way of doing paperwork too, and called him a slob.

A lump formed in his throat, remembering his reply. *Yeah, but cute with it, right?* She had to be all right. He'd never forgive himself if she wasn't.

The crates provided the cover he'd thought they would. He checked for signs the enemy was still present. There were none. He gave Ken and Liang the all clear and began moving again. Ken knew about Matt's history with Elise and understood why he had to do this. They'd need to meet once he got Elise clear. He liked the idea that his two best friends would finally be given that opportunity.

Poor Elise. Holm and his men would be too concerned with tracking the fugitives to worry about her. He'd probably left her bound and gagged so she couldn't interfere with his plans. She wasn't a threat. Matt's eyes narrowed. Bastard. If Holm had hurt Elise, Matt would kill him slowly, piece by piece.

Matt cautiously opened the door to the Kaffeehaus and peered inside. "Elise?" he whispered, half expecting to hear her muffled curses through whatever she was gagged with.

"Elise?"

He checked the kitchen first, noticing the upturned table. The vase he'd given her for her birthday the first year they were together was in pieces on the floor. Shit, Elise was going to love this.

"Elise?" Where the hell was she?

"Elise?" Of course, the Kaffeehaus. Why hadn't he thought of it before? Keeping his gun at the ready, he swung the dividing door between the two areas open, scanning the room frantically for any sign of her.

"God, Elise, you scared the shit out of me." Matt offered a silent prayer of thanks when he made out the slender figure sitting slumped in the chair behind the counter. "Elise?" Holm must have knocked her unconscious. It would have been faster and easier than the time it would have taken to find something with which to restrain her.

He placed one hand on her shoulder. Cold. Why did she feel so cold? "Poor baby," he murmured soothingly. "I'll take you somewhere warm after this. You'll never have to worry about cold Berlin winters again." He put his gun down on the counter, making sure to leave it within reach in case he needed to grab it. For the moment, his concern was for Elise, and he needed both hands free so he could move her somewhere more comfortable.

Her head fell back limply when he took her into his arms, the moon catching her in a sudden illumination. He ran a gentle hand through her hair, brushing it from her forehead so he could see her properly.

Congealed blood from the single bullet wound spread over his hand in slow motion.

He took a step backward, wiping her blood on his shirt. His breath hitched, and he let out a sob. "No, please," he whispered hoarsely. "Elise. Please God, not her, not now."

CHAPTER EIGHT

Michel glanced between the gun at his feet and Kristopher. Müller had taken a step back, but his finger was on the trigger, and the gun was too close to Kristopher. "Don't give them the information they want," Michel told Kristopher.

"I have no intention of cooperating with these gentlemen." Kristopher clenched his fists, his voice calm and icy.

"We have the plans, so your cooperation is no longer required, Herr Dr Lehrer." Reiniger laughed again. "Your intentions are not my concern."

Motioning with his weapon, Reiniger indicated an area further into the park. Michel chanced a quick look at Kristopher, wondering if he realised the reason the Gestapo officer was moving them somewhere more isolated. Their planned execution had less chance of attracting attention there, and if justified by a story of them attempting to escape while resisting arrest, there would be no witnesses.

Kristopher's shoulders briefly sagged then he took a couple of steps forward so he was standing next to Michel. "Herr Dr Kluge is dead," he pointed out. "Your superiors are fools if they believe the plans are all they need to build this device." His gaze met Michel's. Kristopher's eyes reflected regret and sadness. He turned to address Reiniger directly. "The plans are not complete. Herr Dr Kluge and I were working on the final calculations shortly before he died. Without them the device is useless. You need me, no matter what you were told to the contrary."

Reiniger digested the new information in silence. Michel stilled, waiting. Making any sudden moves would be paramount to a death wish as Reiniger would most likely interpret the action as a reason to kill both of them now, rather than in a few moments' time. The longer they could stay alive, the better their chances of survival became.

"My orders come from Herr SS Standartenführer Holm, and since he's under the impression your presence is no longer required for this project to continue, I am going to disregard your comments," Reiniger smugly informed Kristopher. "Nice try, Lehrer, but you'll have to do better than that. If you want to beg for your life, I suggest you try getting down on your hands and knees."

Kristopher shook his head. "Obergefreiter Schmitz..."

What was he trying to accomplish? Michel didn't believe for a moment that Kristopher had any intention of begging for his life. It didn't fit with what Michel had observed of him over the past few months, nor his words and actions of the last day.

"Schmitz is a traitor to the Third Reich and will be dealt with accordingly." Reiniger's mouth thinned. "As are you, Herr Dr Lehrer."

If Kristopher was bluffing, he was playing a very dangerous game. How complete were the plans? With Kluge dead, it would take time before Holm could find out whether Kristopher was telling the truth or not. Knowing the techniques Holm would use to extract information

Kristopher was not prepared to give made this a game he would be hard-pressed to win. Holm's concern would be getting the version of the truth he wanted. It wouldn't matter if it didn't exist.

He couldn't allow Kristopher's inner light to be killed slowly and painfully. Even a quick death by a firing squad of two would be preferable to a series of interrogations by Holm. "Kristopher...," Michel began, trying to warn him, but Reiniger took a step closer and backhanded him across the face. Michel hissed in pain yet stood his ground.

"As I said, Lehrer, traitors will be dealt with accordingly."

"And as *I* said, Herr SS Obersturmführer Reiniger, the plans are not complete. You need me." Kristopher was silent for a moment. "I can't allow any more people to die." His voice lowered to a whisper. "Let Herr Schmitz live, and I'll cooperate."

What was Kristopher trying to gain by this? His conscience had been one of the deciding factors bringing him to the conclusion he needed to leave the project. Surely doing this would undo everything he'd managed to achieve so far?

Reiniger stifled a snicker and lowered his gun. Kristopher tensed, then adopted a look of resignation, his shoulders slumping still further, for all appearances acting as though the fight had gone out of him.

"Herr SS Standartenführer Holm will be interested to hear of your proposition." A tiny smile crept across Reiniger's face. He relaxed his stance. "However..."

Giving Reiniger a hopeful look, Kristopher took a step closer to Müller, tilting his head to covertly meet Michel's eyes. To his surprise, Kristopher's eyes were bright and focused; he wore the expression of a man who had nothing to lose and everything to gain.

What the...?

Reiniger motioned to Müller to restrain Kristopher, who held out his hands as though bowing to the inevitable. Müller smirked and produced a pair of handcuffs. "Hands behind your back," he ordered, moving to twist one of Kristopher's arms around behind him sharply. Kristopher cursed under his breath and doubled over in pain. When Müller loosened his grip, Kristopher uncurled and launched himself at the SS officer. Both men hit the ground with a thud.

They wrestled for the gun, Müller's grip on it loosening when he was knocked off-balance. Kristopher grunted when Müller kicked at him, but managed to grab the gun before Müller when it fell to the ground. He rolled and pulled himself upright, aiming his newly acquired weapon at his former captor.

Michel dived at Reiniger, hitting him hard several times on his gun arm, trying to throw off his aim. Several shots were fired in Kristopher's direction. Reiniger fell backwards, Michel on top of him as they struggled for control of the weapon.

"Damn you," muttered Reiniger, hitting the gun hard against Michel's shoulder. He winced in pain. Reiniger tried to stand, but Michel brought one foot up behind his opponent's just as he struggled to his feet, tripping him again. Reiniger fell against a nearby tree. He cursed, and attempted to slam his knee into Michel's groin when he came within range. Michel moved quickly, just managing to dodge the blow, his fist connecting with the SS officer's jaw, slamming his head back against the trunk of the tree.

Reiniger grunted, then went limp, the gun falling from his grasp to hit the grass with a thump.

Reaching inside Reiniger's pocket, Michel retrieved a set of standard-issue SS handcuffs identical to the ones Müller had attempted to use on Kristopher, and cuffed Reiniger roughly, leaving him slumped at the foot of the tree.

Only then did he allow himself the distraction of glancing at Kristopher. "Are you all right?"

Kristopher nodded quickly and looked up from where he was securing Müller to another tree with the same handcuffs he'd narrowly escaped wearing himself. He stood up shakily, using the tree as leverage. Michel frowned.

"Are you sure you're all right?"

"I'm just not used to all this exercise." Kristopher smiled sheepishly. "I've spent the last few years sitting behind a desk. I'll be all right in a moment once I've caught my breath." He rubbed absently at his left shoulder, not quite hiding the sharp intake of breath, and bit his upper lip. "The ground is harder than it looks."

"Do you want me to look at that shoulder for you?"

Kristopher shook his head.

Once they found somewhere safe to hide for what was left of the night, Michel would insist on examining it. He and Kristopher needed to get out of the park as quickly as possible before the Gestapo arrived. The Sankt-Michael-Kirche was probably the wisest choice for shelter under the circumstances. Hopefully the two Allied soldiers had already reached Matt, and the mission could proceed even though the plans their superiors were expecting were now carried in the mind of a man who could reproduce them.

If not... Michel mentally shook his head, working

through possible options. Apart from Father Johannes, Elise and Clara were his only contacts in Berlin.

"If you change your mind, let me know." Michel wasn't going to push the issue just yet, but he kept an eye on Kristopher all the same. They began walking briskly, each with one hand resting on a hidden firearm that hopefully wouldn't be needed. Curfew was in force, and anyone caught breaking it would be automatically arrested.

Only a few moments later, Kristopher began to slow his pace. Something was definitely wrong. His hand dropped to his side. He seemed to be favouring his shoulder.

"Kristopher?"

"I haven't changed my mind. We need to get out of the park." Kristopher was certainly stubborn. He winced again, his steps becoming more deliberate.

"Are you sure you're all right?"

"I'm. Fine." Kristopher answered through gritted teeth. Michel placed a gentle hand on his arm, making him stop under a nearby light. Kristopher let out a small moan of pain and swayed. Michel hooked his arms around Kristopher's waist, pulling him close. Resting his head on Michel's shoulder, Kristopher leaned in, allowing himself to be held.

"I've got you," Michel whispered soothingly. Kristopher's breathing was ragged, his face covered in beads of perspiration. Now his attention wasn't totally focused on putting one foot in front of the other, he couldn't hide whatever was wrong.

His eyes glazed over; he was fighting to stay conscious.

"Kristopher?"

Jerking free from Michel's embrace, Kristopher reached inside his shirt, his hand brushing gingerly against his shoulder. He bit down on his lip but didn't manage to hide a murmur of pain. A frown creased his forehead when he removed his hand and held it up to the light, staring at it. "Michel," he said slowly, "is that blood?"

Blood? Oh God, no. Michel's mind returned to the gunfight and the shots Reiniger had managed to fire in Kristopher's direction.

Kristopher stared at his hand as though he didn't believe it belonged to him. His eyes began to close. He blinked, whimpering. "I don't feel right," he whispered faintly. His hand dropped to his side.

"Kristopher, you need to stay awake." Michel slid his arm around Kristopher's waist, trying to help him stay upright, but Kristopher pushed him away and pulled the borrowed jacket more tightly around himself. His eyes fluttered, and then he slowly reopened them.

Michel gently replaced his arm around Kristopher's waist and held him close again. This time Kristopher didn't argue. "I'm sorry." He gave Michel a shaky smile. "I'll try, but I'm so tired." He groaned, his head drooping before he jerked awake once more, leaning more heavily on Michel. "I just need to sleep. I'll be fine once I sleep. I only wanted to make the world a better place." He looked up at Michel, his expression pleading, his fingers gripping Michel's sweater. "I tried to stop the nightmares. Please, you have to help me... put... things... right." Kristopher's eyes began to close. He shivered. "It's cold. Why is it so cold?"

"Kristopher... please. Look at me." Michel lowered Kristopher carefully to the ground. His pulse was fast and irregular, and his skin cold and clammy to the touch. "You need to try and focus." Michel's fingers shook as he eased the jacket from the shoulder Kristopher had favoured. The inside of it was soaked with blood. Michel's breath hitched, but he forced himself to examine it more closely. He was no doctor, and so couldn't tell how bad the wound was, just that it had obviously been seeping for some time.

God, how had Kristopher managed to get this far? He was strong-willed and stubborn, but this... Michel bit his lip. If he didn't get Kristopher to a doctor and soon... He grabbed a handkerchief from his pocket and rolled it into a makeshift pad, then pressed the cloth against the wound in the hope that pressure might at least help staunch the flow of blood.

"Thank you." Michel barely heard the whispered words before the grip on his sweater loosened and Kristopher slipped into unconsciousness. He bent and lifted Kristopher into his arms, cradling him.

Nearby a dog barked, and men shouted. "The dogs are picking up on something. It looks like blood!"

"Matt?"

This couldn't be happening. Any minute Elise would open her eyes and tell him he was having another bad dream. Matt glanced down at the stains on his shirt. Black was really good at hiding the dirt. If he squinted, he could easily pretend none of this was real. After all, it couldn't be her blood on there, right?

Right.

"Matt?"

Couldn't whoever was calling his name see he was busy? He had to look after Elise and make sure nothing bad happened to her. Matt wiped his hands down his shirt. Black was also a good colour for shrouds, he remembered absently. Black was the symbol for death.

Black and red. Red flames from the fire that killed his family. Red blood caused by the bullet that killed Elise.

He stifled a sob.

"Matt?" The voice grew more insistent. Why couldn't it just leave him alone? Matt felt a hand on his shoulder. He tried to shrug it off but without success. "Matt?" asked the voice again. He turned to tell it to go away, only to meet Ken's expression of concern.

"She's dead, Ken. I didn't get here in time." He choked back another sob. "The bastard killed her, and I wasn't here to protect her."

"It wasn't your fault," Ken insisted. "You probably couldn't have done anything even if you'd been here." His voice softened, a quality to it Matt hadn't heard before. "War is an evil thing. People die, Matt. Good people die, and there's nothing you and I can do to stop that."

Matt shook his head and cradled Elise in his arms, rocking her back and forth. "I won't believe that. I can't believe that." Why were they fighting this war if they couldn't save people? All of this had to make a difference and to the people who mattered. He'd joined up to protect the innocents and to fight so they wouldn't have to. He'd known at the time he was naïve, but he still clung to it on some level. Just to be able to save one person who would have otherwise died would make it all worthwhile.

He hadn't saved Elise.

His voice grew bitter, his tone hardening. "I am going to take her killer apart piece by piece."

"And what will that achieve?" Liang asked. "It's not going to turn back the clock. She's still going to be dead, Bry —Matthew."

"Go to hell, Zhou." Matt spat out his reply. "What the hell would you know? You've never seen your loved ones die, never held them in your arms knowing you should have tried harder to save them." Damn them all to hell. He drew her closer to him. Maybe if he talked to her and told her how much he was going to miss her, it might make things better.

Liang took a step back, his voice hoarse. "You know nothing about what I know or what I've been through." He sounded angry. "Revenge is not the answer." He swore under his breath in Mandarin. "I..." Liang shrugged. "Do what you bloody well want."

"This isn't the time or place." Ken stepped between the two men. "Zhou, I suggest you return to the church and make sure Walker and Palmer are staying out of trouble. I'll follow you shortly."

"I don't believe you have the authority to give the orders, Lowe." Liang snorted. "I know I don't belong to your precious OSS, but I refuse to be treated like an inferior because of it. This is a joint operation between our two organisations. Don't forget that."

Matt interrupted. "Guys, please. I just need..." His voice hitched. "I need some time to..." To what? What did he need the damn time to do? It was too late to *do* anything. He didn't even have the luxury to ensure she received a decent burial.

"I'll go to the church," Liang conceded. "Someone with more common sense than those two needs to be there in case Gabriel and Dr Lehrer decide to put in an appearance." He walked over to the door and turned to look back at Matt before opening it. His expression and tone lightened into something akin to sympathy and understanding. "Take as long as you need. It might help you to find the peace I couldn't." Then he was gone, leaving Matt alone with Ken and Elise.

"Ken..." Matt didn't want to be alone, but he needed to be to do this properly. Saying goodbye to Elise was going to be difficult, but he couldn't leave her here without explaining to her why he'd left. He owed her that much.

"It's all right. You need to say your goodbyes in private." Ken gave him a small nod. "I understand." He raked one hand through his hair, suddenly hesitant. "Do you want me to wait outside?"

"Thanks, but I'll be fine." Matt appreciated the offer, but he could look after himself. He'd feel better knowing Ken was safe. He sighed, wishing Ken would get on with whatever he wanted to say. But then, he wasn't doing much better himself. Too much was left unspoken between them, both of them avoiding a conversation past needing to be had.

"Take whatever time you need." Ken's gaze lingered on Elise, but his expression was unreadable. "Be careful, and remember where you are." He picked up the gun from the counter where Matt had left it and handed it to him.

"I will." Matt stared after Ken for a moment before refocusing his thoughts and emotions. The gun felt heavy in his hands, but was necessary. Tucking it back into his waistband, he took Elise in his arms, carried her out to the living room, and laid her gently on the sofa. He stepped back to look at her and then covered her with a blanket so only her face was exposed. "Got to do it properly, you know," he told her, picking up the hairbrush she'd left on the side cabinet. He arranged her hair so it covered the bullet hole.

The gun in his waistband dug into the small of his back, although he'd carried it there countless times before. "I'm sorry, Elise," he whispered, retrieving it and putting it down on the floor next to the sofa. Ken was right about being careful, and it would be easier to grab it from there if needed.

The cassock was beginning to annoy him, in part because he shouldn't be still wearing it. Elise probably wouldn't have approved of his disguise either, but he was stuck with it until he could return it to St. Michael's, as he couldn't risk being stopped and asked what he was carrying. Dumping it somewhere ran the risk of providing Holm with a scapegoat. Matt wouldn't do that to Father Johannes. He was a good man and too valuable to the Resistance.

"I know it's not the way you like your hair done." He ran the bristles of the brush through her dark hair until it was smooth and free of knots, kissed her cheek, and stood to review his handiwork. "But I want to remember you like this, with no reminders of how you... died." He swallowed, rubbing at his face with one hand. "I want to remember the good times, Elise. I just hope you still remember them too." The brush fell from his fingers to land with a thud on the rug under his feet.

Elise had always loved that rug. He'd hated it. She'd told him he had no taste.

He cleared his throat, needing to get this over and done with. Ken and the others would be waiting for him, and the longer he took, the greater the risk. Time to move on. He placed one finger to his lips, then gently caressed her face. "I guess this is it, Elise. Give them hell, baby, and save me a place in heaven."

Footsteps sounded behind him. He looked up, cursed under his breath, and reached for his gun—too late. A leather boot stamped down hard on his fingers, and he yelped in pain, instinctively cradling them to his chest after his hand was freed.

The man kicked Matt's gun out of range, then studied him with interest. He was taller than Matt by at least two inches, and well-built. He had short, cropped blond hair, and his eyes were a very pale shade of grey. His lips were turned up into a cruel smile, as though he was amused by what he saw. He pointed the 9mm Luger in his hand directly at Matt.

"Go to hell," Matt told him. "My friend is dead. Just leave me alone." Part of him knew he wasn't acting logically, that he should at least make some attempt to escape, but the rest of him no longer cared.

The man grabbed Matt, forcing his arms behind his back, and he felt the cold steel of handcuffs click into place. As the SS officer spoke, Matt finally recognised his captor to be SS Standartenführer Holm.

"I am arresting you for the murder of Fräulein Schuster." Holm retrieved the Colt .45 from the floor, and his smile grew wider. "How interesting, to find a priest not only at the scene of a murder, but in possession of an American-issue firearm."

CHAPTER NINE

The knocking grew louder. Clara frowned, wondering who would be foolhardy enough to be out after curfew. If they sought medical help, fortunately this was the end of a long day or she'd be home by now. She quickly crossed the floor of her official surgery and walked into the back room. This entrance was only known to a few, most of whom had connections to the Resistance. Whoever it was, their situation had better be urgent enough to warrant the risk. She opened the door, intent on reminding the person on the other side of that, but the words died on her tongue.

"Michel? What on earth?"

Michel glanced behind him before stepping over the threshold, his companion leaning on him heavily for support. "It's all right." Tightening his grip around the shorter man's waist when he staggered and almost lost his footing, Michel's tone was reassuring and soft. "I've got you."

Helping the injured man onto the examination bed, Michel continued to speak softly. The man swayed again, shaking his head in response to whatever Michel had said.

The stranger's face was hidden by a jacket wrapped around him as a makeshift blanket, which made it difficult to determine clearly what had passed between them.

"Clara." Michel's voice hitched, which in itself was unusual. He'd always amazed her with his inherent calmness and his ability to stay collected under any circumstances. "Clara," he repeated a little more firmly. "I'm sorry..."

The man groaned. She caught sight of blond hair when Michel lowered his companion's head onto the pillow very carefully, murmuring more reassurances. The tone of his voice reflected a gentleness and regret she'd never seen from him before. Michel sighed and moved quite deliberately to block her view of the figure on the bed.

"Don't you 'Clara' me," she started. "This man needs medical attention, or you wouldn't be here in the first place. You don't have to worry about my safety. I chose to do this. I'm a doctor first and foremost."

Michel reached out and laid a hand on her arm. "Kristopher..."

"You're supposed to be watching him. Yes, I know that, Michel." Clara stopped, her mind suddenly putting the facts together. *Blond hair.* Michel was standing in front of the injured man so she couldn't see him.

God, no.

The blond man groaned again, his eyes fluttering before he croaked out a single word. "Michel."

Kit? Clara shoved Michel to one side, brushing her brother's hair off his forehead with her shaking hand. "It's all right, Kit. I'm here." Clara shot Michel a glare, then ran a practiced medical eye over Kit. "What the hell do you think you were doing? You're supposed to be watching him and keeping him safe. You weren't supposed to allow him to end up like... like this."

"It's not his fault, Clara." Kit cut across her thoughts, his voice no more than a whisper. "It was mine. If I hadn't..." His brow creased into a frown. "Clara? You knew Michel was watching me?" The tone wasn't accusing, but instead more curious. Kristopher looked around the surgery, seeking out Michel. "Michel? Are we safe? Are you all right?" The fear in her brother's eyes visibly lessened when he saw Michel there with him, and safe.

"I'm fine," Michel said softly. "You fainted, and I brought you here." He shook his head when Kit began to protest. "You needed a doctor, and Clara is the only one we can trust." Michel turned to Clara. "His wound was seeping for some time before we discovered it. I think the bullet only grazed him, but I'm no expert."

The questions could wait until later, or at least until she'd made sure his initial assessment was correct. "No, you're not." She fixed Kit with the glare she reserved for difficult patients. He could be extremely stubborn once he set his mind to something. "You can explain what happened later."

Kit opened his mouth to argue as she suspected he would, but then he winced and laid his head back on the pillow instead. "Later," she repeated, hoping she sounded more in control than she felt. The action of washing her hands gave her the few moments she needed to remind herself of the techniques her teachers had taught her in medical school to help her relax when faced with a difficult situation. She hadn't needed to use them in years, but then she'd never had to treat her brother for gunshot wounds.

Gunshot wounds. Michel was supposed to look after Kit, not just watch him from a distance. She'd been clear about that. Michel's instructions were to seek assistance once Kit's doubts about the project reached the point where he could be approached, not to take on the local Gestapo alone.

She was going to give him a piece of her mind once she'd dealt with Kit's injury.

"A, B, C," Clara murmured under her breath, working her way through the basics. Obviously Kit's airways were fine, or he wouldn't be asking awkward questions. She took his hand in hers and felt his pulse, which was fast and thready, probably due to blood loss, but not as bad as she had expected. His chest moved symmetrically, which was also a good sign. She placed her stethoscope on his upper chest, listening for a few minutes. His heartbeat was strong.

So far so good.

"You acted well," she told Michel, a little guilty for her initial anger. "Keeping him warm was the best you could have done under the circumstances." Noting the makeshift field dressing, her opinion of his actions rose another notch. "Pressure on the wound was good thinking too. At the very least it prevented further blood loss." She frowned, realizing the implications of Michel's words. Why hadn't Kit noticed he'd been shot sooner? And, more importantly, who was the bastard who had pulled the trigger?

"Sorry, Kit, this might hurt." Clara removed the dressing cautiously, making herself ignore the sudden hiss of pain from him, and examined the wound. "Michel was right. It grazed your muscle but appears to have missed the bone and vessels. You're very lucky, little brother."

Kit made a noise of disgust, and she couldn't help but smile. He hated it when she called him that, but this time it wasn't her problem. There were consequences for worrying her like this.

She motioned him to keep quiet. He glared at her through clenched teeth. "What caliber was it?" she asked Michel.

"Luger 9mm," Michel informed her calmly. He seemed to have regained a little of his usual demeanour, at least outwardly.

Standard-issue Gestapo? She was definitely going to have a chat with him, and sooner rather than later. The idea of the Gestapo firing at her brother was disturbing, to say the least.

"I've seen the results of these weapons before," she replied, putting on her best lecturing tone. "A 9mm round to the shoulder will cause a huge amount of bruising, ruin most of the muscles, break most of the bones, and probably tear several large vessels. If that had happened, little brother, you would have bled to death in minutes, and we wouldn't be having this conversation."

"*You* wouldn't be having this conversation, you mean." Kit gripped the side of the bed tightly and took a sharp breath.

"When I say lucky, I mean lucky." Her mind was already working through the list of what she had on hand to clean and sterilise his wound. "Don't argue with the doctor, *Kristopher*."

Kit looked shamefaced for a moment. "Sorry," he said, wincing again when she continued her examination. He was pale and trembling slightly, a delayed reaction to what had happened, most likely.

"This looks and feels a lot worse than it is." Clara gave him a smile before indicating a bottle on the shelf where she kept her supplies. "Michel, could you pass me the seventy percent surgical spirits solution, please, and the small tin next to it? Thank you." Kit followed her eyes and pulled away from her touch. He knew what was coming. Years ago, when he was only a child, he'd seen her clean out a little girl's badly infected wound. He hadn't reacted well to the blood or seeing her patient in pain. The girl had been terrified, and the procedure had upset both of them.

"I have to clean this, Kit," she insisted firmly. "If it gets infected, it is going to become a problem." She swallowed, wishing she could lie to him but knowing this was not the time to do so. "This is going to hurt. I'm sorry." Michel handed her what she'd asked for. "Do you think you might have been followed?"

"I hope not, but it's likely, yes." He laid a hand gently over Kit's. "It's important you don't make any noise. If you cry out and are heard, it will make it easier for them to find us."

"I'll... try." Kit grasped Michel's hand firmly. He was scared, and she didn't blame him. The poor boy was out of his depth. Nothing he'd experienced in life or anything he'd read could have prepared him for the reality of what he must have gone through since they'd spoken at breakfast that morning.

She reached into her medical bag and brought out a leather strap. "Bite down on this when the pain gets bad," she suggested, watching Kit and Michel carefully. Did the body language between the two of them suggest what she thought it did? If so, the attraction between them was definitely mutual. Pushing the idea away, she gave Michel further instructions. "You'll have to be prepared to restrain him if needs be. He must be still if I'm going to do this properly. Keep holding his hand, Michel." Her voice softened. "Talk to him. He's taking comfort from your touch. Use it to help him focus and to distract him from the pain."

Michel nodded, moving closer to her brother. "Kristopher," he began, but Kit shook his head.

"Kit. Call me Kit... please."

He was giving Michel permission to use *that* name? Clara almost dropped the strap she was handing to Michel. She was the only person allowed to call her brother Kit. Busying herself cleaning his wound, she remembered the reasoning he'd given.

"When you use that name, I feel as though you accept me for who I am. I don't have to hide behind the façade of being who everyone expects me to be. I don't have to pretend anymore." His voice had dropped to a shy whisper. *"It's the name I like to imagine Mama would have called me. Because... she loved me."*

Kit tensed when she carefully poured the sterilising solution over the open wound. It wasn't too deep but was still going to require packing with gauze. Clara nodded towards Michel who was watching Kit carefully, their joined hands strengthening their grip around each other.

"Clara tells me you play the violin... Kit." Michel gave Kit a wistful, hopeful smile before continuing. "I used to play the flute, but I haven't for a while. Maybe after we get through this, we could play a duet together."

Hopefully, for Michel's sake, his suggestion was sincere, as Kit would hold him to it. His love of music had taken second place to his work for far too long. Clara missed the vibrant sounds of his violin and the way he could touch her so deeply with his music. At some point in his life, he stopped listening to himself and to what was right. Otherwise he would not have been a part of the madness responsible for the creation of such a dangerous weapon.

Kit bit down on the leather strap, his eyes gazing over as he attempted to distance himself from the pain. Michel continued speaking softly. Clara couldn't make out all the words, although she recognised one or two. They flowed from him almost as though they were sung, not spoken, and Kit began to calm, his eyes closing as he anchored himself with, and took solace in, Michel's voice.

With a silent prayer, Clara liberally sprinkled sterile sulfa powder into the wound before packing it with prepared cotton gauze. Finally she bound it firmly with clean dressings and hoped for the best. If it didn't become infected, he should be all right. He had to be all right.

Michel grew quiet after Kit slipped into sleep. "Thank you," he finally said. His expression made it difficult to tell what he was thinking. "He should be all right if the dressings are changed regularly and the wound is kept clean?" It sounded like a statement despite being phrased as a question.

"You're planning to leave," she said flatly. Although he didn't have a choice, she didn't have to like it. Given the current situation, she might never see Kit again or know of his fate.

"Yes. It's only a matter of time before they track us. I'm sure the dogs have picked up our trail by now, and we don't want to place you in any more danger than is necessary." Michel disengaged his hand from Kit's, his gaze lingering for a moment. Kit stirred in his sleep, his brow creasing into a small frown before settling again. "He would never forgive himself if something happened to you. I think we both know that." Michel looked at her directly. "I'm not prepared to take that risk either."

Clara nodded. He knew her brother much better than she'd given him credit for. She reached out her hand and drew him closer. "My brother trusts you, Michel." While she suspected Kit's feelings for Michel were very much more than just that, they needed to figure that out for themselves. "If you do anything to betray that trust, I'll hunt you down and kill you myself. Do I make myself clear?"

He attempted to free himself from her grasp, but she tightened her grip. "I would never do anything to hurt him."

"Not intentionally," Clara agreed. The emotions behind the words he'd spoken seemed genuine. "Just be very careful. Kristopher has a difficult path ahead of him, and I'd like to know he's not going to be alone." Did Michel understand what she was trying to tell him? Putting what she wanted to say into words was too dangerous, yet she suspected he did. She also knew her brother well enough to guess what inner demons he must be fighting and hoped this time he'd find the courage to make the decision he needed to be true to himself and follow his emotions.

"He won't be, not if I have any choice in it." Michel glanced over at Kit again, then continued softly, the tone in his voice similar to when he'd spoken about the music they hoped to play together one day. "I'll protect him with my life." Silence hung between them for a few minutes. "We need to go now. I'm sorry."

"I understand." She wouldn't ask where they were going. If she didn't know it would be safer for all concerned. The Gestapo couldn't retrieve information she didn't possess. "I believe one of the doctors on the night shift has the unfortunate habit of leaving his keys in his car. If someone were to borrow that car..." Motioning him to wait, she quickly got together the medical supplies he'd need and handed them to him in a small duffel bag.

"Thank you." Michel swung the bag over his shoulder before bending to lift her sleeping brother into his arms.

Clara walked over to the door and opened it slowly to check it was safe for them to leave. "Both of you take care," she told him, giving Kit a quick kiss on the cheek. He smiled in his sleep and snuggled closer into Michel's embrace. "What did you say to Kit before to calm him?"

Michel wrapped the blanket he'd retrieved from the examination table more firmly around Kit. "My mother used to recite it to me when I couldn't sleep as a child. I thought it might help."

"It did." Perhaps more than he'd realised. Clara watched them disappear into the night. "May God go with you," she whispered, "with both of you."

Ken edged closer to the Kaffeehaus, cursing under his breath. Why the hell had Holm decided to return? For the last ten minutes the building had been swarming with Gestapo, and he wasn't able to ascertain whether Matt was all right, or even still in there.

He was a fool. A fifty-fifty chance as to which was the better entrance to watch and he'd made the wrong choice. Despite Matt insisting he didn't need anyone to keep lookout for him, Ken hadn't felt comfortable about returning to the church with the others. It would be too easy for Matt to get caught up in the moment, and Ken wasn't about to lose him because of it.

But he'd still screwed up and might anyway. No, he wasn't going to follow through on that thought. Too much had been left unsaid between him and Matt. Selfish as it might be, Ken wanted closure with at least one person in his life. He wasn't good at relationships and at times was a lousy friend, but he cared about Matt, more than he had for anyone else in his life, his parents aside.

The Germans' first priority was Lehrer and Gabriel.

The logical assumption was that they'd returned, although that scenario was highly unlikely, Ken would have heard them approaching and warned Matt in time. Holm must have entered through the back door, making his way back to the Kaffeehaus on foot, as there was no sign of any vehicle. Those had come later when the Gestapo had returned in force, and by then it was too late.

He heard voices coming from the Kaffeehaus, and strained to hear what was being said. "He said what?" Holm was annoyed, and his tone held an edge of disbelief.

"Lehrer said the plans were incomplete, sir. He implied we still needed him, and proposed a trade..." Reiniger paused. "He proposed trading his services for Schmitz's life... sir."

Holm laughed. "That's an interesting proposition, but I doubt it would work in practice." His tone became very calm. It sent a shiver down Ken's spine. "When we find Lehrer, we need to show him that the Gestapo do not negotiate with traitors."

The muffled cry of pain from someone else in the room was followed by a muttered "Go to hell."

Matt.

Ken raised his binoculars again, but couldn't ascertain what was happening in the dimly lit building. Matt had wanted to take whoever killed Elise apart piece by piece. If Holm was responsible for that *and* hurting Matt, Ken wanted him first. Matt would have to stand in line.

"You will change your mind about cooperating with us, Priest," Holm told Matt. "If that's who you really are."

"I don't have any information to give you." Matt's voice carried clearly across the still night air, followed by another muffled cry, then silence.

Damn it! He needed to know what was happening, but

risking discovery wouldn't help Matt. The best plan, as much as he didn't like it, would be to observe, then determine a suitable rescue plan after rejoining the rest of his team. He couldn't achieve anything on his own and was vastly outnumbered and outgunned. He also had a responsibility to his team. Now Matt was in custody, Ken was in command of this mission.

"I will kill you slowly and painfully, Holm," Ken muttered under his breath. "That's a promise."

A transport truck pulled up in front of the building. The door of the Kaffeehaus swung open, and two members of the Gestapo exited, escorting a hunched-over figure in black between them. Matt's arms were cuffed behind him; his feet dragged as though walking were an effort. He stumbled, and one of the soldiers prodded him in the ribs with a rifle butt. Matt struggled to regain his footing, his eyes darting in all directions as he desperately sought a way to escape. Ken stepped forward instinctively, catching Matt's gaze, and attempted to give him a reassuring smile. It came out more of a grimace, and Matt shook his head very slightly. He mouthed, "Leave me," before his eyes glazed over, and he turned away.

One of the soldiers urged Matt onward, but not before following his gaze to see what had got the prisoner's attention. Ken quickly took refuge in the shadows. "It's probably a good idea to admire the scenery while you still can, Priest. I doubt you're going to see it again once Holm has finished with you."

Matt let out a choked laugh. "May God have mercy on your soul, my child, because no one else will." The soldier opened the door of the truck, roughly pushed Matt inside, and slammed it shut.

Although Matt had given Ken an order to leave, he

didn't intend to obey it. Matt was no longer running this operation, and as far as Ken was concerned, the original mission parameters had not changed.

Retrieve the plans and return home.

Patrick Lowe would never have left a colleague in the hands of the enemy, and neither would his son. Ken stepped out of the shadows and tilted his head at the sky, remembering the words Matt had used in St Michael's church earlier when he'd outlined the so-called simple mission.

"Retrieve the schematics for this weapon, head for home, and give the Nazis a good kick where it hurts, if required."

"I'm not going home without you," Ken promised. "If that means we have to give the Nazis more of a kick where it hurts than we originally intended, so be it."

CHAPTER TEN

"If there is anything else you require, Herr Werner, be sure to let me know."

Michel nodded his appreciation to the nun when she turned to leave the small room. "Thank you, Sister. I... we... appreciate the risk you are taking in allowing us to shelter here." With no one else to turn to, Michel had contacted Father Johannes, who had sent them to the Klosterkirche, a nunnery at the site of another church in Berlin.

Sister Brigit smiled. She'd promised they could stay until Kristopher was fit enough to travel, and that she would also supply them with the identity papers needed to do so. "God doesn't turn away those in need. Your friend needs somewhere to rest. You are welcome to stay for as long as you are able. Sleep well." She paused in the doorway. "Are you sure you wouldn't be more comfortable using the bed in the room next door? You'd still be able to hear him if he wakes."

Michel shook his head. "I'll be fine." He needed to be here if Kristopher woke. "Thank you for your concern.

Goodnight." He watched her go, then carefully closed the door behind her. After locking it with the key she'd given him, he extinguished the only light in the room. Kristopher had woken again while Michel was talking with Father Johannes at the rectory, and had stayed awake and on his feet until Sister Brigit showed them to their rooms here.

The side of Michel's mouth turned up into a slight smile as he recalled the events of the past twenty-four hours. Kristopher was a good man, but he needed to think about his own needs too. Clara was right in her assessment of her brother. He was stubborn and extremely strong-willed, qualities that were a double-edged sword when it came to his own welfare.

Leaning over Kristopher, Michel adjusted the blankets to ensure he was properly protected from the cold night air. The little heating barely took the chill off the air, and Kristopher had refused to take Michel's sweater when he'd offered it. At least for now, the room was quiet, and safe. Michel gently brought his hand up to brush a stray lock of hair from Kristopher's... Kit's face. With the worry of the last few weeks finally absent from his expression, he was beautiful. It had not been a great hardship to watch him over the past six months. Something about Kit had drawn Michel to him. Michel wished he could have made all this easier for Kit and saved him the heartache he'd experienced while wrestling with his conscience.

He hadn't done a great job protecting Kit either. Michel would never forget the expression on Kit's face when he'd found the blood, or the sick feeling in the bottom of his own stomach when it became obvious Kit was injured.

Michel had known for a while he was falling for Kit but had tried to deny it. He didn't dare hope those feelings might be mutual, but Kit giving him permission to use that name showed an enormous step of trust. Hopefully it would be the first of many to come. Clara was right in urging caution. It was sad the world had come to this—a dangerous place where care had to be taken even to admit to someone how you felt about them.

The moonlight shone through the small window, illuminating Kit's hair in its pale light. Michel brushed his lips against Kit's cheek, and he stirred in his sleep, smiling as though giving his approval to the act of affection before wriggling further down into the blankets. The arm he'd tightly gripped around his pillow fell to lie limply at his side as he relaxed into deeper sleep.

Puffing up the pillow Sister Brigit had given him, Michel settled into the chair and arranged his blanket firmly around himself. "Goodnight, Kit," he whispered in French. "Take care, my dear friend." He allowed himself one more look at Kit before closing his own eyes. "I love you."

Although all he wanted to do was crawl into a corner and nurse both his physical and emotional wounds, Matt was determined to stand upright. While military logic dictated the importance of not showing any sign of emotion in front of Holm, the orphan who had lost his family and now one of his closest friends wanted to tackle the smug bastard and break his fucking neck.

"If you answer my questions correctly and without hesitation, you have a much better chance of enjoying your stay with us," Holm reminded Matt. The corner of Holm's mouth twitched as he examined his captive closely. "Your vocabulary is very extensive, Priest, and you need to be taught some manners." Running the back of one hand across Matt's cheek, Holm dragged the sharp tip of the ring he wore over the skin to leave a shallow cut. "I see you are also capable of silence when it suits you." Holm nodded his approval and smiled when Matt didn't react to the pain. "I'm interested as to whether these stories of the self-sacrificing tendencies of the Catholic clergy are correct." He shrugged. "Or perhaps they are merely myths." He gestured to the two soldiers who were flanking Matt. "Remove the priest's handcuffs."

What the hell was the bastard up to? Matt flexed his fingers in an attempt to return a sense of feeling to his hands.

Holm poured a glass of water from the pitcher on his desk, offered it to Matt, and then gestured for him to sit in the chair in the center of the room.

Matt refused both the request and the water.

"Who are you working for?" Holm asked in heavily accented English.

Matt remained silent. At this point it would be prudent to feign ignorance.

"*Für wen arbeiten Sie?*" This time the question was asked in German.

Matt made no reply.

Holm sighed. He studied Matt carefully, looking him up and down before nodding curtly at one of his men. The soldier undid the flap of his holster and rested his hand on the handle of his gun, reinforcing the idea that sitting and taking the glass of water was an order, not a request, and therefore not open to debate. "I think you'll find cooperation to be a far more healthy option," Holm pointed out. "I apologise for the way you've been treated so far. I'm only doing my job, and I dislike violence as much as I suspect you do."

"So killing a defenseless woman doesn't equate to violence?" Matt lowered himself into the sturdy leather-backed chair with deliberate slowness.

Holm laughed. The sound sent a shiver through Matt. "You forget, *I'm* not the one under arrest for the murder of Fräulein Schuster." Holm placed one hand on Matt's shoulder, his thin smile reiterating the sick pretense of sympathy.

"Go to hell," Matt muttered, attempting to pull away. Fingers closed around his chin to hold his face in a viselike grip while Holm used his free hand to trace the bloody pattern his ring had made.

"I see you priests still enjoy preaching about fire and brimstone." Holm leaned in still closer, his breath hot and heavy with the stench of death, his eyes the colour of grey, icy, tempered steel.

For a moment, Matt was sure he could smell Elise's blood on Holm. It had to be his imagination. It took all his willpower to stay calm. He gripped the edge of the chair. The odour permeated the air, seeping into his skin and through his hair—everywhere Holm touched.

"We like to ensure those such as yourself are well prepared for what awaits you in the afterlife." Matt was unable to keep the tremor from his voice. He took a sip from the glass one of the soldiers placed in his hand.

Holm stepped back and leaned against his desk. He crossed his arms over his chest and examined his ornate dress ring with an intensity Matt still would have found disturbing under different circumstances. "My father left me this ring when he died. Family is important, don't you think?" An unintelligible emotion reflected in Holm's eyes for a moment before disappearing. "I consider those I serve with to be a part of my family, and I'm sure you feel the same way about your congregation." He laughed. "Although, of course, a priest isn't going to understand the concept of what it's like to lead a squadron of men into battle and have them depend on you for their very lives."

His knuckles white, Matt kept holding the glass and tried to ignore the implications of where Holm was going with this. It would not be wise to admit he did understand, only too well, regretted the men he'd lost, and hoped like hell Ken and the rest of their team were still free.

His team, along with Gabriel and Lehrer, should by now be making plans to leave the country. Matt had given Ken an order, and Ken always followed those by the book and to the letter. Whatever happened, Matt was on his own.

"Who is your contact in the Resistance?"

The question, coming directly on the tail of Holm's earlier rambling, took Matt off guard. The tone was precise and cold. It suggested none too succinctly the only correct answer was one Matt was unable to give.

"What is your name?"

Matt bit his lip to fight the automatic response of name, rank, and serial number. Fortunately, apart from the Colt .45, he didn't have anything to identify him as American. Giving any name, either his own or an assumed one, at this point would only make it easier for Holm to discover that no one by that name was currently attached to the parish of St. Michael's.

"You may call me Father, my child." The smartass comment that rolled off Matt's tongue was answered by a sharp slap across his face. The glass fell from his fingers and smashed into tiny transparent slivers at his feet.

"Hmm," mused Holm. "It's interesting that a mere priest is so much more uncooperative than his colleagues."

He smiled cruelly. "I don't know why you persist in refusing to tell me your name. I already have the other information I need." He laughed, the sharp staccato sound echoing through Matt's mind long after the noise itself was silent. "Today was a great disappointment to me." He shook his head sadly. "But blood makes it so easy to track one's prey, don't you think?"

"Blood?" Matt couldn't help but ask the question.

"Surely you aren't so arrogant as to presume that those who cross the Third Reich will be allowed to walk away unharmed? Bullet wounds can be so messy." Holm shrugged. "All I require is your name. As I said, I already have the other information I need."

Then why ask about the Resistance? Wouldn't that be part of the information you needed? Despite the reminder, Matt couldn't stop his mind working through various scenarios.

Was Holm playing games or telling the truth? The glimpse Matt had gotten of Ken at least was reassuring. He hadn't appeared injured then, but Matt had no idea how long ago that was, as they'd taken everything from him he might have used to keep track of the time. Liang should be at the church with Walker and Palmer. Hopefully St. Michael's wasn't compromised. That left Gabriel and Lehrer. Was it possible one of them, if not both, had been shot? Matt had no way of knowing whether Gabriel had gotten Lehrer clear. The Germans had recovered the plans. The success of their mission now hinged on getting Dr Lehrer to safety.

Please no. All of this couldn't be for nothing.

Lifting his head, Matt met Holm's gaze directly but kept silent.

"Do you deny, then, that you knew the Fräulein?"

"I knew her." Matt's voice cracked. He couldn't bring himself to deny it. "But I didn't kill her, you bastard, and you know it."

"Are you aware that she was working for the Resistance?"

"Are you aware that murder is a sin... my child?" The comment was rewarded by another slap. Matt knew he was treading on thin ice but didn't care. His chances of getting out of this mess grew slimmer by the minute, and his temper was getting the better of him.

Holm sighed. "I am a patient man, and yet you repay my kindness with such rudeness. You disappoint me."

"Tough. Life is full of disappointments." For some reason, once he'd started on this slippery slope, he found it difficult to stop. Was this some kind of delayed reaction to the shock of Elise's death? He had to get a grip on himself while he still could. He needed to stay focused. Annoying his captor further would only serve to hasten his date with death.

He hadn't finished with life yet. He'd left too much unsaid to those who needed to hear it.

"Especially for you." Holm nodded in agreement. He gestured to his men. They pulled Matt to his feet and forced him to stand behind the chair he'd been sitting in.

"Remove your cassock, drop your trousers, and spread your legs."

"Fuck off," Matt exclaimed. "What the hell do you think—" He gasped when a fist connected with his stomach.

"When Herr SS Standartenführer Holm gives you an order, he expects to be obeyed," the soldier explained calmly. "I believe he asked you to remove certain items of clothing."

"Fuck off," Matt repeated. The soldier who had spoken aimed his Luger at Matt's head and cocked the trigger.

"Do as you are told," Holm ordered. "Blood stains are so messy, and brain matter is even harder to remove from the carpet." He sighed. "Perhaps Fräulein Huber is correct, and it is time I changed the decor to something easier to keep clean. Polished wooden floors might be a better option, after all."

Better to do this than to die. Matt removed the priest's cassock and dropped it on the floor to the side of the chair. His fingers shook as he then started to slowly undo his belt buckle. Surely Holm wasn't about to do this in front of his men. He was bluffing. He had to be.

Matt bent and awkwardly slid his trousers down so they pooled at his ankles.

"You're still overdressed, Priest," Holm informed him. "Would you like some assistance in removing your undergarments?"

It wouldn't be a good idea to remind Holm that wasn't part of his original order. Matt did as requested. The room was cold, yet it did nothing to relieve the heat of embarrassment stealing through him.

"Place your hands on the arms of the chair," Holm ordered, and the soldiers pulled Matt's hands into the required position when he refused to follow the instructions given to him.

Two loud clicks and the coldness around his wrists told him he was cuffed again. With no room to wriggle, he was forced to lean over the top of the chair with his head bent down. The leather had been cleaned with a chamois cloth recently, and the smell of the polish did nothing to help the nausea growing in his stomach.

With the distance between the chair and the door, he'd

be lucky to reach it if he could get free from the cuffs, and doubted Holm's men would miss a target at this close a range even if they were lousy shots. The window to his rear, although open, was further away from the door so wasn't an option either.

Who the hell had designed the decor of this room? The white shag-pile carpet needed to go and be replaced by something more in keeping with the dark red of the walls.

He yanked at one of his restraints, hiding a gasp of pain when the added strain on his arm sent a barb of fire through it. *Damn it.* This must be why the heavy and well-crafted chair was at odds with the simple lines of the desk. Its position in the center of the room was also well-thought-out to leave no object within range that could be used as leverage.

Matt turned his head to the other side, glanced downward, and froze.

The crimson stain ingrained into the carpet pooled outward like the ripples caused by the stones he and Elise used to enjoy throwing into the clear waters of their favourite swimming hole at home in Pennsylvania.

Oh God, no. Matt closed his eyes for moment. When he opened them again, he felt a shutter go down tightly over his emotions. If he didn't feel this, it wouldn't hurt. If he pretended it wasn't real, then it wouldn't be.

"That will be all. Thank you, Müller," Holm said quietly. "Your presence is no longer required, and I believe you have other more pressing matters to attend to."

"Yes, sir."

Please, no. The bastard couldn't be serious. He couldn't be. Matt twisted his head to look at Holm, to try and read his expression. He didn't want his first time with another man to be like this.

Holm just wanted information. That was it. It had to

be. Didn't it? That was the reason for the blood on the carpet.

"I expect a full report on our other guests in the morning. Use any means necessary to ensure their continued cooperation." Holm smiled at Matt, his expression devoid of any warmth whatsoever. "As I said earlier, blood is so easy to trace..."

CHAPTER ELEVEN

"Remember your priorities are the textbook and parcel, *not* Toto." The final message from London repeated through Ken's mind as he removed his headphones. Reaching a decision, he repacked the radio set in its box and walked out of the sacristy to join Liang, who was keeping watch from a pew near the door.

"Well?" Liang visibly relaxed, shifting his hand from resting on his gun to fall at his side. He frowned, catching sight of Ken's expression. "Do we go after Bryant or focus on our original mission?"

"Both," Ken said evenly. "We do not abandon our own, and we need to complete our mission." He would find a way to do both. "Our instructions are to retrieve the plans from the hands of the Gestapo while we mount a rescue attempt. Matt and the plans are likely in the same location, since they were both taken by the same Gestapo officer, so combining the two missions makes sense." Although their orders were transmitted from London, this mission was a joint one between the British Special Operations Executive and American Office of Strategic Services, so any decisions reached by their superiors had been discussed and agreed on by both.

"Good," replied Liang, much to Ken's surprise. In the short time they'd known each other, Liang had given the impression of a man who preferred his own company. He was capable and knew how to use a gun, although he was not a soldier, but that was all Ken knew about him. Ken tended to leave the social niceties to Matt, who was better at building friendships and getting to know people. "I may be vocal about my disagreement with the way your armed forces conduct themselves at times, but I would not have condoned leaving a comrade at the mercy of the enemy." He glanced around the church before continuing. "Walker and Palmer are still keeping surveillance outside. Now would be a good time to tell me the exact wording of the instructions from London."

"What?" Ken glared at Liang. "Why do you have to question everything? You're putting the mission at risk with your attitude." He needed to save Matt, and couldn't risk someone on his team hesitating at a crucial moment because he didn't agree with their course of action. Ken sighed. At least Liang had enough sense to bring this up while Walker and Palmer were not within earshot.

"I think I am entitled to the truth if I am to follow you in this madness," Liang pointed out, "and I doubt the instructions you just relayed were exactly what you received." He placed a hand on Ken's shoulder. Ken pushed it away. "Matthew Bryant is a good man. I give you my word I will do everything I can to help rescue him. However, retrieving the plans has to continue to be our priority. There is too much at stake."

"Our instructions are only to rescue Matt if we are able to do so without endangering the mission." Ken leaned against a nearby pew. "If we make Matt's welfare our priority, our superiors made it very clear they will not be impressed." He snorted. Impressing their superiors was not *his* priority. "I am well aware of the importance of this mission and what is at stake," Ken said, keeping his tone even and polite, "but I don't see a problem in retrieving both him and the plans."

"What about Lehrer?"

"According to what I overheard at the Kaffeehaus, the Gestapo aren't sure the plans they have are complete." Ken shrugged. "It may well be that Lehrer was bluffing when he told them they still needed him, but there is no way of knowing for certain."

"I can give you a better idea once I've sighted the plans," Liang confirmed. "It would be helpful to speak with Lehrer too, but that is looking very unlikely, at least in the immediate future." He paused before continuing. "I do wonder if the Germans truly have the technology and know-how to match what has been achieved so far with our own project."

While the idea of the plans for a weapon of such mass destruction in the hands of the enemy didn't thrill Ken in the least, he wasn't exactly enthralled with the idea of the Allies having that same capability either. He might be an American, but he'd seen firsthand just what his own people were capable of against those who could not defend themselves. What had happened to the so-called Bill of Rights? Damn Roosevelt and his executive order. Ken would never forget his mother's plea for him to take his father's name rather than hers.

"You're American, Ken," she had told him. "Remember that and make your father proud." He'd protested, remembering how enthusiastically she'd taught him about Japanese customs and history, but she'd insisted his safety came first. He took after his father in looks and could pass as a white American. She couldn't. "You can't fight this war in an internment camp."

That final appeal had eventually swayed his decision, yet he still felt guilty for denying his heritage and using a name that, although legally his and on his birth certificate, didn't feel like his own. He'd spent most of his life as Ken Tsukino. After this war, he would use that name again.

"Getting Lehrer out of Germany and delivering him safely to the Allies is also a priority. We are to ascertain he is capable of reproducing the research undertaken by this project." Ken hesitated for a moment, then decided if Liang was prepared to help save Matt, he needed to be aware of the situation. "London had no clue about Lehrer's defection. Gabriel hadn't passed along the information as he implied."

Liang raised an eyebrow. "I thought we were supposed to be able to trust Gabriel." He frowned. "Do they believe that still to be the case?"

"That depends on his motivations, and there is no way of knowing what they are." This mission was quickly becoming anything but the simple retrieval outlined in their initial briefing. "Lehrer is considered too high a risk to be allowed to remain in Germany. If he falls into the hands of the Gestapo, he might be persuaded to assist them."

"So they aren't sure he can be trusted either?"

"Gabriel is convinced Lehrer is trustworthy, but I am not so sure, especially considering his own position at present. He and Lehrer have both disappeared. Lehrer has worked on this project since the beginning, so why the attack of conscience now?" Ken had reservations about the entire scenario. If the Germans had received intelligence about the Allied mission, it wasn't unlikely or unheard of that they might plant a spy. Not all defectors were honest about their reasons for doing so, and either Gabriel or Lehrer could be a double agent.

According to Palmer and Walker, Lehrer spoke fluent English, with a British accent, so he could have undergone training to prepare him for his role. His ability to pinpoint which part of England Walker came from had unnerved both men. Ken mentally rolled his eyes. It was difficult to figure out how Lehrer could have some kind of inside information, and why would he reveal he understood and spoke English if he was a spy? All English accents sounded the same, at least to Ken's ear. Then, of course, Palmer observed that Gabriel and Lehrer seemed to be working together and had referred to each other by their first names.

That, in particular, fueled Ken's doubts about the whole situation and made him rethink his initial conclusions. While it wasn't unheard of for an agent to form an attachment towards... He shook his head. Was he projecting because of his worry for Matt? Gabriel losing his objectivity could be another reason for his willingness to believe Lehrer was keen to change sides and defect.

"I agree." Liang nodded. "He will require watching. Both of them will."

The door of the church opened, and a woman entered. She walked up the aisle and paused to genuflect when she reached the front of the church. She made the sign of the cross, then knelt in the front pew.

Dropping his voice to a whisper, Ken continued. "A member of the Resistance is to meet us here with information regarding the current situation. Hopefully this person might know something of the whereabouts of the elusive Herr Doktor."

"Hopefully," agreed Liang.

The woman crossed herself again, rose to her feet, and made her way to the exit, pausing when she reached their pew. "Excuse me, but I've lost my dog. Have you seen him? His name is Toto."

"I haven't seen him, but I'm told he's following a yellow brick road." Ken examined the woman carefully after giving the counterphrase. She seemed about ten years older than either of them, but as she kept her head down and glanced around nervously, it was difficult to ascertain much more about her.

"Tinman?" Her voice was soft, yet firm.

"Dorothy?"

The woman nodded, one hand tucking a stray lock of dark-blonde hair back under her scarf.

"I believe you have information for me." Ken indicated Liang in answer to the woman's frown. "This is Scarecrow. He can be trusted."

"I will be brief," Dorothy said, "as I suspect I could well be under observation by the Gestapo." She glanced around again before continuing. "Your friend is being held at Holm's offices at the institute research compound. Several of the office staff frequent a local Kaffeehaus after hours called the Süße Ecke. It's on Unter den Linden just before you reach Brandenburger Tor." She paused. "One of his secretaries might be willing to help you."

"And that secretary's name?" Ken asked. Her information sounded a little too good to be true, but he couldn't afford to disregard it under the present circumstances.

"Fräulein Dunst," Dorothy replied. "Be cautious. I'm not sure how much of what I've told you is accurate, and even if she is approachable, she will be understandably wary."

She turned to leave, but Ken placed a hand on her arm

to detain her. "Can you give us any information regarding the parcel we are supposed to transport?"

"Parcel?" Her expression hardened. For some reason, she didn't seem impressed by the codeword he'd used. Was she connected to the Herr Doktor in some way? "Herr Dr Lehrer, or your parcel, as you so nicely refer to him, can be trusted. I've known him for a considerable length of time."

"Do you know of his whereabouts?" Liang asked. "It's imperative we find him before the Gestapo do."

Shaking her head, Dorothy met his gaze directly. "It was safer I didn't know. Kristopher..." She sighed. "Herr Dr Lehrer is unable to travel at present, and I doubt Michel... Herr Schmitz will be in contact until he is certain it is safe to do so. Rescue your man, recover the plans, and get across the border to Switzerland. When they are able to meet you there, they will."

"You sound very sure of yourself." Ken noticed she'd referred to Gabriel as Michel, which was the same name Lehrer had used.

"I'm very sure of *them*, Tinman. Kristopher's a very stubborn man and so is Michel in his own way." She pulled her arm free.

"I'm sorry, Fräulein, I did not mean to insult either you or Herr Dr Lehrer, but we have very little information about him." According to the Walker and Palmer, Lehrer was also a lot younger than Ken had expected. He would have said almost too young to be one of the key researchers for the project, but Dr Zhou Liang had proved that line of reasoning to be a foolish one. Although only three years older than Ken, Liang had two doctorates, one in physics and another in linguistics. "Our original mission was only to retrieve the plans and did not include his safe passage out of Germany."

Dorothy nodded her acceptance of his apology yet did not offer any further information about Lehrer. "I'm putting you at risk the longer I stay here." She glanced nervously at the door. "It's only a matter of time before the Gestapo begin tracking my every move."

"Thank you for your help."

"Take care." Dorothy turned to leave. "May God go with you. All of you."

Before she'd reached the front door of the church, it opened and two SS officers entered. Ken and Liang quickly slipped into the nearest pew, knelt, and bowed their heads in prayer in an attempt to appear inconspicuous.

"Fräulein Dr Clara Lehrer?" asked one of the officers.

Lehrer?

No wonder she was so sure the Herr Doktor could be trusted. Ken fixed his gaze on the altar, interlacing his fingers tightly to fight the urge to turn and see what was taking place behind him.

"Herr SS Standartenführer Holm wishes to ask you a few questions."

"Holm? He's head of security where my brother works, isn't he? Has something happened?" Clara's surprise seemed as genuine as her concern. "Is Kristopher all right?"

The man ignored her questions. "This way please, Fräulein." The heavy door shut behind them.

Her brother?

Ken swore under his breath. Lehrer's sister was part of the Resistance? They needed to leave immediately. This church had outlived its usefulness. Fräulein Lehrer could describe them to the Gestapo. How loyal would she remain to the cause if her brother's life was threatened? If Lehrer was a double agent and she didn't know, she might also unwittingly pass on valuable information to the enemy.

"There are several empty rooms in the apartment building by the park." The quiet voice of the parish priest took Ken by surprise. "You will be safe there until you are able to leave Berlin." Father Johannes Hanson had given them permission to use the church as a base of operations when they'd arrived. "Clara Lehrer is a good person and would not intentionally betray you. However, I am aware this is of little reassurance. I've seen strong men and women crack under Gestapo interrogation." The question that followed took Ken by surprise. "What is the name of the other young man? I believe he was still masquerading as a member of the clergy when he was arrested."

"Why?" Ken asked, unable to keep the suspicion out of his voice.

"If the Gestapo ask questions, I can corroborate his cover but tell them he had only just arrived and therefore I do not know him well enough to give them much in the way of information. It is safer for all of you the longer the deception remains intact." Hanson frowned. "I know of Holm's methods. It is only a matter of time before your friend reveals information of some kind."

"He would never—" Ken began in protest.

"We hope he would never, but unfortunately, there are no guarantees." Liang shook his head. "If he has his wits about him, he'll give as little information as possible. Father Johannes has a point."

"You'll be putting yourself in danger with this information, Father." Ken still wasn't convinced.

"Your friend is dressed as a Catholic priest. It's only a matter of time before the Gestapo begin searching the churches in Berlin for more information about him. When I first offered the use of this church, I placed myself in danger. If I need to, I can always suggest that perhaps the credentials he showed me were fake. After all, I am a mere priest. What would I know of such things? It's a shame I have no idea where those identity papers are now. The ruse should at least buy you and your friend some time." Hanson placed a hand on Ken's shoulder. "Our Lord would never turn away someone in need, my son. We help where we can. What is his name?"

"Brandt," Ken replied. "His name is Matthäus Brandt."

"I'll keep young Father Matthäus in my prayers," Hanson assured him. "Now go while you still can. You can't help him if you are occupying the cell next to his."

"Thank you, Father," Liang said, bowing slightly. "We appreciate your support."

"Thank you, Father," Ken echoed the sentiment, his thoughts already racing ahead to formulate a plan based on the information they'd received from Clara Lehrer.

"I'm not going home without you, Matt." Ken's promise repeated itself in his mind. The revised mission parameters weren't impossible. They would just require some adjustments from the original to take into account the changes in circumstances. To hell with worrying about what their superiors thought. The only person Ken had ever wanted to impress was someone he'd never met. Sadly, his father had died in France in 1918, and probably hadn't known he had a son. However, that had not prevented Ken from taking Patrick Lowe's name and doing his best to live up to the legacy of a man who had died a war hero. Inspired by the stories he'd heard of his father, Ken had risen to every challenge life had thrown at him thus far, and this time would be no different.

~

Matt watched the door close behind Holm's men. He bit down on his lower lip in an effort to hide his growing sense of dread.

Still smiling, Holm opened the bottom drawer of his desk. "I hope you don't have sensitive skin," he remarked casually. The drawer shut with a thud. Matt jumped. "It will be so much more satisfying for the both of us if you last the distance."

"No," Matt whispered, barely realising he'd spoken aloud.

"Did you say something, Priest?" Holm asked. "Keep in mind that it is your choice as to what happens next."

"My choice?" Matt's voice sounded hoarse. "I've already told you I don't have the information you require."

"And I've already told *you* that all I require at this point in time is your name." Holm sighed. "It *is* your choice. Tell me your name now, or I'll extract it later, either from you or from my other... guests."

"You're bluffing." Matt moved his head to meet Holm's gaze directly.

For a moment, they stared at each other in a silent battle of wills until Holm chuckled, pushed back his chair, and rose to his feet. "Am I?" he asked. "I quite assure you, Herr...?"

"I told you to call me Father, my child." Matt couldn't help but smirk when he repeated his earlier comment. Surely Holm didn't think he was that stupid?

"You are definitely more uncooperative than your colleagues." Holm stood and walked around the side of his desk. "It's a shame," he said conversationally. "I'm a reasonable man, but you have to understand, *Father*, that I have responsibilities to the Fatherland I cannot permit you to jeopardise." He sighed.

Matt wriggled, straining against his restraints so he could get a better view after his captor moved back into his line of sight.

Please, no.

Matt's mouth went dry. His heart thumped.

Holm ran one finger down the length of the thin black leather whip before caressing it with a tenderness that sent a shiver of terror down Matt's spine. The finger stopped, the tip of the whip resting in the palm of Holm's hand. He moved closer, the look in his eyes calm and clear, his footsteps muffled by the carpet under his feet. "It's so difficult to get the blood stains out." He walked behind Matt, out of his line of sight. "You will cooperate and save me the effort, won't you?"

"Go to hell." Matt tensed. Something cold traced a line slowly across his exposed buttocks.

"Interesting." Holm paused. "Your friend also seemed to share your preoccupation with the afterlife."

Matt bit his lip and focused his attention on the stained carpet. Holm was attempting to discover any weakness that could be used to further his agenda. If Matt focused hard enough, he could pretend it wasn't blood at all but something else entirely. Perhaps the colour was a trick of the light. Perhaps it was really dark blue, like cold, clear water. Matt closed his eyes, remembering the time he'd swum in the ocean with his father. It was beautiful, with depths that up to then he'd only dreamed about.

He and Elise had come to Germany by sea, but in the middle of winter. One day, Matt had told her, they'd do all those things they'd dreamed about. They'd swim in the ocean and travel the world. Their life together was only beginning. They always had tomorrow.

But they'd run out of tomorrows. All Matt had of her

now were his memories of a relationship that hadn't lasted, of a friend lying dead in his arms as he'd wept, knowing he was too late to save her.

He'd be damned if he would give the bastard who killed her any of the information he wanted. Once, he would have vowed to join her in death first, but not now. He couldn't do that to Ken, not when there was a chance they could have a future together. He'd failed Elise. He wouldn't fail Ken.

He bit his lip, tasting blood. He had to believe the feelings he had for Ken were mutual, that the glimpses of emotion Ken let slip when he thought no one was watching were not the product of wishful imagination and a yearning for a what-if that had no chance of becoming reality.

Even if he couldn't completely believe Ken might love him, they were still close friends, and friends didn't desert each other. Would he disobey Matt's order, and rescue him? A glimmer of hope rushed through him that he couldn't afford to lose . Once he did, the enemy won. Holm would win.

Shit!

It took all of Matt's willpower to stop from crying out when the leather connected with his buttocks. Pain spread through his body, the searing heat like...

He screamed silently, a whimper escaping his lips. He'd spent years trying to forget. He didn't want these memories. He'd never wanted them.

The edge of the whip cracked against his skin again. Matt choked back a sob.

Everything around him was burning, the smoke making him cough as he crawled along the floor toward the door. Mommy had told him to stay low, where the air was. She always knew what to do. If he was good and did what she told him, he'd be all right. They'd all be all right.

"What is your name?"

Matt opened his eyes, desperately seeking anchor in reality to escape his memories, but the room spun sickeningly around him.

The crimson stain burned red, reaching for him, wanting to devour him.

He groaned. He wouldn't answer Holm's question. This wasn't real. It was just another part of the nightmare. There was no fire. No whip.

Elise wasn't dead.

The whip bit into his skin again. Matt felt his body jerk.

"Mommy, you said you'd stay with me." The stench of the smoke was overpowering. It permeated his pajamas, his hair, and his body. He crawled faster to escape the wall of fire. Glancing behind him, he searched for any sign of his mother and his sister but couldn't see them. "Where are you?" Where was his father? Why wasn't he here to save them?

Another lash. Then another.

Stop the fire. Stop it. Stop it.

Matt buried his face in the leather of the chair. He shook, gasping for breath, trying to force air into his protesting lungs. Water ran down his forehead, into his eyes. His skin felt hot and clammy.

"Tell me your name!"

The air around him was heavy. He struggled to breathe. *It's not real. It's not real. It's not—*

Another wave of pain hit. Someone screamed.

His stomach lurched. Matt tried to yank at his restraints, but his body wouldn't obey him.

Make it stop. Make it stop.

The darkness was coming for him. He didn't like the dark. There was no escaping the fire in the dark. It burned like a beacon, bringing the monsters, bringing the nightmares.

Elise?

He reached for her.

And then everything went black.

CHAPTER TWELVE

Kristopher shivered and wriggled further down under the blankets. He felt hot and sweaty, yet his hands and feet were freezing. Trying to get comfortable, he gasped at the sharp pain in his shoulder when it rubbed against the hard mattress beneath him.

Hard mattress?

He opened his eyes with a start. Where was he? Definitely not in *his* bed. He eased himself up on his right elbow, gritting his teeth against the wave of pain the action provoked.

He blinked, his eyes adjusting to the dimness of the room. It looked barely light outside, so couldn't be much past dawn. Lowering himself back carefully onto the pillow, he touched his sore shoulder with his other hand, only to feel a slight wetness when he removed it. He stared at it, straining to see in the half dark. Blood. He was bleeding?

The memories tumbled over each other. Kristopher groaned aloud. Dr Kluge was dead, Holm and his men were in pursuit, and the plans for the project were in the hands of the SS. Kristopher's life had turned upside down in less than a day. He couldn't go back to what he'd had or the person he'd been, and wasn't sure he still wanted to.

Michel.

Kristopher visually searched the room in a panic, relieved when he saw his friend asleep in the chair by the bed. Michel sighed in his sleep, his breathing deep and even. The blanket he'd draped around himself had fallen to the floor, leaving him uncovered. Michel shivered, tiny clouds of white smoke forming from his breath, but he didn't wake. The room they were in was very spartan in appearance. The single bed was pushed up against one of the walls, which seemed to be made of brick. A plain wooden cross looked down at him from the wall above the head of his bed. He couldn't see any paintings or photographs, and yet his surroundings gave the impression of being well cared for. A cabinet stood next to the bed, a few inches to the left of the doorway. The doorframe took up most of the rest of that wall, not leaving much space on the other side of it. The floor was concrete, with not even a mat on it to offer any warmth.

Michel's chair was the only other piece of furniture in the room. The old rocker had a carved headrest, but it was difficult to make out any detail in the wood with Michel sprawled back against it. His hair was mussed up at angles where he must have shifted to try and get comfortable during the night.

Had Michel spent the entire night in the chair? Kristopher smiled, brushing his hand against his cheek. He remembered the touch of something soft against his skin as he'd drifted off to sleep, and words whispered in a language he hadn't understood. For the first time in years he dared hope someone besides Clara truly cared about him, or was that merely wishful thinking? Denying his growing feelings for Michel was becoming more difficult, although it was highly unlikely they would ever be returned.

Michel was a friend, and Kristopher was foolish to contemplate anything more than that. Someone being decent and kind didn't give him the right to read anything else into it.

Michel shifted in the chair and sighed again. He was a good man; he deserved a happy life.

Kristopher watched him for a while, fighting the urge to move closer, to run his fingers over the night's growth of stubble already growing on Michel's chin. Had he imagined last night? The touch against his cheek had felt like more than a caress, and closer to a light kiss.

He was definitely allowing his imagination to get the better of him. Given their present situation and that they would both be lucky to survive, now was not the time to be hoping for a future that had little chance of happening. He needed to focus on the task at hand, which was no different than the mathematical problems he was so practiced at dealing with. Then, once they were safe, he and Michel would go their separate ways.

Had Reiniger believed the story about the plans not being complete? Or, more importantly, would Holm realise that Kristopher, in his desperation to buy time for his and Michel's lives, had in fact told the truth?

With Kluge dead, the plans the Gestapo had were now useless without the page of formulae Kristopher had memorised and then destroyed. He'd hidden the rest under the floorboards in the attic room at Elise's Kaffeehaus. Even if another copy existed of that final page, they still needed the equations he and Kluge were working on before his death. Those had never been committed to paper. The only place they existed was in Kristopher's head.

He'd done the right thing in betraying Kluge's trust. He should have never tolerated what they were doing or allowed the project to get as far as it had. If the device was completed, his nightmares would become reality.

He already had too much blood on his hands. Kluge was dead. Kristopher hoped Elise had escaped, although he suspected she'd been caught or killed. Clara was also at risk because she'd helped them.

It didn't alter the fact that, whatever the cost, the Nazis could not be allowed to possess the information they needed to build this device. But how could he trust the Allies not to use it in the same way?

Kristopher shook his head, unsure of the answer to that dilemma. For the moment, he'd focus on his and Michel's safe passage out of Germany. The other decision would have to wait until he knew enough to hopefully make the right one.

A sliver of sunlight crept through the window, its rays highlighting Michel as he slept.

Clara was involved with the mission to retrieve the plans and had told Michel to keep watch. Kristopher sighed. Perhaps that was the only reason for the concern for his welfare. Michel would be under orders to get those plans, and by extension, Kristopher, to safety.

Clara had promised an explanation, but he doubted that would happen now. Kristopher was barely conscious when they'd arrived here, wherever here was. If it wasn't for Michel, Holm's men would have caught up with them hours ago.

He touched his cheek again and blinked back tears. God, he was such an idiot. How could he believe Michel cared for, or was interested in, him romantically? Michel was a member of the Resistance doing his job, and Kristopher was part of that mission. That was all.

His hands shook. He wasn't a coward. He would take whatever came his way without any show of weakness. Once Michel woke, Kristopher would demand answers. If he was to play his part, he needed to be fully informed. Clara had trusted Michel. Kristopher couldn't believe that trust was misplaced. Whatever the reason for Michel's kindness, he was at least owed the chance to offer an explanation for it. They could then work together to do whatever was needed to complete this mission.

The rising sun wasn't helping the icy temperature of the room. If anything it was growing colder. Kristopher swung his legs over the side of the bed and took a deep breath. Steadying himself, he took a tentative step towards Michel. The cold would wake him soon, and he needed his sleep, especially if he'd kept watch for most of the night.

Another few steps and Kristopher's breath grew ragged. This was ridiculous. After all he'd gone through the previous night, he should surely be able to walk the short distance needed to cover Michel with the damn blanket.

The room spun. Kristopher reached out instinctively to stop falling.

Unfortunately, Michel's chair was the only thing within grabbing distance.

"What the...?" Michel was awake instantly, pinning Kristopher's arms behind him. Kristopher cried out in pain. "Kit? What on earth?" Michel released his grip, running one hand through tousled hair.

"I'm sorry," Kristopher mumbled, stumbling backwards to collapse on the bed. "I didn't mean to—"

"It's all right." Michel rubbed at his eyes and squinted at Kristopher. "You startled me." His words were slurred, his yawn changing to a frown when, suddenly alert, he noticed Kristopher's shoulder. "Your wound is bleeding again. Why are you out of bed?"

"I'm not a child, and I would prefer you didn't address me as though I were." Kristopher's voice shook, either from embarrassment or because of Michel's tone. "I was merely attempting to cover you with the blanket. I didn't expect to be attacked for my trouble."

Michel sighed. "I didn't attack you. I can't afford not to react like that, considering our present situation. What if you were the enemy?"

"I would have drawn my gun and shot you as you slept." Kristopher couldn't help but add a sarcastic tone to his reply.

"It's fortunate for me we are on the same side, then." Was Michel being serious or not? He examined Kristopher's wound. Kristopher winced and pulled away. "Clara was right." Michel glared at Kristopher with undisguised annoyance. "You're very stubborn and uncooperative when you want to be." His voice softened. "I'm only trying to help. Your wound is seeping and needs to be redressed. We can't afford it to become infected."

"It hurts." Kristopher lowered his eyes, suddenly ashamed. "I'm sorry. I should be thanking you for what you've done instead of..." He trailed off, remembering the other thoughts he'd had before Michel had woken. "I just don't know what to believe anymore."

"Stay here. I left the medical kit with my bag in my room and need to go fetch it."

"I doubt I'd get very far if I tried." Kristopher gave Michel a shaky smile. "Where is here anyway?"

"We'll talk once I've redressed your wound, I promise." Michel returned the smile. "It's normal to feel this way after what you've been through. Don't be so hard on yourself. You're coping a lot better than you think you are. I've seen men cry and shake due to the aftereffects of shock."

"Hmm." Kristopher still wasn't convinced. He was a scientist who had led a very sheltered life, not a trained soldier. He wasn't equipped to cope with this, and both of them knew it. Was Michel trying to placate him and put him at ease before telling him the truth about their situation?

When Michel unlocked the door and opened it, Kristopher caught a glimpse of a painting hanging on the wall outside. He'd seen the painting of the angel before but couldn't remember the name of it. Two nuns walked past slowly, their heads bowed in prayer. In the distance, someone was singing a cappella, which was soon joined by a chorus of several voices answering in two-part harmony. It sounded simple but beautiful.

Michel stopped in the doorway, exchanging a few words in a low tone, his body blocking Kristopher's view of whomever Michel was speaking to. When their conversation finished, he moved to one side before leaving the room to allow a middle-aged nun to enter.

"How are you feeling this morning?" The nun smiled at Kristopher. "Herr Werner seemed quite..."

"Herr Werner?" asked Kristopher, convinced he was missing something obvious.

"He'll return in a moment," she confirmed. "He was right. That wound really does need redressing."

"Thank you for your concern," Kristopher said politely. If Michel was using an assumed name, how much could she be trusted? Appearances could be deceiving, and he couldn't lower his guard just because she was a nun. "Sister... I'm sorry, I don't know your name."

"Sister Brigit." She frowned. "How much do you remember about last night?"

"Very little," he answered truthfully, hoping she wouldn't ask for too much information.

"Herr Lehrer," she began.

Why would Michel have trusted her with Kristopher's name and not his own? Kristopher edged back towards the wall. The Gestapo were after both of them.

Sister Brigit attempted to place a hand on Kristopher's forehead. He pulled away. "Do you feel hot?"

"No." Kristopher sighed. Lying was not one of his strengths. "Yes." If he was running a fever, it was a very mild one. He didn't feel ill, just tired. Turning away from her, he examined the wall, running one finger along the cement between the bricks. He didn't feel up to being sociable at the moment.

"Would you like some time alone before your friend returns?" She didn't offer to redress his wound herself, for which Kristopher was grateful. Michel would do it when he returned.

He nodded but didn't turn around. "I'm sorry," he mumbled, hoping she understood he did not mean to be rude.

"Get some rest," she advised. "It will help. I'll tell Herr Werner to take his time."

After her footsteps died away, Kristopher realised he hadn't thanked her for her kindness. What was wrong with him? He usually had better manners than this. He grabbed his pillow and threw it at the wall, immediately regretting the action when his shoulder protested the sudden movement.

How could he have allowed himself to get into this situation? His former superiors would not let him flee their project. He knew too much. He and Michel would be lucky to get out of Berlin alive, let alone Germany.

Verdammt!

If the Gestapo found them now, he was in no condition to fight them off, let alone run. His failed attempt of the simple task of covering Michel with a blanket had proved that. He had no clue how to proceed from here or where here was. He hated being so helpless.

He could hear church bells through the open door, the timbre and tune both familiar. Usually he'd stop and listen and enjoy the music they made, but now his inability to give a name and place to them only served to further bring home his present situation.

Kristopher buried his face in his hands. Giving in to his despair risked the attention of anyone who might pass his room, but he no longer had the energy to keep hiding it.

"A l'aise, Kit. Je suis ici." Kristopher didn't understand the words, but he leaned into the strong arms encircling him, and let himself be held. "Ssh, tout est bien."

Unsure of how long he'd cried, Kristopher wiped his eyes on his sleeve before taking the offered handkerchief and blowing his nose loudly. "I'm sorry. I'm not normally this emotional. You must think I'm a weak idiot."

"No, I don't." Michel brushed Kristopher's hair from where it had fallen over his face. "As I told you earlier, mon ami, shock can be a nasty thing." Michel studied Kristopher for a moment. "You're not weak, Kit. Don't ever think that. In the past twenty-four hours, you've given up everything important to you and had your mentor die before your eyes. You're also recovering from a gunshot wound. Many would have given in long before now."

"Thank you." Kristopher searched Michel's face for a sign he was telling less than the truth but couldn't find one.

Perhaps his earlier fears were unfounded, and he hadn't given up everything important in his life, after all.

Michel smiled and shuffled down the bed, putting some distance between them. Kristopher was tempted to ask him not to move but decided against it. While he'd enjoyed the closeness, he didn't to dwell on or discuss that just yet.

His curiosity getting the better of him, Kristopher broke the silence between them. "Michel?"

"Yes?"

"Why were you speaking French?" Kristopher waited for an answer, but Michel wasn't forthcoming with one. "That was French, wasn't it?" He pressed for a reply, wondering if he was mistaken. He'd recognised the sound of it rather than the words and was certain Michel had spoken the same language softly the night before.

"Yes." Michel spoke hesitantly. "I didn't realise you spoke it."

"I don't," Kristopher confirmed. Michel seemed to relax after the admission. "I have heard it once or twice." His tone grew wistful. "It's so wonderfully lyrical I've never forgotten it. I haven't a clue what you said, but it made me feel better, thank you."

"I was reassuring you that I was here and everything is all right." Michel smiled. "Mon ami means my friend." He was silent for a moment. "French is my native tongue. I haven't used it much over the past several months, as it would be dangerous to do so. It seemed to settle you last night, so I thought it might help now." He cleared his throat. "I can teach you some basic words and phrases if you'd like. Having something to focus on will help to distract you while you heal."

"I'd like that, thank you." Kristopher blushed a little, warmth spreading across his face at the thought that Michel considered him his friend. "I'm not sure what I can offer in return. I only speak German and English."

"I don't speak English," Michel admitted, "only French and German. You could teach me some English. It's a language I'm curious about, but I've never had the time or opportunity to learn."

Kristopher nodded his agreement, wondering how to put his next question into words. Better to get straight to the point. "Sister Brigit called you Herr Werner. Why did you give her my real name yet use an assumed one yourself?"

"Part of me is pleased to see you're learning not to trust, yet I'd hoped by now you trusted me." Michel shifted across the bed to rest his back against the wall. He crossed his arms, then met Kristopher's gaze and sighed. "Sister Brigit already knew who you were. You're the son of one of the richest men in Berlin."

"That's going to be a problem, isn't it?" Kristopher remembered Elise's initial reaction when he and Michel had asked for her help.

"Yes, but at present, it's the least of my concerns." Michel didn't elaborate, and Kristopher didn't ask. He had other more immediate questions he wanted answered first.

"Herr Werner?"

"You're persistent, I'll give you that." Michel sounded somewhat amused. "Using my real surname could lead Holm to my family in France. I was not prepared to take that risk."

"So your name isn't Werner or Schmitz?"

Michel hadn't mentioned his first name so presumably it was his real one.

"No." Michel unfolded his arms. "My name is Michel Faber. You are the only person in Germany I have trusted with that information. My contacts in Berlin know me as

Gabriel, although Clara and Elise knew my cover name too." He studied the worn ribbon at the side of the blanket. "With the Gestapo after us, it is no longer a good idea to use Schmitz's name."

"Use Schmitz's name?" Kristopher shivered, suddenly wondering what had happened to the real Schmitz.

"Leo Schmitz was a casualty of a raid by my Resistance cell six months ago. He was travelling to his new appointment at the institute. It was a simple matter to alter his papers and for me to take his place. I kept my own Christian name, as it was important I react to it by instinct. Any suspicions that I wasn't who I appeared to be could have been fatal. If Holm was suspicious enough to check my credentials further, my cover would already be in jeopardy before he discovered the discrepancy in first names."

"You killed Schmitz?" Kristopher felt sick.

"He was killed in a raid." Michel's voice was calm, yet firm. "We're fighting a war, which means there will be casualties." He looked up. A flash of pain crossed his face, then was gone. "On both sides."

"The end never justifies the means," Kristopher protested. "Was it really necessary to kill him?"

"We didn't target him specifically and didn't intend to kill him." Michel shook his head. "He was in the wrong place at the wrong time, and the opportunity to use his identity was one we couldn't afford to ignore. He pulled a gun. If I hadn't killed him, I would be dead. Sometimes you don't have a choice."

"I'm not sure I could have killed him. I'm sorry there wasn't another way."

"In an ideal world, maybe there might have been another way, but we're not in an ideal world. As I said, we're fighting a war, and that is something you need to remember." Michel frowned. "When you overpowered Müller and aimed the gun at him, surely you would have shot him if you'd had to?"

"I don't know. I couldn't shoot a man in cold blood." Kristopher looked away. "I'm sorry. I'm not a killer."

"No one is until they have to be." Michel placed his hand over Kristopher's. Kristopher glanced up, surprised at the action. "I'm not asking you to be something you're not. I don't expect you to compromise your morals, but I need to know that if you're threatened you'll defend yourself." He squeezed Kristopher's hand. "We're leaving here in a few days, as it's too dangerous to stay once you're well enough to travel. I can't watch your back as well as my own for the entire time." He grew quiet, his words choked as he looked away. "I've already lost someone I care about…"

"I'm sorry." Kristopher reached out to give Michel a brief hug. "Do you want to talk about it?"

Michel pulled away. His eyes were vacant, his mind elsewhere. "I've been told that sometimes it's necessary to sacrifice someone for the greater good, but it's not something I'm sure—"

"Would you sacrifice me for the greater good?" The words were out of his mouth before Kristopher realised he'd spoken.

"No!" Michel's reply was sharp. He slid off the bed, his tone and demeanour suddenly very matter-of-fact. "I need to change your dressing." After collecting the duffel bag from the floor, he found the supplies he needed.

He'd overstepped and asked about something he had no business knowing, Kristopher was certain of it. A verbal apology didn't seem the right way to respond, as it wouldn't be enough, so instead he said nothing.

Michel eased off Kristopher's shirt, then carefully began

to remove the bandage from his shoulder. "This might hurt."

"Do what you need." Kristopher gripped the headboard with his right hand, his thoughts returning to the implication of what Michael had said. Michel cared; his actions had shown it several times. Kristopher gritted his teeth against the pain, deciding the distraction a change of subject would provide might be good for both of them. "You still haven't told me where here is."

"We're at the Klosterkirche," Michel answered absently, concentrating on the task at hand. "You weren't in any state to travel very far last night."

That explained why the bells sounded familiar. Kristopher had heard them often before, and visited the adjacent church, although he'd never been inside the Klosterkirche itself.

"How safe are we here? Surely if the Gestapo are thoroughly searching the city, it's only a matter of time before they find us. We need to leave Berlin." Kristopher bit his lip and tried not to wince, despite Michel being as gentle as possible.

"I didn't have a choice. We can't risk travelling until your health improves. It's going to be dangerous as it is. We'll review the situation in a few days' time after you've rested and regained some of your strength."

"If the Gestapo come before then, I want you to leave me and at least save yourself." Kristopher watched Michel for his reaction. "You're a traitor to the Third Reich. I don't want to be responsible for your death."

"It is my decision to be here and to stay with you." Michel finished changing the dressing and began tidying up. "If I have to leave, you're coming with me, even if I have to carry you over my shoulder. In the meantime, try to get some rest. I need to go talk to Sister Brigit about the arrangements for our journey." He returned the medical kit to the duffel and stowed it under the bed. "Kit?"

"What?" Kristopher's tone was sharper than he intended.

"I promised Clara I'd protect you with my life, and I intend to do just that." He left the room and closed the door behind him. Kristopher listened to his footsteps fade into the distance.

"I'd protect you with mine too," he whispered.

CHAPTER THIRTEEN

Karl Holm shook his head, trying to clear his memory of the priest's expression before he'd lapsed into unconsciousness. Such a shame the man was so stubborn. Often it only took one glance of the whip, the light touch of it on their bare skin, to make a prisoner cooperate. Karl had only intended that, all he'd hoped would be necessary, but of course once he started, he didn't have a choice but to see it through to the end.

The fear in the priest's eyes when Karl had dismissed his men also irked him. Karl was no fool. He knew what went on elsewhere, but although he did not condone it, his own sphere of influence was much more limited than others believed.

He was a man of honour, and he loved his country, almost as much as he did his family. His last memory of his father was being told very solemnly about the importance of both. His father's lesson was one Karl had never forgotten.

The pen he held between his forefinger and thumb fell to his desk with a clatter. Would his father have approved of the actions his son had taken over the past twenty-four hours? Karl sighed. He was fighting a war, and the threat of this weapon had the potential to ensure victory for the Fatherland and in doing so save many lives. Unfortunately, sacrifices would have to be made for the sake of the greater good, but sometimes that was how things were.

He regretted too many things in his life, yet he could not afford the luxury of dwelling on them. He had a job to do and would not shirk his responsibilities, even if the actions he needed to take were sometimes less than pleasant.

A sharp knock at the door interrupted his thoughts, but instead of acknowledging it, Karl retrieved his pen and returned his focus to the task at hand. His visitor was expected, but she could wait until he finished writing his report. The few minutes that would take would be enough to allow her to ponder the potential of the position in which she now found herself.

Karl gestured to the woman to take a seat once she was shown into his office. He noted her outward calm with interest. He'd expected her to be fidgeting in her chair at the very least. How close was Clara Lehrer to her brother? Knowing that would make all the difference in choosing the approach he should take.

Sibling bonds were not always as they appeared.

"I am Herr SS Standartenführer Holm, head of security for this project." Karl placed his pen on his desk and closed the dossier.

"I'm aware of who you are," Clara answered. "Do you have news of my brother?"

"What makes you think that was the reason I wished to see you?" Karl raised an eyebrow. Her response was interesting.

"You are the head of security for this project," Clara said calmly, "and my brother works here. Therefore, it stands to reason that either you wish to inform me something has happened to him, or you think I may have information as to his whereabouts." She waited for him to answer, but continued when he didn't. "Has something happened to Kristopher, Herr SS Standartenführer Holm?"

If she knew anything about the recent events concerning her brother, she hid it well.

"Herr Dr Kristopher Lehrer is a traitor to the Third Reich." Karl kept his tone casual and watched carefully for a reaction. "He killed his superior in cold blood and then stole the plans pertaining to the specific part of the project they were working on."

Clara shook her head. "There must be some mistake. Kristopher is not a killer."

"We all have the potential to kill, Fräulein Doktor. Given the right motivation, it is surprising what a person is capable of." He picked up his pen and rolled it between his fingers, this way and that. "Money is often a reason."

"My father is one of the wealthiest men in Berlin. The very idea is ridiculous."

"What do *you* think would motivate your brother to kill?" A solitary ray of sunlight caught the gold plating on his pen, and he smiled. Motivation was always such an interesting topic of conversation, and something he was very familiar with. Everyone could be bought for a price. One merely had to find that price.

"Kristopher is not a killer," Clara repeated firmly, averting her eyes.

"I'm certain his superior would disagree." Karl shook his head sadly. He stood and slowly pushed his chair out from the desk. "You're a doctor and as such, aware that a vicious blow to the head is not a particularly pleasant way to die. Your brother was with Herr Dr Kluge at the time of his death. If Herr Dr Lehrer is not responsible, then why did he flee the scene? Surely the humane thing to do would be to call for help and at least attempt to save a life."

"Do you have witnesses placing him at the scene?"

"Yes," Karl confirmed, "several witnesses." He walked around the desk, leaned against it, and rubbed the heel of one boot across the carpet. Fresh bloodstains were quite difficult to remove, and this particular one was proving most obstinate. "These witnesses are prepared to testify he was the last person to leave the room before the body was discovered."

"Witnesses are not always truthful. As you pointed out earlier, given the right motivation, it is surprising what a person is capable of." Clara watched the movement of his boot, her eyes widening very slightly, but she didn't comment. She also didn't attempt to explain why her brother had not remained at the scene. People tended to run only if they had something to hide. Clara Lehrer obviously knew more than she was prepared to divulge.

"Witnesses who are not personally involved with the perpetrator tend to have fewer problems with honesty than those who are." Karl smiled. "Of course, things are also not often as they appear."

"Oh?" Clara didn't return the smile yet remained calm. Her response revealed much about her state of mind. If she could not believe her brother was a killer, she might be open to alternative explanations for his disappearance.

"You have been a surrogate mother to your brother since your mother's death, have you not?" Karl returned to his seat and opened the second dossier. "It must have been difficult. Family is very important."

"Yes, it is." Clara didn't answer all of his questions. Did she presume they were rhetorical?

Karl turned a page, the paper smooth against the roughness of his fingertips. He glanced at Clara and then at the information in front of him again. "Herr Dr Lehrer was last seen in the company of a German Obergefreiter who we have since discovered is an impostor. It is possible he did not leave by choice. This same person was also seen in the vicinity of the crime scene."

Interestingly, she didn't protest this new theory. Perhaps she was more prepared to believe this scenario?

"Are you concerned for your brother's welfare, Doktor?" Karl nodded before she had a chance to reply. "I know I would be if our situations were reversed. This must be very trying for you." He allowed concern to enter his voice. "If he was taken against his will, I fear for his safety once he outlives his usefulness."

"Yes, I am concerned for his safety," Clara answered after a long silence. "However, I can't help you. As I've already told you, I have no idea as to his whereabouts."

"Of course you don't," Karl agreed sympathetically. "How could you if he was abducted?" He closed the dossier, adopting a grave tone. "If you wish to save his life, you need to give me any information you possess. We've had dogs tracking the traitor, and they've found blood. If Herr Dr Lehrer is injured, we need to find him quickly. It is difficult to survive on the run and only a matter of time before his captor decides your brother is a burden he cannot afford to carry." He studied her closely. "You do want to save your brother's life, don't you? Or am I mistaken in thinking he's important to you?"

"He's my brother, Herr SS Standartenführer. Naturally I want him to live."

Karl nodded. "I too would prefer him to live. It seems we are in agreement on this."

She didn't reply, but he would be surprised if she had. Loyalty was important between family members and could be exploited from several angles. Clara Lehrer had seen her brother recently, of that Holm was certain. Her reaction to his questions was too calm. Surveillance suggested the Lehrer siblings were close. For the moment, Kristopher's location was unknown, so Clara would be more useful if allowed to continue with her work. She was a doctor, and if her brother needed medical attention, he might go to her.

He stood. "Thank you for your assistance, Fräulein Doktor. Our discussion has been most enlightening. I will be sure to contact you if any more information comes to my attention."

"Thank you." Clara rose to her feet but waited to be dismissed. She was well mannered, as was her brother. Almost a shame that a family of such standing was involved in something like this, but Herr Dr Lehrer should have considered the consequences before making the decision to betray his country. Enemies of the Third Reich were always caught, and justice was always served. It was a simple fact of life.

"Before you take your leave, I have need of your skills." Karl was amused by her startled reaction. People often lowered their guard once the interview appeared at an end. "I have a prisoner in need of medical care."

"How severe are his injuries?" Clara's tone was all business. She covered her slip well. "Unfortunately, I don't have my medical bag."

"That won't be a problem. We have medical supplies here, if you require them." He opened the door for her. "If you'll follow me, I'll take you to him."

"Thank you." Clara nodded. "I'll help him, if I can." She followed Holm into the corridor to the holding cells.

"That would be greatly appreciated." Karl hoped she would be able to make good on her promise. "This prisoner is extremely uncooperative. I've tried to help him but to no avail." He sighed. "He won't even tell me his name."

Ken took another sip of coffee before surveying the patrons of the Süße Ecke once more. He was comfortable in his role as a wireless operator and could put together a working radio set from the most basic of materials. He'd always had an affinity for communication devices. They fascinated him, and he prided himself that he could handle most related technology once he was familiar with it.

He wasn't an undercover operative, and as an American soldier in enemy territory, hiding in plain view made him very nervous. Ironically, although his forte was communications, he'd never had much success with social interaction. Matt would usually be the one doing this, but now it was up to Ken to push his own shortcomings to one side and rise to the occasion. If the mission was to proceed, this had to be done. They had to discover if Matt was still alive, and if so, formulate a plan to rescue him.

The door to the Kaffeehaus opened, and a young, blonde woman entered. She ordered coffee and something to eat before taking a seat near the window. Ken observed her carefully, comparing her description with what he'd been given. She appeared to be in her mid to late twenties, slim without being overly so, of average height, and smartly dressed. The clientele of this Kaffeehaus appeared to be, at first glance, representative of the upper class of German society. Uniform aside, the soldiers he'd seen also had that air about them. Even so, the décor, while not ostentatious, was very different from Elise's Kaffeehaus. Not that he was very knowledgeable of such things, but he was not blind.

Taking another sip of coffee, he refocused on the task at hand. At this moment all other thoughts were a distraction better ignored. Liang, at least, had given him some supposedly helpful advice about how to talk to women. Ken wished, for the first time in his life, he had more experience in starting conversations, considering what he was about to attempt.

Not attempt. Do. He couldn't afford to fail. Not with Matt's life at stake.

Taking a deep breath, he picked up his coffee cup and walked over to Fräulein Dunst's table. "Is this seat taken?" he asked, cursing how pathetic the pick-up line sounded aloud.

"No, not yet." Fräulein Dunst smiled. She seemed amused, and Ken mentally groaned. This did not bode well. She nodded towards the waiter when he placed her hot coffee and pastry in front of her. "Thank you," she told him politely.

Ken decided to try again, this time more directly, an approach which usually worked better than small talk. "I hope you don't mind the intrusion, but you seemed to be alone and so was I."

"But I've only just got here, Herr...?"

"Gerber, Dieter Gerber." He took the seat opposite her and held out his hand. "I'm pleased to make your acquaintance, Fräulein."

"My name is Juliane," she replied, shaking his hand. "Juliane Dunst. It's nice to meet you too, Herr Gerber."

"Dieter. Call me Dieter, please."

"Only if you call me Juliane." She took a sip of coffee,

nodding her approval that the taste was to her liking. "You're American, aren't you?"

"How did you know?" Ken hadn't expected her to figure out who he was quite this quickly and had hoped to at least win her trust before she did. He glanced around nervously, prepared to launch into his cover story if necessary.

"Your accent is good but not quite right."

"There is nothing wrong with my accent." He glared at her before remembering he was supposed to convince her to go out on a date with him. The glare faded quickly to be replaced by a sheepish smile.

"It's not local," Juliane explained. "I knew someone with an accent similar to yours. He came from Chicago."

"Oh." Ken leaned back in his seat, trying to think of something witty to say that wasn't insulting her by denying the truth. He'd never had a girlfriend, and he and his friends always went out socially as a group. Later he'd figured out he wasn't interested in girls romantically, but it wasn't until he met Matt that he started to hope that maybe there was someone special for him after all.

"So what brings you to Berlin?" Juliane appeared to be doing most of the talking, although Ken was certain it should be the other way around.

"Business." Ken gave her a curt nod before forcing a smile. She didn't seem surprised by his admission of his nationality and didn't seem troubled by it. So far this was going better than he'd expected, so he didn't think it would be a good idea to remind her that their two countries were at war.

"That's a shame." Juliane turned her attention to the outside of the Kaffeehaus. "It's supposed to rain later today. I miss the rain. It's been unusually dry for this time of year."

"Why?" Ken blurted out. When women began talking

about the weather, it meant they were changing the subject. At least that was what Liang had said.

"I don't know." Juliane's response made Ken wonder if they were talking about the same thing. She lowered her voice. "Is the change of weather impacting your business here?"

"No." Now Ken was very confused. How could she have thought the weather had anything to do with his business in Berlin? "Why did you want to know that?"

"Because if you're here on business and it isn't, you probably don't have time to take me out for dinner tonight." Juliane shrugged and studied the sidewalk outside.

"What? How?" Ken stared at her, completely taken aback. He pushed away his growing indignation. This wasn't how the conversation was meant to proceed. The plan was for him to pick her up, not the other way around. He followed her line of sight, hoping for a clue to what had initiated the comment, but her attention seemed momentarily taken by the lime tree just beyond the Kaffeehaus. The tree was not particularly interesting and looked no different from the others of its kind lining each side of the boulevard.

"Dinner," Juliane repeated. "Tonight. You do eat dinner, don't you?" She smiled at him. "You sat down at this table with the intention of asking me out on a date."

"No, I didn't." Ken felt his face grow warm. "I'm not..." He trailed off. She had it all figured out. "Umm, yes, I did." No point in further denying the obvious, and Juliane clearly found the situation amusing.

"You're not very good at it." Juliane chuckled. "I've seen a fifteen-year-old do better."

"Maybe you'd prefer a fifteen-year-old take you out to

dinner, then?" Ken turned his head away and folded his arms. He wasn't sure whether she'd just insulted him or not.

"I'd prefer to have dinner with you," Juliane answered quietly. "If you're interested, that is. You must excuse me if I've misread your intentions."

"You haven't." Ken felt a moment's guilt, considering his true intentions towards her. She seemed like a nice woman and was attractive and intelligent. The only reason he was considering doing this was because she might be able to help him free Matt and enable his team to gain access to the plans. "I would be honoured if you'd allow me to take you out for dinner tonight."

"That would be wonderful." Juliane smiled. "Thank you for your invitation." She reached into her handbag for a pen and scribbled down an address and telephone number on the back of a small card. "I'll be ready at seven."

Ken took the card, read the address, nodded, and turned it over. "I will see you at seven, then." He stood, hoping like hell Clara Lehrer's information was correct and both women could be trusted. "I need to go. Until tonight, Juliane."

"Until tonight, Dieter," she repeated, watching him leave the Kaffeehaus.

Once he turned the corner of the street so he was out of sight, Ken leaned against a wall and took several deep breaths. "What the hell have I done?" he wondered aloud. She worked for Holm, the same man who'd captured Matt.

Either she could help them, or he'd just sold himself, his team, and the man he considered his best friend and more, for the price of a dinner date with a woman he barely knew.

CHAPTER FOURTEEN

Kit wrinkled his nose in disgust, then dutifully repeated the phrase. "My accent is terrible," he complained. "When you say the words, they're so lyrical. I sound as though I'm trying to kill your language."

"And here I was thinking that was what I sounded like when I attempted to speak English." Michel couldn't help but chuckle at Kit's expression.

"Your English is very good," Kit protested.

"Say that again and look me straight in the eye." Michel was enjoying this opportunity to spend time together. With two days rest behind him, Kit had regained his strength and his sense of humour, but he was still very tired. Michel tried not to focus on the fact they would have to leave tomorrow and would have a long journey ahead of them to St. Gertrud's convent in Alexanderdorf. Kit's slight fever had lifted, although his wound was still seeping and probably would continue to do so for a while yet.

"Your English is excellent." Kit's mouth twitched, and Michel rolled his eyes. Kit laughed. "I'm sorry. I am not a very good liar. It was easier when I didn't have to look at you." He took a sip of water. "Your English isn't that bad, though. I swear that is the truth."

"Your French accent is terrible." Michel loved the way Kit's eyes sparkled when he laughed. "However, it is much better than it was when we began these lessons." He made sure to look at Kit directly, so he knew Michel spoke the truth. "Certain phrases you speak well, others just need a little more work. Your understanding is growing quickly." Kit was a fast learner and very intelligent.

Kit opened his mouth to protest, and Michel placed a finger on his friend's mouth to quiet him.

"We've done enough of this for today. You need to rest."

"I feel fine." Kit drank more of his water, draining the cup before studying the bottom of it. "You don't need to leave yet, do you?"

"I can stay for as long as you need," Michel reassured him. "The preparations for our journey tomorrow are well in hand. Sister Brigit is very capable, and I fear I would be in her way if I offer any further assistance." They'd already gone over the plan in detail. Too much of it depended on them not being stopped by any German soldiers. Their disguises were makeshift at best, and if they were recognised, they stood no chance of fleeing, especially with Kristopher's ill health. They needed more time to allow him to heal, but that was a luxury they could not afford. Holm's men were searching Berlin and, according to Sister Brigit's contacts, would be closing in on their location within the next day.

"I'm enjoying your company." Kit smiled, a slight flush spreading across his face. He had something on his mind, but Michel was not about to push the matter. When Kit was ready to speak of it, he would.

"And I, yours." Michel refilled his own glass and offered Kit more water, but he shook his head.

"Tell me more about your family." Kit leaned back against the wall, and Michel shuffled over to sit closer. He wished he could take Kit into his arms, but that would not be a good idea. This situation was complicated enough without sharing how he truly felt. He couldn't, however, resist leaning over and brushing an errant lock of hair from Kit's face. "Was your brother very much like you in appearance?"

"We were nothing alike." Michel closed his eyes, remembering. He'd looked up to Corin. His brother was five years older, and as a child, Michel had thought Corin could do no wrong. Although that changed as they grew older and the rose-coloured spectacles matured into a sense of reality, the two had remained close. When Corin died, Michel retreated into himself and focused completely on his work with the Resistance. He still occasionally had nightmares where he watched Corin die, unable to stop it, the scene replaying in slow motion.

"Michel?" Kit asked softly, his hand gently resting on Michel's. "We can talk about something else if you wish."

Michel normally would have shifted Kit's hand, but this time he took comfort in the touch. "I'm fine," he said, opening his eyes to meet Kit's concerned gaze. "You're the first person I've spoken of him to since he died. It's time I did." He was silent for a moment, sipping from his water glass before leaning over to place it safely on the floor. "Corin was nothing like me. My parents often wondered how we could be brothers."

"In looks or in personality too?" Kit prompted.

"Both." Michel found it easy to talk to Kristopher. He listened but didn't judge, and his questions did not strike

Michel as invasive. "He has... had dark hair and brown eyes. He was shorter than me, but still a little taller than you. His temper could be fiery at times but only towards people he felt deserved it. He was very protective of those he cared about."

Kit smiled. "That last part sounds quite a lot like you." His head was almost resting on Michel's shoulder, a position they'd found themselves in several times over the last two days. It felt comfortable, although a small voice reminded Michel it hinted at more than a feeling of friendship between the two. Kit hadn't appeared to notice, so Michel didn't point it out or attempt to move away. Once Kit was fully recovered, things would return to how they should be, but for the moment, Michel was giving in to his own needs. If they were caught tomorrow, this could be the last evening they had together. He wanted good memories and at least a glimpse of a future that most likely would never be.

"I don't have a fiery temper."

"You are very protective of those you care about."

Michel shrugged. "I didn't do a very good job keeping you safe." He glanced quickly at Kit's shoulder and sighed.

"It was my decision to tackle Müller, not yours. I knew he and Reiniger were armed." Kit's eyes narrowed.

"It was a big risk," Michel said. Attempting to argue with Kit when he wore that expression would be a waste of time.

"I wanted to at least keep *you* safe." Kit shook his head. "They were going to kill us. A wounded shoulder, which will heal, is inconsequential compared to that." He shivered and leaned in closer. Michel drew him into an embrace without thinking. "This might be the last chance we have to spend time together." Kit looked at Michel directly. "If they capture us, I will not give them the information they need. I wasn't bluffing when I said they need me and the plans aren't complete." He took a deep breath. "I destroyed some of the calculations and memorised them, but even if they have copies of those missing pages, the device will not work."

"So they still can't use it?" Michel tightened his embrace, not wanting to think about what the Gestapo would do to Kit if he were caught. With how stubborn he could be, he would suffer horribly at their hands.

"No." Kit bit his lip. "Only Kluge and I knew the final formulae, and I solved the one we were having problems with shortly before he died."

Michel joined the pieces and then spoke slowly, sharing his thoughts. "So when you told them they needed you, you meant it. Is there a chance Kluge gave them what they need?"

"No. We didn't have the opportunity to discuss it." Kit sighed. "As far as I know, and I've gone over the equations in my mind several times, my calculations will solve the problem, but there is no way of knowing for certain until the device is tested. I can't allow that to happen." He pulled out of Michel's embrace, putting some distance between them. "If there is no hope of escape, you cannot allow me to be taken alive."

"No! Don't ask me to do that. I can't."

"I cannot afford to run the risk I will tell them what they need." Kit's tone was flat. "It is not just my life at stake here. I've had nightmares about what this device will do." He turned his head away. "You have to act for the greater good."

"To hell with the greater good." Michel shook his head. Although Kit was right, Michel didn't want to contemplate this as an option. "We're in this together. Until we are caught, there is always hope." Once they were, he doubted he would be given the opportunity to do what Kit asked of him. He cupped Kit's chin, forcing him to turn so their eyes met. "If our situation were reversed, would you be able to kill me?"

Kit's eyes widened. "No, of course not." His lower lip trembled. "I couldn't hurt you. I..." The reality of what he'd asked seemed to register. "I'm so sorry." He pulled Michel into a tight hug, holding him close.

"It's..." The words *it's fine* died on Michel's lips before he could speak. It wasn't fine. Logic be damned. If they were caught, while he couldn't allow the information Kit carried to fall into the hands of the enemy, this mission wasn't about just that. It hadn't been for some time.

They held each other for several minutes, neither saying a word until Kit pulled free of their embrace and wiped his eyes. "Je t'aime," he whispered.

Michel stared at him, certain he must have misheard. "What did you say?" he asked hoarsely.

"Je t'aime." Kit gingerly reached out to caress Michel's face. "I'm not exactly sure what the translation is, but it's what you said to me the first night we were here."

Oh God. "You were asleep. I didn't..." Michel took Kristopher's hand in his. "I love you," he murmured. "It means 'I love you.'" He searched Kit's face, waiting for his reaction.

Kit leaned in and softly kissed Michel on the lips. "I guessed... with your reaction to what we've just discussed. I hoped..." He was flushed, his hands trembling.

None of the words Michel could find would be enough. They could not have a future together. If they survived this, Kit needed to go to the Allies and share the information he possessed. Once the war was over, Michel would return to his life of taking care of his family's farm outside Paris. He had nothing to offer Kit. Their backgrounds were very different, and they could never admit to their relationship in public. He couldn't ask that of Kit now. They'd only known each other a short time, and once they had to part, their feelings for each other might not last.

"Kit..." Michel was tired of hiding. He'd spent the last six months pretending to be someone he wasn't. He couldn't keep doing this. Three days ago he'd known exactly what he should be doing and was completely focused on his mission. Kit Lehrer had turned all of that upside down.

He returned the kiss, deepening it and threading his fingers through Kit's hair, holding him close. "I'm so sorry," he whispered after they finished kissing. "I wish things were different."

"I know. So do I." Kit glanced at the door. "Stay with me tonight? I can't promise you anything. I'm too tired, but I want to sleep with your arms around me. Just..." His voice broke. "This might be our last night. I want to spend it with you."

Michel smiled softly. He slipped off the bed, walked over to the door, and locked it behind them. Sister Brigit would presume he was spending the night in the chair again, like he had since they'd arrived. "I'm not leaving you." He wouldn't ask for more. They both knew Kit wasn't up to it, and they needed their sleep for the day ahead. He climbed into bed and took Kit into his arms. "For as long as you'll have me and we can be together, I am yours."

Ken read the address on the card again, checking it against the number on the door of the restaurant. Surely this couldn't be right. When Juliane had given him the address, he had presumed they'd be meeting at her home. This establishment looked expensive. The curtains hanging from the windows were dark velvet; the tables inside were laid with fine china and crystal glasses. He felt very underdressed and did not possess enough German currency to pay for one meal here, let alone two. He cringed, imagining the explanation that would be forthcoming when asked to justify his expenses for this mission. Sighing, he glanced at his watch again. She was already two minutes late. Liang had warned him that ladies often made a point of keeping a man waiting and not to mention it if she did.

"I'm sorry I'm late." Juliane smiled when she saw him. He relaxed when he noticed she didn't appear to have dressed up for their date either, then frowned when it occurred to him to wonder why.

"It's fine. I haven't been here long." He offered his arm. She slipped her hand into his instead and led them inside. "I was surprised you wanted to meet here." Better to be honest with her, at least about this. "This is a fine-looking restaurant. I'm sorry if I've given the wrong impression, but I suspect it might be a little out of my price range."

She shrugged. "Don't worry about it. I know the owner. He'll find us a private table where we can talk."

As if on cue, a middle-aged man greeted her enthusiastically, offering to take their coats. Ken declined at first, in case he had to leave quickly, but surrendered it when Juliane frowned at him and shook her head. The man, who introduced himself as Robert, led them to a table in the back of the restaurant, handed them menus, and promised to return shortly to take their order. The restaurant was almost deserted, with only one other couple finishing their meal in the opposite corner, which negated the risk of being overheard.

Ken picked up the menu and studied it carefully. While his spoken German was passable, his ability to read the language was not. His briefing had covered the basics he might need to succeed in his mission, but there were words on this menu he had not seen before. He couldn't see any prices either.

Frowning, he turned it over, wondering if they were on the back.

"Would you like me to order for you?" Juliane did not seem surprised by his reaction.

"Please."

She spoke pleasantly when Robert returned, ordering for both of them. Ken declined her offer of wine, preferring to keep a clear head, and asked for coffee instead. Once Robert left, Juliane lowered her voice. "Thank you for meeting me here. It is better not to risk you being seen at my home."

"Why?"

"Are you always this abrupt?"

"Yes." He had the grace to look embarrassed. "I'm sorry, I'm not very good at social niceties. It's not personal."

"I noticed," she commented dryly. "It's lucky one of us is, then, isn't it?" She thanked Robert when he reappeared with coffee for Ken and a glass of wine for her. Sipping it slowly, she watched him for a moment. He found the action disconcerting. His mother, he was sure, would applaud and encourage her. Cho Tsukino preferred people to be direct, and acted that way herself.

"You still haven't answered my question. Why did you want to meet here rather than at your home?"

"People would notice if you were seen there. Here they

will not." Juliane peered at him over her wineglass. "As much as I am flattered by your pretense of wanting to spend an evening with me, I know the only reason you are here is that you need my help." She put the glass on the table. "I believe we have a mutual acquaintance."

"Perhaps," he confirmed cautiously. "What is it you think I need your help for?" He cleared his throat. "I could be exactly as I appear to be, an American here in Berlin on business."

"I don't doubt you are American or here on business. The question is, however, what that business is, exactly." She sighed. "I'm not one for using codes to communicate, despite my associates reprimanding me for it."

Ken raised an eyebrow. He couldn't imagine anyone having the nerve to reprimand her for anything. "You're not exactly what I was expecting. I was told you are a secretary for an officer of the Gestapo."

"I am." Juliane matched his eyebrow with one of her own. "However, I do help those who ask nicely for my assistance upon occasion. Just because I work for the Gestapo does not mean I condone what they are doing." She took another sip of wine. "I'm not a traitor to my country, Herr Gerber, but I cannot sit back and do nothing while men, women, and children suffer because someone decided certain people are worth more than others. We are all equal in the sight of God, and so I do what I can."

"I'm asking nicely for your help." Ken wanted to believe she was prepared to help them rescue Matt. Surely Clara Lehrer would not have set this up as an elaborate trap. Liang had pointed out, quite rightly, that as part of their mission was helping her brother to defect, it would be in her best interest to cooperate with them. If she signed their death warrants, it would most likely include doing the same for him.

"Then I will do what I can."

Robert approached their table, more loudly than was necessary. Juliane changed the subject of the conversation to a piece of music she'd heard recently and enjoyed until Robert finished serving their meal and departed.

"I need help in rescuing a prisoner from Herr SS Standartenführer Holm's custody. Can you get me access to the institute, and more specifically, to the area he's being held?"

"Which prisoner and what is your interest in him?" Juliane carved a bite-size piece of meat and chewed it thoughtfully, her tone not dissimilar to the one she'd used when they'd discussed the weather earlier that day.

"Why do you need to know my interest in him?" Ken wasn't ready to give her all the information she'd asked for. He wasn't as trusting as Liang.

She shrugged. "I'm curious, and I like to know the type of person I'm dealing with. I have just as much to risk in doing this as you do."

"That sounds fair." He poked at the food in front of him with his fork, not having had much of an appetite since Matt was captured. "He was arrested by Holm for the murder of Elise Schuster." Ken scowled. "At least that is the excuse they are holding him on."

"You are convinced he is innocent, then?" Juliane's question seemed genuine enough.

"Matt is not a murderer!" Ken let his fork fall to his plate with a loud clunk. "He and Elise were close friends, and he was upset by her death. The very idea is ridiculous. Besides, she was already dead when he found her."

"So that is his name," Juliane said softly. "He is the one dressed as a priest, yes?"

"Yes." Ken swallowed, relieved she at least knew of Matt. "Is he all right? How badly has Holm treated him?" He couldn't help the anger that crept into his voice.

Juliane looked up at him. "If I help you, you have to promise me something."

"Anything."

"Don't promise something you will not be able to adhere to," she warned him.

"As long as you do not either, I can't see we will have a problem." Ken hadn't expected to have to bargain for Matt's release, but it made sense she would have a price for her services.

"He is a friend." She phrased it as a statement, not a question, then emptied her wineglass.

"Yes." Ken placed his hands on his lap so she wouldn't see him clench his fists. Whatever price she asked, he would find a way to make the payment. Saving Matt was all that mattered. Unfortunately, his superiors might not agree, but they were not here. He would not readily give up information that would put anyone else at risk, but hopefully it would not come to that.

Juliane sighed. "I will help you, but it may take a few days. Karl is a patient man, but he grows frustrated with your friend. He can be a little... focused when the information he needs is not forthcoming."

"Karl?" Surely she wasn't referring to Holm?

"Herr SS Standartenführer Holm." She leaned in closer, her voice dropping to a whisper. "If I help you to rescue your friend, you must promise me no harm will come to Karl. Otherwise access to the institute is out of the question."

"What business is his welfare to you?" Ken did not like

this condition at all. If Holm had harmed Matt, the man deserved whatever happened to him.

"Promise me first."

Ken hesitated but realised he had no choice. She would not back down from the argument easily, and she was obviously involved with Holm in some way that was not strictly professional. "I promise."

"Thank you." She stood, the rest of her meal forgotten. He pushed out his chair, wanting to end this conversation as quickly as possible. "I will be in touch. Father Johannes will inform you of the details of our next meeting."

He nodded curtly, wondering if he should offer to pay for the meal. "I should go," he said stiffly.

"Yes," she agreed. "Do not look so concerned. There is no charge for this meal or for anything else. I am not a mercenary, Herr Gerber. I merely want to keep those close to me safe, the same way you do."

From Ken's perspective, that was payment enough. Her supposed reassurance did not do anything for his current state of mind. "You still haven't answered my question. Why are you so concerned for Holm's welfare?"

She sighed. "Sadly, Herr Gerber, we can choose our friends, but we do not always have the luxury of deserting our family." She had a hint of sadness in her eyes. "I might not agree with Karl's actions, but there is no escaping the fact he is still my brother."

CHAPTER FIFTEEN

The truck lurched, and Kit bit down on his lip. "Are you all right?" Michel asked after Sister Brigit apologised for the state of the road.

Kit nodded but didn't reply with words. The long journey was taking its toll on him. Although they'd both slept well the night before, this was the first time he'd ventured very far out of bed since arriving at the Klosterkirche.

"Brother Dominic?" Michel asked, using the cover name they had agreed on. Hiding in plain view wasn't an ideal situation, but it at least gave them more options. Michel hadn't thought Kit would fare well crouching down for an extended length of time among the supplies they carried. Those supplies would also very likely be thoroughly searched. So for the duration of their journey, Kit would be Brother Dominic, Michel was Brother Bernard, and they were helping Sister Brigit deliver much-needed supplies to a neighbouring convent. The heavy brown robes of the order would also help to hide their identities and that Kristopher's wound was still seeping.

"I'm fine," Kit mumbled, turning his head away from Michel's gaze. "Just tired." He gripped the wooden beads hanging from his robe, his breath hissing after the truck jerked again. Discreetly taking Michel's hand in his, he squeezed it tightly.

Last night, Michel slept better than he had since Corin's death. He'd found Kit's presence comforting and stayed awake for a while after he fell asleep, listening to the sound of his breathing and feeling the steady rhythm of his heartbeat. Waking that morning, Michel found Kit propped up on one elbow, watching him. Although Kit's hair was mussed up and he needed a shave, starting the day like this was something Michel could well become used to, especially when greeted by a kiss.

They hadn't shared much more than a few kisses and gentle caresses, given Kit's health, but those brought with them whispered promises of more once their situation allowed them that opportunity.

After a quick breakfast, Michel had shaved and then helped Kit to do the same, spending a little more time than necessary. Now he could, Michel enjoyed touching Kit; the simple task of shaving him felt very erotic. He loved the feel and shade of Kit's hair. Unfortunately, they would have to do something about changing the colour of it before leaving Alexanderdorf.

"We talked quite late last night," Michel said quietly, squeezing Kit's hand reassuringly.

"Yes." Kit faced him again, this time managing a shaky smile. "I slept very well, more so than I have in a while." The truck hit another bad stretch of road, and Kit hissed again when the movement jarred his shoulder. His complexion paled.

Michel placed a hand on Kit's forehead and frowned.

"You're very warm." Hopefully the slight fever had not returned and Kristopher had only overextended his energy levels. Michel reached behind them, pulled out one of the water canteens they carried, and offered it to Kit, then watched him drink.

"This particular stretch of road isn't very well maintained." Sister Brigit crunched the gears and muttered something under her breath very unfitting for a nun. "We still have a few more kilometres of this, I'm afraid."

Kit returned the canteen to Michel. "You should drink too."

"I'm fine, and it's important you look after yourself." Michel retrieved Kit's rosary beads when they fell from his hand into his lap. "You need to rest."

"I'll rest when we reach Alexanderdorf." Kit's eyes began to close, but he opened them again, his body jerking awake with a start.

"If you need to sleep, do so," Michel suggested gently. "I'll wake you if necessary."

"But I wanted..." Kit glanced at Sister Brigit, who was focusing her attention on the road, before his eyes closed again. Michel put his arm around Kit's waist, making sure the action was as inconspicuous as possible while holding him in an upright position to avoid arousing the suspicions of anyone they passed on the road. While Michel wasn't sure whether the Gestapo were aware of Kit's injury, it would be difficult to explain the reason for his condition if pressed for an answer.

"The medicine seems to have helped with the worst of the infection." Sister Brigit took her eyes off the road for a moment to nod in Kit's direction. The cab of the truck wasn't very large. Michel eased Kit closer, careful not to wake him, in order to give her more room. "It's going to take a while for him to rebuild his strength, though."

"Yes, it is." Michel brushed Kit's hair from his face and adjusted the hood of the monk's robe so it covered him properly. "I'm hoping we do not have to leave the convent until he's fully recovered." The journey to Switzerland would not be easy, and he doubted Kit would survive it otherwise. They could not risk any further infections, as the Gestapo would be watching any hospitals or doctors in the area. The supplies Clara had given them would also not last much longer.

If they were discovered, he would not leave Kit. Michel had told him they were seeing this through together, and he meant it. Corin had always told him that in a situation such as this, it was important to think clearly, react quickly, and not allow any emotional attachments to cloud his judgement. Although he'd lost the ability to distance himself, which made this all the more dangerous, Michel didn't want to return to how things were before. He and Kit had discussed the situation the previous night, and they'd both agreed they'd prefer to have whatever time they could together than to live a long life alone and apart.

Kit shifted in his sleep, his head slipping to rest on Michel's shoulder. Without thinking, Michel brushed his fingers against Kit's cheek. Kit smiled, but he didn't wake, his breathing remaining slow and even. Michel glanced quickly at Sister Brigit, but she was watching the road ahead.

He gave in to the luxury of letting his mind wander, of wondering how this would all play out. Although Kit said he wanted to try to see if they could have a future together, they both had an obligation to see through the rest of this mission. The Gestapo weren't the only side aware that Kit could reproduce the plans for this device. Michel doubted they or the Allies would be prepared to allow Kit to disappear quietly without giving up the information he carried. Michel sighed. Kit had needed to talk last night, and in doing so, he'd told Michel about this device and its potential for destruction. Michel was horrified, not wanting to believe someone would consider using it. He'd held Kit as he'd berated himself for his part in its creation. Kit carried so much guilt, not only for his part in the project, but for believing the people he'd worked for would only ever use its potential to benefit mankind.

Michel knew why. Kit was caring, gentle, and wanted to see the good in people. He'd allowed those traits to cloud his judgement. While understandable, Michel suspected it would take Kit a lifetime, if that, to forgive himself.

Considering the circumstances, there was nothing *to* forgive.

Sister Brigit slammed on the brakes. Michel grabbed Kit so he wouldn't fall. She cursed under her breath, and Michel wondered, not for the first time, about her background before she'd joined the order.

"Brother Dominic, wake up!" she whispered urgently. "We have company."

Michel took a deep breath, trying to appear calm. His heart thumped. They had to appear as though they had nothing to hide and hope like hell the Gestapo didn't realise who they were. Holm was very efficient. The first thing he would have done was circulate their description. Too much of their escape plan depended upon this not happening.

The road ahead of them was barricaded. An armed Feldgendarmerie unit guarded the roadblock. A metre of barren ground stood between the side of the road and nearby trees. It would take several moments to reach cover, and Michel doubted Kit would be up to running that quickly. The only chance they had was to meet their enemy directly and hope their cover story was believed.

He adjusted his disguise and Kit's, placing the rosary beads back in Kit's hand before waking him.

"What?" Kit's eyes were unfocused. He seemed confused. "Where am I?"

The Oberfeldwebel exchanged several words with his men and walked over to the truck. "Heil Hitler," he said in way of greeting. "You are all to exit the vehicle slowly."

Karl looked up at the firm knock on his office door. He wasn't surprised to see the door already opening and Margarete Huber walking into the room. She was the only person working at the institute with the nerve to enter his office without waiting to be invited. Part of him was amused, while the other knew from experience it also meant she had the potential to be a dangerous foe if she put her mind to it.

"Fräulein Huber, what a pleasant surprise." He gestured for her to sit.

"Why thank you, Herr SS Standartenführer Holm," she said politely. Margarete was always polite, although the words she spoke were often not as straightforward as they appeared. She was a complex individual and very ambitious. Part of that ambition, however, meant she had developed connections that could be exploited.

"Do you have some information for me?" Karl indicated the folder on her lap. While they could have wasted more time on small talk before getting down to business, he didn't see the point in it. Neither would she.

"Yes, I do." Margarete looked particularly pleased with herself, more so than usual. "I received this dossier from my contact by a trusted courier this morning. I thought you would appreciate seeing it as soon as possible."

"Thank you." He waited for her to hand it to him. Although he was keen to see it, he didn't want to give her any advantage by making that obvious. He kept his voice calm and even. While he'd waited a very long time for this information, a few more minutes would not make much difference.

"I took the liberty of looking through it first." Margarete tapped the file with one perfectly manicured fingernail. "After all, it would not do to get our hopes up with information that is, for want of a better word, *useless*, would it?"

The folder potentially held the answers *he'd* hoped for, not she. If he wasn't more desperate for the truth than he wanted to admit, he would have corrected her. Unfortunately, though, she was the one with the contacts for this particular research, and was not above holding that over him. Allowing her to read the information now was something that could be dealt with later. For the moment, she was useful to him, and he to her.

"Your concern is appreciated." He nodded at the folder. "Your contact was able to find the records without too much trouble, I hope."

She leaned over to place the folder on his desk so it sat in a no man's land between them. He would have to make the next move. "I didn't ask." She shrugged. "He was paid well. The details are none of my concern." He had suspected they wouldn't be. Margarete never concerned herself with those kinds of details. If someone collecting information for her was caught and executed for treason, she'd merely shake her head, comment on how good help was difficult to find, and move on to the next person placed well enough to be of assistance.

Karl did not want to get on the wrong side of her, especially with the connections she had within the Nazi hierarchy, courtesy of her grandfather. He picked up the folder and opened it, his eyes widening when he saw the details of the information she'd provided him, which was far more than he'd anticipated. His breath caught. He stopped skimming and re-read the words properly, once, then twice, to make sure he wasn't imagining it.

"Unfortunately the man you sought died shortly after your father." Margarete sounded regretful. He looked up in surprise, but her tone seemed genuine. "Given the date on his death certificate and the related newspaper article, it appears he lost his life at the Battle of the Marne."

"In the line of duty, I see." Karl skimmed the clipping and rolled his eyes in disgust. The American had been given an award for bravery and honoured as a hero. He doubted many knew the truth.

Heinz Holm had died the same way he'd lived—with honour—despite his murder at the hands of an American soldier during the Battle of Belleau Wood in France during the last war. Karl peered closely at the faded photograph included in the file, committing the face of his father's murderer to memory. At last he at least had that and a name. He sighed, his dream of confronting his father's murderer slipping quickly from his fingers. Revenge was not an honourable trait, but he'd wanted to at least make the man pay in some way for what he'd done.

Margarete raised an eyebrow. "That really isn't surprising, Herr SS Standartenführer. War forgives many atrocities, and history is often not an honest retelling of events. However..."

"However?" Karl finished reading the eulogy and looked up at her. It hadn't mentioned a wife or children either, more the pity. *His* mother had remarried hastily after his father's death, his half-sister, Juliane's, existence a reminder of the former Frau Holm's infidelity.

"My contact was able to find a birth certificate listing him as the father of a male child born in 1914. Given the information at hand, it is doubtful the parents were married or that the child was officially acknowledged as such." Margarete shrugged. "I have always believed the sins of the father can still be paid for by the son. Others may disagree, but for a crime such as this one, there need to be consequences."

"I will take that under consideration." The chances of meeting this child were very remote. Perhaps, once this war was won, he might consider it further. But in the meantime, he had much more information than he'd ever thought possible.

"Please do." She stood and smiled at him, as if waiting for something.

"Yes?" he asked politely, keen for her to leave so he could have some time alone to digest what he'd just learned.

"I believe there is a matter of payment for my services, Herr SS Standartenführer." Her eyes were cold, the blue of them reminding him of ice.

"We agreed to discuss that at a later date, Fräulein." He met her gaze directly and did not flinch. "I believe there was nothing specific I could offer that you wanted at the time."

"The situation has since changed. You now possess something I want, or rather you will soon. It is just a matter of time."

He sighed. Everything in life came at a price. It was foolish of him to think this would be different. Margarete was not concerned simply for the good of the Fatherland. "Name it," he said, hoping it was something he could give her. After all, he was now in her debt, and he did not want the details of his father's death to become common knowledge.

Her smile hardened. "I wish to be present at the interrogation of Herr Dr Kristopher Lehrer."

The Oberfeldwebel gestured towards them, his action one of impatience when his initial order was not followed immediately. "Now!"

Kristopher shook his head minutely when Michel offered him assistance. Although his shoulder ached and he was still groggy from having dozed off, he was determined not to show any sign of weakness. He slipped his hand under his robe and pressed the loosely taped cloth more firmly to his wound, hoping it would absorb enough of the seepage so it wouldn't show through the rough material. He bit down on the instinct to wince. His shoulder wasn't as sore as it had been, but the jarring from the truck on these roads had aggravated it.

Sister Brigit stepped down from the driver's side, careful to keep her hands raised and not to arouse suspicion. Michel followed her, keeping his head down. Adjusting his robes, Kristopher joined them as quickly as he could, ignoring the wave of pain from his injury.

The Oberfeldwebel eyed them for a moment before motioning to his men to search the truck. Kristopher heaved a sigh of relief he'd agreed to Michel's insistence that it wouldn't be a good idea to hide among the supplies they carried.

"Travel papers, please, Sister." The man had manners and, now they were following his instructions, seemed almost apologetic. "We are hunting two fugitives wanted for murder. Have you seen anyone suspicious?"

"Heil Hitler." Sister Brigit's eyes widened. "Murderers? Certainly not...? We haven't seen anyone at all, Herr Oberfeldwebel. These back roads are very quiet. It's dreadful what the world is coming to these days, is it not?"

"Very." Although the Oberfeldwebel's Walther P38 was still in its holster, he wouldn't hesitate to draw it if necessary. Disagreeing with him or attempting to flee the scene would not be a wise move. They had little chance of overpowering him beforehand, and even if they did manage to, there were the other four men with him to consider. They each carried MP40 submachine guns slung over their shoulders, and as German military police, they would most likely have had both military and police training.

The only other option was to try to escape, but it would take too long to reach the safety of the trees beyond the road, and Kristopher was under no illusions about his inability to make a run for it. Michel would not attempt to escape on his own, a decision not worth arguing over, even if they had the time for it. If the situation were reversed, Kristopher would not leave Michel to face the brunt of the soldiers' displeasure either.

He fingered his rosary, more for something to calm his nerves than his being a spiritual man, although he'd prayed more in the last few weeks than he had in a very long time. His legs wobbled like jelly, his heart beat quickly, and his breathing sped up.

The Oberfeldwebel walked around them, examining them closely. Kristopher's rosary fell from his fingers. He didn't move to pick it up. The edges of his vision darkened.

He looked straight ahead, determined to stay on his feet. His weakness could not be allowed to put all of them at risk.

"Are you not well, Brother?" The Oberfeldwebel asked the question softly.

Kristopher bit down his panic. If he were examined, his wound would probably be discovered.

"Brother Dominic has been ill," Michel answered calmly. "He is still recovering."

"I believe I asked Brother Dominic the question." The Oberfeldwebel repeated the question, watching Kristopher carefully.

"As Brother Bernard said, I am recovering from an illness," Kristopher confirmed, unable to keep the tremor from his voice.

"Perhaps you should not be travelling, then." One of the soldiers who had searched the truck signalled his superior that they hadn't found anything untowards. "Travel and identification papers, please."

Kristopher swallowed. God, this was exactly the scenario they'd hoped to avoid. Their travel papers were in order as were Sister Brigit's and Michel's identification papers, but his would most likely not pass close inspection. Michel was prepared for a possible escape from Berlin and so already had the papers he'd need, but his original assignment did not include Kristopher. Sister Brigit's contacts had managed to forge some for Kristopher, but with the time constraints, they were far from perfect.

He fumbled in his pocket and pulled out his papers, not daring to catch Michel's eye. His skin was clammy; he swayed on his feet. "I'm sorry," he mumbled.

The Oberfeldwebel's tone sharpened to one of suspicion. "From what illness are you suffering?"

Kristopher's shoulder twinged again. An idea occurred

to him, but it was risky. Yet what choice did he have? If they were captured, Holm would use any means necessary to extract the information he needed. That could and probably would entail torturing Michel to ensure Kristopher's cooperation. While he would not give up the missing equations to save himself, he could not be the cause of Michel's suffering.

"Brother Dominic...," Michel warned, but Kristopher ignored him. He coughed, making sure some of the spittle sprayed across his identity papers. They fell from his fingers and dropped to the ground. Reaching into his robe, he quickly retrieved the cloth pressed to his wound, careful to hold the bloody side so it couldn't be seen. Making a show of coughing loudly, he held it up to his mouth with an apologetic look and spat into it. When he brought the supposedly clean "handkerchief" from his lips, it was covered with a combination of blood and phlegm.

The Oberfeldwebel backed away quickly. "You should not be travelling with such a complaint," he mumbled, fear in his voice.

Sister Brigit interrupted smoothly. "Brother Dominic and Brother Bernard kindly offered to help me transport supplies. I will, however, be insisting Brother Dominic rests upon our arrival." She frowned. "It appears he is not as well as he claimed to be. I apologise."

Following Kristopher's cue, Michel bent to retrieve the identity papers, picking up the forgotten rosary at the same time. He wiped the papers with his fingers before giving them to Kristopher. His expression was one of concern. "I believe you dropped these, Brother Dominic."

"Thank you, Brother Bernard." Kristopher returned his "handkerchief" to his pocket along with his rosary and offered the papers to the Oberfeldwebel. "I believe you wished to see these, Herr Oberfeldwebel," he said politely.

The Oberfeldwebel took the papers gingerly, barely glancing at them, as though wanting to be rid of them as quickly as possible despite the gloves he wore. He looked at Kristopher with a mix of fear and sympathy, and spent only a moment longer examining Michel's identification. Sister Brigit offered her own papers and their travel documents. The Oberfeldwebel nodded in response, scanning them briefly.

"You need to be on your way." He seemed a lot more nervous than before and kept his distance. "Be sure to report anything out of the ordinary." He saluted. "Heil Hitler."

"Thank you, Herr Oberfeldwebel." Sister Brigit climbed back into the truck and waited for Michel and Kristopher to join her. Both men were careful to return the phrase signifying their loyalty to the Third Reich first. Although Kristopher's ruse appeared to have worked for now, if the Oberfeldwebel or any of his men mentioned the incident, Holm probably wouldn't react with the same caution. He was not the kind of man to allow the risk of sickness from preventing him from carrying out his duty.

The Oberfeldwebel's men didn't waste any time removing the barrier to let the truck pass or in replacing it. Kristopher looked straight ahead, not wanting to interact on any level with them as Sister Brigit drove through. Once they were clear, he slumped in his seat, shaking.

"That was very brave, Herr Lehrer," Sister Brigit commented softly. "Thank you."

"Very brave," Michel repeated. He sighed. "It also drew their attention almost completely towards you. But I expect that was part of your plan, wasn't it?"

Kristopher didn't see the point in denying the truth. "Yes." He moved closer to Michel. Sister Brigit again focused her attention onto the road. Had she guessed something of the nature of his and Michel's friendship? She was a good person, and from the few conversations they'd had, he doubted she would be one to pass judgement. In that regard, she put his past reactions to shame.

"Sleep if you need, Kit." Michel slipped his hand into Kristopher's and held it tightly. "This is not the first time you have risked yourself for others." Something in his voice made Kristopher look up so their eyes met. For a moment, Kristopher glimpsed Michel's fear. His usual calm expression was absent.

"I only did it because there was no choice." He tried to reassure Michel, but he responded with a shrug. "If he'd taken a good look at my papers, it wouldn't have been just me who would have been taken into custody."

"I know." Michel looked down. He opened his mouth as if to say something but didn't. Whatever he wanted to say could not be said in front of Sister Brigit.

They would have to talk later.

CHAPTER SIXTEEN

Despite his intentions to stay awake, Kristopher dozed on and off for the rest of their journey, his head slipping to rest on Michel's shoulder. The adrenaline rush brought on by his fear of impending capture and worse had worn off faster than he'd anticipated, and suddenly he felt very tired again.

Michel was not happy, but for the moment nothing could be done about it. Neither of them was prepared to have that conversation in front of an audience. Nor was it one Kristopher was looking forward to. He'd taken a risk in what he'd done, but hadn't seen a choice. Better to take a chance on something that might work than do nothing and face a certainty far more dangerous. He still wasn't sure how he'd found the presence of mind, let alone the energy, to do what he had, but it was done.

"We're nearly there, Kit." Michel shook Kristopher gently, whispering the words.

Fields stretched on either side of the road, with the hint of vast forests in the distance. A brick wall was directly ahead, a section of it built up to provide support for the bell hanging from wooden struts. The open wrought iron gates welcomed them into the long driveway leading up to what appeared to have been once the manor house of a country estate.

"Welcome to St. Gertrud's, gentlemen," said Sister Brigit. "This should be a safe haven for a while. At least as safe as it is anywhere, with the way things are at present." She slowed down as they passed through the gates, then continued at that speed until they reached the end of the driveway and came to a halt in front of the building.

The place looked peaceful, the trees very noticeably beginning to lose their foliage, signalling the rapid approach of winter. The house itself consisted of three levels, and the topmost of those seemed to be some kind of annex. An iron outline of a cross was attached to the brickwork above the sturdy wooden door. Below that was a Latin word Kristopher recognised from his studies and translated as *peace*. Whether it referred to the atmosphere of the convent itself or represented the belief of the order residing there, the symbol was well chosen.

The door opened, and two nuns hurried down the front steps. "Sister Brigit!" the older of the two exclaimed, giving Sister Brigit a hug when she got down from the truck. "I'm so glad you made it safely." She smiled at Kristopher and Michel. "Brothers Dominic and Bernard, I'm presuming? Welcome to St. Gertrud's. I'm Sister Magdalene."

"Thank you, Sister. It's nice to meet you," Kristopher said politely. Her age was difficult to guess, but her face was lined with creases, especially around her eyes.

The other nun took a step closer and also greeted Sister Brigit with a hug, although much more reserved than the one Sister Magdalene had given. "You must be tired from your journey," she said. "Sister Magdalene will show you where you'll be staying. Don't worry about unloading the truck. We'll look after that." She smiled at Kristopher. "Brigit tells us you're recovering from an illness. Rest is important."

"Thank you, Sister…?" Kristopher wasn't about to argue with her. Something in her eyes told him it would be a waste of time. He'd learned very early on it didn't pay to argue with a nun. "My name is Sister Claire." Her tone was kind yet firm. "I'll bring supper up later." Her attention refocused on Sister Brigit but not before she scrutinised Michel carefully. He sensibly didn't respond. "Brigit, we have much to talk about. Please come and I'll make us some tea."

Michel waited until both nuns were out of sight before retrieving his duffel bag from under the front seat of the truck. "Is she always like this?" he asked Sister Magdalene.

She chuckled. "Sister Claire likes to think she runs St. Gertrud's and knows everything that goes on under its roof and within ten kilometres of it. She's a good soul, and there's no harm in it." She began walking up the steps, and they followed her. "I remember your sister's first days at the hospital after she'd graduated. You're very similar in looks, Brother Dominic. I would have recognised you anywhere."

Kristopher froze. "Excuse me?" he spluttered. Had their cover been compromised already? "I'm sure you must be mistaken."

Michel discreetly placed himself between Kristopher and the nun.

"I'm sure I'm not," Sister Magdalene said casually. "I hadn't heard you'd entered an order either, but don't worry, young man, I'm not about to ask any awkward questions. We are here to help those in need, and so that is what we will do."

"Thank you, Sister," Michel replied softly, seeming to

relax again, but he held on to the strap of the duffel tightly, his knuckles white. He also kept very close to Kristopher, ready to support him if he tired. Kristopher smiled, trying to make his expression as reassuring as he could. He felt much better after resting, although the tiredness would hit again much quicker than usual. His shoulder still ached, but at the moment the pain was bearable.

The inside of the building was as striking as the outside and also served to provide a good distraction. Kristopher couldn't help but look around with interest. He'd always loved old buildings and their history. The brickwork was more noticeable now they'd passed through the front door, and the exposed wooden beams were impressive, to say the least. "Is this original?" he asked, his curiosity getting the better of him.

"We presume so, yes," she said. "This used to be a country estate, and the previous owners have slowly worked at renovating and adding to it, so it is an ongoing project. It is a beautiful building, as are the surrounding grounds." She led them through the main foyer to the kitchen area. The steep set of steps about a metre inside the back door appeared to lead up through a square hole in the ceiling above. "This is the way to the attic, where you will be staying. If you'll follow me, I can show you where everything is." The first landing of sorts was midway up, at about the level of the first floor, but there didn't appear to be a way off the steps to that floor, the access to which was probably the more conventional staircase Kristopher had glimpsed from the foyer. Three of the steps near the very top creaked loudly. "If one of us comes to bring you food or whatever else you need, we'll call out a warning. If that warning does not come, it means you need to hide quickly."

Michel nodded his understanding, helping Kristopher

up the final steps when he stumbled. The attic room was bigger than expected and had to be at least twice the size of the foyer on the ground floor, although it only looked to be half the length of the roof of the first floor. Exposed beams crisscrossed the ceiling, the light from small windows between those at each end of the room providing enough illumination for reading, but not enough to keep someone awake if they slept in the middle of the room.

"Where would you recommend we hide?" Michel asked, noticing as Kristopher had that the room was a large open space. If they were caught there, it would be as rats in a trap with the stairs being the only way in or out.

He was answered by a smile. Sister Magdalene walked over to the old candlestick secured to the wall closest to the stairs and twisted it. A section of the wall slid silently open to reveal a space about the size of a large wardrobe. "There is another candlestick inside. The mechanism works the same way on both sides so it can be opened by either. I wouldn't recommend lighting the candle in there, as the light can be glimpsed through the slight gap at the bottom of the wall. After all, the air has to get in somewhere. There is no point in having a hiding place you cannot breathe in, as it defeats the purpose of it."

"Yes, it does." Kristopher hoped they would not have to hide in there for long. He suspected it would also be very dark inside once the wall slid back into place. Clearing his throat, he glanced around the rest of the room, noticing the starkness of it. The old bed, to his surprise, did not look out of place, but as though it had been left there in storage rather than used recently. The entire room had that look about it. He doubted anyone stumbling onto it would guess its true purpose. They would have to be careful to clear anything away as they used it. If it were discovered, they would not have much warning to hide.

He shivered, not wanting to think about spending too much time, if any, hiding while Gestapo or the like searched for them. He was not keen on small, dark enclosed spaces.

As though reading his thoughts, Sister Magdalene closed the secret room and quickly changed the subject. "I'm afraid there is only the one bed, although it is a double. I hope you gentlemen do not mind sharing."

Michel's voice sounded huskier than usual when he finally replied. "We're grateful for your hospitality, Sister." Kristopher kept his head bent. His face was flushed, and his thoughts had gone in a direction very unsuitable for a man currently dressed as a member of the clergy.

"Someone will bring supper in a while. In the meantime try to get some rest." She removed the dust cover from the bed, folded it, and placed it on the table in the corner, which was the only other piece of furniture in the room. Her voice betrayed her amusement, and Kristopher did not dare look at her directly, certain his expression reflected his thoughts.

"Thank you, Sister," he managed to mumble instead.

The door also creaked loudly as it closed, but Michel waited another minute before pulling Kristopher into his arms and holding him tightly. He kissed the top of Kristopher's head. "I shall enjoy having you in my arms tonight." His voice hitched, and he buried his head on Kristopher's good shoulder.

"Michel?" Kristopher asked quietly. He stroked Michel's back, trying to offer comfort. Michel leaned into the touch.

"You can't keep taking risks like that, mon cher." Michel looked at Kristopher. "This is the second time you've put yourself in the line of fire. The next time your luck could run out, and they will kill you."

Kristopher kissed Michel softly. "I had no choice. He was already suspicious, and if he'd discovered my identity papers were false, it would have put all of us at risk." He bit his lip, unsure how to put what he was feeling into words. "I know this mission is important, and this might be selfish of me, but I don't want it to succeed at the price of losing you. Your life is important too."

"It's not to Holm and his men, and I'm not so sure it is to the Allies either." Michel's face shadowed for a moment. "All sides in this war are focused on the job that needs doing, rather than the people involved. It sounds harsh, but I realised that after Corin died. Whatever happens, those who are left keep going and pick up the pieces. They work around whatever or whoever is lost and adapt their plans to fit the new situation."

"That doesn't make it right." Kristopher stroked Michel's hand. "I know no one is indispensable, and that includes me. If I were killed, they'd have to find another way."

Michel swallowed hard. "I don't want to think about you dying." He laughed with a choked, hoarse sound. "This whole situation is crazy. I want a future with you. My mind makes up scenarios for it, although it's never going to happen."

"Why isn't it?" Kristopher shrugged. "There's no harm in planning a future. Hell, I've been doing that too. I thought the feelings I had for you couldn't possibly be mutual, and I was wrong. Je t'aime." He leaned in and kissed Michel long and hard, lingering as long as possible. Michel still tasted of the coffee they'd had over breakfast that morning, and of something else Kristopher couldn't discern. He linked their fingers together and gestured for them to lie down on the bed.

A groan escaped Michel's lips. He wrapped his legs around Kristopher's once they were lying down and in each other's arms, and broke the kiss. "I have nothing to offer you. Once we get to France and the coast, you'll need to go with the Allies to give them the information you have. I belong with the Resistance. What we do is important."

"I could come back to France after the war." Kristopher studied Michel's face for a moment. "We could find a way to be together."

"You're a brilliant man, a scientist. I work on my parents' farm. We could never publicly admit to our relationship. Can you live the rest of your life like that? You've already given up so much." Michel closed his eyes but not before Kristopher saw the pain reflected in them.

"I don't care who knows. I know you love me, and that's all I need." Kristopher blinked rapidly to stop the tears threatening to spill over. "Why can't that be enough?"

"I won't ruin what is left of your life." Michel shook his head. He opened his eyes. He was crying. "I don't know how long that is. Please, Kit, let's just make the most of what we have left together, and let us both cling to our illusions for as long as we can."

"I think," Kristopher said softly, "that it should be my decision as to how I spend the rest of my life." He ran a finger gently under Michel's eyes and wiped the tears, then kissed each cheek. "Neither of us knows what our future will bring, but what we have now, that's our reality. I'm hoping we have at least a few days here. Whatever happens, I want those memories to be good so I can take them with me." He undid the top button of Michel's shirt, kissing the skin there. "I want you to have good memories you can treasure too."

Michel placed his hand over Kristopher's, stilling it. "Are you sure this is something you want to do, mon cher? Your shoulder is still sore. I really should check your dressing first."

"Later." Kristopher took their joined hands and placed them on the top button of his own shirt. "I'm not sure I'm asking for what you think. I will in time, but not now." He wanted their first time to be good, although he had no clue of the details needed to make it so. "I just want to touch you and be touched. I think we both need that."

"Someone could walk in... When I touch you, I want more. I get lost in you. I'm not sure I'd hear anyone until it was too late." Michel glanced nervously at the door. They were already wanted by the Gestapo. If they were caught like this, it would be another excuse for them to be hunted down and captured. "This is a dangerous game."

"We're already playing one just in being here." Kristopher had no intention of risking that either. "If we were under the blankets no one would see. There is only one bed. Sister Magdalene already told us we'd have to share."

Michel was still hesitant. "I'm supposed to be keeping you safe." He brushed back a lock of hair from Kristopher's face. "If something happened, I'd never forgive myself, and I don't trust myself to be able to do that at the moment." He averted his eyes. "I'm tired. I think these last few days are catching up with both of us."

"Then let me look after you for a while." Kristopher placed one finger over Michel's lips when he tried to protest. "I'm tired too, and sore, but there is no harm in touching each other under the blankets before we sleep. We'll both be better for it."

"All right." Michel helped Kristopher stand, and together they pulled back the blankets and crawled underneath them. He placed his arms around Kristopher, drawing him close. "You do need to look after that shoulder, though. Promise me that if it starts to hurt, then we will stop?"

"I promise." Kristopher snuggled in, taking care to lie on his good shoulder. He rested his head on Michel's pillow so they were facing each other. Michel pulled the blankets up over them, then began undoing the buttons of Kristopher's shirt.

"Let me. Please." Michel gently moved Kristopher's hand when he curled it gently around one of Michel's shirt buttons, intent on mimicking the action. "Your shoulder."

"You are beautiful," Kristopher whispered, watching Michel undress.

Michel blushed. "I've never had someone say that to me before." He kissed Kristopher tenderly. "Je t'aime, Kit."

"Je t'aime, Michel," Kristopher replied softly. Their future together might not stretch into the distance like some, but for now, this snatched moment was their reality. It would have to be enough.

Liang continued pacing. He did not like this current situation. While he agreed they had to use whatever available means to rescue Matt from the Gestapo, working with the sister of their enemy was far too high a risk.

"You should sit down," Ken remarked dryly. "You're only going to draw attention to yourself."

"There is no one here apart from us, Lowe," Liang pointed out. They had agreed to meet with Fräulein Dunst in these supposedly safe offices. The last occupant must have left in a hurry. Paperwork was still spread across one of the desks, and an empty, unwashed coffee cup sat on the windowsill. Liang suspected there might be some new life form breeding in it but wasn't about to take a closer look to be sure. "I don't see why it matters."

"It matters because it's distracting as hell." Ken shrugged and seemed to consider his next words carefully. "My name is Ken. We need to trust each other and work together closely."

"So using our first names will magically ensure that happens?" Liang snorted, and immediately regretted his words. He sighed and sat on one of the two chairs in the room. Ed Walker and Trevor Palmer were keeping watch outside. He'd heard them talking before, wondering if they were going to get through this alive.

"Of course not, but I've been told that it's a good start."

"It sounds like something Matthew Bryant would say."

"It was... is." Ken's expression changed to something totally unreadable. "I'm sorry. Shall we start this conversation again?"

Liang could well imagine his grandmother's disapproval of his behaviour. He'd kept to himself since joining this team, not wanting to volunteer any personal information or form any bonds. He was not a trained soldier like the others, and his two PhDs had not prepared him for the reality of being out in the field. He was also well aware that because of his Chinese heritage, he risked far more than they did if his presence was noticed. The part he played in their mission might be an important one, but he still felt like an outsider. "All right."

Ken had always given Liang the impression of not being very interested in social talk. He was a difficult person to get to know, but then Liang was no better. Matt's personality smoothed over the differences within their team, and with his leadership, they worked well together, each getting on with the job required of them.

Liang wasn't convinced they could pull off a mission as complex as this without Matt, but unfortunately his survival depended on them being able to do just that. It wasn't that they were not capable men, but more they were loners rather than team players. This war had forced many people to take on tasks that made them uncomfortable. Liang wasn't sure that was altogether a bad thing. He hoped in this case it was not.

His grandparents were proud of him, and that he was serving his country, although, of course, he could not tell them any details. They would only worry anyway. Having lost their only son and his wife to the influenza epidemic, they doted on Liang, whom they had raised since he'd lost his parents.

Wasn't Ken supposed to be continuing the conversation they were supposed to be starting again? Not that Liang was any better as he'd let his mind wander instead of contributing anything to it. He cleared his throat. "Do you trust this woman?"

"Do we have a choice?"

"That wasn't what I asked. Do you trust her, and if so, why?"

Ken shrugged. "Her words did seem sincere. It's possible to be loyal to your country but not agree with decisions they've made. Those decisions are often made by a minority and inflicted upon the majority."

"She is Holm's sister." Their relationship was the big problem with this scenario, at least from Liang's perspective. "If she has to choose between him and us, or saving

Matthew, she will put family first. She has already shown that by insisting he not be harmed."

"What would you do in her situation, Liang?" Ken picked up a piece of paper off the desk closest to where he was sitting and started to read it.

"My family comes first, but..." Liang wondered why they were having this conversation when Ken was not giving it his full attention. "I could not kill someone. My conscience would not allow it."

Ken looked up at him. "So if someone walked in here now, and you both had a gun, you'd let him or her shoot you because you couldn't kill someone?"

"Of course not."

"Exactly." Ken looked smug, but Liang wasn't finished yet.

"I'd aim for somewhere that would wound rather than kill." Liang couldn't help but feel pleased at the surprised expression on Ken's face.

"Is your aim that good?"

Although tempted to retort with of course it was, Liang honestly didn't know. He could handle a gun, but firing at another human being would be completely different. "Let's hope neither of us ever has to find out, hmm?"

The sound of footsteps in the corridor outside saved Ken from replying. They exchanged a glance, drew their guns, and took cover behind the desks. From their hiding place, they had a good view of the door, but hopefully wouldn't be seen if someone entered.

While they were expecting to meet with Juliane Dunst, it would be foolish to assume she was their visitor. Neither Walker nor Palmer had given the prearranged warning signal, but that did not mean anything. Liang was not ready to trust his life to someone else on the team, and judging by how quickly Ken responded to the interruption to their conversation, neither was he.

The door to the office opened slowly, and someone peered around and scanned the room before entering. The slender blonde woman was impeccably dressed in clothes that clung to her in all the right places. Ken had forgotten to mention how beautiful she was.

"I'm alone," she said.

"You're five minutes early," Ken pointed out, but didn't put his gun away. He stood so she could see him.

"It's impolite for a lady to keep a gentleman waiting twice." She glanced over at Liang and smiled. Her face lit up, and the warmth of it reflected in her deep blue eyes. "Are you going to introduce me to your friend?"

"Fräulein Dunst...," Ken began.

"My name is Zhou Liang, Fräulein Dunst." Liang rose to his feet and bowed slightly. "It's a pleasure to meet you."

"A gentleman with good manners; I'm impressed." Her eyes reflected her amusement. She took a closer look at him and frowned. "You're taking a risk being in Berlin, Herr Zhou." Liang was impressed she was aware of the traditions of his people and had addressed him by his surname. He'd lost count of how many times he had to explain that one to people at the university where he worked.

"We are all taking risks, Fräulein." Liang studied her carefully. She didn't avert her eyes after what he'd said. "It is the way of this war, unfortunately."

"That it is," she agreed, clearing a space on top of the desk where Ken had sat only minutes before. She reached into her bag and brought out a large notepad, which was soon joined by a pencil. "I did not want to be caught with a map of the compound or the institute, as it would be difficult to explain the need for it, so I will have to draw you one." She began sketching a rough map of corridors and offices. "This needs to be destroyed as soon as we are done. If it is discovered, our plan will be compromised before you have the chance to carry it out."

Ken moved closer and examined the map in detail. He ran his finger down one of the lines she'd drawn, noting the corridor separating the sections between where the scientific staff worked and where the prisoners were held. A way would have to be found through the locked doors at each end of it. "I'm presuming entry to this section is well-guarded on both sides. Getting in there and through to the holding area will not be easy. The men will be well-trained."

"That is why we need to wait another day before acting." Juliane sneezed. "Goodness, the amount of dust in here is atrocious. I'm tempted to get someone in to clean." She sighed. "Which reminds me, please remember to not leave patches without dust before you leave, or it will alert anyone who finds this place that someone has used it recently."

"What happened to the previous occupants of these offices?" Liang asked.

"They were Jewish." Juliane ripped the paper from her notebook, repeating the action with the two pages beneath it in case the imprint of the pencil marks had gone through. She wrote an address at the bottom of the map. "There will be two uniforms left here together with identification papers you will have to personalise for whoever uses them. The institute will be having issues with its telephone system over the next day or so, and you will be employees of the company who we call to fix the problem. You'll have to trace the fault from the switchboard and test the cabling leading to each handset in the institute in order to fix it." She glanced at Liang. "You need to keep out of sight. Find someone else to work with Herr Gerber on this one."

Liang snorted. "I'm not foolish enough to volunteer. I know my limitations." He wasn't about to admit he wished he could be a part of this. He respected Matt. He would do what he could to ensure this rescue was a success.

"So we have a plan to get into where Matt is being held." Ken frowned and studied the map. "There is only one way out. Surely someone will notice if we walk out with him? We will be outnumbered, and the chances of winning any kind of gunfight are slim."

"That is the reason you need to wait. The guard on duty tomorrow is sympathetic and prepared to look the other way while you rescue your friend. However, you will need to knock him out and restrain him. This is for his protection, rather than your own." Juliane leaned over the desk and drew an X on the map. "This is the cell where Matt is being kept. If something goes wrong, I can't help you and will deny any knowledge of this plan. Karl trusts me, and if he knows I am betraying that trust, I will not be in a position to help anyone else in the future."

Ken nodded slowly. "That's fair," he agreed.

"I suggest when you find him and overpower the guard, one of you wears the guard's uniform when you leave the building. It would be better if Matt dresses in the clothes you discard. The soldiers at the gate will be expecting two workmen to leave. I have checked the roster and they haven't seen the prisoner, as he was brought in on a shift they weren't there. When you leave in the guard's uniform, keep your head down and don't enter into conversation, or they will be quickly alerted to the deception."

This plan still left too much to chance and good luck. Liang peered at the map, trying to figure out how long it would take them to reach the cells and then make their way out. Passage through the two locked doors was the only escape route, so if things went wrong they'd be trapped. He'd seen the compound very briefly from the outside, but from a distance. The institute building inside was a sturdy structure, built of brick and very well secured. Soldiers guarded the only entrance into the compound, which was surrounded by tall wire fences with barbed wire on top to discourage intruders.

A thought occurred to him. "Is Matthew in a fit condition to make this escape? He will have to walk briskly with no support, at least from the building to the gate. That is a good distance, from what I was able to see."

Ken raised an eyebrow. "I thought I told you to keep out of sight." He sounded more annoyed than concerned.

"I did." Liang shrugged. "I went for a stroll while you were enjoying dinner out." Ken made a nondescript noise that voiced his disapproval more than words would have. "I kept my head down, and did not draw attention to myself." Liang allowed his annoyance to creep into his voice.

"I'm sure you did." Juliane's mouth twitched around the edges. The woman was amused by their conversation. Liang wasn't sure whether he should be insulted or not.

"I'm quite capable of looking after myself," he muttered. "So, is he in fit enough condition to do this or not?" A change of subject seemed in order. He chastised himself for his reaction. This was a serious situation. Why did Ken have to question everything?

Juliane sighed and looked from one to the other. She shook her head. "I'm not entirely sure," she admitted. "I suspect he could be in bad shape. But it is this or he stays where he is, at least until Karl moves him to another location. Once that happens, it will be too late for you to mount a rescue."

"Then we attempt this rescue." Ken tapped an impatient rhythm on the edge of the table with one finger. "We're out of options, and I, for one, am not prepared to leave him there and do nothing." For a moment he sounded desperate and very tired. Liang quietly slid the other chair in next to Juliane's so Ken could sit. He took the offer wordlessly.

"We will not leave him," Liang promised. "As far as I'm concerned, retrieving him is as much a part of this mission as the—" He stopped abruptly, suddenly remembering this was not a subject they should be discussing in front of Juliane.

"It's a terrible thing, this whole business with Dr Lehrer being accused of murder," Juliane said softly. "It has everyone talking."

Ken and Liang turned to stare at her. Did she suspect the nature of their original assignment? Ken had mentioned hearing some of that gossip in the Süße Ecke. "Do you think he did it?" Liang asked cautiously. They knew nothing of the elusive Dr Lehrer, and this might be a good opportunity to rectify that.

"No, I do not." Juliane sounded convinced. "I've known Kristopher for years, since we were children. Our families attend a lot of the same social functions." She smiled wistfully. "I heard him play the violin once. He made the instrument sing in a way I've never heard before. I could never understand why someone of that talent could give it up to dedicate his life to science."

"Sometimes," Liang said slowly, choosing his words, "you have to follow a different path for a while and put your heart's desire to one side."

"Maybe." Juliane shrugged. "Is that something you believe or something you've been told?"

"My grandmother believes it to be true." Liang smiled at the memory of sitting at her knee while she told him stories of her childhood and her life in China before she moved to Britain and then later met the man who would become her husband. "She is a very wise woman."

"I think if you follow that different path, then you also need to make sure you return to your heart's desire." Juliane seemed thoughtful. "There is no point otherwise."

"Sometimes we don't have the luxury to do that," Ken noted, an edge of bitterness in his voice. "None of us chose this war, or the bigotry that has come with it."

"According to Herr Zhou's grandmother, that means we're still on that different path, I would think. Sadly a lot of that bigotry already existed. The war has merely made it more difficult to ignore."

"Yes," Liang agreed. Juliane was not only beautiful but intelligent. He wished they had the time to continue this conversation further. Examining the map again, he wondered whether he should ask her directly about the whereabouts of the plans they were meant to retrieve. "Is there a specific place important paperwork would be kept? I'm presuming with Dr Lehrer now missing, whatever remains of his work would be closely guarded."

"All the papers pertaining to the project are in the safe in Karl's office." Juliane looked at Liang thoughtfully for a moment. "However, I would focus your energy on rescuing your friend. From what I gather, the only person who can provide you with the information you need is Kristopher Lehrer. The plans that were retrieved are incomplete, which is why Karl is so focused on finding him." She glanced at her watch. "I need to go." She stood and both men did likewise. "Be careful and good luck."

"Thank you for your help," Ken told her. "It is appreciated."

"Yes, it is," Liang reiterated. "I hope to see you again one day." If what she said was correct, it made sense to follow her advice. What they needed to undertake in order to free Matt was dangerous enough.

"I'd like that." She cleared her throat, all business again. Was he imagining the slight pink dusting her features? After all, the light was not the best. It did suit her, though, and added a pretty warm glow to her pale complexion. "Don't forget to burn the map and commit all of the information I've given you to memory. When we meet again, I will not know you."

They both nodded their understanding of her position and watched her go. After the door closed behind her, Ken turned to Liang. "Why did you talk to her about your grandmother? I thought you weren't sure we could trust her."

Liang's response was simple, although he couldn't explain the reasoning behind it. "I changed my mind."

CHAPTER SEVENTEEN

Matt stayed silent while the guard was in the cell. The darkness returned once the door slammed shut. He'd lost track of time, and had no idea how long ago the woman doctor had tended his wounds.

It could have been weeks or merely hours.

He ached all over. The cell was cold, the stone floor of his prison freezing against his bare skin. After the doctor had left, they'd made him strip off his clothes and taken everything. He hadn't the energy to protest, or the state of mind, although he did regret the loss of his boots, and with them the small knife hidden in one of the soles.

He brought his knees up to his chest and let his head fall. He hated the dark. Usually he could distract himself long enough to sleep, but that wasn't working here. When he closed his eyes, he not only saw the flames of his childhood nightmares but Elise as a part of it. He couldn't save her. He couldn't save anyone he loved.

A couple of times, he nodded off, finally able to snatch a moment's sleep only to be woken by the guard giving him a swift kick. The man seemed to enjoy the violence he inflicted at regular intervals, but it made Matt all the more determined not to show any weakness.

The doctor had seemed genuinely concerned about him. She'd tended to him as best as she could. He saw her disapproval in the dim light. Holm had referred to her as Dr Lehrer, but that couldn't be right. Surely that was the name of the scientist working on the project?

God, he felt so confused.

Reality and nightmares. Wishful thinking and fact. They were all mixing and merging so he couldn't tell the difference anymore.

Holm could go to hell. He'd said he was only doing his job, but Matt had a mission to complete too.

A groan escaped his lips. He shifted, shivering, the hairs on his back standing on end. Fuck, it was cold in here.

His eyes fluttered closed. He could see Elise. She was smiling, holding out her hand to him. He reached for her, but she was too far away.

Her expression changed, a frown creasing her brow. She looked behind him. He turned, straining to see what had caught her attention. Ken stood there, his hands over his head, raised in surrender.

The three of them were back in the Kaffeehaus. But instead of it being as Matt remembered, the air around them seemed hazy, as though memories and reality were fighting to win their rightful places. The living room was that of the Kaffeehaus, but the stairs off it led to the landing of his childhood home.

Smoke filled the air. Elise and Ken were both coughing. He turned, unsure who needed him more. Elise brought her hand away from her forehead. It was covered in blood. Ken shook his head and took a step further back into the smoke. "We needed to talk, Matt," he whispered. "We needed to talk, and now it's too late. I don't know what I am to you."

"Come back!" Matt called, glancing at Elise, needing direction. He was adrift, treading the uncertainty his life had become. Elise pointed to Ken, then disappeared into the smoke.

Flames flared, growing taller. Ken crumpled to the floor, surrounded by fire, the heat threatening to consume him. Matt dropped to his knees, crawling along the floor where the good air was, just as his mother had taught him.

He had to save Ken before it was too late. Their future was burning, their present already a manuscript of hope blackening to ashes.

Something hard kicked him in the shins.

He woke with a start. Where was he? He looked around for Ken, for Elise, but they weren't there.

The guard placed a small candle on the floor, put his fingers to his lips, and left the cell.

The light burned brightly, giving out tiny wisps of smoke.

Matt whimpered and backed away slowly, yet couldn't stop looking at it. He didn't like the dark.

Ken repacked his radio set into its suitcase. He had not given London all the details of the plan to rescue Matt, but enough so they were aware of the situation and it might be a while before contact was made again. So far he'd managed to make his daily transmissions. He couldn't risk not doing so, in case his superiors took the silence to mean the mission had been compromised. Sending in another team was not the answer. He'd told London he and Liang had the situation under control, although the statement was a bold one and a considerable stretch of the truth. However, if the extraction went according to plan, they would have to leave the area quickly, as Holm would not take kindly to his captive disappearing.

This would probably be the last time he'd use this particular radio. The suitcase was airtight, and Liang had promised to bury it deep so it would not be found. Safe houses were scattered between here and Switzerland. Ken would use one of their crystal sets if necessary or barring that, build one. London had passed along a coded message to a trusted member of the Resistance and arranged a meeting in several days' time. If a member of Ken's team did not turn up for that meeting, London would presume the mission was a failure. They would be on their own.

"It's done," he told Liang, handing him the suitcase. Walker and Palmer had kept watch while Ken made the transmission. He suspected they wanted the time to have one final cigarette to calm their nerves. Walker would be accompanying Ken to the institute. His German mother had taught him her language—he had a Berlin accent like Matt's, and he could read and write German fluently. Palmer had also volunteered, arguing they might need his medical skills. He might not be a trained doctor, but he was a good medic with some experience under fire. However, in the finish, they'd decided Walker should go, as his ability with the language meant he had more chance of passing as German. Ken's first encounter with Juliane had confirmed he would not.

Ken regretted not having taken the time to get to know

Walker and Palmer better. He remembered Matt striking up a conversation with them upon occasion while Ken did not know anything about either of them apart from their names, the reason they'd been chosen for this mission, and they were both British.

"Did they approve of the rescue plan?" Liang had agreed it was a good idea to give sketchy details. Although their transmissions were coded, they still couldn't risk them being intercepted.

"I told them retrieval would be taking place today, nothing more." Ken shrugged. "They asked whether we'd gotten any further in our mission to retrieve the missing 'parcel.' Unfortunately, reception wasn't very clear at that point, so I'm uncertain as to how much of my answer they received."

Liang nodded approvingly. "Once we rescue Matt, we will regroup. Hopefully his recovery will be speedy, and we can continue with the task we were sent here to do."

"Hopefully." Ken wasn't as convinced Lehrer would be easy to find. He and Schmitz had disappeared completely. Perhaps the meeting with the Resistance in a few days' time would shed some light on the matter. But for the moment, it was the least of his concerns. He'd feel less on edge knowing Matt was safe.

Their conversation grew silent, and Ken didn't push to continue it. If Liang felt there was anything more to be said, he'd say it. Ken had gotten to know Liang much better in Matt's absence. Even so, he still didn't know much about him, but then he hadn't shared a lot with Liang either. Their friendship was comfortable, if that was the right word for it. Considering the last few days, Ken thought maybe it was.

Once Ken and Walker entered the institute, Liang and

Palmer would take up position, keeping watch from a safe distance. Juliane had provided not only the uniforms and equipment for their ruse but a vehicle too. When Matt and Walker had driven far enough so they wouldn't be seen, Ken and the others would join them. The truck would be abandoned on the outskirts of Berlin to give the appearance they were attempting to flee the city, which would hopefully make it easier to hide within it.

Ken glanced at his watch and took several deep breaths. So much hinged on this, and there were far too many variables for his liking. One slip and their cover could be blown. He did not like trusting his back to a man he barely knew, especially one as inexperienced as Walker, but as Liang had put it rather bluntly, Ken hadn't exactly been in this situation before either.

"Nervous?" Liang asked softly.

"Yes." Ken picked up his toolkit and checked it over for the last time. Everything in there would pass inspection, but they were not going into this without weapons. His training had shown him how to fight dirty if needed, and he mentally thanked the Technical Division of the OSS for the innocuous-looking pen attached to his clipboard. Hopefully the Germans wouldn't suspect the pen was actually a miniature .22-caliber gun.

"I wish you good luck, my friend." Liang bowed slightly. Ken was pleased Liang hadn't attempted any cheerful reassurances neither of them could guarantee. They understood each other, at least where that was concerned.

"If we are not at the arranged meeting place within twelve hours, you and Palmer are to presume we've been compromised and act accordingly."

"Yes, I know." Something in Liang's expression wasn't as convincing as it should have been, but Ken wasn't in the mood to discuss it further. If this all went to hell, he would have enough to deal with without worrying about the safety of the two remaining members of their team. Liang was an intelligent man and had a high level of self-preservation about him. He'd survive this. He had to.

"Ready when you are, sir." Walker was waiting for them just outside the building. He hid his nervousness well. The institute was a fifteen-minute drive from the apartment where they'd been staying, but they were going to head well away from the area before turning towards their destination from a different direction. It would be safer that way. The time taken for their detour would also give Liang and Palmer the opportunity to get into position.

"Be careful, Ed." Palmer seemed more nervous than Walker. Ken didn't envy the waiting. He'd always preferred to be in the middle of the action rather than sitting on the sidelines not sure what exactly was going on. "You too, sir."

"Drop the formality, hmm?" Liang suggested. "Although Ken's cover is the more senior technician, it would arouse less suspicion if you don't automatically lapse into calling him that or his rank if you get nervous."

Walker nodded. "Yes, si—Dr Zhou." Palmer grinned, amused by the slip. Walker mock glared at him. "Remember, Trev, you owe me a pint."

"How can I forget?" Palmer's grin faded to be replaced by something more solemn. "Get yourself back in one piece, all right? You too, Sarge."

"I was planning to." Ken wondered what the two of them had talked about while he and Liang were having their own conversation inside. He hadn't seen Walker and Palmer this informal, but he'd found from experience that people coped with approaching danger in different ways. Perhaps when this mission was over, they should meet up somewhere for a drink. He suspected Matt would approve of the idea.

Ken handed Walker one set of keys to the van. Liang already had the other, in case. Walker took them, his earlier mood suddenly forgotten. He climbed into the van, started the engine, and waited silently for Ken to join him.

They'd driven several blocks, the figures of Liang and Palmer growing smaller in the rearview mirror, before Walker spoke again. "What do you think the chances are of completing this part of the mission successfully?"

Ken shrugged. "To be honest, Walker—Ed—not good. Although we have a plan and inside help, it's still going to take more luck than anything else."

"Then we'd better start praying, I suppose, Sarge." Walker didn't take his eyes off the road.

"Ken," Ken reminded him softly. He wasn't a religious man and had barely set foot inside a church, apart from the meetings with their contacts here in Berlin, but he wasn't about to argue that point now. "And yes, we had." He shuffled down in the heavy jacket he wore over his overalls. Although yesterday had felt warmer, the cold had returned today. "Perhaps you could pray for both of us."

"You're not a religious man, then?" Walker turned a corner. Another couple of streets and they'd be on a direct route to the institute.

"No." Ken wondered if it was normal to be speaking of these matters under the circumstances. He wasn't ready to be thinking about his own mortality yet, and talk such as this tended to be a prelude to that kind of conversation. He cleared his throat, deciding to shift Walker's thoughts onto other things. "Once we leave the van, conversation needs to be kept to the matter at hand and nothing else. We don't want to draw attention to ourselves."

"The idea of being there makes me nervous," Walker admitted. "I've never been undercover before. I don't know how that bloke, Gabriel, or whatever his name is, managed it."

"You'll be fine," Ken reassured him. "Remember who you're supposed to be rather than you really are, and follow my lead."

"I'm Uwe Breiner and you're Dieter Gerber," Walker said obediently, repeating the cover names on the identity papers they carried. He rattled off the rest of the information they needed to know without hesitation.

Ken opened the bag he carried and double-checked the contents for the last time. His hand shook slightly, but he ignored it. Matt hadn't had the chance to prepare for this role in the same way. What if he wasn't well enough to stand, let alone walk out unaided? There were too many variables in this plan. Another five minutes and there would be no turning back. They'd gotten this far, and Ken had no intention of getting this close to Matt only to leave him behind.

If this failed, so would the rest of their mission. He couldn't allow either of those to happen. Failure wasn't an option. Ken sighed. Three of them against a compound full of trained soldiers. He remembered a story he'd heard as a child about a man walking into a lion's den. While he doubted they'd get the same happy ending, at least he could make sure theirs was a quick and honourable death. God, he hoped it wouldn't come down to that.

He shivered, closing his eyes, and then wished he hadn't when his imagination helpfully supplied images of how the situation might play out. *No!* Until the worst happened, it wasn't real, and he'd hang on to hope with both hands tightly so it had no chance of escape.

A whimper must have escaped his lips.

"Are you all right?" Walker asked. The van was slowing down. Ken's eyes snapped open. He schooled his features into a calm, inexpressive mask.

They were there.

CHAPTER EIGHTEEN

Ken examined the telephone cabling. Whoever had done the repair the last time was good. He mentally gave a low whistle of appreciation. They'd fixed it all right, but ensured the job would only last for so long, therefore leaving an opening to anyone else who might need access to the compound or the institute building within it. No wonder Juliane had been able to provide uniforms and the repair truck to go with them. The guards at the front gate glanced at the identity papers before ushering them in with a comment about "fixing it properly this time."

He straightened and studied the map they'd been provided. Finding the location of the telephone closest to the switchboard, he ran his finger along the cable path to the next one. "The problem isn't just the switchboard," he announced, making sure he was loud enough to be heard, "but I suspect compounded by a fault in one or more of the cables running to the telephones directly connected to it."

"So we'll have to check all of them?" Walker leaned over the map, playing his part well. He had more of an idea of how it all worked than Ken had given him credit for, and knew which tools to hand over when required.

"It appears so." Ken sighed, shaking his head. "I hope this isn't going to be a big job." He made a point of glancing at his watch.

"Is there a problem?" The woman took them both by surprise, as neither man had heard anyone else enter the room. The guard standing by the door hadn't registered her presence either. One of the women operating the switchboard looked up briefly before returning to her duties.

"No, Fräulein," Ken replied politely. "There is more to this job than we anticipated, though."

"Isn't there always?" She was a blonde woman, fairly tall and slim, with an air of authority about her that was probably not wise to ignore. "Do what you need. It is tiresome when the telephone malfunctions, and I am losing patience over it." She peered at Ken closely, looking him up and down.

He repressed the urge to shiver, feeling rather like a small bug being scrutinised before being devoured for supper.

Walker kept busy collecting the tools they'd need and attaching the smaller ones to his belt. He kept his head down but need not have bothered. She ignored him completely.

"We will have to check the cabling throughout the entire building to find the origins of the fault." Ken kept his tone very matter-of-fact.

"Of course you will." Her eyes narrowed. They were a darker blue than Juliane's and as cold as ice. "You seem familiar, Herr...?"

"Gerber, Fräulein." His heart sped up. Surely their cover couldn't be compromised already? She couldn't know who he was. Could she? "I've worked in many different places in Berlin. Perhaps that is why."

"Perhaps." She seemed thoughtful and then shrugged. "Perhaps not. Just find the fault and quickly, Herr Gerber." She turned on her heel and walked out of the room, but not before saying something quietly to the guard on duty.

He clicked his heels together, came to attention, and gave her a salute. "Yes, Fräulein Huber."

Whoever this woman was, at least some of the authority she projected was genuine. The guard's reaction had shown that clearly. Ken hoped they would not run into her again. She did not strike him as someone who would miss much. Not only that, but she'd already had a close look at him, which didn't bode well as he needed to change clothing with the soldier guarding Matt.

Ken pursed his lips. "Come on, Breiner, let's get this job finished as quickly as possible." He grabbed the map, rolled it up, then slid it into one of the pockets of his overalls. He'd already worked out the direction they needed to head in to be closer to the corridor leading to the security wing where Matt was held. They'd test the cabling and telephone jacks along that route so they didn't arouse suspicion, then make their move.

He kept his head down and led the way from the room, Walker following closely. For all his talk of being nervous, once they'd gotten inside the compound, Walker appeared very calm, apart from the slight tremor in his hands.

Pretending to test each telephone jack in turn was a slow job, but Ken didn't want to risk their cover by giving in to impatience. As much as he wanted Matt freed, another half an hour would not make much of a difference.

For the most part, the guards left them to get on with their work yet still did not let them out of sight. One of the offices they passed had the name "Dr Kluge" on it. The door was closed, and a guard was posted outside. When Ken asked about access to the office in order to do his job, he was told it would only be allowed if the fault could not be found elsewhere. What had really happened between Lehrer and Kluge? Once they finally found Lehrer, Ken intended to ask him, although Lehrer's account of the events that day would be tarnished by his point of view. Distinguishing the truth in such situations was difficult, but with the way this mission had gone so far, Ken was more than curious to meet Lehrer and form his own impression of the man.

Juliane passed them at one point. She had on her coat and hat and was carrying her handbag, a file folder tucked under her arm. Ken glanced at her briefly, taking care his interest wasn't long enough to be noticed. As he expected, she kept walking and ignored him. At least she would be out of the building when Matt escaped. Probably a deliberate move on her part, and a wise one at that.

"The next telephone jack should be the right one," Walker said softly, already putting together the one they'd just taken apart and tested. "If it isn't, the fault must be in the cabling in either Kluge's or Lehrer's offices." Lehrer's office was further down the same corridor and as well-guarded as Kluge's. Ken doubted they'd be allowed access to it either.

"I know." Ken wiped his hands on his overalls. He was deliberately taking longer to get to this point of the plan than he should be, yet couldn't push forward, despite sternly reminding himself he was playing with Matt's life. Matt had suffered enough. The time to rescue him was long past.

What the hell was wrong with him? He was scared, but

that was no excuse. They'd gotten this far and wouldn't be turning back.

"Ready?" he asked Walker.

Walker nodded. "As much as either of us will ever be." He finished what he was doing and picked up the tool bag, waiting for Ken to make the next move.

The section of corridor outside the room they were in was empty, save for the guard at one end of it. Another guard approached and engaged him in conversation, both men moving away from the door while they talked. This gave Ken the opportunity he'd waited and hoped for.

Trying not to draw any more attention to themselves, Ken and Walker briskly walked to the next office, making a show of marking it off their list. Once inside, Walker dismantled the telephone jack by the door, spreading his tools out more than usual. Ken glanced at the two guards outside. They were still talking.

He quietly made his way to the unguarded door leading to the next section of the corridor and slipped through it. Walker would remain in his current position, working and keeping guard. If someone asked, he would tell them Ken had needed to use the bathroom and would be back in a few minutes. When Ken returned, they'd finish fixing the telephone jack they had open, discover it was the problem, and then they would walk out of the compound.

If all went well, it wouldn't be Ken who walked out with Walker, but Matt.

The drop in temperature was obvious as soon as Ken closed the door behind him. He'd expected the corridor to be longer. A row of single lightbulbs illuminated the windowless area. He cautiously tested the door at the other end of it and peered through once it was open, but as Juliane had promised, it was unguarded. It didn't take long to make his way down the flight of stairs leading into the lower level that housed the prisoners. Staying on the same level would have led him to Holm's office and command center. With the way the two sections were separated, the scientists involved in this project in one part of the building wouldn't have needed to venture into the other.

If a prisoner was lucky enough to escape as far as the connecting corridor, it would also be fairly easy to lock both ends of it once they were inside. Ken shivered, not wanting to focus on that right now. He was all too aware he and Matt could still be caught in that same trap.

The holding area was a dismal place, consisting of a row of doors with what appeared to be an air vent at the top of each one. A separate square metal flap, with a handle attached to open it, was also built into the top of each door. No doubt it was there to check on the prisoners without the need to actually open the door itself.

The one guard glanced up when Ken entered, and reached for his gun. Ken took a deep breath and whistled the opening phrase of Glenn Miller's "A String of Pearls." The guard stared at Ken as though he had lost his mind. Could he be overpowered before raising an alarm? God, which of these cells was Matt in? The guard had a ring full of keys hooked onto his belt. Even if he could be subdued, it would take several minutes just to find Matt, let alone free him.

Ken tensed, ready to fight, but then his potential opponent smiled crookedly and whistled the answering phrase— the last five bars of the piece.

The guard put one finger to his lips when he saw Ken visibly relax, a reminder they needed to be silent. If the other prisoners heard their conversation and were persuaded to share that information, it would compromise the guard's cover. He was already taking an enormous risk helping Matt escape.

Ken nodded to show his understanding and followed the guard to the second door from the end of the row. The guard opened the door, and its occupant blinked rapidly against the sudden light.

Oh God.

Although Ken had expected the worst, he still wasn't prepared for this. Matt's eyes looked wild. He edged back against the wall, a not-quite whimper escaping his lips. His hands were cuffed behind him, and he was naked. A single candle must have lit the room at some point, but had burnt down to nothing. Matt shivered and tried to turn away.

"It's all right," Ken whispered hoarsely. He knelt beside Matt, and looked him up and down, checking for injuries, then wished he hadn't. His face flamed and his breath hitched. Even like this, dirty and bruised, Matt was breath-taking, just the right combination of lean yet muscular. Ken swallowed, a mixture of embarrassment and annoyance running through him. This definitely was not the time or place for having those kinds of thoughts. He averted his eyes, hoping Matt hadn't noticed. "It's Ken."

Lips pressed against his as Matt leaned in and kissed Ken hard. *What the...?* Ken froze, too shocked to react, to even return the kiss.

Matt was breathing heavily when he broke it. "Ken?" Relief and terror crossed Matt's face in rapid succession. "Oh God, you're real." He stared behind Ken and tried to stand. "I told you to leave me! You fucking idiot. Get out of here."

"I'm not leaving without you."

"I gave you an order." Matt pulled away, a tone in his voice Ken hadn't heard before, a tremor that suggested he was fighting his own emotional battle. "Now get out." Matt looked down, as though embarrassed to meet Ken's eyes, or scared of what he'd see there.

"No." The word came out little more than a whisper. This must be a dream, it had to be. Matt had kissed him. Ken stood, then turned to the guard, who was waiting in the corridor just outside. The cell was very small, barely enough room for both of them, let alone a third person. "Do you have the keys to his handcuffs? I need your uniform too." He hesitated. The cell was very cold and the man might be here some time. "Don't worry about removing your under-garments. You'll need them."

"I don't have the keys. Only Holm does, sorry. You'll have to pick the lock." The guard began to remove his uniform.

Inside the lining of Ken's overalls was a fine wire that could be used for the job. Palmer had sewn one into both uniforms, insisting they might need it. Ken mentally thanked him and crouched on the concrete floor, gesturing for Matt to turn around. The cold seeped through the coarse material of his overalls as he shuffled closer. It would be far worse against bare skin. How long had Matt been in here? Ken's eyes narrowed. He swore under his breath, wishing he could kill the person responsible.

His fingers fumbled, his vision suddenly blurring. He blinked, clearing it. They didn't have time for this. Matt was not going to stay here a moment longer. Focusing, he jiggled the wire with more force than he'd intended, and the lock opened. The handcuffs fell to the floor.

"Ken?" Matt stared at him. Distracted, Ken hadn't noticed Matt had changed position so they were facing each other. Not sure he could trust himself to speak, Ken began to remove his clothes. "What are you doing?" Matt looked over Ken's shoulder, watching the guard outside do the same. "This is too dangerous. What the hell are you thinking? Are you even thinking?"

"No." Ken replied. "We don't have time for this conversation now. We can argue about it later. You're not staying here to do…"

Matt stood, leaning against the wall for support. He swayed. Ken instinctively put out his arms to offer support. Matt turned into the wall, and Ken got a clearer look at his back. "Oh my God," he breathed.

"I don't want that bastard near you," Matt said roughly, not moving. "Please, Ken. Get out now while you still can."

Matt could be stubborn as hell when he put his mind to it, although he didn't often show that side of his personality. Usually he used humour to defuse a situation, but it was past that now.

Ken was determined to win this argument, at least for now. He finished removing his overalls and the vest he wore underneath and handed them to Matt. "Get dressed," he ordered. "This is decided. Don't waste your breath arguing as it won't work."

As Matt took the clothing, he brushed his fingers against Ken's, then glanced at the door. The guard had his back to them, probably to give Matt some privacy, considering the state they'd found him in. A look crossed Matt's face— desperation, sadness, and something else Ken couldn't place.

"Get dressed, Matt." Ken glanced at his watch and took a step towards the open door. This was taking too long. He cupped Matt's face, lifting his head so they were facing each other directly. "I love you, you idiot," he murmured so only Matt could hear. Making sure they did not have an audience, Ken kissed Matt gently on the lips.

"I won't leave you. I expect you to be dressed when I come back in here with the guard. Do you need any help?"

Matt shook his head. For once he didn't seem to know what to reply. His eyes were bright, with a hint of their usual sparkle. He began to pull on his clothes. Ken turned and walked out, struggling to comprehend what had just happened.

The guard was growing impatient. "You are running out of time," he muttered. "Is he well enough to do this?"

"Yes." Ken took the uniform and put it on quickly. The fit was a little loose in places, but it would have to do. He only needed to play the part for however long it took to walk out past the guards at the gate. "Ready?" he asked the man. "Thank you for doing this."

"Make it look good. If I'm caught, then I can't help anyone else." His tone sounded light, yet it was impossible to miss the underlying edge. If the assistance he'd given was discovered, the penalty for collaboration with the enemy would be harsh.

Matt stood in the doorway of his cell. He still looked unsteady, yet seemed determined not to show it. Once he slipped into character, he would show no sign of being anything but the telephone technician he was supposed to be. Matt was good at pretending to be something he wasn't and had the inner strength needed to be convincing. Ken doubted Holm would have learned anything from Matt about the true nature of their mission. Matt was far too stubborn for that.

The handcuffs dangled from one hand. "You'll need these." Matt slipped out of the cell, allowing Ken to cuff the guard. Once the guard was secured, Ken muttered an apology and threw a punch. He caught the unconscious guard and lowered him to the floor as gently as he could, not wanting to injure him any more than necessary.

The cell door clanged slightly when he shut it. "There is a door leading to a corridor on the first landing of the stairs. On the other side of that corridor, you'll find Ed Walker finishing off work on a phone jack in the office closest to the door. His name is Uwe Breiner. You're Dieter Gerber. You got lost trying to find the bathroom, which is why you were not where you were meant to be. I'll follow once you're clear so we're not seen together." He managed a smile. They were alone. He caressed Matt's face. Whatever happened now, at least they both knew how they felt about each other.

Matt placed his hand over Ken's for a moment. "I'm sorry."

"It's done and I'm not." Ken shook his head. "You shouldn't be either. Now go." He watched Matt turn and walk out the door, his footsteps growing steadier, although he didn't quite hide the cautiousness in the way he moved. Once they were out of here, he would get the medical attention he needed. Ken would make sure of it.

That woman was beginning to irritate him. Karl grimaced and drained the remainder of his nearly cold coffee. He'd sworn to take no notice of her, but now the idea she'd planted in his mind was taking hold, and he could not get rid of it.

He'd talked to the guard posted on the gate. The men fixing the telephones had shown their identity papers, and nothing was out of place. Margarete's notion that one of them seemed familiar was ridiculous, yet when pressed, she refused to explain the reason why. He knew her well enough to know she was hiding something, but she was stubborn, even more so than the man presently residing in one of the cells who kept insisting he was a member of the clergy.

His pile of paperwork was already behind schedule, and he needed to obtain the peace of mind required to finish it. He sighed. He didn't have time for this. But did he dare do nothing when there could be a security breach in progress?

Damn the woman. Karl slammed down his cup and stood. He'd make an unscheduled inspection of the compound and ensure the route he chose took him to where these men were working. He'd then return to his desk and put the conversation behind him.

She'd be amused, and no doubt her contacts would not hesitate to keep her informed of what he'd done. Nothing happened without her knowledge. He smirked. That, of course, was one reason why this whole incident with Lehrer annoyed her so much; she hadn't foreseen it. No wonder she wanted to be present for his interrogation. No one made a fool of her without there being a price collected for it.

Upon leaving his office, he noticed Juliane was not at her desk. The files he'd asked her to deliver were taking a little longer than anticipated. Still, it was nothing unusual, as often she would stop at the Süße Ecke to buy coffee on her way back to the institute. She claimed it was better than what was available at the institute, but he didn't agree. Since the war had begun, nothing tasted quite the same. They'd all had to make sacrifices for the good of the Fatherland. In the grand scheme of things, this was not one of much significance.

Juliane had led a sheltered life. He would have expected her duties here to have widened her outlook somewhat, but her priorities had changed little since he got her the position. Very few staff members knew of their relationship, and it was better that way. Karl might have done the right thing in looking after his sister, but he could not allow any appearance of favouritism to risk the authority he possessed in his role as head of security. He had worked hard to prove his loyalty and would do whatever was needed to keep doing so.

His first stop would be the switchboard. If the technicians were still fixing the fault in the cable, they would not yet have returned there. If the job was finished, it would be easy enough to locate them at a point between there and the front gate of the compound. With Lehrer still to be apprehended and the prisoner uncooperative, Karl was not about to take any chances.

A brief exchange with one of the switchboard operators confirmed the fault had been found and the technicians were on their way out. Karl nodded his thanks, having discovered very early on that people tended to give more information if spoken to politely rather than given an order. He glanced at his watch and smiled. He'd take the shorter of the two routes between here and the front gate and intercept them before they got that far. Another five minutes and this foolishness of Margarete's would be dismissed, and he could return to his paperwork.

The shorter of the technicians looked up in surprise when Karl stepped out in front of them. "Heil Hitler!"

"Heil Hitler!" Both men replied in unison, although he couldn't help but notice the taller one kept his head down. That in itself was suspicious. Perhaps there was something in what she'd told him after all.

"Identity papers, please." Karl kept his tone pleasant and nonthreatening. He'd had enough of having to resort to other means to attempt to ensure cooperation of late, and wanted this over as quickly as possible.

The shorter man handed over his papers. Karl looked over them carefully, noting everything seemed in order. "Thank you, Herr Breiner." Breiner seemed relieved when they were returned to him. That was nothing unusual. The harsh penalties were in place with good reason, for those caught without them. Karl gave the technician a final visual examination. He definitely did not seem familiar. If anything, his appearance was unremarkable, although he did appear to be rather more nervous than Karl expected. "You haven't worked here before?"

"No, Herr SS Standartenführer," Breiner confirmed. He adjusted the tool bag he carried, his knuckles whitening almost imperceptibly around the handle.

Karl smiled. "There is no need to concern yourself, Herr Breiner, unless you have something to hide. This is merely an extra security measure. One can never be too careful."

"Yes, sir." Breiner relaxed a little, but did not quite lose the tremor in his voice. His reaction after being stopped by a SS officer was not unusual. Their reputation tended to precede them.

The other technician held out his hand, offering his papers. He had anticipated the request for them and acted accordingly. Karl nodded approvingly. Some degree of initiative was to be encouraged, even if too much risked disrespect towards a superior officer. Finding men who possessed the right balance between the two was the key.

Karl scanned the papers quickly. They, too, seemed in order. "Thank you, Herr Gerber." Gerber nodded, but kept his head down. "Look up when you're spoken to," Karl ordered. Breiner glanced at Gerber, but kept his own expression neutral. Something was definitely going on here. Karl instinctively reached for his gun, but didn't draw it just yet, although he kept his hand on it, just in case. "Gerber?" he prompted when the man did not immediately comply.

"Herr SS Standartenführer Holm." The tone was polite but resigned, the voice instantly recognizable.

"Priest!" *Verdammt.* How had the prisoner managed to escape custody? Karl narrowed his eyes. He drew his gun and gestured for both men to raise their hands. A ripple of annoyance chased his anger. Margarete had nearly cost him his prisoner. She should have raised the alarm the very moment she'd seen him, not merely hinted he was posing as a telephone technician.

Gerber—although it was doubtful that was in fact his name—glanced behind Karl, his eyes widening in what could only be fear. Careful to keep his gun trained on his prisoners, Karl turned to the side to see what had got Gerber's attention.

Margarete walked towards them with two guards several steps behind her, flanking another man. She smiled when she saw Karl's prisoners, her eyes sparkling as soon as she recognised Gerber. "My," she exclaimed, "I see you've had your own successful hunting party, Herr SS Standartenführer."

"Fräulein Huber, what is the meaning of this?" Karl did not bother to hide his displeasure. He'd had quite enough of her games for one day.

The guard in custody raised his head. Karl gasped. "Lowe?" *But how?* The man standing in front of him was the spitting image of the American who had killed his father.

CHAPTER NINETEEN

Michel pulled the woollen coat around him more tightly. The sun would be setting soon, and the weather was definitely deteriorating. Despite the coolness, he did not regret taking Sister Claire's suggestion that he and Kit get some fresh air. The front gates were shut and would remain so until the bell rang to let the sisters know they had visitors. That gave ample warning for them to make their way to the back stairs and into the safety of the attic, especially as the pond and the land around it at the back of the convent couldn't be seen from the gate or the driveway.

"Are you warm enough?" Kit sat on the wooden bench next to the pond, shuffling along to give Michel room to sit next to him.

"I'm fine." Michel couldn't help but smile. In the few days since they'd arrived, Kit had regained a lot more of his strength. The wound would take a bit more time to heal, but the seepage was much less than it had been. His shoulder was still sore, and he favoured it when he moved, but it was only noticeable when he was tired.

Kit glanced up at the windows overlooking them and

slipped his hand into Michel's, squeezing it. With having to sit close to share the bench, their linked hands would not be seen from a distance. They couldn't risk anything else. One day when the world was a different place, they would be able to share a kiss in public without having to hide their relationship. Michel wondered if that would happen within their lifetime. He hoped so.

"It's beautiful here," Kit said softly. "It's been too long since I've taken the time to enjoy the simple things in life. It's only now I'm realising just how long."

"You will love the countryside outside Paris." Michel wanted to see Kit's reaction to it. They'd spoken a little about music the night before, and Michel had glimpsed how Kit must have been before he'd become so absorbed in his chosen path. He was a brilliant scientist, but in his dedication to that had obviously prioritised it over another, equally important, side of himself.

"I want to see it." Kit smiled, a genuine expression Michel enjoyed seeing. Although they both knew their time here was limited and merely a temporary refuge from the reality of their need to escape from Nazi Germany, Kit seemed determined to make the most of each day they had together. The weariness associated with his wound wasn't the only thing lifting from him. So was the stress of his work. In the months Michel had watched Kit, he'd only taken one day's break. Even that had been because he was sick and sent home and told to rest.

"Perhaps you will be able to return to France after the war," Michel suggested. They would have to pass through there on their way to the Channel, where they would say their goodbyes. There would probably not be time for another respite like this, and certainly no opportunity to stop and admire the scenery.

"I will come back to you." Kit bit his lip, his eyes clouding over with the change in his mood. One or both of them would probably not survive this war.

"I'll wait for you." Michel tried to keep his tone light, but it came out hoarser than he intended. He didn't want Kit to leave, but it was unreasonable to put his own wishes and desires first. Too many people depended on the success of this mission.

Kit was quiet for a moment. "I keep visualising the life I want. It's not the path I know I will have to take." His grip loosened on Michel's hand. He stood and walked over to the pond, staring out across it. "The water here is clean and clear on the surface, but you look beneath, you become aware of the weeds and the darkness underneath. They threaten to swallow everything about it that is good."

"Then we have to make sure they're kept trimmed back to a level where that won't happen." Michel put his hands in his pockets before joining Kit at the edge of the water. He wanted so badly to pull Kit close and hold him tightly. To kiss him and reassure him he wasn't on his own in this. God, it was so unfair that they couldn't share a simple gesture of affection unless they were alone.

"I'm not sure that's possible. There's too much darkness." Kit wasn't only talking about the water. "Being with you these last few days has given me more hope than I've had since all this started."

"It's not a path that needs taking yet, mon cher." Michel surveyed their surroundings. The convent was quiet; the sisters were at evening prayer. He risked brushing his fingers against Kit's cheek. Kit leaned in for a moment before moving back to an acceptable distance. "Tell me about the future you want, Kit."

Kit nodded slowly, yet didn't quite meet Michel's gaze.

"It's after the war. We're in France, living together. It's in the country so we can sit outside in the evening if we please. There is enough privacy so it is safe to hold each other or kiss if we want to." He looked out across the water again.

"That sounds very much like the future I want too," Michel confirmed softly. "I also promised you a duet." One of his cousins had an old violin. He was sure a few words would ensure Kit would be able to play it, if he so wished.

"I'd like that." Kit sighed wistfully. His voice dropped to a whisper. "I put my violin down, and you wrap your arms around me, holding me. We kiss, and you ask me whether I'm happy with the choices I've made in life."

"Are you?" Michel couldn't help but ask the question.

"I don't know." Kit shook his head and turned to look at Michel directly. "I can visualise those few moments, but that's all."

"We've all done things we're not proud of." Michel wondered if Kit would ever completely let go of the guilt he carried for his part in this project. "You're happy with that future, though?"

"Yes. I want it so much, but I'm not sure how we're going to get there. If you'd asked me whether I was happy with our life together, I could say yes, but as to the choices I've made..." Kit shook his head. "I don't want to hurt you."

"You love me, and you want a future with me," Michel said firmly. "The rest of it is just details of the journey along the way. We'll face those together."

"I hope so." Kristopher grew quiet again. He had a tendency to brood, often becoming lost in his own thoughts and emotions, especially when contemplating situations over which he felt he had little to no control.

"Do you want to still watch the sunset together?" Returning to the safety of the attic was becoming more of a temptation, especially as they did not need to be as guarded there. Distracting Kit from his mood once they were alone would be far easier.

"Yes, of course." Kit sounded surprised. Realisation crossed his features, followed by regret. "I'm sorry. I didn't mean to inflict my melancholy on you."

"You haven't." After checking once more they didn't have an audience, Michel took Kit's hand and led him back over to sit on the bench. "When you love someone, it's for better and for worse. I have my moments of melancholy just as you do." He leaned in closer, lowering his voice. "Once we're inside, I intend to distract you from your mood."

Kit's eyebrow rose. "How are you going to do that?" The innocent smile on his face was belied by the humour in his voice.

"Perhaps I need to remind you of what we did last night, hmm?" Michel chuckled at the speed with which the smile was replaced by a much more eager one. Although they still hadn't done much more than kiss and caress, exploring each other's bodies was very enjoyable. Kit was extremely responsive and loved being touched. He was also a quick study and had already learned where Michel's sensitive spots were. Despite the chance they were taking, and what would happen if they were caught, Michel found it difficult to stop. He didn't dare risk completely losing himself in Kit by allowing them to move to the next step in their relationship. As much as he wanted it, being with Kit completely wasn't safe. At least with the covers over them, and still partially clothed, they could feign sleep if the attic door opened.

"I enjoyed what we did last night." Kit studied Michel intently. He definitely had something on his mind. His next words were hesitant with a hint of shyness. "Have you ever been with another man?"

"I've been with you," Michel replied cautiously, not ready to have this conversation unless Kit truly wanted it.

Kit shook his head. "We've kissed and touched, but we've not given ourselves to each other completely." He swallowed, pink tingeing his cheeks. "We haven't... made love."

"I've had sex with another man, but that's all it was." Michel had no intention of hiding his past from Kit, but didn't want to hurt him either. "We were friends, but we weren't in love with each other. I didn't have the same feelings for him I do for you."

"I see." Kit seemed to relax, although he was still flushed. He looked down. "It was foolish of me to think I was your first. I'm sorry."

"There's nothing to be sorry about." Michel sighed. "I wish you could be my first, but at the same time, I'm pleased I have some experience because I don't want to hurt you."

"You wouldn't. I trust you." Kit's words were spoken with such emotion they made Michel's breath hitch.

"I trust you too." Although most of his memories of François were good, they were tinged with sadness and grief.

"Tell me about him." Kit genuinely seemed to want to know. He frowned, his voice softening. "Did something happen between you?"

"He was a friend." Michel's thoughts drifted back to the past. The more intimate he and Kit became, the harder it was for Michel to hide his emotions. He'd shared more about himself over the past week than he had in a very long time. It took a moment to form his words. Kit didn't prompt any further, but instead waited patiently. If Michel didn't want to share any more, he didn't need to, but he didn't want any secrets between them. "François and I had known each other since we were children. By the time I was out of my teens, I knew without a doubt I wasn't interested in girls."

"Did anyone else realise?"

Michel shrugged. "I didn't think so. I already had a reputation for not being very social, and I was careful to hide the reason why. But I wasn't careful enough. François and I were celebrating my birthday, and we were both very drunk. He..." Michel's cheeks grew warm. "He kissed me. It felt good." It hadn't taken long for one thing to lead to another, especially as they were alone. He'd had no idea François had felt that way. The shock of it had quickly been followed by relief he wasn't alone, to guilt that François had feelings Michel could not return.

"Kissing you is wonderful." Kit's matter-of-fact tone lacked any sign of jealousy.

"Are you sure you want to hear this?" Michel still missed his friend some days. He'd lost too many people he cared about over too short a time. François was another reason Michel was scared of losing Kit to the likes of Holm and his men.

"Yes. I don't begrudge you being with someone else." Something in the way Kit spoke made Michel look at him directly.

"We had sex in the barn, more than just once. It was good, but I didn't love him." Michel still remembered the moment he'd admitted as much to François, and the hurt expression he'd seen before François had covered it.

"But he loved you." Kit sighed. "That was my fear when I first realised I was falling in love with you. I hoped you felt the same way, but I wasn't sure."

"That was my fear with you too." Although François hadn't begrudged him his feelings or lack thereof, Michel still felt bad about it. "We remained friends and trusted each other with our secret, but it wasn't the same after that." Michel had vowed he'd never again have sex with a man he didn't love. He wouldn't risk hurting someone the way he'd hurt François.

"Je t'aime." Kit squeezed Michel's hand. He was silent, obviously thinking through something. "It's going to hurt François if he sees us together, isn't it? He knows you, and he might figure it out."

Michel shook his head. "No." He took a deep breath. "François is dead, Kit. He died at the same time as Corin." He closed his eyes, the memory as clear as the night it happened. The meeting was a trap, and they'd walked right into it. Michel had escaped merely because he'd gone back to pick up something Corin had forgotten. Even so, he arrived just in time to duck for cover before Corin, François, and three of their friends were gunned down by the Germans.

"Oh God. I'm so sorry." Kit's eyes widened and a look of frustration crossed his face. He moved closer to Michel.

"So am I," Michel whispered. Damn, he was tired of this, of all the months of hiding his grief and pretending he was all right. No wonder it hadn't taken Kit long to break through all those barriers. Elise had noticed the difference merely watching Kristopher and sharing a few words with him made. Hopefully no one else would. He would do whatever it took to prevent the love he and Kit shared to be used against either of them. Holm already had enough reason to hunt them down without giving him another one. However much Michel wanted Kit to hold him right now, risking it in the open where they might be seen was not an option.

He was scared they might lose each other before they'd had the chance to be together properly. Being with François, a man he liked but did not love, had still felt so very good. Michel wanted that and more with Kit. He wanted to give himself to Kit in a way he hadn't been able with François. But once he did, he wouldn't hold anything back.

"Je t'aime, Kit." He wanted to say so much more, but they were both already frustrated with not being able to kiss or hold each other. To hell with the sunset. Michel stood. "Let's go inside." The sky was beginning to darken quickly, faster than expected. Already fine rain was beginning to fall. The clouds above them looked angry. A storm was brewing.

Kit didn't move. He murmured something under his breath, hesitantly almost nervously. "You... I want to be able to... Dear God, I'm sick of this."

"I want to hold you, to kiss you when you're hurting, to walk out here and hold your hand." Michel sat down again.

"Is it ever going to be truly safe?" Kit swallowed. Even in private, it wasn't really, no matter how much they tried to convince themselves they were being careful. "I want you, Michel. Every time I touch you, that feeling grows stronger. But I'm scared if we keep putting it off, it will never happen."

"It will." Michel wasn't as convinced as he hoped he sounded. "We'll find a way. I promise." He slid along the bench, closing the distance between them. "I don't know how much longer I can wait."

"Then don't." Kit brushed his fingers lightly across Michel's knee. "Each morning I wake up in your arms and wonder if this will be the last time it will happen. I feel as though we're living on borrowed time, that Holm and his men will find us and we'll lose what we have together."

"You want to make love."

Kit was right. The longer they waited, the less chance they'd get the opportunity to do so.

Kit nodded. "I know the risks. We can bolt the attic door and make some excuse for why we have. If…" His voice faltered. "I want to be with you. I don't want to…" He trailed off.

"Die without knowing we've at least had that," Michel finished the sentence, putting what they both feared into words.

"It's not just me taking the risk." Kit's fingers trembled. He shoved his hands into his pockets. "Do you really think we should wait?"

Michel licked his lips. A drop of water trickled down Kit's forehead onto his nose. Michel wondered what it would be like to lick it off. "Yes. Logically I think yes."

"But?" The hope in the word was unmistakable.

"Life is short. I want my future to be with you, however long it is." He leaned in, his voice dropping to a whisper. For the moment, they were safe. With what was ahead of them, things could, and probably would, get a whole lot worse. At least if it did, they'd have this memory to cling to, even if they no longer had each other. "Just for tonight, I say we ignore that logic and follow our hearts instead."

He clung to her, crying her name over and over. When she wouldn't open her eyes, he called for his father, hoping he, at least, would wake. Finally, worn out, he crawled into bed with them, knowing they'd keep him safe. The room was chilly, his mother's skin cool to the touch, his father holding her tightly in his arms, as if he never wanted to let her go.

The bed shook. He heard someone scream. Someone tugged at him. He lashed out, not wanting to be pulled away, not this time. If he let go, he'd never see either of them again.

Why was it so cold? The screaming grew louder, a wail that could not be silenced. He closed his eyes tightly, willing it to go away, to leave him alone.

"Dr Zhou?" The voice grew more urgent. "Liang? You have to wake up."

Liang opened his eyes, disorientated and still lost in the dreams and memories of his past. "Let me go," he muttered crossly, the ghost of the little boy still lingering as he groggily focused on the reality of his present.

"Sorry, sir."

His vision swam in and out. He focused and saw Trevor Palmer's face in front of him.

"I should be the one apologising." Liang hadn't had one of those dreams in years. The current situation was taking its toll on all of them. He frowned. The noise was still there. With a jolt, he realised what he was hearing. All around them was darkness, the torch Palmer held barely enough light to see by. "What's happened? How long is it since the air raid sirens started?"

"A couple of minutes ago." Palmer glanced around, moved back to the window, and peered outside, trying to get a good look at the sky above. He was nervous, and rightfully so. "I can't see anything because of the cloud cover."

"You did the right thing in waking me." Liang stood, his limbs stiff, sharp pain running through him when he moved. The hard concrete floor was not an ideal bed in any sense of the word. He'd feel better once he began moving properly. They had to get out of here. The apartment building would not survive a direct hit, and he'd prefer to be closer to the ground once the bombs began to fall.

A bright flash momentarily lit up the darkness.

Palmer swore under his breath. He tilted his head to the side as though listening.

The air around them was still and silent. The earlier storm had blown over but left low-lying clouds over Berlin that would play havoc with the visibility needed by aircraft, either friend or foe.

"Bloody hell." Palmer grabbed Liang's arm.

They ran for the door.

"What?" This day was going from bad to worse. They'd waited for several hours watching the institute, hoping for a clue as to what was going on. Ken and the others had been in there too long. Something had definitely gone wrong. The van was still parked where Walker left it, which was also odd. The façade of normalcy made Liang more uneasy than if Holm obviously sounded an alarm and started to search the surrounding area for any sign of accomplices. What was the man up to?

In the end, he and Palmer had retreated for the night, taking refuge from the weather in a nearby apartment house. No point in all of them being caught, and they'd reassess the situation in the morning. Liang knew the name and location of the restaurant where Ken and Juliane had met. Tracking her from there would not be easy, but they only had the one lead, apart from the Süße Ecke. While Liang was not happy about involving her further and compromising her position, he would if there was no other choice. Surely she'd be able to shed some light on the matter or point them in the direction of someone who could.

He didn't want to contemplate leaving the rest of their team in the custody of Holm and his men.

Palmer didn't reply until they were at the bottom of the staircase and clear of the building. A pale blue light shone in the distance, signifying the entrance of an air raid shelter, but if they took refuge in it, there would be too many questions. "Thought I heard engines," he explained, still catching his breath. "Lancaster. Still can't see anything, though. Bloody weather."

Searchlights lit up the sky. Storm clouds flashed white. The ground shook. A loud booming noise filled the air.

"Down!" Palmer yelled, dragging Liang further away from the building. Glass shattered from the windows, shards hitting the pavement below. Both men covered their heads with their hands and ducked down.

"The institute!" Liang said. "Come on." If the building was damaged or destroyed, it might give Matt and the others a way out in the confusion. Liang started to run, Palmer behind him. The ground shook again. A woman screamed in the distance, and a baby began to cry.

A wall crumbled, missing them by barely a foot. Palmer prayed as they ran, pausing to dodge rubble and people.

The streets were still dark. The blacking out of streetlights must have gone into effect as soon as the Germans had picked up the potential enemy in their airspace through the first of their network alarms.

Liang stumbled. Palmer steadied him and offered the torch. Liang shook his head. Another flash was closely followed by yellow flames as the timber of internal walls started to burn. The fire lit up the sky, providing the light he needed to see.

He hesitated just for a moment, trying to get his bearings, and then began to run again. With all the confusion, no one was paying any attention to two men sprinting through the streets. Ahead of them, the institute and the compound around it came into view. The front gates were open, one of the surrounding wire fences flattened.

The building was on fire.

CHAPTER TWENTY

Matt banged on the door of his cell, frantic for a response. What the hell was going on out there? The ground shook again. His shoulder hit the wall, and he bit back a cry of pain. At least, this time, he wasn't handcuffed. Not that it made it any easier for him to escape.

Where was Ken? How did Holm know him? Matt didn't believe for a moment Ken could be a double agent, but none of this made sense. Holm had referred to Ken by name, although Ken had seemed just as shocked by that as Holm. When Holm had then asked Ken for his father's name, Ken seemed to close down, a curtain falling over his features, and he refused to answer.

Matt and Walker had been dragged away then, leaving Ken alone with Holm, who ordered his new prisoner be taken to his office. Walker seemed just as confused as Matt, if not more so, and scared. The discovery of the guard, restrained but now conscious, in Matt's cell earned both him and Walker a punch in the stomach before they were shoved into separate cells. Holm would deal with them later.

Fräulein Huber looked extremely satisfied when Holm had seen Ken. She'd smiled and looked Ken up and down after making a comment about how much he looked like his father. Could his father have been the double agent? Matt shook his head in frustration. As much as he wanted to know what was behind the fixation with Patrick Lowe, he was more terrified of what they'd do to Ken.

The look Holm had given Ken when he'd "recognised" him was disturbing, to say the least. The realisation had given way to a mixture of triumph and anger, which wasn't a good combination, especially with Ken on the receiving end of it.

"Open the damn door!" Matt hissed after yelling the words, the sharp intake of breath sending pain through his chest. He was sure one of his ribs was bruised, if not broken. The rest of him wasn't feeling that great either. His back was better than it had been but was still tender. He was tired, hungry, and thirsty, not having eaten or drunk anything since first thrown into this hellhole.

He banged on the door again, this time kicking it as well. The panicked voices outside were muffled by the thickness of the door and walls between them. The flap in the door opened. One of the guards peered in. Keys jangled, and the door opened. Behind him, chaos erupted as an explosion rocked the cell block. He could smell smoke.

Matt bit his lip, instinctively taking several steps back. Not fire. Anything but that.

The guard waved his gun. "Out!" he ordered.

Matt shook his head. "Like hell," he muttered, not about to give this man an excuse to kill him under the pretense he was attempting to escape. He wanted to know what was going on first.

"Do you want to die?" The guard gestured with his gun. Movement behind the guard made him whirl just in time for a fist to connect with his jaw, and he dropped to the floor, a look of surprise on his face.

Ed Walker stood there. "The building's on fire," he explained urgently. "We need to get out of here." He wiped at his forehead. A thin trickle of blood ran down his face. His expression was grim.

"What happened? How did you get out?" Matt wasn't sure what to believe. Surely Walker was still supposed to be in the next cell? This must be a hallucination. As they went, it wasn't as good as kissing Ken, but then as that had turned out to be real, this could too.

"I was being taken to be questioned." Walker bent over the guard to retrieve the key ring from the man's belt. "All hell broke loose, and I managed to escape in the confusion. I headed down here, figured I couldn't leave you and these other poor bastards to die."

"Thanks." Matt grabbed the gun that had fallen to the ground with the guard. "Are we under attack?"

Walker nodded. "Bombing raid, from what I've seen and heard." He waved Matt away. "Go find Ken. I'll get these prisoners out. No point in both of us being here." He'd already turned his back to Matt and was trying one of the keys in the next lock. The ring was welded closed, with no way to remove individual keys. Matt staying to help wouldn't speed things up.

"Good luck." Matt thought quickly. "We'll meet on the corner of Mauerstraße and Leipziger, but stay out of sight." They would have passed that intersection on their way here from Elise's Kaffeehaus, so they should find it easily enough yet be far enough away from the institute to be clear.

"Good luck to you too, sir... Matt." Walker cocked his head at Matt for a moment before returning to the task at hand.

Another blast rocked the building. Someone screamed. It sounded like a woman.

Matt gripped the weapon he carried, already thinking through the route between the cell block and Holm's office. At the top of the stairs, he turned towards the door that would lead him to the administration offices of the security wing. He stepped through it and a chill ran up his spine. Part of the outside wall of the corridor was missing. Men were running, trying to get clear of the building dying around them. A wooden beam fell from above, hitting the ground with a sickening thud. One of the soldiers yelled a warning too late.

Matt turned his head away, unable to watch. Ken had to still be safe. He had to be. Matt set off at a run, focused on finding Holm's office. Soldiers passed him, running in the opposite direction. Matt kept his head down and prayed he wouldn't be stopped.

The lights flickered, once, twice, before plunging the corridor into darkness. Outside, the fire kept spreading, its glow growing to provide Matt with adequate light to see the way ahead. He was breathing heavily, his heart thumping by the time he reached the double doors leading to the next section of corridor. No one questioned him; they were too busy trying to get clear. After all, only an idiot would run further into a burning building.

He took a moment to catch his breath. Timbers creaked on either side of him. He forced himself to focus and ignore the pain shooting through him. Medical treatment would be a luxury, even if they did manage to get out of here. At the very least, his ribs would need strapping, but if necessary, he'd get Trevor Palmer to do it for him.

Both the left and right door handles were warm to the touch. Matt let go of them quickly. The fire must have spread more rapidly up here. Someone had thought to close the double doors dividing these two sections in order to prevent the smoke and flames getting through. "No," he whispered. Despite the growing heat, he began to shiver. He couldn't face this again. Once had been more than enough. The flames had tried to claim him, reached for him, the heat searing him.

He took a deep breath, picturing Ken in his mind. Ken hadn't pulled away from Matt's kiss but had returned it with the whispered words Matt had thought he'd never hear. Bringing his hand up to his cheek, Matt remembered how gentle Ken's touch had been and the look in his eyes when he'd told Matt he loved him.

Another image entered his mind, of Ken lying injured somewhere on the other side of the door. Matt's breath hitched. He gritted his teeth, another wave of fear rushing through him. If he left now, he might be able to save himself, but the price would be too high. He hadn't been able to protect Elise; he couldn't let Ken die.

Damn it. Damn this fucking war. He'd already lost too much. He'd hidden the fears of his nightmares behind a façade of humour for too long now. Time to shatter the mask and fight for what was important. He and Ken deserved the chance of a future as much as anyone, and he was not going to let Holm or some fire take it from them.

He tried one of the door handles again. It was definitely hotter than it had been a few moments beforehand. "Shit." He'd already wasted more time than he should, Matt rolled down the sleeve of his overalls—thankful uniforms the world over were not a great fit—and covered his hand with it. The handle still felt warm through the fabric, but at least now he'd lessened the risk of it burning him.

Luckily the door was not locked. Matt opened it and immediately began to cough. The air was thick with smoke. He dropped to his knees and began to crawl through the corridor, his lungs straining to find breathable air. He shivered despite the heat, his vision blurring. His mother's voice whispered to him, telling him to be careful, urging him to save himself. It would be so easy to listen to her, to head back the way he'd come, but he couldn't. He couldn't leave Ken to die.

The smoke reached for him—it wanted him just as it always did. He ignored it and his rising panic. This wasn't a dream. This wasn't like last time. He wasn't a child; he could do this. He closed his eyes. They itched with the heat. It would be so easy to give up, to go back.

But that would also mean giving up on Ken.

A low groan sounded somewhere up ahead. Holm's office should be the second door on the right. Matt was torn between hoping Ken was still there, and that he'd already managed to escape. Crawling as fast as he could, he headed towards the sound. The door to Holm's office was open. Matt ducked inside, looking around frantically for any sign of life.

"Ken!" Matt stood to get a better view. The air in here was a little clearer, but it wouldn't stay that way for much longer.

"Matt?" Ken bent over a wooden beam, muscles straining as he tried to lift it. Flames danced around a hole in the roof. Part of it must have given way in one of the explosions. He grunted, easing the beam back down. "I need help. It's too heavy."

Matt was by his side in an instant. "Are you all right?" He peered at Ken anxiously, placing a hand on his arm, making sure this was real, not just another dream that would soon darken into a nightmare.

"I'm fine." Ken's jacket was missing, his shirt ripped, his cheek bruised, and his top lip was split. Matt's eyes narrowed. Was the explosion responsible for Ken's current state, or Holm?

Another groan caught his attention, distracting him from none too charitable thoughts. Holm lay under the beam, one of his legs caught by it. He was barely conscious, his face covered in perspiration and tiny splinters of wood. Shattered glass surrounded him. The window must have given way when part of the ceiling collapsed.

"You're trying to save him." Matt attempted to keep the emotion out of his voice but failed. Where were Holm's men? Had they left him here to die?

"Yes." Ken sighed. "Help me, will you?"

Matt had planned to find Ken, but hadn't a clue how he was going to deal with Holm. It would be so easy to leave him. After all, the beam was heavy. They'd be doing every prisoner Holm had interrogated, or would in the future, a favour.

"I am not my father." Ken shifted position, again trying to lift the beam. Something in the tone of his voice warned Matt not to broach the subject further. None of this made sense. Ken didn't talk about his father. As far as Matt knew, he was some decorated war hero who'd died during the last war. What the hell had Holm said? "I'm not going to leave him."

"Then I'll help you."

Ken was determined to do this, and working together gave them more chance of success.

Matt gestured towards Ken's injuries. "Did he do this?"

"No," Ken said very calmly and matter-of-factly, but that was no surprise. They'd discuss the details later, and then the emotion behind them would come out.

"Good." Matt turned his attention to the task at hand. While he had intended to keep his promise to help, it was easier to do so knowing Holm wasn't responsible for hurting Ken any further. At least not physically.

Holm's eyes were closed. He appeared to have lapsed into unconsciousness. If the beam pinning Holm's leg could be lifted and held for the short time needed for him to pull free, then they'd only have to worry about getting out of the building before it collapsed around them.

"Wonderful," Matt muttered. Even if they got that far, they still needed to escape, and having Holm with them narrowed their chances considerably. Matt preferred to avoid using Holm as a hostage, and not only because he doubted it would work. Holm would probably order his men to shoot him themselves to avoid being used as leverage.

Matt examined the beam, making sure nothing else hampered Holm's movement. For once, luck was on their side. He attempted to lift the beam, but it barely budged. Damn, it was heavy. It would take both of them just to lift it. Holm would have to pull his leg free as there was no other way to hold the beam off any longer.

Matt swayed in a momentary wave of dizziness. He had to stay strong. He didn't have time to give in to what he'd been through the last few days. Once they were out of here, he'd rest. He coughed, then licked his lips, the dryness of the air catching his throat. He looked around the room, shaking his head in surprise when he noticed the desk and that damn chair were still intact. That figured. Maybe...

He walked over to the chair and dragged it to where they were. The workmanship was solid, and the thickness of its back adequate for what would be needed. Neither of them had the strength needed to lift the beam high enough. However, if Ken could ease it up a little further, jamming this underneath would give them the rest of the height they needed to free Holm.

They'd need help. Matt bent and slapped Holm across the face. "Wake up," he ordered, refusing to enjoy the action too much.

Holm groaned, his eyes fluttering open. He stared at Matt in disbelief. "You!" he exclaimed hoarsely. "What are you doing here?"

"Helping a friend," Matt muttered. He couldn't help but glare at Holm. During his captivity, Matt had thought about everything he wanted to do to Holm. It would be so easy to leave him here to die. He didn't owe Holm anything, except maybe a slow, painful death. Holm had killed Elise and done God knows what to Ken.

Matt raised his hand, ready to slap Holm again, as Holm could do little or nothing to stop him. The beam had trapped him just as securely as the handcuffs and that chair had trapped Matt.

Another explosion rocked the floor. Matt stumbled. Ken caught him, holding him for an instant before letting him go.

"Let's get on with this," Matt said testily. The faster they were away from here, the happier he'd be. He struggled to breathe, and wasn't sure the smoke beginning to fill the room was the only reason. The adrenaline he was running on would not last much longer, and he'd prefer to be somewhere safe when he collapsed in an undignified heap on the ground.

"I'm going to lift the beam," Ken told Holm, "then we're going to use the chair to lever it higher. You need to pull your leg free immediately."

"I understand." Holm gritted his teeth. He was obviously in a lot of pain but determined not to allow it to stop him from doing what was needed. For that, at least, Matt had to admit a grudging admiration. Despite there being more to this Holm than met the eye, he was not someone Matt wanted to get to know better.

"Ready?" asked Ken. Matt and Holm both nodded. Slowly Ken began to lift the beam, grunting from the exertion. Matt watched it rise, ready to shove the back of the chair in at the right time. He had considered breaking the chair, but doubted he could do so easily. Better to save his energy for as long as possible.

The beam kept rising. Perspiration ran down Ken's face, his muscles straining visibly under his shirt. Holm tried to pull free, but the beam wasn't high enough. "Now!" urged Ken. Matt edged as close as he could, put all of his weight behind the chair, and shoved it hard into the gap between the beam and the floor. Once it was secure, Ken stood, his hands on bent knees, breathing heavily.

Holm wriggled back. He cried out in pain yet still wasn't free. *Damn it!* Matt moved behind him, grabbed under his arms, and helped to ease him out. The chair groaned in protest against the weight slowly crushing it. One final yank and Holm was clear, both of them thrown backwards when, with a loud crack, the chair broke into pieces.

Bits of it flew in their direction. Matt put up one arm to protect himself, ducking when a shard of wood narrowly missed him. His vision spun, darkening around the edges at the sudden movement. He got to his knees to catch his breath.

In the distance, something rumbled. The building shook. They had to get out of here. Ken glanced at the still-open office door. Flames danced around the frame, eager to find their way inside. He ran over to it and slammed it shut to put something else in the path of the flames.

"There's another way out of here," Ken said urgently to Holm. "Where is it?"

Holm looked up in surprise. "I see you've had access to the plans for the building." He studied both of them for a moment. "Yes, there is." He pointed to the bookcase in the corner. "It's behind there."

"Can you walk?" Ken was already helping Matt to his feet, ignoring his protestations it wasn't necessary. The question, however, was directed to Holm.

"Not on my own, but with help, I should be able to, yes." Holm tested his leg and winced in pain. It was at least badly sprained, if not broken.

After making sure Matt was all right, Ken examined the bookcase and pulled it out from the wall. The door behind it was not locked. Ken opened it and cautiously peered through. Matt caught a glimpse of what could have been stairs leading down, but the light was too dim to see properly. Ken disappeared through the door for a moment before reappearing. "As far as I can tell, the stairs are still intact."

From his expression, he didn't think they would be for much longer. Matt slipped his arm around Holm, offering, and at the same time using him for, support, although it meant he would be more likely to be caught than Ken. "You have more mobility," he said in way of explanation when

Ken gave him a questioning look. "Lead the way, and we'll follow."

Ken hesitated, but then he nodded. Holm adjusted his weight against Matt, and they began to stumble towards the door. Matt bit his lip, glancing at the office and corridor behind them. The fire would soon have its appetite back as it was already making short work of what it was now consuming. He closed his eyes, counting to five slowly. His heart raced, and he was beginning to shake. They weren't walking into the fire, but away from it. They would survive this.

"You need to pull yourself together," Holm said quietly, "and you need to do it now."

Matt's eyes snapped open. "I'm fine." He wasn't about to give Holm the satisfaction of showing any outward sign of weakness.

"Of course you are." Holm's reply had a degree of smugness to it, but Matt didn't have the energy to care he'd been played. Let Holm have his games. If they didn't get out of here, none of that would matter.

The journey down the dozen or so steps seemed to take forever. Ken kept glancing back, waiting for them no matter how many times Matt urged him to go on ahead. Ken had found a working flashlight in a boxlike compartment near the beginning of the handrail, and used it to light a narrow path ahead of them. They needed to focus on one step at a time. Holm slipped halfway down. Matt strengthened his grip, the shake in his hand becoming more pronounced. Not much longer.

The building around them creaked and groaned. They were all breathing heavily, with no energy to waste on conversation. Matt coughed. His ribs screamed in pain. He was tired, so tired.

Finally the flashlight showed another door. Ken opened it as another explosion rocked the building. Matt stumbled, losing his footing, the stairs disappearing from under him. He fell. Ken yelled something... and then everything went black.

CHAPTER TWENTY-ONE

Liang watched in horror as another explosion rocked the building. The fire was spreading quickly, despite all efforts to extinguish it. A couple of soldiers talked about the armoury and what would happen if the flames reached the weapons and ammunition store.

No one had questioned his and Palmer's presence. Several civilians were pitching in and doing what they could to help, but it wasn't enough. Other buildings in the area slowly burned, their ashes picked up by the wind and spread across the cold night air so it was impossible to tell how much damage had been done. Morning would give a better idea, but Liang didn't intend to stay that long. Up to now, the dim glow of torches had helped to hide their identities, but the fires lighting the sky were bringing with them a false dawn.

"There's no sign of any of them yet." Palmer looked around frantically. "No one could survive that." He shivered, pulling his coat around him. He'd wanted to go into the building to see if he could find any survivors, but it was too dangerous. Liang didn't see the point in risking their lives to retrieve corpses.

He noticed movement from the rear of the building, yet couldn't see what it might be from this distance. Hope niggled at the back of his mind. He squashed it quickly. Perhaps someone had gone to examine the damage there, although the Germans seemed more focused on the front where the fires burned more fiercely.

Palmer followed Liang's gaze and began to run. Had he seen something Liang hadn't? Not about to waste time, Liang caught up to him quickly. Two figures slowly took shape in the darkness the closer they got to the building.

Not two figures. Three, with one man carrying another. The man in front wore a German uniform, the insignia on it showing his rank to be SS Standartenführer. His left trouser leg was ripped, blood seeping into the grey material. He was limping.

Liang pulled his gun. While he did not recognise the man, his identity wasn't difficult to figure out. "SS Standartenführer Holm," he spat. This was the Gestapo officer who had killed Elise and arrested Matt. A bullet between his eyes would be far more than he deserved for what he'd done.

"Don't shoot!" Ken barked the order, but Liang did not lower his gun. Holm raised his hands, watching Liang warily.

"Have you forgotten what he has done?" Liang wondered if Ken had lost his sanity in the fire.

"No, and I'm not about to." Ken cradled the man he carried closer to him when he moaned quietly. "Matt is hurt."

"It's not just Matt who is hurt." Ken's lip was split, his shirt ripped to show angry scrapes and bruises. Another bruise shadowed his face. Liang's grip tightened on his gun. "How can you trust this man?"

"Where's Ed?" Palmer interrupted. He too had his gun drawn and was eyeing Holm suspiciously.

"I don't know," Ken admitted. "We got separated. The last time I saw him he was with Matt."

"He must be still in the building!" Palmer gave Liang an apologetic look, and before Liang could stop him, took off at a run in the direction Ken and the others had come from.

"Bloody idiot!" The chances of finding anyone in there, let alone alive, were slim. Liang hesitated, torn between going after Palmer to stop him or staying to help Ken.

The ground beneath them shook. What was left of the back of the building shuddered and collapsed completely, flames devouring it with renewed hunger.

"It's found the armoury," Holm said flatly. "If your friend was alive, he won't be now. I'm sorry, but no one could have survived that."

Liang handed his gun to Ken. "Watch him. I'm going to get Trevor before he does anything stupid." Palmer would not have made it back into the building in time to save his friend, and the dead could not be brought back to life. The best way to honour Walker would be for the rest of his team to complete their mission and keep his memory alive. This mission had already cost too much. Liang wondered, not for the first time, if Lehrer and the plans for this device were really worth the price. War and death went hand in hand. What gave the Allies more of a right to a weapon with the potential to wipe out an entire city? The firepower they possessed could already do enough damage. Tonight was proof of that.

"Be careful." Ken rearranged Matt in his arms, then took the gun. His expression was unreadable. He gestured with his weapon for Holm to move with them back into the shadow provided by what was left of one of the smaller outbuildings. Matt was still unconscious but mumbling words under his breath, obviously caught in some kind of nightmare. His face was bloodied, and he was pale and shivering. They needed to find him medical assistance and quickly.

"You too," Liang replied.

By the time he reached Palmer, he was hugging himself and sitting on the ground. He seemed dazed. Had he been thrown by the explosion? "Trevor?" Liang asked cautiously, not wanting to alarm him too much. "Are you all right?"

Palmer shook his head. "Ed wasn't supposed to die," he whispered hoarsely. "This wasn't meant to happen. Bloody hell, we'd only just celebrated his twentieth birthday before we were both called up." He stared at the building. Although there had been no more explosions, it was still slowly burning and would probably continue to do so until morning. "He still owes me a pint."

"I'm sorry." The words weren't enough. They never were. "Is this the first time someone close to you has died?" Liang asked gently, helping him to his feet. He hadn't realised Ed Walker was so young. He hadn't even had the chance to live properly. Bloody war. The sooner it was over, the better, even if, sadly, it would always be followed by another.

"Yes. I've seen death before, had a bloke die on me in the field, but it wasn't someone I knew. I went to school with Ed's older brother. Told him I'd look after him." Palmer wiped his eyes on his sleeve while they walked. "Stupid, really. After all, we're fighting a war, and not everyone comes back, do they? I thought... it was supposed to be someone else, not him."

"It always is." Liang knew far too much about loss. Not only had he lost his parents at a young age, but he remembered all too clearly his grandmother's anguish when many of her family died at the hands of the Japanese in Nanking. While he hadn't had the chance to meet most of them, he'd grown up hearing stories about them and looking forward to the day when he could. The massacre had ripped that away from him, and taken an extended family he'd now never know. He'd wept alongside his grandmother and listened to his grandfather's vow that one day the price required for such a despicable act would be paid.

"There's no chance he got out in time, is there?" The minute hope died in Palmer's eyes when Liang shook his head.

"If he did, we should have seen him. We were watching the building the entire time." Liang placed a hand on Palmer's shoulder; the man was still shaking. "We need to think about our own survival now. Ed wouldn't want us to put our own lives at risk." He'd try and get to the arranged meeting place later, just in case, but didn't want to give Palmer false hope. That would be cruel. "He was a good man, Trevor. He will be missed."

"Yes, he will." A mask came down over Palmer's face. He was pushing his emotions aside until they were safe. It might be a while before he'd have the luxury to grieve properly. He didn't have time for it now. They'd already left Ken and Matt alone with Holm for longer than they should. Palmer glanced at what was left of the building behind them and whispered, "Goodbye, Ed. I'll have that pint for you."

Ken looked up as they approached. Holm was already gone, probably to sound the alarm, although he couldn't have got far with his injured leg. "The fence has been compromised on the south side. Holm is giving us half an hour before he sends his men after us."

"How kind of him," Liang said dryly. Holm had got a good look at all of them so now had an added advantage when he began hunting them again. Giving them a head start wouldn't hinder him now he had their descriptions. "Do you know if he's aware of the reason we are in Berlin?"

Ken nodded. "He's no fool." He adjusted Matt's weight, murmuring something under his breath when Matt moaned softly. "Matt needs medical attention urgently." His expression briefly reflected the fear and concern he was hiding. "After all this, we can't lose him too."

"No, we can't," Liang said.

"He needs a doctor," Palmer added. "I know enough to patch him up, but that's all."

Liang hoped his original plan was still viable. Juliane had to have survived this. She was Holm's secretary and would have finished for the day and be safely at home before the bombing began. He refused to consider the possibility she might have been trapped in the building like Walker. "I have the address of the restaurant where you and Juliane dined together. You said she was known there. Perhaps they know of her whereabouts. With the air raid tonight, it's doubtful many questions would be asked about your appearance. You could claim to be concerned about her safety." That part, at least, wouldn't be a lie.

"She might know of a doctor who can be trusted." Ken considered the idea, and came to the same conclusion. Trying to find her was risky, but what choice did they have? "Trevor, lead and take point." He returned Liang's gun. "Liang, take the rear and watch our backs."

"Do you want me to take Matt?" Liang offered. Ken

would be the better shot and have more of a chance of keeping them safe.

"No," Ken said sharply.

Liang wasn't about to argue with him. Something about the way Ken held Matt niggled at him, but he didn't have the time or energy to pursue it further. Besides, considering their present circumstances, it hardly mattered.

They'd need all of their skill, energy, and luck just to survive what was left of the night.

Liang banged on the door of the restaurant again. It was closed, with no sign of life inside. The streets around it were deserted. People were reluctant to venture from the relative safety of their shelters, in direct contrast to the mix of soldiers and civilians still combing the wreckage for survivors in the area that had taken most of the damage in the night's raid.

"We need to get off the streets," Ken said, trying not to sound as desperate as he felt. He was tired, his arms ached, and his face throbbed, yet he still refused to let either Liang or Palmer take a turn with Matt. Soon he would have no choice, as his body was protesting the extra strain of carrying his friend, but he was determined not to deal with that until he had to.

A noise sounded from inside. Palmer took several steps back onto the pavement, and peered up at the first floor, trying to find a sign of life from inside. One of the curtains pulled back briefly to reveal an indistinct face.

"Another minute," Liang insisted. He called out, "Please, we're looking for a friend."

"We haven't got another minute." Ken glanced at his

watch. The head start Holm had given them was almost up. If they didn't find shelter of some kind soon, they'd be caught.

The front door creaked open a fraction, and the waiter who had served him and Juliane peered out.

"Robert, you have to help us." Ken took a step forward. Robert put his hand to his mouth, and Ken remembered the uniform he wore. "I'm a friend of Juliane's... Fräulein Dunst. Do you know where I can find her?"

Robert hesitated, his gaze travelling over each of them in turn. He shrugged. "You'd better come in. Juliane said you might come looking for her."

"Is she here?" Liang asked. "Is she all right? I... we were worried she might have been injured in the raid tonight." He and Palmer had holstered their guns before knocking on the door so not to alarm someone who might be able to help them.

"She is fine." Robert gestured to a padded sofa in the corner of the dining room after they followed him inside. "Do you wish to lay your friend down?" He shut the door behind him. The restaurant was lit by candles, none of them visible through the heavy curtains that covered each window.

"Thank you," Ken replied politely. He swallowed a moan of pain when Matt's weight was finally free of his arms. Matt was heavier than Ken had imagined and hid a well-muscled physique behind his ill-fitting uniform. Even so, the technician's overalls hung loosely on him, more so than expected. He'd drifted in and out of consciousness since they left the institute, having brief periods of lucidity before giving in to sleep again. When the stairs had given way, Matt hit the ground with one hell of an impact, although Ken managed to pull him clear before any rubble fell on top of him. It had been a close call. Even Holm had seemed unnerved by it.

A glass of water was pushed into his hand, Robert having disappeared into the kitchen to get it. "For your friend," Robert explained, "in case he wakes."

Ken nodded his thanks. "I have no way of contacting Juliane. Can you help us?"

"Perhaps." Robert frowned. Finally he came to a decision. "Your friend needs a doctor. Worry about that first. I know of one who can be trusted and will help. Be aware, though, that you are putting her at risk, as well as yourselves."

"Thank you." Liang took over the conversation when Matt stirred. Ken eased him up into a sitting position, encouraging him to take sips of the water. "Once our friend has received treatment, we will be on our way."

"Yes, you will." Robert watched Matt for a short time. He managed to drink some of the water, but winced with any little movement. His eyes were focused, and he leaned into Ken to steady himself. He was finally awake, which could only be a good sign, if he managed to stay alert. "He can be moved. You've already stayed here long enough." Robert glanced at the door. If they were discovered here, he risked being labelled a collaborator.

"Where do we find this doctor?" Liang asked.

"Clara has private rooms at the hospital not far from here." Robert gave them the address, and directions for the safest route there, nodding approvingly when Liang repeated them flawlessly without prompting. "She will also be able to give you the address of a safe house where you can hide for a few days while your friend recovers."

"Clara Lehrer?" Ken asked sharply. He'd already had a suspicion she'd be the doctor Robert was referring to, but was surprised he referred to her by her first name rather than the code name she'd used when they'd met at St. Michael's shortly after Matt had been taken into custody.

Robert smiled. "Yes. Do not let her family name and background fool you. Clara is nothing like her father." He hesitated. "Neither is her brother, despite the recent rumours. A word of warning, though... Do not speak ill of him in her presence if you want her help."

"I wouldn't be that stupid," Liang commented dryly. "I am aware of the loyalty that exists between family members. I admire her for standing by him, considering the circumstances." Holm had ensured it was common knowledge the Gestapo wanted custody of Lehrer so they could question him in connection with the death of Herr Dr Kluge. Wherever Lehrer was hiding, it was with someone who was aware of the penalties of being caught doing so.

"My concern is more that the Gestapo are still watching her because of her brother." Ken placed the water glass carefully on the floor and slipped his arm around Matt's waist again, helping him to stand. Matt gave him a shaky smile. He was definitely improving, but not quickly enough for Ken's liking.

"They probably are, but there is no other doctor I would trust. There is a back entrance to her clinic. It's the one we usually use, and I'm not sure the Gestapo are aware of it." Robert shrugged. "With the events of tonight, my hope is that they are busy elsewhere. You won't get far with your friend in his current state anyway."

"The patrol has just passed, so we're safe to leave now." Palmer had been keeping a careful eye on the comings and goings outside the restaurant. He let go of the corner of the curtain and opened the door a fraction, then peered around cautiously before closing it again.

"We'll take the chance with Clara." Although Ken spoke, Liang and Palmer both nodded their agreement. Matt frowned, ready to protest, but Ken silenced him with a glare. He'd already nearly lost Matt once; he was not ready to chance it again. At least this way, if Matt got the attention he needed, they could then focus on finding a place to hide until he'd fully recovered.

"Be careful," Robert warned. He retrieved the water glass, no doubt preparing to get rid of any evidence he'd had company. "I'll get word to Juliane that you were asking after her. She will appreciate your concern." He blew out the candles as soon as Palmer opened the door, plunging the room into darkness.

The directions Robert had given them turned out to be a succession of back alleys, for which Ken was thankful. Matt was quiet and leaned on Ken heavily, but at least for now he didn't need to be carried. Dawn was approaching, the sun trying to break through the clouds, its rays colouring the grey skies with a hint of red.

Closer to the hospital, more people were on the streets. Hopefully Clara would still be there, although Ken wouldn't be surprised if she'd been warned they were coming.

Several soldiers walked past, and Ken and the others ducked back into the shadows to wait until the danger was gone. The air of unease in the atmosphere could have been his, rather than a reflection of the people around him. One building they'd seen still stood tall and undamaged while another next to it only remained in skeletal form, a blackened, shadowed outline of what it had once been. The cloud cover would have made it difficult for the Pathfinders to locate and mark their targets. Most of the bombs had probably been dropped blindly. He and his team should have been clear of the institute before the attack if everything had gone according to plan.

This could still be used as a diversion. At least Holm would be immobilised for a while, if nothing else, but then he had men at his disposal to do his duty for him in the meantime.

Once they reached the door Robert had described, Liang knocked quietly, then stood back and waited for a response. The others kept out of sight until he signalled it was safe. After several minutes, the door opened slowly. Ken could see Liang talking with someone, although the person couldn't be seen. Finally, Liang nodded and gestured for them to come forward.

The time taken to cover the short distance between their hiding place and Clara's rooms was more nerve-racking than the several blocks they'd walked to get this far. Once inside, it would be safe, but only for as long as no one knew they were there. Palmer closed the door behind them and scanned the room for another exit. The other door was ajar. The room through it was stacked with shelves of books and medical journals, a desk, and a bed similar to the one in the area they were in. The door beyond that was presumably the entrance usually used for the public. The one they'd come through was painted to match the wall, the handle not obvious until examined closely.

"Help your friend to the bed," Clara ordered. "Your scrapes could do with some cleaning too... Tinman."

"My name is Ken Lowe, Fräulein Dr Lehrer." Ken corrected her once Matt was settled and she'd begun examining him. Under the circumstances, he didn't see the point in referring to each other by code names. They trusted her to treat Matt, and knew who she was. Offering his identity in return only seemed fair. She could already describe them, and Holm would put two and two together anyway.

"Matthew Bryant," Matt said, then shivered when she placed her stethoscope on his chest. "It's cold," he complained.

She rolled her eyes. "You'd better get used to it, as I intend to give you a thorough examination." Following her directions, he lay back down again, while she shook her head and felt carefully around his chest and stomach. "Your ribs are badly bruised. They'll need strapping and will be sore for a while. I can give you something to help with the pain, but take it sparingly."

"Yes, Fräulein Doktor."

"Do any of you have any medical training?" Clara gestured towards Ken. "If so, you can make yourself useful by cleaning his scrapes. The less time you spend here, the safer it is for all of us."

"I have, and I'll help you," Palmer said, washing his hands in the sink by the bed before retrieving the cotton swabs and a small bottle of surgical spirits. Ken sighed, sat down on a chair, and removed his shirt. He knew better than to argue with a doctor about such matters.

Clara nodded her approval, glancing in his direction with a smile before continuing to treat Matt. Liang, not having received any further instructions as yet, took it upon himself to keep an eye out for any unwelcome visitors. Ken heard Matt whisper something to her. It sounded like a thank-you, but something about the way he worded it suggested he was not just referring to the way she was helping him now.

"Have you any news of my brother yet, Herr Lowe?"

Clara asked quietly.

"No." He looked up in surprise, adding softly, "I'm sorry," when he saw the worry reflected in her eyes. "I can promise you we will do what we can to find him and keep him safe when we are able to do so." That wouldn't happen until Matt was well enough to travel, but in the meantime, London might have some information that could prove useful.

"I'm glad there is someone else looking out for him." She finished strapping Matt's ribs and began to clean the cuts on his upper chest, muttering a few words of disgust when he turned and she saw his back. "When you find him, you'll find Michel. I doubt they'll be travelling separately. Michel promised me he would look after Kristopher, and I believe him."

"They did act as though they were friends," Palmer commented, not looking particularly apologetic when Ken winced as a swab dowsed with a liberal amount of the surgical solution was wiped against one of his cuts. He gritted his teeth, certain it didn't have to sting quite that much.

Clara smiled. "One can never have enough friends, young man. Speaking of which, you'll need to go to a safe house once you've left here, and keep a very low profile until Herr Bryant regains his health and is able to travel. I know of someone who can help." She gave Palmer a nod. "I have a bag I will give you with what he might need for the next few days. If you'll come with me, I'll show you once you've cleaned up. It's in the adjoining room."

"Thank you." Palmer finished what he was doing. None of Ken's injuries needed dressing, although they looked angrier than he'd expected. Still, it was a small price to pay for rescuing Matt and escaping from a burning building.

"I can clean up," Ken offered, wanting to be on their way as soon as possible.

"That would be very helpful." Clara pointed to a container at the side of the bed. "Everything that cannot be reused goes in there, and all instruments," she said, indicating a metal tray on the counter by the sink, "in there to be sterilised. Your friend also needs some help getting dressed. Any sudden movements are going to hurt until he's healed." Matt's wounds dressed, she pulled a notepad and pen out of her coat pocket and scribbled down an address, then handed it to him. "Once you've memorised this, destroy it."

"Thank you," Ken said. He read the note, committed it to memory, then shoved it in his pocket. He'd destroy it once they left.

Clara nodded, then gestured to Palmer. "If you'll follow me, please."

They walked through the door into the outer room, Palmer mumbling something when Clara remarked about the good job he'd done and began asking how much training he'd had. Liang stifled something suspiciously like a grin after the overheard conversation. "I don't think Palmer's used to handling compliments," he noted.

"Probably not," Matt agreed, easing his arms back into his undershirt. He cleared his throat. "Could you check outside to make sure we haven't been followed? I'd like to get out of here as soon as possible. Dr Lehrer has taken enough risks for us as it is."

Liang nodded his agreement. "She is a good woman, which gives me hope her brother's intentions may be what they appear." He watched Matt for a moment before adding softly, "It's good to have you back, Matt." Without waiting for a reply, he opened the door and peered out into the alley, then disappeared outside when it appeared to be still deserted.

"I seem to have missed quite a bit when I was away," Matt commented as Ken helped him finish dressing. "Liang seems a little more... mellow, than he was."

"We've worked together better than I expected," Ken told him. "He's a friend." The dynamics between not just him and Liang, but also within their entire team, had subtly changed in Matt's absence.

Matt raised an eyebrow. Ken wouldn't use the word lightly. "Thank you for ignoring my orders and not giving up on me." Their fingers brushed together but not for long enough that anyone else would notice. "Once we have some privacy, we need to talk. It's a conversation we should have had a long time ago." He seemed nervous, as if unsure about what had happened between them.

"It can wait," Ken reassured him. He bent closer and whispered in Matt's ear. "I love you. I meant what I said in that cell, and it's not going to change."

Relief reflected in Matt's eyes. He smiled, a more genuine quality to his expression than usual. Ken couldn't help but smile in return. While Matt's mood was often contagious to those around him, this was a glimpse, Ken suspected, of the man behind the humour few had the privilege to see. He hoped he was right.

"I meant what I said then too." Matt squeezed Ken's hand. He seemed thoughtful, but he'd had a lot to digest during the last few days. Glancing at first one door, then the other to make sure they were alone, Matt cleared his throat.

A loud noise came from the outer room. Liang ducked back inside the surgery, ready to investigate the cause of it. Ken helped Matt to his feet immediately. Once off the bed, they took shelter behind it, hiding against the wall. He signalled for Matt to stay where he was, and carefully peeked through the slit left by the open door. Clara had partially closed it once she and Palmer had left the room.

"Fräulein Dr Lehrer." The voice was instantly recognisable. Obersturmführer Reiniger was accompanied by four armed Gestapo. His weapon was drawn, the door behind him off its hinges. It appeared he hadn't bothered to knock and risk giving any warning of his presence.

"Yes." Clara's voice was steady, with a hint of politeness to it. "What can I do for you, Herr Obersturmführer?"

"You are harbouring fugitives of the Third Reich, Doktor." One of the men moved behind Palmer, ready to secure him.

"I forced my way in here," Palmer replied. "Dr Lehrer had no choice. Let her go."

Reiniger shook his head. "That is doubtful, especially as we are already aware this is not the first time she has done so." He moved closer. Palmer stepped between Reiniger and Clara. "Where are the others?"

"I am alone." Palmer raised his head defiantly. The soldier behind him handcuffed his hands together and pushed him forward onto his knees.

"You lie," Reiniger said. He glanced at the door, and Ken withdrew quickly. "There is a penalty for lying." He raised his voice. "Surrender or I will show this man what it is."

When Ken turned, Liang was already by Matt's side. "It's too late for him," Liang hissed. "If we give ourselves up, they'll kill us all."

Ken hesitated. He hadn't abandoned Matt. Did he have the right to decide differently in this situation? Did Reiniger already know they were here? He was aware of the door and yet had done nothing. At least not yet.

The single gunshot made him jump. A cry of pain followed it. "There is no one here," Palmer hissed loudly, "but me."

"He's telling the truth," Clara said coldly. "Shooting him in the leg won't change his answer. Even if it did, do you think they'd be stupid enough to still be here after this?"

Palmer was breathing heavily, each rasp interspersed with a gasp of pain. *That bastard!* They couldn't just leave Palmer and Clara to the likes of him. Had this performance been because he knew he had an audience?

Running footsteps sounded outside the door to the other room. Liang grabbed Matt and Ken and shoved them towards the outer door, then closed it quickly behind them. On the other side of it, soldiers called to each as they looked for a hidden exit and Reiniger barked orders.

Liang was right. They couldn't stay here. Reiniger and his men would kill them, or worse, take them back to Holm for questioning. It wouldn't take the soldiers long to find their way outside. Even if they didn't find the door, they'd surround the building within minutes.

Silently apologising to both Palmer and Clara, Ken sighed and offered his support to Matt, Liang doing the same from the other side. The sun had broken through at last, its rays illuminating the alley, limiting any place they might hide.

In the distance, Ken saw a gap in the row of buildings to their left. He had no clue where it led, but it better to at least try to escape through it than wait for the certainty of being captured if they didn't.

He pointed it out to Matt and Liang. Both of them nodded, already moving.

Around them, the air filled with the sound of raised voices as Reiniger called his men to the hunt.

CHAPTER TWENTY-TWO

Kit sat on the floor under one of the small windows at the far end of the attic. A book lay on his lap, although he hadn't paid it any attention for quite some time. His eyes were glazed over, a sure sign he was deep in thought.

"Do you want to talk?" Michel looked down from where he was watching the activity outside. One of the chickens that provided eggs for the convent had escaped, and several of the sisters were chasing it around the grounds in an attempt to catch it. So far the chicken was proving evasive. He would have offered to help, but with it being the middle of the day, couldn't risk venturing outside the attic.

"If you don't mind listening." Kit indicated a spot on the floor next to his, moving over to give Michel room to sit. "With the events of the last week, my thoughts keep returning to Clara and my father. I'm worried about them."

They'd watched the night sky light up for several nights in succession and heard the sirens when fire engines had sped to Berlin to offer aid to the city. It had been difficult to get much information, but the sisters had a few contacts who passed along news when they could. While the first air raid caused some damage, that from the bombings three to four days later had been much more extensive. Fires still burned, buildings were in ruin, and many had lost their lives or homes.

"I know you are." Michel slid his arm around Kit's waist. He snuggled in closer, his head resting on Michel's shoulder. Michel threaded the fingers of his other hand through Kit's hair, playing with the fine strands.

"The last time my father and I spoke, we argued." Kit sighed. "I still stand by what I said, and although all we've done is argue over the last few years, he's still my father."

"You can disagree with and even dislike members of your family," Michel pointed out gently, "without changing the fact you love them."

Kit nodded slowly. "I used to want him to be proud of me." He shrugged. "I still do, I think, but I've come to the realisation that I need to be proud of myself first. How can I expect someone to feel that way about me if I don't myself?"

"You have a lot to be proud of." Michel frowned. Kit had a tendency to see the negative in himself. "You're a brilliant scientist and a very caring and compassionate man. *I'm* proud of you."

"I've made a lot of decisions I regret." Kit shook his head. "I've also turned my back on *who* I am for so long, focusing on one part of my life to the exclusion of the other."

"We've all made decisions we aren't proud of, and everyone struggles with the other. Depending on where you are in your life, often there isn't the luxury to focus on more than one thing." Michel wished Kit could see himself through someone else's eyes. "I love you, Kit Lehrer, and there are good reasons for that."

Kit looked up, meeting Michel's gaze. "Sometimes I

think you see me as I want to be rather than who I am now. It's as though I'm two people. Kit is the person I used to be and ran away from by burying myself in my work because I couldn't face what I should have years ago. Kristopher is the result of that. I want to be Kit again, but it's going to take time. That sounds crazy, doesn't it?"

"Not at all." Michel leaned in and kissed Kit slowly. "Even in the time I was watching you, I could see you struggling with something. At first I thought your conscience was trying to come to terms with the project you were a part of, but perhaps it was also this? Accepting ourselves for who we are is an ongoing journey, and finding a balance we're happy with between that and the responsibilities we take on." He took a deep breath. "I can promise you that while we're together like this, you can be whoever you want to be. My feelings for you are not going to change, wherever your destiny ends up taking you."

"I know, and that makes me happy." Kit threaded his fingers through Michel's. "Being with you makes me happy, but everything that has happened has made me think about a lot of things I've avoided for a long time." He was silent for a moment, his thumb stroking Michel's hand. "You aren't the first man I've been attracted to, but I wasn't ready to admit I could be before."

"David?"

They'd talked about David before, very briefly. He and Kit had attended university together and they used to be friends. Kit hadn't been very forthcoming about the details concerning why they'd drifted apart, although Michel had wondered about it.

"Yes." Kit curled in closer, his head once again on Michel's shoulder, a position they both enjoyed, and an intimacy Michel treasured. "I pushed him away instead of being honest with myself. According to the teachings I was raised with, wanting another man in that way is wrong." He shook his head and sighed. "I can't see how the love you and I feel for each other can be. It's beautiful and feels so good."

"You can't help who you fall in love with." Michel remembered the conversation he'd had with Corin when his brother had confronted him about it. For all their intention to be careful, Corin had seen François leaving the barn one night, followed by Michel shortly afterwards. Corin had always known Michel a little too well, and Michel had never succeeded in hiding anything from him. "Corin told me that."

Kit's eyes widened. "He knew?"

"Yes." They'd only talked about it once. Michel had promised to be more careful, and the subject had never been brought up again. "He accepted me for who I was." He doubted anyone else knew. If their parents did, they certainly had not broached the subject, and he wasn't looking forward to having the discussion with them. He would, though, if Kit found a way to stay in France.

"I wish I could have met him." Kit shifted, pulling Michel into his arms and holding him.

Even now, it wasn't easy talking about Corin. He always felt very melancholic afterwards, though he tried to focus on the good memories instead of that final one.

"I think he would have approved of you." Michel couldn't help but smile. "He'd also tease you and ask you what you saw in me. Corin was a terrible tease, but only in fun. He wasn't mean with it."

"That's another thing you have in common with him." Kit ran his hands up and down Michel's back; it felt very good. Michel shuffled closer, then onto Kit's lap, straddling him. This war had cost them both so much already. At least knowing what had happened to Corin had given Michel some closure. Kit didn't have that, and couldn't return to Berlin to find out.

Once they were on their way to Switzerland, Michel planned to ask his contacts outside Berlin to get that information for them. He would also ask for any news about Matt Bryant and his team. Hopefully they'd already left Berlin, although news had come through Sister Brigit that a priest fitting Matt's description was arrested for Elise's murder.

He'd had more time to think since their arrival here, and he and Kit needed to make plans to leave. Kit's health continued to improve, and soon he would be fit enough to travel. Neither of them wanted to impose on the sisters' hospitability more than was needed or put them in any unnecessary danger.

"Hmm," he murmured appreciatively when Kit slid his hands under the shirt. "Keep doing that."

"You were deep in thought. I figured you needed some distraction." Kit kissed along Michel's jawline before brushing their lips together. "Unless you want to talk about it?"

"We've talked enough." Although Kit was the one who had needed to talk before, he was also sensitive to Michel's moods. One of the things Michel liked about their growing relationship was their awareness of each other's needs as well as their own. It also didn't hurt that Kit was an extremely good-looking and passionate man as well as being a good conversationalist.

"You're still thinking too much," Kit teased, deepening the kiss. Michel moaned softly, wanting more. He wriggled further up Kit's lap and started to undo the buttons on Kit's shirt. Kit's breathing sped up. He broke the kiss and licked his lips, a hungry look in his eyes.

Michel loved it when they both wanted each other so badly.

He pulled Kit's shirt from his trousers and reached for his belt.

A loud creak echoed through the attic, followed by another.

They both froze, waiting, hoping one of the sisters would call out a greeting.

Matt glanced at the door when it began to open, his body tensing in case he needed to hide.

"It's me." Ken waited a moment before entering the room. He carried two cups full of steaming liquid. "Coffee," he explained. "I thought you might like something to drink."

"Thanks." Matt shuffled over on the sofa, making room. Although they were supposed to be safe here, he couldn't stop reacting to every noise he couldn't identify. This room was at the rear of the apartment, and its wardrobe had a false back, the wall behind it opening onto stairs leading down into a cellar. "Is Liang busy?"

Ken grinned. "He and Juliane are playing chess. From what I could see, she's winning. He's still deciding whether to be impressed by her ability or annoyed she's better at the game than he is."

"If he has any sense, he'll go for the first option." Matt took the coffee and sipped it slowly so he could savour it. They hadn't expected the address Clara gave them to be Juliane's home. She, however, wasn't surprised to see them and had ushered them in quickly, showing them the several escape routes and hiding places within the building. Liang had expressed his concerns about how safe it would be to stay with her, but she'd shrugged and smiled. She then told them the Gestapo tended to think twice about searching the home of the sister of their commanding officer. A year ago, one soldier had fired his gun at one of her sofas, convinced a fugitive could be hiding in the storage unit underneath it. The sofa was a present from her brother—luckily the bullet missed the Jewish man curled up in the hidden compartment by inches. The soldier wasn't so lucky when Holm found out one of his men had dared accuse his sister of harbouring an enemy of the Third Reich.

"Robert has made contact. He has news from the Resistance about Clara and Trevor." Ken changed the subject abruptly after a brief silence. He studied his coffee.

"And?" Matt prompted.

None of them had wanted to leave anyone behind, but they'd had no choice. As it was, they'd barely escaped their pursuers and made it to safety, despite several instances when Matt had been certain they would be caught, with soldiers searching mere feet from where they were hiding.

"They're both in custody at Gestapo Headquarters. Holm is being very careful." Ken shook his head. "Our chances of breaking them out of there are very slim, and that was before all the security was tightened. Trevor has gotten medical treatment for his wound, but..." His voice trailed off.

"He'll know we would have rescued him if we could. You took such a risk in coming after me. He knew how that nearly ended." Matt would order a rescue mission if he thought they had any hope of one.

"First Ed and now Trevor." Ken wouldn't meet Matt's eyes. "I didn't do a very good job leading this team."

"Yes, you did. Every mission we undertake is a gamble. Some you get lucky on, others you don't." He put down his cup and took Ken's hand in his own. "Ed was a brave man. He died trying to save others. Trevor isn't dead yet. I'm praying he'll survive this war in a POW camp. I'm not giving up on him yet."

"And Clara Lehrer?" Ken stared into space, his eyes unfocused. "Although she knew the risks and we weren't the first people she's helped, we were the reason Holm took her into custody."

"Holm wants her brother. He's not above using her to achieve that." Matt wished he felt as matter-of-fact as he sounded. "We need to find Kristopher and Michel and complete this mission." With the institute and everything within it destroyed, Kristopher Lehrer was now the only source of the plans their team had been sent to retrieve. Ken had also promised Clara they'd find her brother and keep him safe. Matt intended to keep that promise.

"At the moment, that's very much like trying to find two needles in a haystack. Wherever they're hiding, there's no sign of them at all. None of Juliane's contacts know of their whereabouts." Ken shrugged. "I still believe this mission is an important one, but..." His voice flattened. "I've always tried to do the right thing, but life doesn't make it easy. It complicates whatever choices you make and laughs at others."

"I'm not sure life is supposed to be easy." Matt eased the coffee cup out of Ken's hand, placed it next to his own, and pulled Ken into his arms, ignoring the way his ribs protested the movement. "Come here." He kissed the top of Ken's head, glad of the height difference between them. "You're not alone in this, not anymore. Whatever happens, we'll get through it together."

"Holm... I couldn't let him die. Even after what he'd done and said, and especially after what he'd said." Ken's voice sounded muffled. The emotions he'd hidden for the last few days were finally breaking through. "My father... I'd always looked up to him, wanted to be like him. Now... I just don't know what to believe anymore."

"What did Holm say to you?"

The way Ken said he wasn't his father implied something had happened. Holm had mentioned Patrick Lowe earlier, too, and figured out Ken's identity because of their resemblance.

"He said my father murdered his." Ken let out a long breath, his voice shaking. "I pointed out calmly that our two countries were at war then, just as they are now. Soldiers are killed in battle. It happens. My own father lost his life during the Battle of the Marne shortly afterward."

"He wouldn't want to believe that." Although Matt had tried to convince himself he'd only helped to rescue Holm because Ken wouldn't have left otherwise, he couldn't have left the man there to die. He had to take any chance to save someone's life. His distress after his father's death meant he understood Holm's need to find someone to take his anger out on, but that didn't mean he agreed with it.

"He didn't." Ken shook his head. "I don't want to believe he was right, but he claimed to have witnesses who saw it happen." He bit his lip. "I never met my father, and he never acknowledged his relationship with my mother. How can I defend a man I know next to nothing about? Perhaps I've wanted to think he was a war hero like the stories say? I just don't know anymore. Does it even really matter?"

"He was your father, so yes, it does matter. Despite what Holm thinks, there are always two sides to every story, and as both your father and his are dead, it's doubtful anyone will ever know the entire truth. It's his problem, not yours." Matt hoped those words wouldn't return to haunt him later. Holm was a driven man, and it was doubtful he'd give up on his need for revenge entirely.

If he hurt Ken...

Matt put that thought out of his mind quickly and refused to dwell on it.

"I've taken his name and pretended to be someone I'm not." Ken's laughter was choked and bitter. "Perhaps I am his son after all, more so than I realised."

"I'll tell you who you are." Matt wished he could hit Holm again, and hard. "You're the man I love and want a future with. You're brave, determined, and damn good-looking." He made Ken look up, then held him at arm's length, a hand on each shoulder, so he had no choice but to listen. "I don't care what last name you choose to use. Whether it's Lowe or Tsukino, it doesn't change who *you* are." Ken had told him about his mother and the internment camp she was in before they'd flown out on this mission. He'd wanted to make sure she was taken care of if something happened to him, and Matt was the only person he trusted with that information. Matt had promised to keep the confidence, but told Ken it wouldn't come to that. "You trusted me before. Trust me now."

"I can't just switch off how I'm feeling. I'm confused, and I don't think that's going to pass anytime soon." Ken managed a slim smile. "I've never talked to anyone about how I feel about anything before I met you."

Matt grinned, trying to lighten the moment. "It's part of loving someone. You'll get used to it." He sobered. "I want you to get used to it. I don't want to think about losing you as well. We'll find a way to make this work. I promise."

They were already breaking so many rules being together like this. To hell with it. Once this mission was over, they'd both be reassigned to different units until the end of the war. Matt would make sure of it. Making a command decision when the person involved was someone you loved made it impossible to stay detached. Those rules were there for good reason.

And once this damn war was finally over, he and Ken would make a life together. They'd find a way they could live together and, at least in private, be honest with themselves and each other about who they truly were.

CHAPTER TWENTY-THREE

Michel held Kit tightly, their breathing loud in their small enclosed hiding space. He prayed the Gestapo searching the attic wouldn't be able to hear them and would leave soon. Kit was shaking and, like Michel, didn't manage to completely hide his fear. Michel kissed the top of Kit's head, offering a reassurance he didn't feel. Kit leaned into him, running his hands in soothing circles over Michel's back.

When they'd heard the creaking of the stairs, they'd grabbed all evidence of their presence in the attic and bolted into the hidden room. Sister Magdalene explained to the soldiers on the other side of the attic door that the door stuck sometimes, and they'd have to be patient. She'd found a way to give Kit and Michel a few extra seconds to hide.

One of the men sounded familiar. Michel strained to hear what was being said. A loud crash echoed through the room, followed by another. The soldiers must have over-turned the table and bed, and were now knocking against the wooden floor, looking for loose floorboards, no doubt.

The man raised his voice. Michel swore silently.

Reiniger. As far as that man was concerned, this hunt was personal. He wouldn't give up until both his prey were found.

"Lehrer," Reiniger called. "It really would be in your best interest to surrender. You can't hide forever, and the longer you persist in this, the more difficult it will be for you... and your friend." Michel felt, rather than saw, Kit shake his head in the dark. The tiny gap to let in the air wasn't large enough to bring any light with it.

"It pains me that you persist in ignoring what I have to say, especially as I bring you news of your family." The noise of the search lulled while Reiniger spoke, hoping to draw out his prey.

Kit's breath hitched, but he did not move. His hands had stilled; he held Michel in a firm embrace. Michel kissed Kit's forehead. This had to be a trick, a ploy on Reiniger's part. Didn't it?

Even if it wasn't, once they had Kit in custody, the outcome would still be the same.

"As you're probably aware, the bombings of the last few days have caused a lot of damage," Reiniger continued in a conversational tone. He sighed. Michel wanted to rub the smug smile Reiniger would be wearing off his face. "I was saddened by the news about your father."

Kit's breathing sped up. He buried his face in Michel's shoulder, smothering the choked noise that escaped his lips.

"Such a loss to the community, but he never stood a chance." Footsteps waxed and waned. Someone was walking around the attic, probably listening for an audible response to Reiniger's words. "Remember that about these people you're planning to work for. They killed your father, Lehrer. No one deserves to die like that, trapped in a burning building with no way out. The entire block where the bank stood is gone."

The bastard! Michel strengthened his embrace around Kit. He wished he could murmur words of comfort but couldn't risk being overheard. Kit sagged against Michel.

But he stayed silent.

Reiniger kept talking, his tone casual and matter-of-fact. Michel gritted his teeth, visualising ways to kill the man, each one more painful than the last.

"I do hope your father was unaware of your actions and those of your sister." Reiniger made a tsking noise. "She's in custody now. I've arrested her for collaboration with the enemy. Cooperation is not a trait that runs in your family, now, is it?"

Kit raised his head. While surrendering would not help his father, Clara was still alive. Michel shook his head, although Kit couldn't see him. Giving himself up wouldn't save his sister. The longer Kit evaded capture, the more likely Clara would be kept alive. A hostage was not worth anything dead.

"I've already had to shoot someone who tried to protect her." Reiniger interjected a sadness into his voice that was almost convincing. "Come now, Kristopher. I can call you Kristopher, can't I? I'd hate to see something happen to such a fine woman. Give yourself up, and we can come to an arrangement for both yourself and your sister. You're an asset to the Fatherland, and this is your first transgression. Herr SS Standartenführer Holm is keen to speak with you."

Of course he was.

Kit's shoulders shook. He was silently crying, his tears falling onto Michel's shoulder. Not able to say anything of comfort, Michel cupped Kit's chin and kissed him softly, trying to put his feelings into the action. Kit leaned into the kiss, returning it and the gesture.

Kit wouldn't surrender. He wouldn't betray them.

One of them surrendering to Reiniger meant giving up the other.

They held each other for what felt like forever, focusing on each other and trying to ignore Reiniger's words and the soldiers searching for them.

Finally, Reiniger stopped talking, and the footsteps died away, the stairs creaking several times as he and his men left the attic.

Michel still didn't dare move, in case the silence was another trap. Someone might have stayed behind, ready to catch the mice as they emerged from their hole. He'd stay like this with Kit for however long it took.

He didn't know how much time passed as they waited until the stairs creaked again. Surely Reiniger couldn't be coming back for another look? Didn't that man ever give up?

"Brother Bernard? Brother Dominic?" Sister Magdalene called. "It's safe. They've gone." She sighed when they didn't reply. "Oh Lord, thou hast searched me, and known me..."

At the words of the psalm they'd agreed on as a code phrase, Michel reached for the candlestick to open their temporary prison. Kit pulled away from him, wiping his eyes. The sudden light, although not bright, made them both shade their eyes for a moment after the darkness they'd become accustomed to.

Sister Magdalene shook her head and muttered something under her breath Michel was pleased he couldn't discern. "I'm so relieved that man didn't find you." She turned the bed over the right way, and Michel quickly went to help her. "He was most unpleasant, in spite of the politeness of his words. It is doubtful he will return soon, but I think it would be for the best if we start making plans for you to begin the next part of your journey."

"We won't stay any longer than is necessary, Sister." Kit's voice sounded flat, his manner very reserved. He was struggling to stay in control.

"You'll stay as long as you need, and it is safe to do so," Sister Magdalene said firmly. She glanced up from remaking the bed, and her expression softened into something that reminded Michel of his mother. "I'm very sorry for your loss, Herr Lehrer... Kristopher. You both look as though you could do with some privacy for a while. Don't worry, you won't be disturbed. I'll make sure of it."

"Thank—" Michel didn't have time to finish the words before she turned away and closed the attic door behind her.

Kit held him tightly. "Michel," he murmured, then kissed Michel hard. "Oh, love." Kit broke the kiss but kept holding Michel, not wanting to let go. His lower lip trembled.

"I'm here for you, mon cher," Michel whispered, his fingers brushing the lone tear falling down Kit's cheek. "If you need to cry, do so." Kit had lost so much already, even without this.

"I've already cried. I..." A sob escaped Kit's lips. "My father is dead, and Clara... They'll hurt her. They'll hurt her, and I can't stop them." He shook his head. "Even if I'd given myself up, it wouldn't have stopped them, would it?"

"No, probably not." Michel hadn't lied to Kit, and he wasn't about to start now. "She's helped the Resistance, and she knew the risks. I know that doesn't make it any easier, but she's a brave woman."

"I couldn't give you to them too." Kit looked at the floor.

"I love my sister, but I kept thinking if they found me, they'd find you. Is this ever going to end?"

"I don't know. I wish I did." Michel wanted nothing more at that moment than to give Kit the reassurance he needed to hear. But he couldn't. Kit wasn't the only one tired of all this. Michel wanted this mission to be over, although that might mean losing Kit for good.

"I'm sorry," Kit whispered. "I'm being selfish. You've lost people you care about too." He bit his lip, let go of Michel, and shoved his hands into his pockets.

"Yes, I have, but I've had the chance to grieve. You haven't." Michel leaned in and kissed Kit softly. "You need to let go properly. I never did until you were there for me." Kit had held him and let him cry himself to sleep one night after they'd talked. "Let me do the same for you. Please."

"I'm not sure I know how." Kit seemed lost, torn between staying strong and letting his grief show. He'd let a tear escape and then pull himself together again. In the darkened silence, he'd still had to keep enough control so they wouldn't be caught.

"Do you trust me?" Michel searched Kit's eyes for an answer. Kit nodded as Michel saw what he sought. He knew what would help Kit to let go. "Make love with me." Kit always gave himself so fully, no secrets and no holding back when they did. "I'll catch you when you fall. I promise."

Kit nodded again. "You always do."

"As you do for me." Being together was the only time they had the freedom to be themselves without worrying about the rest of the world going on around them. They could escape into each other and be who they wanted to be at that moment—two people who loved each other. To hell with anyone who thought they shouldn't be together in this way. Kit was right when he'd said something that felt so good couldn't be wrong.

"Je t'aime, Michel." Kit never seemed to tire of saying those words. Michel didn't want him to. Each time he heard them his breath hitched. While Kit still struggled with the pronunciation of many French words, those always sounded perfect.

"Ich liebe dich auch, Kit." Michel returned the sentiment in German, wanting to say it to Kit in his mother tongue just as Kit had done for him. He reached for the buttons on Kit's shirt, Kit already starting to undo Michel's belt.

God, he was so beautiful. Michel let his gaze linger as each bit of skin was revealed, not hiding the need in his eyes. Kit blushed, held out his hand, and led Michel over to the bed. "With you I can be who I'm meant to be," he whispered, lowering Michel onto the bed. "Stay here."

He quickly walked over to where Michel had dropped his duffel bag and retrieved what they'd need for their joining. Michel watched him, his breathing speeding up, his body already reacting to what they were going to do.

"You want me so much." Kit smiled, almost shyly. "It makes me feel very loved."

"You are very loved." Michel opened his arms when Kit came closer again, embracing him when he lay down on the bed. It didn't take long for them to finish undressing each other. Michel rolled them over, kissing Kit gently at first and then more demanding as they touched and caressed, taking their time, memorising each other's bodies.

Their joining came quickly. Although he'd planned to go slowly, once he had Kit in his arms, Michel didn't want to stop. Kit cried out as he let go, emotionally as well as physically, holding Michel tightly. The tears rolled down Kit's cheeks. He sobbed while Michel made soothing noises and stroked his hair, murmuring endearments.

"It's all right, mon cher, I love you. I'm not letting you go." Michel didn't know how long he could keep the promise for the latter, but for the former, he didn't make it lightly. This man in his arms was his life, and while they both still drew breath, that would not change.

"I won't let you go either." Kit began to calm, but he was still quiet. "I was wrong," he murmured. "I'm so sorry."

Michel froze. "Wrong about what?" he asked slowly, remembering the words he'd spoken to Kit that first night they'd admitted their love for each other. *For as long as you'll have me, and we can be together, I'm yours.*

"About the journey to Switzerland." He caressed Michel's face. "I know I need to get these plans to the Allies, but I had thought about leaving you here to keep you safe." He looked embarrassed. "I know it's selfish, but I can't leave you. I don't want to. If we travel together, they could catch both of us and hurt you to get me to cooperate."

"If you travel alone, there's more chance you'll be caught."

"Ssh, love." Kit placed one finger over Michel's lips. "You're not listening. I said I'm not going alone."

"You're... not?" Relief flooded through Michel. He would have found a way to follow Kit, to keep him safe, but didn't want their last words to be in anger.

"I don't know what our future will bring or how much time we have, but I want to spend it with you. Even if we only have a few days or weeks together, no one can take those memories away from us."

"No, they can't." Michel smiled. He kissed Kit slowly, putting as much love into it as he could. "I love you, Kit Lehrer." His heart beat fast, and he licked his lips, suddenly nervous. The words he really wished to say could probably never be spoken by one man to another, at least in their lifetime, but that didn't change the sentiment of what he asked. "Be mine?"

Kit's breath hitched. He threaded his fingers through Michel's and laid their joined hands over first his own heart and then Michel's. "I already am."

ABOUT THE AUTHOR

CONNECT WITH ANNE

Contact me at: annebarwell.wordpress.com
darthanne@gmail.com

Anne Barwell lives in Wellington, New Zealand. She shares her home with Kaylee: a cat with "tortitude" who is convinced that the house is run to suit her; this is an ongoing "discussion," and to date, it appears as though Kaylee may be winning.

In 2008, Anne completed her conjoint BA in English Literature and Music/Bachelor of Teaching. She has worked as a music teacher, a primary school teacher, and now works in a library. She is a member of the Upper Hutt Science Fiction Club and plays violin for Hutt Valley Orchestra.

She is an avid reader across a wide range of genres and a watcher of far too many TV series and movies, although it can be argued that there is no such thing as "too many." These, of course, are best enjoyed with a decent cup of tea and further the continuing argument that the concept of "spare time" is really just a myth. She also hosts and reviews for other authors, and writes monthly blog posts for Love

Bytes. She is the co-founder of the New Zealand Rainbow Romance writers, and a member of RWNZ.

Anne's books have received honourable mentions five times, reached the finals four times—one of which was for best gay book—and been a runner up in the Rainbow Awards. She has also been nominated twice in the Goodreads M/M Romance Reader's Choice Awards—once for Best Fantasy and once for Best Historical.

Who do you trust when no one is who they seem?

Germany 1944

Fleeing German physicist Dr Kristopher Lehrer and his lover, Resistance fighter Michel, are caught up in an Allied bombing campaign. Separated from Michel after discovering an injured RAF pilot in the Black Forest, and pursued by the SS for the information he carries, Kristopher is frantic to reunite, unaware that Michel has been recruited by the Allies for a rescue mission.

Time is running out. The Gestapo is closing in. How can they decide who to trust, when the dagger pointed at Kristopher's back could be wielded by a friend?